W9-ACL-998

Sea
of
Hooks

Sea
of
Hooks

a novel by

Lindsay
Hill

McPherson & Company
Kingston, New York

Published by McPherson & Company,
Post Office Box 1126, Kingston, New York 12402.
www.mcphersonco.com
The publisher gratefully acknowledges the assistance of
a grant from the Literature Program of the New York
State Council on the Arts, a state agency.

3 5 7 9 10 8 6 4 2   2013 2014 2105 2016

MANUFACTURED IN THE U.S.A. BY THOMSON-SHORE, INC.

Library of Congress Cataloging in Publication Data

Hill, Lindsay, 1952-
Sea of Hooks : a novel / by Lindsay Hill.
pages cm
ISBN 978-1-62054-006-0 (alk. paper)
1. Life change events—Fiction. 2. Self-realization—Fiction. I. Title.
PS3558.I395S43 2013
813'.54—dc23
2013029189

The author and publisher express thanks to the editors of
Conjunctions *(web),* New England Review, New American Writing,
and Peep/Show, *where portions of this book appeared first.*
Acknowledgments continue on page 351.

*This book is dedicated
to Nathaniel Tarn*

A boy grew up
beside a sea of hooks
and he learned to swim
in that sea
and to notice the hooks
as they rose
and fell
and twisted in the tides

And he learned
to feel his way
at first very slowly
in the sea of hooks

And he noticed
that all around him
people had hooks
in their skin
and were being pulled
in many directions

And many of the hooks
were small and hard to see
barely silver in the glinting
light down deep
barely visible
and numerous

And some
from the place of his birth
would not put a toe
in that sea

And some lived
their entire lives
full of hooks
in the underneath

Sea
of
Hooks

GLASS

Of the great Victorian conservatory in Golden Gate Park, known formally as the Hall of Flowers, Christopher Westall's mother had once said, "This is a place where glass is safe." For some reason he thought of this first on finding her body, the plastic bag fitted so snuggly over her face. He held her hand awhile there in the cold. It felt reef-stiff. Her eyes were closed. She had somehow managed to tuck herself in quite tightly. Her face was soft, expressionless and tired. No hint of how it had been for her to die, there on the bed in his room, the bed under which he once thought knife-people slept.

PLASTIC FINGERS

When Christopher was in the second grade he told a first grader that his parents had taken him to the country *and that all his fingers had been chopped off by some farm equipment and they had been replaced by a very special doctor with plastic ones and if you looked really hard you could see that his fingers were really plastic and you could see the little crisscross stitch marks at the base of each finger where they had been sewn on.* The first grader started to cry and wouldn't stop and told the other kids, and they told the teacher, and the teacher called Evelyn, so this created quite a stir. But nothing compared to when Christopher told his fellow second graders about the secret passage that ran from the play yard to his den.

OTHER PEOPLE'S DREAMS

When Christopher was a child he had dreams some nights that were not his own—dreams filled with people he didn't know, places he'd never been, and circumstances that were unfamiliar to him. Christopher called this *having other people's dreams.*

SALT

And once when he was twelve and studying Genesis for his confirmation, Christopher asked his mother if she'd ever actually seen a pillar of salt and what did it look like because he was having trouble picturing it. Was it glistening and transparent like a pillar of glass or rough and cloudy or gray and rough and sparkly like a granite slab?

GONE

Early one morning in late September, before the markets opened, on a trading floor in downtown San Francisco, a disheveled banker, still drunk from the night before, stood slouched against his desk, staring through a wire mesh window into the shaft of a light well. He was experiencing, however hazily, the somewhat unfamiliar sensation of worrying about someone else. He was worried indeed, about his friend, who had dropped from sight after the suicide of his mother—sending only an envelope with the keys to her still fully furnished house folded in a note—saying only that he'd had to go to Asia. Now weeks without word—gone—no details of where—no explanation of why—not even a hint of whether he ever expected to return.

VENTRILOQUISM

When Christopher apologized to the first grader for the plastic fingers story, the teacher was standing right behind him with her hand in the middle of his back. She was saying "Christopher has something to say to you and he is going to say it now," and Christopher said the words that the teacher had told him to say in a voice more hers than his, so it was more like ventriloquism than apology, and he knew that her lips were moving very slightly as he spoke. The first grader was anxious and shuffling and he would not look at Christopher's face, and he would not look at his hands.

KNIFE-PEOPLE

Even as a child, Christopher knew that knife-people lie so flat that you cannot see them. But he could just hear them, sharpening themselves against each other like hands washing—that wispy, metallic, sweep, sweep, sweep, almost indistinguishable from their breathing. In the morning he would go under the bed and collect the shavings and take them to the trash, and he never said anything about it to anyone.

FURNITURE

Her arms were out of the blanket and her hands lay flat, palms down. She had removed her rings, he knew why, and placed them like little weights on the folded note that lay in the cloisonné dish they'd purchased together on McAllister Street when he was ten. He sat by the bed in the numbness and the slowness, in that feeling of feelings falling into depths and not diving in to retrieve them, that feeling of falling over spillways where the lights on the water are scissors chopping the surface to bits and bits and bits. How the shattered shapes are whole things in themselves. He could not look at her face through the plastic bag. Everything in the room seemed crisp and vivid: the light on the corner of the worn red Persian rug, the gunmetal blue of the bed. Everything singled-out and standing by itself. Furniture was steady like this. All the things in the house were steady and factual like this.

FURNITURE BODY

And he knew that it was OK to be dead in his mother's house; it was OK for your body to be furniture or part of some piece of furniture or becoming furniture.

THE DREAM OF THE DROWNING CHILD

And one night when Christopher was eight and having other people's dreams, he dreamed that a child was being swept down a river, and the child's mother was running along the bank just keeping up and keeping eye contact with the drowning child as he was carried in the rapid currents. And the mother was running along the bank, running alongside her drowning child because she had no arms.

VOICES

Evelyn left a list with the names of two friends and their numbers and some instructions. And they were friends from long ago in her life, and there were no other names on the list, and he saw how long ago her life already was. He told them she died in her sleep, *and their voices were far away, as if a pound of gauze were stuffed in their mouths, or in the phone, or in his ears, or all of these—so far away and so indistinct that what they said didn't seem like human speech, was barely speech, or another kind of speech that couldn't carry what was meant like water falling through fingers or a language where what was meant was like a landslide or the workings of organs or trickles or a little inward-facing orchestra with a choir behind tin curtains—that kind of speaking; or a language where putting words in order was not the goal, or again, a kind of singing, but it wasn't exactly singing, but singing like the singing of certain objects when rubbed together, but not metal objects but objects wrapped in cloth, like the rubbing together of gloved hands as a kind of speech.* He told them she died in her sleep and after a little while of listening he hung up.

RUBICON

The Rubicon is the point of no return.

TIME AND THE DEAD

If you could ask the dead about time what would they say? Time does not always seem the same when you are alive—you know that time is different for one who is asleep. You know that the dead cannot sleep. Does time always seem the same when you are dead—is that the difference?

A BOY HAD A BIRD FOR A MOTHER

A boy had a bird for a mother, an ice age, a smoldering fire; a boy was raised by a bird, a glacier, a fire; he learned nervousness and patience and hunger, and he learned to keep her safe and to withstand the cold and to offer whatever he could find to keep her going.

THE SECOND FIRE

After the second Thorn fire, Christopher stopped being able to cry.

TRIPS TO JAPAN

Christopher's passport had never been stamped. He had acquired it, at Evelyn's insistence, a few years before, during one of her periods of planning trips to Japan—the making and subsequent canceling of reservations, the gathering of ship schedules, ports-of-call, the maps with the railway lines, the maps with the circled cities with dates penciled in, the brochures of the little inns and the temples and the museums, and she would have to insist on rounds and rounds of vaccinations and how petulant she became at the suggestion that they were not needed because Evelyn said there was no telling where they'd end up once they departed; the making and canceling of reservations over and over because of scheduling concerns, because of health concerns, because the accommodations weren't quite right, the travel brochures, the letters to the consulate, the trips to Japantown asking shop owners, in a Japanese that was like someone walking on stilts for the first time, where they were from and what they would suggest that she not miss and what she should avoid.

TRIPS TO JAPAN

And finally she simply couldn't go. Days of silence—days upon days of icy empty silence.

BHUTAN

In early September, 1974, on a side street of the capital, Thimphu, in a small house, in the pitch dark before dawn, Dorji, a slender Bhutanese man of twenty-two, stirred to the cries of his infant daughter, Chuke, pulling himself reluctantly from the salt-sweet embrace of his wife. They had fought the night before, as they had often in the past, over his choice to become a tourist guide for the government. Today was his first day at that work, and he had argued that any contact with Westerners, now only newly admitted to the kingdom, would lead to opportunities in the future and a better life. Namita had responded sharply, that his precious youth, his education and competent English, would be squandered in tending to spoiled curiosity seekers. And, now that their financial sponsor, Dorji's uncle, Prakesh, was dead, they would have to watch out for themselves and not waste time on empty dreams. Dorji rose, lifted Chuke from her crib and placed her in Namita's arms.

BHUTAN

The Kingdom of Bhutan, known to its inhabitants as the *Land of the Thunder Dragon*, is located in the Eastern Himalayas, between Tibet and India. Fortress-monasteries, called dzongs, dot the valleys of the otherwise mountainous landscape, and house traditions and artifacts among the most ancient and honored in the Buddhist world. During the British colonization of India, various military expeditions were made in an attempt to conquer Bhutan. All were unsuccessful, defeated not primarily by the force of arms, but by the difficulties of the terrain.

DORJI

Dorji had secured his position with the State Tourist Bureau through his uncle, Prakesh, the same uncle who had loaned him the money for his education in India and who, like Dorji, hoped for economic gain now that the kingdom's doors, after over one thousand years of isolation, had finally been opened.

DORJI

Namita held Chuke to her breast, and Dorji, feeling his way in the dark room, washed his face in a basin, donned his traditional robe, whispered goodbye to his wife and daughter and hurried from the house. He was more preoccupied than actually awake, but no matter, he'd rehearsed these minutes, and the hours of the coming day, over and over in his thoughts and now had only to enact them. He walked, half-ran, through the dark and empty streets of Thimphu, past shuttered family restaurants and closed shops stocked with traditional Bhutanese clothes, textiles and dry-goods—shops that he envisioned would one day be filled with radios, televisions and consumer goods. Now that his uncle was dead, killed in a car crash in India, he would have to keep such thoughts mostly to himself. He walked quickly toward the newly designated tourist office, which now stood lightless and closed. In front, a small bus idled, coughing bursts of white exhaust and the piercing odor of diesel. In the front passenger seat sat Sonam, a slightly older man whom Dorji did not admire—thinking him dull, undereducated and tradition-bound. Standing at the door of the bus, awaiting Dorji, was the tourist supervisor who was waving Dorji along as if asking him to hurry even more. They spoke briefly, with the supervisor wishing Dorji good luck and emphasizing the importance of the mission—that all the visitors must be made welcome and comfortable and, above all, kept safe. Dorji slipped behind the wheel and embarked on the long curvy journey, south to the Indian border. It would take nine hours; they would meet and retrieve twelve travelers, put Sonam behind the wheel, and come straight back on the same road.

PRAKESH

As Dorji drove, he thought of his father, how largely indifferent to anything new he was—preferring mundane agrarian tasks, repeated dutifully, and wanting to not make a stir of any kind. But, his father's brother Prakesh, could not have been more different—always on the lookout for opportunity, always advancing a new scheme in careful steps, always engaged in anticipating what others would someday want and planning to have it on hand to sell to them. Not surprisingly, this had resulted in his becoming a very successful merchant—even with customers among the royal family. His sudden death had left Dorji rudderless. Now he was driving through the dark, struggling against an impediment with no remedy but to somehow find another plan, another ladder, with rungs reaching even higher.

DORJI

Dorji had a perfunctory relationship with Buddhism and its rituals. Mostly, he found them tedious, eroding hour after hour in a droning litany. His uncle had felt the same way, and his elaborate cremation felt like it belonged to someone else. There had been a certain rough affection between them, the way pragmatism can serve as a kind of affection between pragmatic persons joined in a mutual project—an affection anchored in action where the enthusiasm for the outcome transfers to the vehicles of its realization. The evening before, Dorji had visited his widowed aunt. She had always been rather cold, uncomprehending and resentful of the attention that Prakesh had lavished on his nephew, especially given his relative indifference to their two dull sons. The visit was sheer duty, the conversation like chipping granite. His aunt was simmering, indignant that Dorji would resume worldly pursuits so soon after the funeral.

THIMPHU

The dusty, rattled, and exhausted passengers climbed off the cramped state-owned bus which had finally traversed the countless valleys and mountain passes that lay between Jaigaon, India and Thimphu. Christopher, now twenty-two, using essentially a bribe had, in San Francisco, arranged to take a graduate student's place on the trip. His mother had been dead for five weeks when the group departed. The student's designation as the tour-guide's assistant had the consequence of leaving the guide, who was a professor of Buddhist Studies at Berkeley, without an American aide, and bunking with Christopher in the same hotel room. When visas were issued at the border, there had been some squabbling, also solved with money, about the name on Christopher's passport not matching the name on the tourist list. With the guide, whom everyone called "The Professor," stiffly withholding assistance, Christopher had to gain entry with the help of a Sikh army officer.

THIMPHU

The hotel itself was a brown latticed jumble of hallways, parlors, rooms, and shared toilets, all smelling of sandalwood and mold. The newly replaced red carpet did little to lend a sense of modernity. The desk-staff was overly formal, as if they were "playing" hotel, and the "bellhops" dropped the bags roughly on the floors of the rooms and, given their shocked expressions, seemed to have no conception of what tips were. The professor, who apparently had a mosquito phobia, lit so many citronella coils that Christopher could barely breathe and, after a brusque goodnight, Christopher pulled the harsh wool blanket over his head, which rested on a pillow he was sure had been stuffed with straw.

THIMPHU

For Christopher, the first breakfast was like sitting down at the meeting of a club of which he was not a member, which is to say, he was invisible and talked-around. He was listening to the scholars and pilgrims comparing notes on their prior travels to India, Nepal and Sikkim, quoting texts and delineating lineages, and he had nothing to contribute but the confession of an upset stomach, which he kept to himself. After moving the pile of eggs, chilies and cheese around on his plate for fifteen minutes, he left the table and went outside.

THE FOLLY OF THE JOURNEY

With alarming speed the folly of the journey descended on him full weight. All the colonial visions of spiritual quaintness dissolved against the reality that Bhutan was grimy, impoverished, listless and feudalistic, even in Thimphu, with its dirt streets, shacks, cluttered shops and squalid public squat-toilets with signs on their outer walls imploring people not to pass stools in the trenches behind their houses. What was he doing here among tattered banners, prim scholars, and pilgrims in a distant stopped-clock capital? What was he doing sitting on a stone bench in an empty square with two letters in his coat? There was nothing for him here—it was just the world, barren and rough, centuries whirring by, rocks stacked on rocks, words stacked on words, people preoccupied with the small-knot concerns of their lives. And expectations were tinsel, and plans were cardboard cars, and memories were false imaginings, and the ground was cold and flat and devoid of promise.

EDGES

She didn't end up in a bus station talking to the luggage racks. She did not wander the streets talking out loud to herself. She did not believe that broadcasts from the Chrysler Building controlled her thoughts. She did not believe that the luminous lines she saw around people's heads from time to time had any meaning, or the ruins she saw in their hearts or the stress cracks in their eyes or the inside hammerings that seemed to deafen them. She did not steal, or drink too much, lie without reason, strike children or cut herself, wash her hands too often or blurt vulgar words. It was none of these. It was a very private, inconspicuous teardown—precise, inside the lines, with words that held their edges against the ice. But the edges could not hold.

SIEVE

Christopher didn't particularly like his mother's orange juice, but asked for it often, because he liked to watch her make it: the sharp, sweet smell that followed the cutting in half of the oranges and their being ground, against the little glass grinder shaped like half an orange, with the twisting motion of his mother's wrist and the small fine sieve that fit exactly over the mouth of the orange juice glass, through which the juice was poured so no pulp or seeds would get into the glass.

LOCK AND KEY

Many things were locked in the Westall House: cabinets, cupboards, drawers. And all the keys were hidden and all the doors to the outside had multiple locks which were always locked.

THE COST OF EVERYTHING

When he was a child, and especially during the year that he was kept home from school, Evelyn taught Christopher the cost of things; the values of antiques; the value of a particular antique based on condition: worn, cracked, broken, repaired or perfect—If this had not been cracked it would be worth a fortune. Many cool clear afternoons were spent browsing through antique shops and going for tea in the Japanese Tea Garden and then to the Hall of

Flowers. Mostly, they went to small shops in rundown neighborhoods, especially on the edge of the tenderloin, but sometimes they ventured to Tea and Rarity, the elegant shop of Margaret and Ceryl Thayer on Bay Street. See how much more you pay for the surroundings—Evelyn would say under her breath just before Margaret offered tea—See how much more you pay because they're British. Journey after journey, this thing that thing, good, better, best, a kind of glacial relentlessness. You have to know the value of everything—she'd say; this versus that; that versus this; which of the two is worth more given their actual condition; which would be more valuable if perfect; how broken things could be repaired but would never be perfect again, would never regain the value they'd had before breaking; how much more would someone pay if a piece completed their collection; how much more do you always have to pay for something you really want.

UNCLE ALFRED

Evelyn's Godfather, Alfred Hopton, whom she called Uncle Alfred, lived with his longtime partner, Doug Sutton, in a house with a lovely garden on Taraval. Alfred, whose wife had died and left him wealthy long ago, had never worked a day in his life or learned how to drive. He seemed to look younger and younger year after year even after all the money was gone, while Doug, who was fifteen years his junior, was haggard, smoked constantly, and worked uncomplainingly in a dingy insurance office on Geary Boulevard. Alfred would take the bus every week or so to have lunch at the Tabasco Taqueria on Polk, where Evelyn and Christopher would sometimes join him. He wore tan suits with freshly cut flowers in the lapels and tightly woven straw hats, and he bought strawberries out-of-season and exotic plants for the garden and exotic spices for the kitchen and black chocolate and freshly ground French Roast coffee. He never had a care and Evelyn revered and adored him.

THE PHILASCOPE

Evelyn told Christopher that she had a philascope with which to watch him during the day.

THE GHOST IN THE HALL

One night when Christopher was five, he woke, climbed out of bed, padded down the hall toward the bathroom and stopped to speak to an old woman who was standing in the space between the end of the low bookcase and the archway of the entry hall *and her hair was wispy and white and unkempt and her face was gaunt and hollowed-out and white and she wore a dark dress with tiny white polka-dots and he could not see her hands and he could not see her feet and she was staring straight ahead and he began to be afraid because she was icy and lonely and lost and she wouldn't speak to him after he asked her her name having told her his and he was starting to measure her height with his hand* when his mother called to him from the doorway of her bedroom and told him to run to her at once.

THE SECOND FIRE

The crowd around the fire had begun to thin. The first firefighters were rolling up their hoses, and some late-arriving engines were starting to pull away. Nothing had yet taken hold through the veneer of shock.

WITHOUT A CAUSE

Dr. Thorn had asked Christopher if he could think of anything that arose without a cause.

WEIGHT

Evelyn would weigh letters in her hand, bouncing them slightly. "It feels heavy," she would say, reaching for a second stamp. Eventually, everything felt heavy. Eventually, everything had to have a second stamp or a third. Eventually, she didn't bother weighing them.

FRANTIC

Sometimes Christopher's mother would become frantic, her word for when the roof came down—like the time when Christopher was nine, and he showed her his penis while she was standing at the sink, and he came into the kitchen, and her back was turned as she did dishes, and he almost absently reached through the little slit in the front of his pajamas and pulled his penis out and took a step or two and spoke to her. When she turned around, he jiggled it a little by rotating his hips, and she exploded in a torrent of tears and shouting. Or the time that Evelyn lost her pearls and became frantic, and Shebee had to be called, and she found them in the torn silk lining of Evelyn's jewelry box—except that *that* time Evelyn wasn't silent for days and days.

BHUTAN LECTURES

In addition to his running commentaries about landscape, history, art, and architecture, the professor delivered a series of evening lectures on the esoteric teachings and traditions of the Nyingma School of Buddhism. These teachings would occupy a central place in the spiritual concerns of the journey.

THE THIMPHU LIBRARY

The professor took the group to the National Library whose attendant spoke little English. Christopher was transfixed by the rows of shelves of silk-wrapped, loaf-like books with their long horizontal pages.

THE PAST

Remembering is never in the past.

TIME AND THE DEAD

Are we one or many? When you are alive there are many. Are the dead a single thing—is that the difference? Do remnants *have* history or is history *made* and *bestowed*? Does something *hold* history? Does something *hide* history like in the folds of a dress? What kind of history do the dead have? Do they find it in the folds of being dead?

FIRE

There is an unforgiving element of fire: the more fire has the more fire wants. Some people try to have a controlled fire in their life, to burn down just a part. But fire never acts to contain itself. The job goes up, the church, the marriage, the fabric of days goes up, the topics of inner talk combust, and the box with all the slots for everything, and the maps with all the streets and all their names. And this kind of fire is not the kind of fire that self-governing people intend to light in their lives, but once it is lit a permission is given that is not easily withdrawn. And those with a stake in this burning-down life will try to stop the fire because the more fire has, the more fire wants, and the weight-bearing walls of this person on fire are interwoven with their own weight-bearing walls, and it is not just the ingenuine, tinsel, bric-a-brac that is burning, but the genuine, the supple, the promising, the beautiful. So those with expectations for this person will not cooperate with fire but will oppose it, not knowing that all their barricades are fuel, and they will not see that something is being celebrated, that with burning there is untangling, that with burning there is a lifting off of weights. They will not see that something is being celebrated: the celebration called *hands full of heat and ash*, called *face streaked with tears*, the celebration called *everything now in cinders, everything now sundered*, called *everything thrown in the air and nothing comes back down*, the celebration called *beginning again*.

GARDENING

Evelyn was not really a gardener because she didn't like to get dirty. It wasn't that she ever bought much to plant, except a daisy or two, but she had a perfect set of red-handled gardening tools— a little trowel and a little hand rake, a black Japanese gardener's jacket and pants, and a broad gardening hat. Sometimes she liked to "putter," as she called it, in the garden behind the flat.

MAGAZINES

The house was chill; the shades were drawn and the shutters closed; on the polished mahogany coffee table, in the living room, the *Antiques* magazines were stacked in perfect stair-steps with the most recent issue on top and the oldest on the bottom.

THE POLICE AND THE CORONER

Not long after Christopher called the police, a slight and slightly rumpled Italian officer, sympathetic to anyone whose mother had passed away, arrived and, after confirming that Evelyn was dead, asked Christopher to accompany him while he dutifully checked all the doors and basement windows for evidence of forced-entry, a procedure to which Christopher tacitly acceded but found to be ridiculous. None was found. The officer called the coroner, who arrived a while later, gaunt and industrious, with an assistant whose face was blank as a canvas tote. He matter-of-factly inquired about Christopher's relationship to the deceased and, taking notes, asked when he had last seen her alive, what was her state of mind, had she ever threatened suicide and had he any foreknowledge of this act? Christopher's answers to the last two questions—which amounted to no—were mostly audible and entirely untrue. And the coroner removed the plastic bag from Evelyn's face and left it on the bedside table with the rubber band that she had taken from the rubber band drawer in the kitchen and used to secure it, and he picked up the suicide note as if it were a sheet of gold leaf and read it solemnly aloud, which startled Christopher, and said he would have to take it with him but would return it when proceedings were concluded.

AFTER THE CORONER

The Canton blue and white porcelain, glistening; the darkly stained hardwood floors, spotless and cold; the early carved Chinese altar in the front hall at the top of the stairs; the most valuable piece in the house, his mother had said again and again; a Japanese fan opened on its stand; a few dried flowers in a cloisonné vase; Persian rugs, lacquer tables, silks laid on armrests; the China Trade oil of Macau harbor over the mantle—all silent and subtracted from the world, all in rooms and hallways already empty, all subtracted out, already belonging to others, already distributed in houses full of talking and boredom, love and fights, laughter and loss and pastimes.

SHATTERING

Every single thing depends on shattering.

EARTHQUAKE

When Christopher was a toddler, an earthquake shook the flat and Evelyn grabbed him, threw him in a doorway and arched over him. Everything was like Jello, and a crack ran up the plaster wall beside them.

THE WALK TO UNION STREET

After the policeman and the coroner were gone, there was a sense of the automatic, of motion without motive. Christopher walked out through the basement and locked the heavy deadbolt behind him, and walked into the gray light and fog-laden steady eastward wind, and down the block, and around the corner, and over the Presidio wall onto the downward sloping poorly paved road past Julius Kahn playground and ball field, and up the hill into the sharply scented eucalyptus forest with ragged gray-brown ecliptic leaves strewn on the sandy ground, and across Presidio Street and up the steep grassy hill to the gate where Broadway dead-ended at the Presidio's eastern wall.

PRESIDIO GATE

And he walked through the Presidio gate to Upper Broadway, where the great houses looked out over the Marina District, the Palace of Fine Arts, Alcatraz and across the bay to Sausalito, Tiburon and Angel Island. Evelyn's grandfather had owned one of these great houses, and massive acreage at Tahoe, and a square block in New York. His brother, Uncle Henry, upon taking the reins after his death, had said when questioned by Evelyn's grandmother about his careless unloading of assets to support the lifestyle of a czar, "It will not hurt us in our time."

WALKING

He walked past the vacant lot where Grant School used to be, down the steep stairs on Broderick Street and past the modern house that had been built to replace the Thorn house after it burned to the ground, down to the level block of Green Street, where they used to live in a flat, and looked up at his old bedroom window on the second floor.

DRIVING THE RICH KID TO SCHOOL

And he looked up the hill at the big wooden mansion where his mother's grandfather had lived and she'd visited as a small girl, which now was owned by some Exxon heirs, and he thought of how she had looked up at that house every day and how the son of those wealthy people had gone to Anglican Academy with Christopher and called every weekday morning to ask if he could have a ride to school and, of course, every morning Evelyn consented, and the boy's mother never offered to drive even once.

THE GREEN STREET FLAT

The flat on Green Street occupied the entire second floor of a three-story building. A long hall ran down the middle of the space. The bedrooms were in the front, facing south, and the living room and dining room were in the back, overlooking the bay to the north.

THE LITTLE GRAY GIRL

Walking toward Union Street and Landry's pie shop, Christopher passed the little cottage placed far back from the street with the white picket fence and gate between two garages and remembered *The Little Gray Girl,* as everyone in the neighborhood called her but whose name was actually Priscilla.

BROKEN

Evelyn wanted nothing to be broken.

THE WOMAN WHO BOUGHT THE DOG SO HER DAUGHTER WOULD BE NORMAL

One afternoon at Grand Central Market on California Street, Amanda Gray, who was a widow, told Evelyn that there was an emptiness in Priscilla, and that she didn't want something bad to fill that emptiness, so she had purchased a puppy so that her daughter would be normal.

CALM

Westy's primary motive in the household was to keep Evelyn calm.

THEORY OF BROKENNESS

Evelyn had a theory of brokenness that a broken thing encouraged other things to break, that breaking was like fire because its nature was to spread.

POMEGRANATE

The pomegranate was an Arabian lamp that turned into a house on fire when opened, the thin paper walls holding back the flames; "I'm eating a house on fire," he'd said to Evelyn.

THIMPHU

The group was taken down dusty, narrow, alleyways, to workshops where young monks and craftspeople, huddled closely together, made paper with embedded flowers, Tanka, and wooden masks. They also wove wall hangings and embroidered robes and quilts with exquisite skill.

ROCKING HORSE CUP

When Christopher was five and chipped his rocking-horse hand-painted ceramic cup, his mother picked it up, and, embarking on her familiar cycle of panic, fury, tears and detachment, and over his urgent pleadings that it could be fixed, took it away to be discarded. The following day Christopher toddled down to the garbage cans to secretly retrieve it. He went through every coffee ground and every crumpled paper bag and cereal box, but the rocking horse cup was not there.

CHINESE MEDICAL CHEST

There was a Chinese medical chest in the corner of the entry hall of the flat. Christopher was fascinated with all the drawers and why there needed to be so many. Evelyn explained how important it was to keep the remedies separated and in their places because things that touched unintentionally became spoiled or diluted or corrupted with the influence of the others.

IMPERFECT DRAFTS

And there, at the bottom of the wire waste basket by her desk, as he had expected, the numerous imperfect drafts of the suicide note lay folded and stacked; he picked them up and crushed them like fists full of flowers and let them drop. *If a wind were to rise and scatter lives—if a tide were to turn and carry everything out—if the moments did not stack themselves in hours but simply scattered outward in all directions like a voice—if nothing could be retained and nothing ever mentioned again* this is what it felt like in that house as he stood there, in the silence, in the chill, watching those crumpled papers fall to the polished floor.

THE THIMPHU LIBRARY

Later in the day, Christopher returned to the library and managed to enlist the librarian in retrieving successive, silk-wrapped, volumes from the shelves and placing them in front of him on a long wooden bench. The librarian was deferential, but clearly confused about the intensity with which this strange foreigner, who knew not a word of the language, appeared to be "reading" the texts. After an hour or so, Christopher rose, thanked the librarian, and left to wander the streets of Thimphu until the light began to fade. When he returned to the hotel, somewhat disheveled and abstracted, the tour guests were just being served a dinner of chilies, cheese, bread and, with no apparent sense of irony, bottled water from India.

WESTY

Christopher's father, who idealized Gauguin, would sit in his living room chair with a drink at the end of the day and read books about Stalin, Hitler, World War II and the great criminals, con men and murderers of the past several hundred years. He did not like to be disturbed until dinner was ready.

EVELYN'S ANTIQUES

Evelyn never had to wonder what they meant. Their needs were steady and clear. They had no motives to interpret. They did not change. Their value consistently increased, and, above all, they were beautiful and increasingly so.

AUNT ELLY

Evelyn's Aunt Eleanor, whom she called *Aunt Elly*, had lived in San Francisco since before the earthquake of 1906 and in the last years of her life had a small apartment on Russian Hill. She was long ago widowed, and her only child, a son, whom she'd had quite late, was killed, at age twenty-seven, test-piloting a plane not long before the Second World War. Evelyn and Aunt Elly corresponded regularly even though they lived in the same city and had telephones. Both thought telephone calls to be somewhat intrusive and rude, like coming to someone's house unannounced and knocking on the door.

EVELYN'S CHERRY DROP FRONT DESK

Two years before her death, Aunt Elly gave Evelyn, over perfunctory protests, her colonial cherry drop front desk, which Evelyn had coveted, saying that she wanted the pleasure of seeing Evelyn enjoy it. Evelyn prized it almost above all else and kept it open. Her envelopes and blotters and paperclips were in the little drawers and cubbyholes; her stationery, silver stamp bowl, silver letter opener, black enamel fountain pen and colonial sterling inkwell were arranged with exactitude on the writing surface, and in the three deep drawers underneath, she kept papers and photographs. She told Christopher that the desk was very valuable because it was American and would have been worth a fraction had it been English. Sometimes Christopher would see his mother sitting with the drawers open puttering with the papers and photographs. He knew that he was not to bother her.

ROUTINE

Weston Mercer Westall, whose name in the business-world was Westy, was a man who liked routine. He never missed dinner and was never unaccounted for. He read books every evening, often while listening to Beethoven, but rarely spoke of what he'd read, and he had season tickets to Candlestick Park.

A BOY WOKE SPEAKING ANOTHER LANGUAGE

Someone at school told Christopher that a boy had woken one morning speaking another language. Christopher asked Uncle Alfred if this could be true, and he said that he had never heard of such a thing outside of marriage.

WESTY BELIEVED

Westy believed in the crack of the bat, the substantiality of made things, the insubstantiality of faith, the neutrality of nature, self-made men, making your own breaks, enjoying your own jokes, helping those who had less, a level playing field and playing by the rules. He did not believe in regret or looking back, in luck, coincidence, clinging to life or fearing death, making more of things than they really were, needing anyone more than you needed yourself, that things were "meant to be" or in crying over spilt milk. And he did not believe in God or in men who did not drink.

WESTY STRODE

Westy strode in a very particular way down Montgomery Street. His frame was slightly sloped to the left—the result, he said, of a collapsed lung during the war. But there was a confidence, a bearing, a self-sufficiency—almost a sense of ownership that he exuded in his stride, but quietly.

RAW EGG

Westy did not teach Christopher how to rebuild a car engine, but he did show him how to prepare a raw egg in a glass with Worcestershire Sauce in the morning.

CHALK

Christopher told his fellow first-graders that chalk was made from the bones of children who were said to have moved away.

THE TREASURE CYCLES

The great eighth century Buddhist saint, mystic and teacher, Padmasambhava, who in Bhutan is commonly called Guru Rinpoche and who founded the Nyingma School of Buddhism, scattered and concealed thousands of treasure troves across Tibet, Bhutan and the greater Himalayan Region.

THE APARTMENT ON SACRAMENTO STREET

Christopher asked Evelyn if she and Westy had always lived on Green Street, and she said no that they had once lived in an apartment house on Sacramento Street. He asked which one, and he asked again, so on their next trip downtown, she pointed out some first-floor windows facing the street in a nondescript brick building across from a park and said offhandedly, that that was where they'd lived. Every time they'd drive by that building, Christopher would look at those windows and try to imagine the apartment behind them and try to picture his parents' life before he was born.

MILLIONAIRE MANY TIMES OVER

Evelyn used the term "a millionaire many times over" to denote very rich people whom she did not like, and the phrase was freighted with envy because these people didn't have to try very hard because everyone around them was trying very hard for them. Certainly no one was trying very hard for Evelyn, at least not that she could notice.

WESTY'S SCHEDULE

Because of the three-hour time-difference between San Francisco and New York, the bond markets opened at 5:30 in the morning in San Francisco. Christopher would lie in bed and hear his father get up, shower and then go into the den. Christopher would listen for the hangers sliding on the rail as his father picked a suit with a folded handkerchief in the breast pocket, and he'd imagine hearing the recently shined shoes being pulled from their maroon felt sacks with the tie-strings, and the shoetrees being removed. He knew that the smell of polish would linger in the room all morning, and he would wait for the sound of the silver shoehorn sliding on the glass top of the dresser where a silver-framed photograph of Evelyn stood by itself. Westy would go to the kitchen to prepare his raw egg in a glass, drink it fast, put the glass in the sink and then down the stairs, raise the garage door, start his sports car, pull out, close the garage door quietly, and drive off into the night. Christopher would listen to the shifting of the gears as the car faded into the fog, and every weekday morning it was the same and, because of the time-difference between New York and San Francisco, work was over by 2:00. During baseball season, when there was an afternoon game, Westy would drive south down Third Street through skid row and along the bay to Candlestick Park where he had the same two seats year-after-year on the second level, a little down the first-base line, and sometimes he would take a business-friend but often he went alone.

TEETH

Christopher was intrigued and confused and repulsed by watching Westy remove the gold and enamel dental bridges from the back of his mouth while brushing his teeth.

REDUCED CIRCUMSTANCES

Evelyn was what a more genteel generation would have called "living in reduced circumstances." She conducted herself with courage, at least in the context of what the rich would consider courageous, yet there were always the remnants. Everywhere things pointed back—the houses in which she did not live, the parties to which she was not invited, the negligent ease. These she had to stand beside again and again in the presence of those who had them and to do so in a way, now formalized, that both acknowledged and diminished their significance.

SOCIAL REGISTER

The little blue book, purporting to be a directory of "polite society," remained nestled just out of sight in the little narrow drawer of the telephone table.

POOL-TOY

Evelyn said that Mrs. Donnelly, "a millionaire many times over," was a pool-toy of a person.

SHEBEE

Chrystabel Eckles, whom everyone called "C.B.", was a short, bowlegged woman with mocha skin, sharp alert dark eyes, and a high voice that sparkled with easy laughter. C.B. was in her sixties at the time of Christopher's birth, and he called her "Shebee" from his first learning to speak. Shebee "worked" for the Westalls in a way that was not quite clear to Christopher, other than that she was often there and sometimes had a cocktail in the kitchen with his parents in the evening. She took him on buses all over San Francisco and looked after him when his parents were away. She came over every Christmas Eve to help decorate the tree, and she and his parents would drink and laugh late into the night, and Christopher would lie in bed and hear ornaments falling to the floor and smashing and everyone laughing harder and harder, even his mother.

THE TREASURE CYCLES

The hidden treasures of Guru Rinpoche were to be recovered in their proper sequence in a progression of concealment and revelation called "The Treasure Cycles."

CHINATOWN

Shebee was widely known and admired in Chinatown. She would often take Christopher to shop in the food markets where, to his grimacing fascination, whole cooked birds hung in windows by hooks in their necks, dripping grease into pans, and live fish swam in tanks, and people pushed and crowded and bickered over prices and the smells were sweet and salty, and for lunch they always ate in the kitchens of restaurants, at tables filled with Chinese, and Christopher never saw Shebee pay for a single meal. She would teach him phrases in Chinese and tell him to say them when she nudged him. They were strings of curse-words coming from the mouth of this little blond white boy, and once he cussed a tong who scolded Shebee and then burst into laughter. After lunch, the big table became a little gambling parlor with cards and bets and everyone smoking and yelling.

SHEBEE

Westy first met Shebee while visiting an old business friend who was down-and-out and living in a shabby hotel on Howard Street. Shebee was caring for him during his final alcoholic decline. Westy arrived one afternoon when she was finishing making his bed, and she told him she had known the man in better times. She said nothing more of why she was there, though clearly he had nothing to pay her. By then she had lost her husband, Wong, and took care of herself. She lived in Chinatown, above a store at Pine and Grant, with her two cats, Goldie and LaFoo, and she and Westy took a liking to each other. Soon, she was coming to the apartment on Sacramento Street and sometimes did the laundry and some cleaning for Evelyn, but mostly she'd share a drink and bring some special food from Chinatown and tell stories of her adventures. Over time, she just became a part of their life, and when Christopher arrived, Evelyn offered to hire her as a sort of a nanny two days a week. She accepted gladly.

SHEBEE'S SON

Shebee had been an opium addict, worked as a maid in a brothel, smuggled religious refugees of every stripe out of Communist China and provided, with her husband, a kind of underground railroad for the new arrivals. She'd had a son, whose name neither Westy nor Evelyn could recall, and though she'd shown them his picture early on, she never spoke of him after that. Evelyn knew what this must mean and did not ask.

COURSEWAY

Shebee lived with depths *and ghosts and guardians and voices and demons and wonders—as if she'd pierced the covering enclosing everything—as if she'd breached the courseway next to us—and sometimes, when you are open in this way, you have to shield yourself—in smoke, in squalor, in forsaking—like dropping to the floor when you've lost your balance.*

COURSEWAY

Westy did not believe in a courseway next to us.

ALCOHOLIC FRIENDS

All of Westy's friends were alcoholic men who were more alcoholic than he.

REPTILE HOUSE

The bond-trading floor at Pacific Bank seemed both steamy and chill, like the reptile house at the Fleishhacker Zoo. There was the sense that those who lived there could live nowhere else and that those who did not live there could hardly bear to linger long enough to view the inhabitants.

CHARLIE DENNIS

One of Westy's alcoholic friends was Charlie Dennis. He not only had two first names, but he had those little burst veins under the skin of his nose and cheeks that Christopher was used to in his father's friends. He was the only person Christopher knew who had an elevator in his house, and Lana Dennis, who wore bright silk turbans and satin pajamas while at home, had retained a nervous little woman, with a petrified-leather-purse-face, whom she called "Garbo," or sometimes "Gabor," neither of which was her name, to operate the lift and exercise stealth in securing a near constant supply of expensive perfume from the City of Paris, which Lana drank, in lieu of scotch, having been cut-off by her doctor for cirrhosis of the liver.

DRIVING TO CANDLESTICK

Westy did not take the Bayshore Freeway to Candlestick, though it was the quickest way. He preferred to drive across Market Street through skid row and the acrid industrial districts that smelled like diesel and creosote and along Third Street. As he drove he'd sometimes tell Christopher stories of his hard-drinking friends in the business who had fallen across Montgomery to skid row. It was sort of the way one might talk about the war that one survived; there was a quiet but steady undertone of pride in all of this, as if drinking was a mandatory thing, like when there's a war and you have to go. How some are not destined to survive this obligation and some are, and no one knows which is which or why, but those who survive present themselves, ever so quietly, as better.

CANDLESTICK PARK

Candlestick itself, which had been built on a landfill, sometimes smelled like garbage, and the wind blew off the bay almost constantly.

CHRISTOPHER'S TREE HOUSE BED

Some nights Christopher put himself to bed by *crawling along the floor very flat because there were men with dogs in pursuit and he pressed himself into the dry sharp crumbling leaves inching along until he reached the secret door at the base of the tree and opened it and, climbing the bedrail, hoisted himself up the narrow ladder into the secret tree house with the bed nestled in the branches out of sight and he would lie very still and hear the predators, the heavy steps and the jingling pulled-tight leashes moving rapidly under him and away.*

EVELYN AND SLEEP

Evelyn didn't really like to fall asleep and anything out of the ordinary woke her. It was not out of the ordinary for Christopher to get up once a night to pee, but if he rose a second time, she woke. Foghorns were not out of the ordinary, but moonlight through the bedroom window woke her, as did the sound of water dripping in the kitchen, even though the kitchen was far away. And once she was awake she could not go back to sleep. So Christopher knew that he must do his part to keep his mother asleep *by not doing anything unusual at night so it couldn't be his fault if she were to wake—it couldn't be a noise he made or a noise that could be placed near where he was or a noise he could have made—if something woke his mother, it had to be something outside or far away or something quick, like the slamming of a door that can't be placed the moment after it wakes you.*

LYDIA MOSIER

Westy's mother was a frightful, gaunt hayride of a woman who came to the flat from time to time unexpectedly and for whom Evelyn harbored a barely hidden enmity. Westy sometimes told stories of how, during the Great Depression, when he was sixteen and working in a sawmill to support her, he would come home to find her being dandled by numerous hangers-on and dog-track types while wearing silk tea gowns she had purchased on credit, and how she insisted on scrambled eggs made with whipping cream. Lydia married often and had never been employed. Byron Westall had been her first husband, and her last had been Bob Mosier, a weak-willed, tag end heir who, in the second year of their marriage, threw himself under a train.

REHEARSAL DINNER

After lots of drinks, as the rehearsal dinner was ending and the guests were departing, Lydia took Evelyn aside and told her that Westy had slept with his boss's wife and that, though she did not doubt that Westy was fond of her and would make a decent husband, she could not count on him to be faithful, "and I know a thing or two about these things my dear," she slurred, taking Evelyn lightly by the wrist. Evelyn pulled away and, steadying herself, faced Lydia squarely and said she thought less of her for the telling than of Westy for the doing, and she proceeded across the room to Westy's side and put her arm through his as he spoke with a business friend, and she never mentioned the exchange to anyone.

DEBTS

At seventeen, Westy closed all of Lydia's department store accounts, and worked for over a year to discharge her debts in full.

SPECIAL EGG CARTON

Evelyn had a special square egg carton into which the eggs from the store were moved from the rectangular cartons in which they came. Since she would use no other, the consumption and purchasing of eggs had to be planned in such a way that she would neither run out nor have any left in the special carton when she brought the new eggs home.

THE TREASURE CYCLES

The Dharma Treasures of Guru Rinpoche, called "Terma," were concealed in earth, water, sky, mountains, rocks and mind. These treasures were to be discovered and revealed at appropriate times across the ages by designated treasure-finders, called "Terton."

ELLY'S GRAND TOUR

Once, when Christopher was a little boy, he brought a finger painting home from school which was entirely brown because he'd swirled all the colors together. He was somewhat downcast about the result, but his mother greeted the painting with adoration and said that she was so proud of it that she was going to put it in a very special place, which he thought would be on a wall in her dressing room or on the refrigerator but turned out to be in a drawer of her cherry desk. After she had carefully pushed back all of her writing things and lifted the draw-bridge writing surface, she pulled the top drawer out and said "See, I'm putting this in the top drawer on the very top. You know it was Aunt Elly who gave me this beautiful old desk before she died, and it is very valuable because it's American and not English. You never knew her, but she would have absolutely adored you," and then she paused and asked, "would you like to see her picture?" He didn't really answer before she closed the top drawer and opened the bottom one. She seemed unusually relaxed. Christopher sat on the floor and saw that the bottom drawer was filled with stacks of papers separated by pieces of cardboard. His mother carefully lifted the top few things from a stack, and, as an aside said just a little sternly, "I keep these things in order, and you are never to disturb them or look in these drawers without my being here." He nodded, and then she showed him a photograph of Aunt Elly sitting sidesaddle on a camel in her wool skirt and sensible shoes with the pyramids in the background and an attendant wearing a fez holding the reins. Evelyn and Christopher started to laugh. "This was part of Elly's Grand Tour in 1950," Evelyn said, and she reached slightly deeper into the stack and brought out a pile of postcards and a large folded map, which she spread on the floor and said, while looking at the card on top of the Tower of London and showing it to Christopher, "her trip ended here," pointing to London on the map, "and before that she was in," and looking at the card of the Eiffel Tower just underneath, "Paris," and she pointed to Paris. The map had lines in blue pencil and places were circled with dates above them, and Evelyn said that she had followed Aunt Elly's trip on this map and circled the destinations as the postcards arrived. Christopher was spellbound by the map and the cards and how his mother knew exactly where Aunt Elly had been and exactly when. And Evelyn said Elly had given her the desk on her return, and she had died not long after he was christened and she had a son, named

Ben, her only child, who was killed flying a new kind of high-altitude plane—"the wings froze, and down he came—an Icarus of ice." Christopher had not seen a look quite like this before on his mother's face—not frantic—but clearly she'd gone someplace else, and wasn't bothering with whether he could follow her—she returned with a start—"he was my friend, Christopher, when I was a girl." Then Evelyn hurriedly put everything back in order in the drawer, closed it, lowered the drawbridge writing surface and exactly arranged her writing things. There was a look of such profound disappointment on Christopher's face—that the adventure was over—that she blurted "Did you know that this desk has a secret drawer?" Christopher began to beam and Evelyn asked "can you find it?"—a remark that she regretted almost at once as Christopher began to pull things out of the cubbyholes. Evelyn, growing nervous, cut the search short. "No, no, it's here," and she pulled on the archway over the cubby in the center, and then she had to tug a little harder because the little drawer was stuck, but then it opened. Christopher looked inside and the secret drawer was empty.

HANSEL AND GRETEL

Pressed against a vast dark forest, a kind woodcutter lived with his hateful wife and two children. Famine was upon the land and they were starving. The cruel wife contrived to abandon the children, Hansel and Gretel, in the middle of the forest so she and her husband could save themselves. The kind woodcutter went along with this. Hansel overheard the plot and stuffed his pockets with luminous pebbles to scatter along the way so he and his sister could find their way back by moonlight.

NOT CALLING WESTY AT WORK

It was a long-standing agreement between Westy and Evelyn that she was not, except in a dire emergency, to call him at the office. Rather, he would call her when he was not busy; which, because he was a man of habit, turned out to be about 10:00 a.m. every morning.

CHRISTOPHER'S BIRTHMARK

Christopher had a small birthmark on the soft space between the thumb and forefinger of his right hand and it allowed him to know right from left.

LOUDON AND SUTTON

The Loudon and Sutton insurance offices on Geary at 24th were a drab and dingy affair, from the names in flaked gold paint on the street-level window to the yellowed, crooked Venetian blinds to the shrill, cranky receptionist to the overflowing ashtrays and the desk blotters soiled with coffee stains and ink. The entryway, where the receptionist had her desk, was small with a rail and a swinging gate that led to two offices at the back. Doug Sutton had the office on the left; Mr. Loudon, as far as Christopher could tell, was never there. Evelyn used to bring Christopher by every now and then on their rounds to drop off a bunch of flowers or a little coffee cake, or they'd just pop in to say hello as a courtesy. Doug was pasty, gaunt and plain, with a flat rectangular face, an easy laugh and a closet full of brown suits. He seemed to live on coffee and cigarettes and those little powdered sugar doughnuts— "Would you like one?"—he asked Christopher somewhat uncomfortably, gesturing toward a small torn-open cellophane package with two leftover from the morning. Christopher was surprised at how cool the sugar felt on his tongue.

FUNERAL INDUSTRY

Westy thought of human remains as nothing more than a sanitation problem, and he held the funeral industry in absolute disdain as senseless, parasitic and exploitative of vulnerable and guilt-rid-den people. For these reasons, he had made arrangements with the Poseidon Society to have his body burned in the simplest wooden box and with explicit instructions that there was to be no memorial service and that his ashes were to be thrown in the Pacific.

THE HOUSE ON TARAVAL

Once, while speaking to Christopher, Evelyn let it slip, in hushed tones even though they were alone, that she would inherit the house on Taraval if Alfred outlived Doug but otherwise it would go to Doug's favorite nephew.

GOOD TO HAVE A SECRET

And Evelyn told Christopher that it was good to have a secret, by which she meant both that there was power in having knowledge that others didn't have and that it was good to be the kind of person who was able to keep a secret.

COAL SMOKE

Christopher's favorite smell was coal smoke and his favorite sound was the knock of the cable car cable on California Street.

SPARK WHEEL

Uncle Alfred gave Christopher *a little grindy spark-wheel with stars and a thumb-pump mechanism: chook chook chook faster and faster until sparks started flying out of the spinning stars.*

WESTY

Westy was never unfaithful to Evelyn.

TERMA

Photographs, paintings and stories are common storage devices for events, but, in the Nyingma tradition, Terma are considered far more powerful than these, because, the Terma store *transmissions*.

GLASS DOG

After their conversation at Grand Central, Amanda Gray called Evelyn and asked if Christopher wouldn't like to come by and see Priscilla's puppy. "Of course he would," Evelyn replied, and after he did of course he wanted one for himself. Amanda had said that Priscilla was less empty now and talk of this vanquished emptiness persisted for days and days. Lydia, who always seemed to find a way to make matters worse, came to the flat one Sunday morning and said "Your grandmother bought you a dog!" Christopher was beside himself with excitement. Evelyn was instantly frantic. Then Lydia held it out from behind her back—a shiny mass-produced ceramic basset hound which Christopher loved more than anything in the world, and "sit," "stay," "play dead," and, about ten minutes later, with "roll over," it smashed into about eighteen pieces on the floor *and Evelyn was unhinged and looked askance at Lydia and Lydia began to shriek that the child should have a real dog and she left in a fit and the following weekend brought Christopher another ceramic dog just like the first; and Evelyn was frantic—you must put that dog on a shelf and leave it there—she said and he did for half an hour and then took it down and was his most careful ever and it was broken all over the floor in about ten minutes.* Evelyn, as with the first dog, threw the pieces in a towel *and she was nearly hysterical, stomping around in the bedroom with the door closed, stammering something about what sort of woman gives a ceramic dog to a four year old and this wicked witch and her wicked wicked gifts*—bits and pieces of speech coming out from behind the door.

GLASS DOG

Evelyn asserted that Lydia would never pay for anything to give to someone else and that she must have secured the ceramic dogs

with coupons from liquor bottles or Pall Mall cigarettes or paregoric or codeine cough syrup or some other thing that she bought
frequently. Westy doubted that they gave away ceramic dogs with
paregoric, but Evelyn could not be dissuaded and told Westy he
must find a way to put a stop to the ceramic dogs.

MORGAN

Finally, Westy took Lydia to a toy store and let her pick out a
stuffed dog for Christopher. She chose a beige basset hound with
black plastic glued-on eyes and a rubbery red tongue. After giv-
ing it to Christopher, she seized it back, pulled off the eyes and
insisted on sewing new ones of her choice, which turned out to be
nested buttons of dark brown, white and red. Christopher paid no
attention to the eyes, played with the dog for hours and named it
Morgan.

THE MESSENGERS

Christopher's habit of picking up scraps of paper and other debris
from the streets started the summer before he entered first grade
at Grant. One afternoon, while he and Evelyn were walking down
Polk, a crumpled laundry list, scuffing along the sidewalk, caught
his attention. He chased it and grabbed it and held it up. "Look,"
he said, "it's a message."

THE MESSENGERS

And Christopher called his collection of debris "The Messengers,"
and he found them on curbs and on sidewalks and in gutters *and
they weren't just papers but bottle tops and foil from cigarette packs and
bits of glass and wood and wire and bolts and he kept them in his pockets until he understood what they were saying and then he kept them in
a special drawer and he kept them with care because to him they were
treasures.*

THE CHRISTMAS GIFT

For Christmas when Christopher was six, Charlie Dennis, who'd made a fortune in manufacturing, gave him a big toy truck with a share of stock inside. Christopher did not know what a share of stock was, but it had the same red PXP as the side of the truck, and it was much more exciting than the many envelopes with money that Westy's other friends had given him. When Christopher was writing his thank you notes, with his mother's help, on his personal stationery, he told Mr. Dennis that the truck was his favorite gift and he hoped to learn about shares of stock someday.

PENCIL MESSENGER

And one time he found the nub of a pencil and the eraser was rounded with use and shiny and the metal casing surrounding it was slightly crushed and much of the bright green paint in the little grooves was gone but the tip was still intact and he could write with it someday if he needed to.

PUZZLE PIECES

The puzzle is the game where something shattered comes back together through your hands, and isn't it really the puzzle itself that decides? Isn't it the puzzle that gets to say which piece fits with which?

THE BANK OF CALIFORNIA

Evelyn would take Christopher to the Bank of California on Union Street, with its ornate ironwork on the outside and marble and nautical paintings on the inside. The branch was small, with only three teller windows. Everyone treated Evelyn with great deference because, he would learn much later, she had placed the money that Aunt Elly had left her, on deposit at the branch in her own name. The manager, Mr. Trent, never failed to invite Christopher and Evelyn to have cocoa and tea with shortbread cookies in a small, richly decorated private room, just to the right of the lobby.

EARACHES

Christopher had frequent earaches as a child, always in the middle of the night, and because he had been told *never to come into his parent's room at night or hover over their bed or touch his mother on the shoulder in her sleep, he would lie in the absolute silence of the flat and waiting to cry out was like holding a rock above a sheet of glass, second after second knowing that you will drop it.*

BANK OF CALIFORNIA

Evelyn told Christopher it was always good to have something that was just yours, and, sitting in the elegant private room at the branch, she would let him hold her prized little blue and gold bankbook with its strange signed entries and plastic sheath. To Christopher, it was more like a messenger than a book. Evelyn said that the money in the account would grow because the bank would pay interest, and it was good to have something set aside for a rainy day. Christopher was mystified because he didn't know what interest was or what money had to do with rainy days, and, anyway, he thought it was more than enough to have cocoa and cookies for free.

ATLAS

Uncle Alfred gave Christopher a small square atlas bound in Moroccan leather with gilt-tipped pages and gold-leaf lettering on the cover. He liked to look at it at night before he went to sleep, focusing on tiny *invisible* countries—the ones never mentioned anywhere—littered among the giants: Andorra, Liechtenstein, Nepal, Sikim, Bhutan, Goa, San Marino, Macau. He wondered how countries so tiny could exist—or even if they actually did—and he liked the strange small maps at the back that showed all the places that spoke the same language in the same color, so it was like the huge countries of languages. Another map showed all the places that were Christian or Buddhist or Muslim, with a color for each religion, so it was like the huge countries of what people believed about God.

SILVER

Westy kept a sterling silver piggy bank in his closet next to boxes of laundered shirts on a shelf above his suits. The silver piggy bank had a hinge on top and a little silver screw on its belly that kept it closed. Sometimes Christopher would see him take it down when he came home from work and put the silver change through the narrow slot. "This money is for your college someday," Westy said.

STAMP COLLECTION

Christopher knew that a box in the closet, on a shelf behind the suits, contained his father's stamp collection. Westy had lost interest in it a year or two before, packing it away, next to the pipes that he didn't smoke anymore. Christopher had recently wanted to take the collection to his room and play with it, and asked if he could borrow it. His father said that one day, which was not today, he could when he was old enough to really appreciate it. The stamps were in rows, each in its little gelatin envelope pasted onto the page: American stamps first, then European, then Asian—colorful country after country, arranged by page, each page arranged by the age of the stamps. Some of the stamps were cancelled; some were not. Christopher particularly liked the entire pristine page of flags of the countries that the Nazis had overrun—especially the flag of Albania with its double-headed eagle. Lots of stamps were just stuffed in the back of the album, loose and in waxy envelopes, disorganized—the ones he'd bought by habit at the end of his interest—towers, ancient archways, flowers and ships, people who were famous somewhere once.

SHAREHOLDER MEETING

A few months after Christmas, Christopher received a phone call from Charlie Dennis asking to speak with Master Westall. He asked if Christopher, as a fellow shareholder, would please accompany him to the Pacific Express Trucking Company shareholder's meeting in Oakland the following month. Christopher was very excited, and Evelyn bought him a little suit and tie *and on the morning of the meeting Charlie's limousine pulled up and the driver got out and opened the back door and Charlie climbed out with a big cigar in his hand and Christopher greeted him at the door, and Christopher climbed into the back of the huge car and it smelled like leather and smoke and the seat that stretched across the back was more like a couch than a car seat and there was a little bar with crystal glasses and it was the only car that Christopher had ever seen that had a telephone.* The headquarters of Pacific Express Trucking was in the drab and grimy industrial district of Oakland near the bay and consisted of several large low gray buildings and vast parking lots and loading docks. The limousine had to cross a dozen railroad tracks to reach it. Charlie made a call to the CEO, a Mr. Glidebar, and notified him that Christopher Westall, the company's youngest shareholder, would be attending the meeting. He also made a call to the Chronicle saying that he had a story for them. The meeting itself was a plodding affair, conducted by smoking old men in a windowless room with numbers and charts and discussions of government regulations and what could be done to defeat them. It was a droning bore and went on and on, but none of this mattered to Christopher because he was introduced to everyone, and he had never been treated with such respect, except maybe at the Bank of California, and a secretary even brought him a Coke, and then another, when the first was finished.

CIGAR BOX

On the way home from Oakland, Christopher admired the wondrous deep wooden box that contained Charlie's Cuban cigars. He mentioned how wonderful it would be to have a box like that to hold the collection of treasures he'd found on the streets, so Charlie instructed his driver to stop by the house and retrieve an empty cigar box for Master Westall, *and the driver was like a wooden man, and his words were like little single blocks falling out of his mouth and he only spoke when Charlie spoke to him and he did exactly as he was asked and Christopher had never seen an adult like that.* The next day in the Chronicle there was a little article about Christopher being the first of the next generation of financiers, which was exciting to Westy and Evelyn, but Christopher mostly just loved the cigar box that Charlie had given him because now he had a place to keep the messengers.

SEPARATE BANK ACCOUNTS

Christopher asked Evelyn how much money his father made, and she insisted that she did not know. He asked her why she did not know, and, after an uncomfortable silence, she nervously launched into a rambling, elaborate explanation about Westy's separate account at Crocker Bank downtown into which his earnings were deposited and how he provided a monthly allowance for her to run the household and that she put this money in her account at the Bank of California on Union Street and how gentlemen kept their financial records at their offices, and she would never presume to ask to see such things because it would be untoward and furthermore such matters were not to be discussed.

BLACKMAIL

Christopher told his classmates that his father was being blackmailed.

ASLEEP WITH A MESSENGER CLUTCHED
IN HIS HAND

And sometimes Christopher would take the messengers out of their cigar box and spread them on the floor, and sometimes he would fall asleep with a messenger clutched in his hand.

AFTER THE SECOND FIRE

Just flesh and bone and time—fabric and wood and fire.

THE MESSENGERS

Foil messenger marked with smeared ink: and you will know shattering; messenger marked with boxes checked in pencil; messenger marked with creases where carefully folded; messenger marked with tire tracks and dirt; messenger marked with lipstick that Evelyn made Christopher throw away: messenger marked with a tiny map of streets of which way to go; messenger marked with a time when two were to meet; messenger marked with numbers; messenger marked with lines that seemed to be random; messenger marked with an X; messenger marked with ash; drenched messenger whose letters had flooded their banks; nail file messenger that Evelyn made Christopher discard; messenger scented with perfume; messenger with what looked like a fingerprint: cloth messenger that had been a piece of a coat: foil messenger that still had bits of tobacco in its folds; messenger of glass with edges that could cut that Evelyn made Christopher throw away: stained messenger; leaf messenger; paper messenger warped inward and made crisp as dead leaves by the sun; blank messengers; torn messengers; crumpled messengers resting in corners, against curbs, or blowing down streets.

DIVOT AND THE MILKBONES

There was a brown and white boxer named Divot who lived down the block, and Christopher liked lying on his stomach on the pavement with Divot next to him. Evelyn hoped that this would solve the dog difficulty, so she called Mrs. Millard, the dog's owner, and asked if Christopher might give Divot a dog biscuit every now and then and—"of course," she said—so Evelyn bought a bag of Milkbones. Christopher would lie on his stomach and Divot's jowls would rest on the pavement, and he would give a biscuit to Divot and then eat one himself.

THE MESSENGERS

And the messengers of stones that did not carry the messages of people; the messengers of barbed wire; the messengers of rain that carried other messengers in their mouths; the messengers that hid in the tosses of coins that could not be found in the coins themselves but only in heads or tails; and the messengers of scattered dirt and scattered dust and scattered sand; that were not paths but were still the stuff of paths, the stuff walked over on your ways to things—that these too were messengers; and the messengers that found no place to rest no place to reside like the scent of the sea; messengers loose in the world like wind except you can't feel them on your skin; messengers housed in memory that you can no longer touch; longing is also a messenger that you carry, that hides in you, that propels your secret goings; secrets are messengers also, that are silent.

SPARK WHEEL

The neighbor's cat liked dogs and was named Neptune because it also actually liked water. It was black and white with half a mustache and it sat on the curb next to Divot, gazing up at Christopher—not at him really but just above and to the right of him, tilting its head to stare into that space. Christopher knew that look; it was the same look he had seen on the faces of the littlest kids when he'd shown them his grindy spark wheel, so he thought there must be something like that wheel just next to him—spinning and sparking and covered with stars that only the cat could see.

SILVER

Evelyn was polishing the silver. Christopher followed the smell of the polish into the dining room. She was buffing a silver bottle with tiny stars stamped out across its surface so the dark inside shone through in black star shapes. She looked up and said "I christened a ship with this bottle when I was seventeen, a submarine, called the Cachalot. I took a train to Boston with my parents, then to Portsmouth, and a throng was gathered at the Navy Yard to witness the event. It was the first ship christened with alcohol after prohibition," and, seeing she'd lost her audience, she continued, "prohibition was a silly law from Kansas, that forbade people to drink."

BHUTAN LECTURES

The professor told the travelers about Patrul Rinpoche's masterwork, *The Words of My Perfect Teacher*, about loving kindness being the image of the mother-bird regurgitating food into the mouths of her young, and about the image of compassion: a mother running along the bank of a rapid river, keeping up with her drowning child, running along the bank because she had no arms.

LUNCH PACKAGES

The sandwiches Evelyn sent to school with Christopher looked like gifts, they were so carefully wrapped—the corners of the wax paper tightly tucked, the twine tugged tightly in a little bow that had to be pulled quite hard to be undone. The lunches inspired many instances of keep-away with Christopher chasing around the play yard trying to retrieve his snatched lunch, but, eventually, the other kids just wanted to know why his mom made lunches that looked like that.

SHOES AND CORNS

One morning, Christopher dared to look through his mother's closet, with the perfumed stole and dresses tight in their zipped-up plastic garment bags with the cardboard tops and double-hooks. Her too-small shoes were stacked in their cubbyholes. Then, he went through the open door with the full-length mirror into the passageway that led to the den and had been converted to his mother's vanity, with its small frosted window, little padded stool, oval mirror, lipsticks, powders and perfumes arrayed on a counter. Behind them was a bottle of mercurochrome for her corns, small circular adhesive pads, a corn-knife, and a scary looking scraper. He knew that he must not smell of perfume when his mother came home, so he *did not linger, and he touched nothing and he did not look through the built-in drawers with her underwear and garter belts and hose and he only briefly opened the door to the shallow linen closet stacked with folded sheets and blankets and white comforters*, and he went through the other door and into the den.

THE SOLID GOLD MONKEY

Christopher's father's bureau was in the den along with the upright piano that his father had wanted to learn to play but, after a few lessons, gave up and hadn't touched in years. An easel stood in a corner with a watercolor painting of a tree because now his father wanted to paint. There was a sofa-bed where Shebee slept when the Westalls went out of town and she stayed with Christopher, an antique chair, and a black and white TV where his father watched reruns of *Victory at Sea*. Looking through the bureau drawers, he found undershirts, handkerchiefs, and cufflinks, and buried at the back of the sock drawer he found his father's solid gold masturbating monkey—a joke-gift, in ill-taste, from a business associate—in its purple felt pouch with the drawstring. It was heavy and shiny and had a little lever protruding from its back, which attached to its arm and partly clenched fist, which was fitted over its erect penis. The hand moved up and down as you moved the lever, which Christopher did several times before putting it away.

PASSAGE FROM GRANT SCHOOL

In the second grade at Grant, Christopher told several of his classmates that there was a secret passage that ran from the play yard to the piano in his den. A few of the kids went home and wanted to know why *they* didn't have a secret passage from Grant and why did Christopher Westall get to have one? It was not long after this that the phone calls started, and his mother froze, and his father asked him what he thought his life was going to be like as a liar.

MONKEY

Christopher wondered if his mother knew about the monkey at the back of his father's sock drawer.

HOUSE OF SECRETS

A house of secrets is a place where glass is safe because in a house of secrets all the brokenness is buried so no brokenness is loose that might attach itself to glass; so the secrets keep everyone safe from brokenness, from being broken, from seeming to be broken, from letting brokenness out where it can rampage, so the glass in the house is safe even if inside everyone is breaking quietly like sticks being broken in towels.

MESSENGER MARKED WITH CREASES

You must learn to say to yourself that you have no arms.

FRANTIC

Because Evelyn was a person without firewalls, any spark ignited the entire world for her—things broken, things spilled, things lost,

Christopher late, things questioned, any rudeness, any surprises, good or bad—Christopher worked hard to be foresightful, to control events and avoid missteps, to avert the hysterical firestorm and the days of icy silence that followed.

BRITTLE

What makes a person brittle? Pain can make you brittle, being like glass or clay, being dropped too many times, being fired at too high a heat, being thrust into the cold, being forced—all these but also this: an insistence on beauty can make a person brittle.

PASSAGE FROM GRANT

Christopher never had to lie about what he'd seen from the back window that day because no one ever asked him.

WEIGHT-BEARING WALLS

Do you think that the past is the weight-bearing wall of the present? Put your hand on the part of the past that bears your weight and try to lean there. What if the present is the weight-bearing wall of the past? What if where weight rests is an origin?

BRITTLE

And all that pushing away of the unbeautiful will make you brittle.

FIRE

And you will not see that something is being celebrated, that with burning there is clearing. There is room in the ash-wake for breathing; there is spaciousness in the fire-wake, a chance to engage the genuine again; that with burning there is untangling—there is a chance to build again or walk away, a chance to engage the genuine again; in that clearing before the making, in that clearing where all the made things stood be-

fore the fire. Now there is only ash and smoke and gutted rooms and un-
hitched motives and scattered history and time shuffled back into cinders.

LYDIA

When Lydia sewed the buttons on Morgan for eyes, Westy said it
was the only work he had ever seen her do.

MINA

Evelyn's sister, whose nickname was "Mina," had drifted up the
coast to San Francisco with her two sons from different, now dissolved, marriages. Evelyn had been keeping Mina out of various
kinds of trouble all her life, usually involving shiftless men attaching themselves to her money, or when she was caught shoplifting
at the City of Paris, or the time she signed a contract to buy a yacht
because the salesman convinced her she could live on it year-round
for free and travel wherever she wanted and pay no taxes.

SUSTAINING THE SMILE

Evelyn had taught Christopher that if someone made a joke, an
appropriate joke, or a witty remark that was tasteful, one was to
smile, in part to make it clear that you got it. But then there was
something else—one must sustain the smile longer than would be
required by simple courtesy. One must sustain the smile longer so
it will be seen as sincere by those who are watching. Christopher
was a bit confused by this. "What if no one is watching?" Evelyn
responded sharply; "Someone is *always* watching. Yes, they will
watch to see if your smile fades too soon, so you must keep smiling beyond when they would likely stop looking so that others
too will know that your smile is genuine; you will notice how often people's smiles are cut short as soon as the person who made
the comment turns away and then you know that their smiles to

you are the same, shallow and condescending." Christopher saw how this doctrine of sustaining the smile came into play in their lives. After Alfred died, Evelyn still invited Doug Sutton to dinner every once in a while, though she did not like him, because if she had not, then her earlier kindnesses toward him would have been betrayed as false, and it would be obvious to those still in her life from when Alfred was alive that she had been interested only in the house on Taraval. So Christopher would hear her on the phone. "We're having Doug Sutton to dinner Wednesday night," and then they would know that she had been sincere.

SILVER

Christopher regularly stole from the sterling silver college piggy bank.

THE JAGUAR COUPE

One afternoon, standing in his father's closet, Christopher pushed through the suits to the shelf in the back and opened the shoebox of pipes, next to the stamp collection. The wood was velvety smooth, and they still had a burnt sweet smell. Christopher put a pipe between his teeth and drew a bitter breath before putting it quickly back. Beneath the pipes were an old photo of Lydia and Westy's father's wallet. Wedged between the box of pipes and the stamp collection was the blue-green wind-up metal Jaguar Coupe made in the British Zone of Germany after the war in its original green and yellow box with the snarling Jaguar logo on the side. Westy had said that the car was not a toy. Christopher brought it out, sat on the floor, opened the end of the box very carefully and, tilting it, let the car roll into his hand. Flipping it over, he moved the little flat toggle switch on the underside, wound it up with the chauffeur-shaped key and released it to perform figure-eights on the hardwood floor.

MEDITATION PRACTICE

The professor had a meditation practice. He sat every morning before breakfast and every evening before bed. A little grudgingly, he gave Christopher some basic instructions for starting a practice himself.

PLAYLAND AT-THE-BEACH

Playland at-the-Beach, San Francisco's only amusement park, was situated on the Great Highway abutting the Pacific at Ocean Beach, and it was like a journey to a place from just before the world became what it was now. Christopher knew that when it was built it fit into the world, but now it was slightly strange—*the warped mirrors in the Fun House, the rotating gallery of mechanical figures above the door, Laughing Sal bellowing over a grainy loudspeaker, the mirror-walk, the air-jets blowing girl's skirts up, the man in the booth controlling everything, the spinning wheel, the barrel rolling everyone over and the long narrow crowded stairway to the huge wooden slide, waxed slick, and the burlap bags you rode down on like flying carpets, the merry-go-round, the mechanical fortuneteller in the turban with hands full of cards and arms moving up and down when you put your nickel in and it dropped a little rolled fortune into a metal dish with flaked paint. The food was awful—hot dogs smothered in chili and cheese, huge ice cream cones and cotton candy the size and shape of the hair of the lady making it, and there was always at least one pile of throw-up in the middle of the walk and next to it a dropped hot dog or elephant ear or ice cream and cigarette butts everywhere, Kleenex and wax-paper hamburger sheaths blowing around, greased-haired kids with packs of cigarettes rolled in T-shirt sleeves and leather jackets flung over their shoulders and the rickety wooden roller coaster that Evelyn forbade Christopher to ride, and a fake Western town with a few uninspired souls standing around in cowboy outfits and the horror ride with the lurching cars and the eyeballs stuck on sticks and the* graveyard with the zombies climbing out of their graves and coming toward the cars and the headless horseman and the scantily clad screaming woman strapped to the gurney in the laboratory being stabbed to death by the mad scientist and the arcade games that no one could ever win and the dusty stuffed animals hanging from hooks as prizes, and it was sort of deserted, except for the stairs to the slide where children packed together like crushed cans and the hideous calliope music and the bumper cars with their piercing electrical smell and sparks and half the cars didn't work and you just sat there getting slammed.

MEDITATION PRACTICE

After the professor's instructions, Christopher shrugged. What could be easier—sitting still and counting your breath—but it wasn't easy, it wasn't easy at all, in fact, it was terribly difficult.

THE STANFORD SCAM

Mina brought her charming, intelligent older son, Scott "Bright" Moreland to the flat one evening with wonderful news; Bright had been admitted to Stanford on a partial scholarship and Mina could cover most of the extra cost but, unfortunately, not all, and she had exhausted every alternative other than coming to them. Would there be any chance that Westy and Evelyn could lend the rest, in three installments, and provide the first one now because the deadline was days away? Bright was there on the couch in the living room—his face was full of promise and apprehension. "I will get a job in Palo Alto," he had said; "I will pay you back as soon as I can." Evelyn thought of all that her sister had been through and how the family had cut her off, yet again, and her discomfort pitched her all at once into a promise that they would help. Mina said "make the check out to me, and I will combine it with my payment and send it to Stanford," and Evelyn had Westy write the check on the spot.

THE STANFORD SCAM

The next morning Westy called Stanford from his office to inquire if the future installments could be written directly to the university and, if so, where they should be sent. No one in financial aid had ever heard of Scott Moreland, and he certainly had never been offered a scholarship. Westy told Evelyn face-to-face when he got home, and the anger and rueful tears that followed led Christopher to understand that it was better to have a secret than to have a secret kept from you.

DIVING BELL

The diving bell was Christopher's favorite ride at Playland. A big metal arm lowered the rust-blotched bell with its portholes into a cylindrical metal tank decorated with an array of painted seaweed and plastic fish, some lying on their sides on the surface because their strings had snapped. The operator nursed a bottle in a brown paper bag under his chair, and the bell just sat on the bottom until everyone was certain that he'd passed out. Then, with a jerk of the metal arm, the diving bell rose like a rocket being fired from a submarine, and massive waves sloshed over the sides spraying unsuspecting people walking by. Nothing about the diving bell was convincing except for the genuine sense of danger when, abandoned on the bottom, seeping water began to pool at your feet.

DIVING BELL

The first time that Christopher excitedly told Evelyn all about the diving bell, she forbade him ever to ride on it again.

FOG HORNS

Christopher lay in bed and listened to the foghorns from the Golden Gate Bridge late into the night. Their baleful, discordant rounds were like a slowly dissolving floor that dropped him into sleep, and he feared and relied on them.

WESTY'S CONTACT WITH CHRISTOPHER

Except for some Saturday mornings and the occasional trip to Playland or the Zoo, it seemed to Christopher that Westy's contact with him was usually the result of Evelyn asking him to transmit instructions or disapproval or questions that had disapproval built into them, such as "Why don't you go outside more and play with the other children?" Or "Why is your room always such a mess?" So Christopher's sense was that Westy was like another voice that Evelyn used to speak to him in a particular way when she didn't wish to speak that way herself.

SATURDAY MORNING DRIVES

Every Saturday morning, Westy went on his rounds through the city and sometimes, though less and less as years passed, he invited Christopher to join him. They would drive to Rinken Annex, where Westy had a post-office box, and then go to Pacific Bank and sign in with the guard, and go up the elevator to the trading floor which, to Christopher, seemed vast. The telephones had multiple lines, toggle switches and lights, and Christopher had never seen phones like these anywhere else. Westy had a small private office, in a row of offices, all exactly the same, overlooking a light well, and he would go into his office, close the door and review the mail and sometimes make phone calls while Christopher waited at the trading desk with an unimportant piece of mail to look at or a blank trading ticket that Westy had given him so that he could pretend to be a businessman. Sometimes Westy would leave Christopher in the office for a while to go across the street to the Traders Exchange Club, because Christopher was not allowed to go there, and the windows of the trading floor looked out on

Montgomery Street so Christopher could look across at the Traders Exchange Building and watch his father go into the little alley with the staircase to the basement marked "Members Only." Once Westy got so involved in a domino game that Christopher was left in his office for two hours. After the office they went to the grocery store, then to the liquor store on California Street, then over the hill to Green Street and home, and they always went to the same places in the same order.

BHUTAN

The professor, who had some familiarity with the native language, carried what he called "another kind of currency," a cache of colored photo-copies of Buddhist saints, scarves, fine incense and other items to offer to the lamas. Dorji, charged with energy and talkative, assisted as a translator, and helped negotiate the group's access to monasteries. Sonam, heavyset and reticent, mostly drove the bus and carried the baggage.

MEDITATION

He sat in the room, by himself, during one of the lectures. Everything rose, fell, and flew apart, like waves slamming rocks. Futile, foolish, pointless—gone again—back—one, two, in, out—the breath in his nostrils, rising, falling—faces, landscapes, narratives, streets—the failed attempts to reach even four, or five.

DIVING BELL

Westy continued to take Christopher on the diving bell, and it was their secret.

KNIFE-PEOPLE

And one night when he was having other people's dreams, Christopher woke to a sound somewhere in his room. It wasn't clear at first what it was or where it was coming from but he realized that something was *actually rubbing like metal filing metal but more animate, like feet scuffing paper or the purr of a distant mechanical cat or the sound before dinner of his father dressing knives, and he felt a glove of ice close in his chest because now he knew that the knife-people lived beneath his bed and they were whispering to each other by rubbing their blades together and it was like listening to people whispering secrets through a wall, and his heart felt tender and tight and hard-at-the-core, like pomegranate seeds or crowds or hail.*

LETTERS

Evelyn was, by training and temperament, of the last generation that still wrote letters as a duty. Time was set aside for correspondence—time to be spent at her cherry desk with her address book, dictionary, and shallow sterling stamp dish. She understood that the letters that one sent were more than a mere platform for relating the current events of one's life; they stood for one; they took one's place in the company of the friend to whom they were sent. As such, the rigors were extensive if one wished to present oneself without a flaw. This was Evelyn's intent with every letter: to demonstrate that the recipient was worthy of a letter without error. She wrote on the finest stationery from the East, with a fountain pen, in the loveliest cobalt ink, using blotters to ensure that there would never be a smear.

SYPHILIS

Driving along Crissy Field in the Presidio, looking across the bay at Alcatraz, Westy mused to Christopher about the death of Al Capone—about how old Scarface had gone from being the most feared man in the country to dying all mushy-brained from syphilitic paresis and that neither his enemies nor the FBI could accomplish what a horde of microscopic screw-worms had managed to do.

THE DARKEST DAYS OF WORLD WAR II

Sometimes on their drives, Westy referred to "The darkest days of World War II," as in "We met in the darkest days of World War II" or "He was lost in the darkest days of World War II." Christopher wondered why these darkest days were so dark and whether these dark days would return like eclipses or ice ages or the times when his mother wouldn't speak for days at a time.

TORNADOES

Christopher tried to read what was written on the surface of the messengers—the numbers, boxes, check marks, the notes and times, the dates and amounts but everything moved around like curtains lifting in wind in front of windows, and there were faces and stories and questions behind the writing in rooms or in fields or at sea, but it wasn't like that really, it was more as if the messengers were magnets pulling everything through him as if he occupied a giant space where tornadoes lived, and the messengers uprooted everything and spun it around and put it down where it hadn't been before and brought things in that came from far away, and the letters and numbers and markings were just the dust kicked up in their wake.

QUAINT

His parents thought that it was quaint when he told them what was written on the scraps, that it was a little childhood game of pretending to read. And when he took them out and spread them on the floor and rearranged them for hours, and talked softly to himself, it wasn't a more serious thing than arranging wooden blocks or joining the wooden tracks of a wooden train or playing with the colorful puzzle that Auntie Mina had given him after losing several pieces at the beach. And his parents even ignored that the things the messengers said were not the kinds of things that a child would say.

HAIL

It hailed one afternoon in San Francisco when Christopher was ten. The kids from the block were yelling and screaming and throwing hail-balls at each other. None of them had gloves and they couldn't believe how cold the hail was on their hands, and boring old Col. Hampton from down the street was talking above the racket, trying to explain how hail was formed by a particle of dust being blown again and again into the freezing-cold sky, so layer after layer of ice is formed until the stone is so heavy it falls to earth. No one seemed to be listening, but Christopher was gathering hailstones and putting them individually on a plate as the hail covered the street, and he crunched his way back to the flat, and while the other kids were building a little hail-man with coal for eyes, Christopher was in his room watching with a magnifying glass as the separate stones dissolved on the plate, looking for the core of dust in each but to no avail. It seemed to him that the hail had formed layer after layer with nothing at the center, and he pressed his tongue to the cold melted water, and it tasted like icy smoke.

INVISIBLE FATHER

Christopher told his classmates that his father could make himself invisible.

THEATRE ON FIRE

One afternoon Evelyn came to Christopher's room with one of her older friends whose perfume was extremely strong, and her skin was so tight and wrinkly that she looked like a papier-mâché puppet, and her nails and lips were the same bright red. Christopher had the messengers spread out on the floor. After a perfunctory smile the friend looked quizzically at Evelyn, and Evelyn said "It's a little game of finding things on the street and making things up about them." "What a wonderful imagination you must have," the woman said, with only the slightest curl of distaste at the edge of her mouth. Christopher looked at her and pointing to a tow truck receipt said, "It says your body is a theatre on fire that you can't escape." The woman rocked back and gasped and covered her mouth. "Christopher!" Evelyn barked, with a punitive thrust of an index finger. But not wanting to make a scene, quickly calmed herself and admonished him saying she was sure he knew very well that the scrap of paper said no such dreadful thing, and she hurried her friend from the room, apologizing all the while, and took her down the long hall to the living room for tea.

THE CLIMB TO THE TIGER'S NEST

Taktshang Monastery, commonly called The Tiger's Nest, clung to a cliff 3,000 feet above the Paro Valley and was, according to the professor, the holiest site in Bhutan. The climb on horseback took hours, and the wooden saddle wore a blister on Christopher's tailbone where he was tilted back by the angle of the ascent. The horse was small, consistent with this country where the size of everything—the Himalayas, the skies, the snows, the vast forests thick with monkeys—worked to diminish the vanity of man. The dzongs were like this too, bringing proportion to human beings, in just the opposite way that skyscrapers do.

THE MESSENGERS

It was never Christopher's experience that he made things up about the messengers.

SHEBEE'S MAP

Shebee had a map that she would unfold and consult sometimes at night. It was a jumble of symbols, tiny writings, arrows, suns, moons, stars, doorways, passageways, oceans and compass-points. She told Christopher that she had many people to watch over and the map helped her keep track of them, like a calendar or clock or like a train schedule. It helped her to know when things were going to happen so she could be there to help.

SHEBEE NEVER NEEDED MONEY

Shebee never seemed to have any money nor any need of it, and her spotless clothes seemed to exist outside of time, the way that certain thrift store clothes seem to have never been in *or* out of style.

THE NATURE OF COMPOUNDS

Christopher learned that there were secret combinations, like water being composed of hydrogen and oxygen—that some things, common and clear, were put-together things, and that this was hidden because water, almost more than anything he could think of, looked like a single thing.

THE DREAM OF THE ANIMAL CUP

Christopher had a dream: he dreamed that Aunt Elly was *standing in front of him, and he asked her how it was being dead, and she said it was OK but could he bring her the silver cup she'd left to Evelyn—the one with the animal faces embossed on it so that she could press their noses to her face because she missed the cold. And he dreamed that he looked for the cup in every cabinet and drawer in the flat, but he could not find it.*

THE DREAM OF THE ANIMAL CUP

The next morning Evelyn found him sitting on the floor in front of the silver cabinet. The fan on the table next to it had been laid gently on its side, and the cabinet door was unlocked and opened. He was sitting on the floor with the cup pressed to his cheek and he was crying. She asked him what was wrong, and he told her about his dream, and her eyes welled up with tears, and she sat on the floor beside him, and cradled him.

LETTERS

There were fewer and fewer opportunities to correspond as the years progressed, friends fell away, and responses to the meticulous letters failed to arrive at the flat.

VOICES

He knew little of the women he'd phoned after Evelyn's death, though he'd met the two of them a few times when he was younger and his mother had taken him to Southern California to visit his grandmother. Of course, there'd been Christmas gifts and thank you notes, and he had been told that once when Mattie, her oldest friend, was kissing her fiancé on a couch a man had snuck in through French doors and grabbed the high-heeled shoes that she'd kicked off and run out with them, and that she and her husband had such terrible fights that they had tape-recorders installed in their house so that they could play back what each had said because they had new fights about what was said during fights, so they wanted to play it all back to prove which one was lying about what they'd said. And he knew that her other friend, Laura, had lost her husband in the Korean War, and she lived a calm and privileged life with their only child, Cynthia, who was about Christopher's age and who had never known her father. He remembered that one evening, on a visit, he and Evelyn had dined with them at the La Jolla Tennis Club, and he and Cynthia had pretended to have rackets and a ball and had played imaginary tennis on a lighted court while their mothers sipped coffee from demitasse cups and shared a chocolate desert.

WAKING PARALYZED

Evelyn told Christopher about a woman who worked at the rummage sale whose son had awakened one morning unable to walk, and the doctors could find nothing wrong with him. Christopher was fascinated and scared and asked how such a thing could be possible. Evelyn said that it must be a hidden flaw in the little boy's thoughts.

VOICES

He said that she died in her sleep, and their voices reminded him of the speaker who came to his bedroom door in the middle of the night when he was twelve, and after a little while of listening he hung up.

RUNNING ALONG THE BANK

You must learn to say to yourself that you have no arms; that there is nothing in the world that you can fix.

THE THROWN-AWAY MESSENGERS

And the rusty tack messenger and the broken bottle messenger and the handkerchief with the pungent scent of cheap perfume, the lipstick tube, and the matchbox messenger with three matches and the messenger caked with mud from having been driven over and walked upon—all of which Evelyn made him throw away. He took great care, when arranging the messengers, to leave spaces for them where they would have been, even though he would never know what they would have said.

THINGS CLINGING TO THEIR USE

Messengers discarded because of rust, sharp edges, filth; messengers discarded because of intimate human use; discarded messengers discarded because they were crushed, crumpled, soiled; messengers discarded be-

cause of fire, because of hard use, because they were used up, because they had been replaced with other things that were fresh and capable of bearing the thoughtless utility of the world—things capable of shining and being blank, of being unbroken, capable of containing and holding and carrying, even while being expendable, disposable, discardable at will, at whim, at first crease or crack—things clinging to their useful-ness, clinging to the closed hands of their users—so as not to be thrown down and trashed, trod upon and unheard, overlooked and made invis-ible—so as not to have their speech taken not for speech but for refuse, background noise, interference, distraction, curled smoke, cracked light, thin air.

FIERCE GUARDIANS

Fierce guardians stand where the world as you have made it will not stand.

THE QUIET KID

Christopher noticed how, in every class, there was always the kid who didn't ever say anything. He wondered if the kid didn't ever say anything to himself either or if he did and just kept it to him-self so it all stacked up in there.

WESTY BUYS A CAR

Westy liked to put his most worn slacks and sweater on and not shave that morning and wear sneakers and go into a fancy British auto dealer and watch the salespeople ignore him as he stood by a sports car and then when someone finally wandered over tap on the hood and say "I'll take it." At first, Westy's method of buying a car amused Christopher and even made him a little proud. But later Christopher realized it was like so many other things in his life, in his growing up, why couldn't his father have taken him along and showed him how to *really* buy a car?

BARBELL

It was as if Evelyn's finding everything to be disturbing brought Westy to the position that nothing was disturbing—a kind of barbell of panic and indifference with Christopher in the middle.

THE SECOND FIRE

The second Thorn fire burned with spectacular intensity.

DAYS OF THE WEEK

Slogging along one foot before the other—Monday, Tuesday, Wednesday, Thursday, Friday, Saturday, Sunday—week after circular week. But the day itself, what was its name, what was the actual name of the day itself? *Day of birds in great number, day of the shadows of trees across your bed as you wake, day of the waterfall thin and small, day of the river of cars, day of fog and walking.* How would you live each day if it had its own name?

STINGY TIPPER

Of a rummage-sale acquaintance tangled in a tawdry divorce, Evelyn had said "She made the mistake of marrying a stingy tipper."

COUSIN TIMOTHY

The first day of the third grade at Grant, a boy approached Christopher with the news that they were cousins. Christopher was very excited and liked the boy, whose name was Timothy, and Christopher knew that Evelyn would be surprised and delighted as well, so he invited the boy home after school to play. When they came into the kitchen, Christopher called happily to Evelyn, "Mom, my cousin found me at school!" But he noticed at once how terribly uncomfortable Evelyn was with all of this, and she could not, of course, explain anything to the children about why, and after allowing the boys to play for maybe fifteen minutes, she made a very formal and somewhat chilly call, feigning a bit of amused bewilderment at how things happen in life, that their children should now be in school together. "Shall I drop him off?" "No, he can find his way home on the bus." It was clear that Christopher was not to bring his cousin home again.

CHRISTOPHER'S COUNTRY

Just after the incident with cousin Timothy, Christopher made a country of his room and would not grant his mother a visa to come in. Her forced entry the following morning to wake him, was viewed by Christopher as an act of war. Uncle Alfred was delighted with Christopher's country and offered to help him design a currency and a flag but Christopher asked instead if he would be his ambassador to his parents.

HOME FOR A YEAR

Christopher's mother kept him home from school for the rest of the year because she thought that the other children were making him sick.

PLAYING BUS

During his year of not going to school, Christopher turned nine. Mostly, he collected messengers and played bus with his bike, going back and forth, up and down his block, stopping briefly here and there except when he played "express." Sometimes a neighbor would ask why he wasn't in school because he didn't seem sick at all.

GOLDEN GATE PARK

And sometimes Evelyn would take him to Golden Gate Park—to the Hall of Flowers or the Natural History Museum or the Morrison Planetarium or the DeYoung Museum of Art.

HALL OF FLOWERS

At the Hall of Flowers, she would lead him along the narrow boardwalks between giant ferns and huge tropical flowers, and they'd sit together on the damp wooden benches and, with all the condensation on the windows, it was as if there were no other world, only this one—quiet, verdant, fragrant, lush and serene— and Evelyn would remark that whole worlds had been this way many years ago, whole structures of social dignity, whole echelons of people who appreciated the sanctity of quiet and how to tend the world properly.

GLASS

Christopher saw that the glass that was safe in the Hall of Flowers was his mother.

BARE MESSENGERS

Some messengers were like the parts of paintings that have no images: slivers of sky, sides of rocks, blank walls that meet to make the corner of a room, sections of bare floor, the light that shines between strands of someone's hair.

THE MESSENGERS

Until after the first Thorn fire, Christopher never thought the messengers were directed to him personally.

GLASS MOTHER

And he thought that a boy with a glass mother should have a glass dog and live in a glass house and have glass motives that were clear to everyone and carry clear memories and carry himself carefully and be mindful of edges and not spill the part of the world that he was assigned to hold and hold the glass tears back so they wouldn't fall and shatter on the floor and be a clear and useful child, an easily seen-through child and not a child who was always about to break.

EVELYN

And he knew that he must shield her, the way your hand in front of your face can shield your eyes from the entire world.

FINGERNAILS

Christopher bit his nails down to the quick, sometimes bleeding when he'd pull a cuticle down the side like a celery string. Evelyn was very concerned about how the appearance of his hands reflected on him as a person, and on her as a mother.

FIRE

How fire is formless and fierce, like time itself, always riding along, holding onto things.

THE ACTION OF FIRE

That making the past of things is the action of fire.

THE ACTION OF MEMORY

Memory is making new, is taking something out of the fire again, each time a new thing out of the fire, each time out of the ash a newly made thing. The action of memory is the action of *walking into being out of vanishing—the fire unmade, the beams unfallen, the smoke retracted, the unsundering, the fire suspended next to everything. The action of memory as the holder of fire in bare hands; in memory the fire walks into being as vanishing—vanishing from Evelyn, vanishing from the hands of Dr. Thorn, vanishing from summers seen through the windows of the M Oceanview. Memory is making again as bare hands make; within that grasp fire walks into being as vanishing, and all that it has touched walks into being as new. Hands extracting fire is the action of memory, so now whole solid things stand free of the fire that had consumed them—people free and whole, as if made new by hands that lifted the fire out of them—but not hands that move like hands across clay, not working hands, but hands that arise in the course of things, like rain—hands that arise like memory itself.*

THE ACTION OF MEMORY

Hands extracting fire is the action of memory. Watch. That which was sundered now stands. You may close your eyes or not. Look. There is a field pulled from the fire and people standing in it. The hand that holds the fire from where they stand is memory.

LIVES OF THE GREAT POISONERS

Westy was reading *Lives of the Great Poisoners*, a biography of Lucrezia Borgia and her clan, and he spoke of slow-acting, tasteless, odorless poisons which, when skillfully administered, pulled the victim into death with no more awareness or concern than a child being pulled in a cart at a pony ride. He left the book on the spotless coffee table, bookmarks poking out of it everywhere.

FINGERNAILS

Christopher made himself stop biting his fingernails.

PENDULUM

There was a pendulum in the Hall of Sciences that proved that the earth was turning because its cable was encased in a frictionless socket so the earth was actually turning under it. It was absolutely silent, back and forth, and a warped reflection of the room would billow and recede in its pointed bulb, and there was a circular row of pins arrayed around it, and in every twenty-four-hour period it knocked all of them down. Christopher would make Evelyn stand with him and wait because he had to see one of the pins knocked down before he would go home.

MRS. POPOVICH

Shebee did some cleaning and shopping for an elderly Russian woman in Oakland who Shebee said loved children. One morning when Christopher was home from school for a year, Shebee came to the flat and said Mrs. Popovich was in a wheelchair and was going to die next week and would Christopher be willing to come visit her because it would cheer her up. After a little breakfast they rode the buses to the grimy bus station next to the Bay Bridge and took a bus to Oakland. The decks of the bridge at the time were two-way, and buses and trains were confined to the lower deck; Christopher had never been on the lower deck of the bridge before, and it was *shadowy and strange and most of the people on the bus to Oakland were black women—some were dressed in fancy clothes as if they were going to church—others wore coats over nurse's uniforms, and they must have worked all night and were going home, and the upholstery of the seats was worn-slick and stained, and the bus smelled of perfume and exhaust.* Christopher huddled close to Shebee because he didn't want to be noticed. Eventually, Shebee and Christopher arrived at a rundown row of apartment buildings on a street with cracked pavement and trash along the gutters. They entered one of the buildings, and Shebee knocked on a ground-floor apartment door, then let herself in with a key and called out "Anyone home… Mrs. Popovich?" Mrs. Popovich was dozing in a wheelchair in the corner of her room. She was dressed quite elegantly in chiffon and silk with a large gold and pearl brooch on her blouse and a feathered hat with a black veil tucked in the curled brim. She startled awake and spoke as if she had not been asleep; "Come, come my child, come, come I am waiting for you, how wonderful!" The apartment smelled like mothballs and apricots. The front room was furnished with only a few stuffed chairs and a rug; the walls were bare except for a single gold icon, and there was a small cage full of parakeets. "Let's get out and see the world," Shebee said, and she took the cage down and placed it on a board which she somehow attached to the armrest of Mrs. Popovich's wheelchair, and Shebee, Mrs. Popovich, Christopher and the birds went for a walk. Mrs. Popovich held Christopher's hand and she seemed as happy as anyone he had ever known.

THE WORK OF THE SPIRIT

After they returned from their walk, Mrs. Popovich was tired but offered refreshments anyway. While Shebee was changing the paper under the birds, Mrs. Popovich leaned close to Christopher, who sat in an extremely uncomfortable red velvet chair that smelled like a very old book, holding a cup of tepid bitter tea that he could not figure out how to get rid of. She said "This I tell to you…remember always…even if it comes to nothing… you must do the work of the spirit." The birds were chirping and fussing, and there was a slight bronchial whistle when she breathed in and out and then, as if he were not paying close enough attention, she grasped his hand quite hard and shook it rather fiercely, and the tea sloshed into the saucer and he was jarred but not afraid at all, and she said "Do you understand…even if it comes to nothing you must do the work that spirit gives to you." And Christopher looked steadily into her eyes, and said that he understood, and, in fact, he did.

MRS. POPOVICH

Arriving at the flat the following week, Shebee told Christopher and Evelyn that Mrs. Popovich had died.

THE TRADERS EXCHANGE CLUB

The club was members-only, and the members were only white men. There was a mummified whale phallus, scrotum intact, sticking straight out over the long, brightly polished bar, numerous booths where members dined on eggs, steaks and sandwiches, and several cavernous rooms filled with felt-topped tables for playing dominoes. The waiters, most of whom had worked there since the war, were exclusively from the Philippines and conducted their duties unhurriedly in starched white shirts and aprons. Near the entrance was a bulletin board upon which the names of all members delinquent in their dues were posted for all to see.

PUBLIC HIGH SCHOOL

Christopher would go to public high school because he would neither have the grades nor his father the money to attend any private school, much less the schools in the East that Evelyn had always had her sights on.

SILVER

Christopher would never go to college.

TIGER'S NEST

Legend held that Guru Rinpoche, in his wrathful form, had arrived at this very spot, in the year 746, on the back of a flying tigress, subdued the evil spirits and local deities, transforming them into Terma protectors, and brought the enlightened teachings of The Buddha to the people. Taktshang consisted of a picturesque jumble of squat buildings with spires and prayer flags adorning tiered roofs, and moss-covered stone steps threading the lip of the gorge.

SILVER

Every month Westy would open and empty the silver piggy bank, put the change in rolls and write a deposit slip. Christopher had to be careful not to steal so much that it would be easily noticed.

FIRE

The Tiger's Nest had been destroyed by fire many times.

MR. BAKER'S

There was a small corner store around the block from the flat; the owner stocked lots of penny candies as well as canned foods, cleaning products, milk, sugar, butter and soda pop, and you didn't have to cross a street to get there, so the kids on the block could go. This was where Christopher bought candy with the money he stole from his father. Fifteen stolen cents would buy a box of Jello and a stinky finger-puppet, and he'd walk to Cow Hollow, sit on a bench, watch the kids on the swings, and eat the Jello powder.

JAPANESE SCREEN

There was a long six-paneled Japanese screen made of paper and wood hanging by itself on the west wall of the dining room. The frame was black lacquer and the richly designed border looked like the curling patterns on the black iron Japanese sword-guards that his mother collected. The hinged panels, each about three feet tall and two feet wide, were painted with both black and brightly colored inks and depicted the single, continuous scene of a bustling town rising in tiers from the banks of a rushing river toward the green rounded mountains that rose behind it. The foreground and the sky were gold leaf, which also intruded as mist across the mountains and upper edges of the town. The scores of people going about their lives, the houses and temples, trees and animals were painted in sharp detail. On the left, the river poured over a small falls, and far to the right, where it had calmed, flat boats, propelled by men with long poles, carried elegantly dressed passengers toward a dock on the bank where men with litters waited to carry them up dirt streets to large houses in the hills where members of their households could be viewed through windows playing board games, sipping tea or lounging on brightly colored cushions while their servants were busy gardening, gathering flowers or sweeping. The houses were mostly tan—the largest had roofs made of overlapping tiles—and the temples were red, as if they had been lacquered; some of the roofs were shingled, some thatched, and some had rocks on them laid out in rows. And there were horses with brightly fringed saddles set on red blankets that carried richly robed noblemen with servants walking beside them, and horses with no saddles at all, carrying large bundles of hay and led by ropes. There were men and women carrying baskets balanced on poles placed across their shoulders, a bridge across the narrows of the river, a family having a picnic behind a pale blue screen by the bridge, and there were men with fishing poles, and men in loosely fitting loin cloths who had just emerged from the water, and oxen, and merchants carrying goods. The trees were covered with blossoms, and the river bulged with snow-melt from the mountains rising behind the town. Somewhere near the top of one mountain were the spires of a temple poking through gold clouds and a path with a halfway house leading up, and pilgrims and worshipers were ascending with gifts in their hands and returning empty handed. Christopher returned to the screen again and again.

JAPANESE SCREEN

Many times Christopher tried to count the figures on the Japanese screen but lost track every time because he couldn't be sure if he'd counted this person yet or this one twice, so he didn't know how many people lived in the town by the river. But the first time he tried to count them was the first time he ever counted to one hundred, and he knew that there were many many more. The screen gave the overall impression of enormous clarity and calm—of a bright, spotless world ascending in tiers from the river's edge to the tops of the green rounded mountains in the distance. And the thing that could not be escaped, but that Christopher did not yet know how to say to himself, was how everyone in the picture had been granted a sense of place, a way of belonging to everything else, and there was no apparent effort in enacting this—this continuously proportional inclusion in the whole—it was given, granted, effortlessly acquired, and given so wholly that no one in the scene was even aware that it could be otherwise, and, aside from its balance and beauty, this was what was calming about the scene, and that, in spite of everything going on, much of it was blank—empty mountains, empty foreground, empty sky—so there was room to breathe, and all the human endeavors were in balance with this spaciousness.

THE GROUNDLESSNESS

You can touch the groundlessness cradling the given; it is right there, just behind your first memory.

MEDITATION

In spite of the difficulties—the pain in his back from just sitting up straight—the burning in his legs from partially folding them—the boredom—the seeming pointlessness—he persisted.

JAPANESE SCREEN

Especially during the year that he stayed home from school, when Evelyn was working at the rummage sale and Shebee was cleaning the kitchen, Christopher could be found sitting calmly in front of the screen or walking in front of it examining it or standing in front of it looking at some detail.

HARPSICHORD

Christopher had a collection of Wanda Landowska 78's that he played repeatedly on his little turntable, and he wrapped the hammers of the piano in the den with foil in an attempt to emulate the sound of the harpsichord.

THE DREAM OF BARRICADES

And Christopher had a dream; he dreamed there were *barricades on the other sides of all the doors in the Westall's flat, and he was in the long narrow hall going from door to door, trying to open them and some would open a little and some not at all, and he could feel the weight of the barricades pressing from the other side.*

SCHRADER'S

On Union Street stood the venerable Schrader's Stationery store— *since 1906*. Miss Schrader, daughter of the founder, had taken over the business when he had died. Business was not good, and the store was mostly empty. Evelyn had commented that fewer and fewer people seemed capable of correspondence, and she would have liked to give Schrader's her business but by custom ordered her stationery from Copley Square Stationers, in Boston, and what with the Woolworth's opening down the street, it was a miracle that poor old Miss Schrader could keep the place going at all.

ATLAS

Christopher loved looking at his atlas, especially at night before going to sleep. He was in a swirl of desert sands or in a wooden-hulled boat beached on the sandbar of an island in the Indian Ocean or being rocked on the back of an elephant or in the canopy of a teak forest in a house built among the trees far away asleep in a land somewhere.

THE MESSENGERS

Only slowly did Christopher come to see that together the messengers actually made a single thing—but not a single thing like a put-together puzzle, but a single thing like a symphony or a city, and he knew that each messenger had something to say by itself, but now he understood that together they had something else to say, and he wanted to know what it was.

KEATSIAN WAIFISHNESS

Christopher was thin, tousled, intense and disoriented, with a Keatsian frailty, a fine-boned waifishness that was endearing or off-putting depending on how you were with waifishness.

THE SHIP STORY

Westy was not keen on waifishness, did not care for waifishness, did not fancy waifishness of any kind. Westy had been tossed by the Great Depression from his upper-class origins into servitude at that sawmill, and he did not fancy weakness or translucence or frailty in any form. During World War II, he had been a signalman on a liberty ship, running the torpedo-infested waters of the North Atlantic. He told a story of how, one morning during the darkest days of World War II, a signal went out in error from the Flagship for the convoy to slow down. As a result, the ship in front of his took a torpedo to the engine room that would have blown his ship to smithereens had the false order not gone out. There was no sense of destiny in any of this because Westy did not believe in destiny; neither was this story a metaphor for anything because Westy was not keen on metaphors. Westy was keen on a world that stood for itself.

LOST BOYS

Christopher wanted to be one of the lost boys on an island somewhere.

THE STADIUM CLUB

The Stadium Club at Candlestick Park was windowless and plush. Originally intended for the exclusive use of season ticket holders, scant business had opened its doors to anyone wearing clothes. In the bar, an ancient, seemingly mummified cocktail waitress hovered in a miniskirt, smoking long, unfiltered cigarettes—the smoke curling from her mouth and gathering in the silver beehive hair that rose like cotton candy above her head. At her elbow, on the bar beside a book of matches, was a cigarette pack holder made of that aqua woven nylon stuff they make toilet seat covers out of. She weighed maybe eighty pounds, and Christopher was sure that she had seen them build the Golden Gate Bridge and maybe even the Palace of Fine Arts. She wore the reddest lipstick ever and caked her face with powder. She'd stand leaning on the bar reminiscing about Old San Francisco and Seal Stadium and how nothing was what it used to be. Westy called her "May," and always ordered double Gibsons on-the-rocks and made it clear that he wanted nothing to do with talk like that.

THE TIGER'S NEST

There was a room in the back of the lamasery at the Tiger's Nest, large enough for only one person to enter at a time, with a single small gold statue of the Buddha on a low, bare table. It was said that any request made there would be granted.

THE CITY OF THE MESSENGERS

Christopher called the single thing that the messengers made *The City of Messengers*, and he built it during the year home from school. He had to find his way in putting the pieces together side by side because each was still a messenger in itself, and it wasn't as if they didn't belong together in a particular way. It wasn't as if they each didn't have a place that had to be found. And the City of Messengers was like the city itself, only it was the city of things that had been thrown away.

STINKY FINGER-PUPPETS

The papier-mâché finger-puppets that Christopher bought at Mr. Baker's were little hollow heads attached to patterned pants and dresses, and they smelled like dental drilling and their faces were contorted and rouged. Evelyn routinely seized them and put them in the trash, and Christopher routinely brought home more. They rested on his fingertips, jabbering and fighting among themselves, but they always took his side in every important thing, and he liked them even better than candy.

THE SAINT LUKE'S RUMMAGE SALE

Evelyn volunteered at the Saint Luke's rummage sale, which was an annual event the preparations for which took many months. Evelyn grew increasingly agitated as the sale approached, complaining about the other women not doing as they had promised and how her opinions were often ignored. Even so, she could not be dissuaded from continuing.

NAILS

When someone has made a lifetime of driving those nails, you can't tell them that what they've made has no value.

TIPTOES

Christopher walked on tiptoes as a child.

THE CITY OF MESSENGERS

And the laundry ticket messenger, the bus transfer, the paperclip and the folded note, the tiny tin box, the bent nail found at a building site in a web of string and sawdust, the messenger that looked like a leaf but was actually oil cloth—missing messengers, vacant spaces arrayed on the City of Messengers, the thrown away messengers now showing themselves to no one, now showing themselves as nothing—hidden messengers, messengers appearing to be things that they were not, broken messengers and vanished messengers whose spaces in the City of Messengers still remained.

THEORY OF SOUND

Because of his theory of sound, Christopher never talked out loud to himself at home about anything that he didn't want his parents to know about, even when he was completely alone in the flat.

WESTY AND THE PAST

Westy didn't believe in regret almost to the point that he didn't believe in the past, or only the past in a war after war kind of way, in that way that war is a way of being in the world without a past, in that way that the action of war is always immediate and never personal, because in war there are only things thrown through *the gigantic*. Westy was in the world in this war kind of way, in this action after action kind of way, in this trade after trade and drink after drink kind of way. And Westy didn't really believe in the past because what can you do in the past?

WORMS

The Chinese medicine chest in the front hall had worms; you could see the little wood-dust on the dark polished floor. Evelyn was ambivalent, year after year, about going to the expense of having it pressure-treated because she said it wasn't really fine or valuable.

THE GIVEN

The given presents itself as that which cannot be otherwise, and you see no need to be grateful for that which cannot be otherwise.

THEORY OF SOUND

Christopher's theory of sound was that all the sounds ever made were still here, humming lower and lower, and you could hear them somehow in a part of yourself, and the sounds hid themselves in thoughts and intuitions and suspicions and things people said to themselves that they thought were their own. So if you went into a room and you started to think of something it was something that someone had spoken of in that room maybe long ago.

SILVER

One afternoon the lacquered straw seat of the antique chair that Christopher used to reach the silver piggy bank began to stretch and tear. Christopher knew that this was sure to be discovered by Evelyn, and probably soon, so he tried to push the seat from underneath to flatten it but it just made a little dome, and he tried to push the straw back where it had pulled out from the frame but it was no use. He knew he would be called upon to explain why the chair was broken because they never used it, and how could they fail to figure out that he'd been stealing because there was nothing in the room but the piggy bank that he'd need a chair to reach. And he knew that from now on he would have to stand on the wooden rim and not on the seat, but he still had the problem of explaining how the chair got damaged because he knew it would be noticed, and he would be called upon to explain how it had happened.

WEIGHT

Westy gave Evelyn a postal scales but she didn't trust it, so she didn't use it. But she left it on the top shelf of her desk and she dusted it.

CHRISTOPHER

Christopher could not keep up with his comb or remember what time the field trip was or to pass along announcements from his teacher or to grab his lunch from the kitchen counter on his way out the door day after day. His features were sharper and more adult that most children, and he liked to talk to himself, and he grew up thinking that everyone drank like his father, and he liked to be alone.

THE SHIP STORY

Christopher understood that if the signalman had not sent the signal in error, he would never have been born.

TIGER'S NEST

Alone in the small cold room, prostrated before the gold Buddha, Christopher wished for snow.

SILVER

Maybe he should take the chair into the closet in his room and stand on it so hard that his foot pushed through and go to his mother and admit to having broken it and she would become frantic but at least it would not be discovered that he was stealing. But why was he using the chair from his father's den instead of the one in his room? There could be no answer.

THE LADY WITH THE PACKAGE

One afternoon when Christopher was playing outside the flat, a thin, jumpy woman wearing horn-rimmed glasses and smoking a cigarette walked up and asked if he would like to make a dollar delivering a package to an address a few blocks away. Christopher said of course he would, so she said that she'd be back with the package in half an hour. Christopher went inside and told his mother about this wonderful opportunity, but his mother was not pleased. When the woman returned. Evelyn told her that her son would not be delivering the package. "Oh, you'd rather he didn't?" "He may not." "Very well," she said and departed hastily. Christopher often wondered what was in the package and why the woman did not just deliver it herself. Or was she part *of a kidnapping ring, and he was being lured away where he could be safely snatched? He wondered if he could have convinced them to let him join. Or maybe the woman had had a bitter falling out with a friend and had something of hers she had borrowed and needed to return, something valuable, and couldn't bear to see the friend's face or have any words, and if she could just find a trustworthy boy in the neighborhood then she could return the item without having any contact with her friend.*

COBALT TABLECLOTH

Evelyn had a cobalt tablecloth that made the sterling silver look almost white. She preferred the little silver bowls with the tiny spoons for shaking salt onto food. You had to learn control to make this work. Christopher was schooled meal after meal: never sing at the table; never interrupt; show interest in what is said no matter what; always leave a little food on your plate to demonstrate that the serving was more than adequate; use the forks from the outside in; eat soup by stroking the spoon away along the surface, then bring it back to your mouth; never slurp; never sing; keep your elbows in and off the table; keep your controversial thoughts to yourself; place your knife, blade pointed in, above your fork at a diagonal on the plate when you are finished.

SILVER

When he emptied the piggy bank the following week, Westy found four pennies. He mentioned them to Evelyn because he didn't put pennies in that bank, and maybe a penny could find its way in by accident but not four of them. Christopher was called into the room and asked what he knew about this. "I wanted to help with college" was all he said as he looked at the floor.

DINNER IN THE DEGRADED WORLD

Evelyn worked hard before company came, and Christopher noticed how delicate and quiet she became when the dinner table was finally set just so. When dinner arrived, there were tightropes to be walked and no nets, and when people fell, it was Evelyn who shattered. Executives, whom Westy entertained, made rough remarks, slopped food everywhere and drank cocktails, instead of wine, during dinner. Evelyn was beset with an almost constant chipping away of the world as she conceived it—a world where everyone knew their part in the choreography of manners and decorum. Just beneath every expression and inflection was the sum of what it cost her to live in the degraded world among debased souls and to have to serve them for her husband's purposes.

WATER RING

The morning after one such occasion, to his horror, Christopher noticed a bright white water ring on his mother's antique coffee table—a guest had carelessly neglected to use a coaster—and he was sure that she would be *frantic* when she noticed it. She wasn't. She was not upset in the least. "The glass left a ghost," Christopher ventured. She smiled and responded resolutely, "We'll be using *all* of the four elements to solve this. We'll start with the first three: *fire*, *ash* and *abrasion*." She took a cigarette from a silver box and, lighting it, set it in an ashtray to burn while she retrieved a soft cloth from a drawer in the sideboard. Then, she picked up the cigarette, held it over the water ring and tapped it lightly, letting the ash fall into the middle of the ring. She then placed the cloth in Christopher's hand and, guiding it in a series of circular motions, spread the ash along the ring's circumference. "See," she said, and, after several times around, the ring was gone. Christopher was gleeful and astonished. Then, after a long pause, he asked "What's the *fourth* element?" Evelyn smiled "It's *care*," she said.

SILVER

A few days later, while dusting, Evelyn noticed that the seat of the chair in the den was broken. She said nothing and took the chair to the storage room in the basement, putting a sturdier chair in its place.

NATURAL HISTORY MUSEUM

Christopher liked to go to the Natural History Museum in Golden Gate Park almost as much as his mother liked to go to the Hall of Flowers, but he didn't understand *what the stuffed animals had to do with history—they were very much there, weren't they? They stood beside each other, quiet and stiff as people on buses—were people standing stiff beside each other on buses about history too? Positioned in their massive dioramas: gorillas, gazelles, giraffes, bears, buffaloes, birds in glassy pools beside tall grasses, cheetahs, wildebeest, all frozen in their habitats. It was like a zoo for people who didn't want to feed things; perhaps it was his mother's kind of zoo, though she didn't like it. No straining to see the animals, no crowds, no strollers, no smells. Maybe it was about what things alive would look like if they were history, if they were already not alive—yes, the displays were more like memory, and they had that behind-glass feeling that memory sometimes has. Maybe it was like a zoo of memory, memories of animals; maybe that was what it had to do with history.*

PENDULUM

The idea that the room, the park, the world, were rotating under the pendulum at the Hall of Sciences was very hard for Christopher to grasp.

THEORY OF SOUND

Christopher lay in the street next to the curb, with his ear pressed to the asphalt, because he wanted to listen very closely to see if there was a pool of sound, even just half an inch deep—if there were remnants of car horns and tire hums and things people had said. The boxer ambled up and lay beside him, and Mrs. Millard called Evelyn, asking if she knew that her child was lying in the street with Divot.

CHRISTOPHER READING

Christopher could not read like other children. He would stare at the page for what seemed a long time but little of what was there seemed to reach him. If other children were reading aloud, Christopher could sometimes keep his place with enormous effort. More often he would slide from the well-marked roadway of the page to the fields on either side where a kind of fragmented movie was in progress all the time, _and it was like looking at the messengers or having other people's dreams, and islands were there, houses with stone verandas, statues and hallways with gilt mirrors, traffic and destinations, alleys, broken bottles and migrations across great deserts, stained glass windows, gardens overgrown behind their walls; laughter was there sometimes along boulevards, caves were there that led to underground rivers, and crowds were storming walls, and climbers were falling from mountains and birds from the skies, and sometimes something familiar was there, like the face of one of his mother's friends at the market and voices sometimes and the smells of smoke and salt and the open sea was there and a man growing smaller and smaller as he walked down the beach and showers of leaves and arrow showers and meteor showers and narrow mountain paths with travelers strung like pearls and chrome and exhaust and hairpin turns and silver wings and rows of sewing machines and herds of animals galloping and parking meters expiring and the earth shaking and glaciers shearing off into the sea and cities falling and someone opening a letter by a window, and he could see the javelin-thrower on the stamp._

CHRISTOPHER READING

But it wasn't a fragmented movie really because it wasn't just pictures moving. _If you dip your hand into hot sand on the beach and let it sift through your fingers_, it was more like that.

CHRISTOPHER READING

And he could look through to the words; and he could make him-self make them out one at a time: this word, this word, that word, *silence, rain, rockslide, firestorm, hallway, mirror, stone steps slippery with moss—the sense of one's weight as it shifts on the back of a horse. If acceleration is the hand of the intended, if the past is a thin silk scarf imprinted with pictures blowing behind that buckles and brushes your face, if breaking into pieces is prayer—so too could Christopher find each word by word on the page somewhere.*

THE WONDER OCEAN

Christopher called the place where he went when he tried to read "The Wonder Ocean."

BOB BOYEUR COMES TO DINNER

As far as Evelyn was concerned, when it came to Westy's boss, Bob Boyeur, Westy might as well have brought a hyena home to dinner. The drunken executive not only repeatedly called her "Evie," but after chowing his way through three servings of Dungeness crab and asking if there was any more, proceeded to drink the finger bowl and fall asleep in his chair. From then on, Evelyn referred to Westy's boss as "That Horrible Bob Boyeur," as in "That Horrible Bob Boyeur called this afternoon while you were at the game" or "That Horrible Bob Boyeur was in the paper again today." Westy would somewhat grit his teeth each time Evelyn spoke this way of his boss, but he did not argue.

WIND

Christopher did not understand how the uneven heating of the earth caused wind; the flat was unevenly heated, and there was no wind in the flat.

SHEBEE'S CLIENTS

Shebee took care of numerous people, mostly elderly souls who rarely left their homes, all over the Bay Area. She would shop for their groceries, pick up their medications, clean their apartments, take them for walks and keep them company. They all had her phone number; if anything was wrong, they could call her, and she would come. Shebee had a client who claimed to have lived two hundred years. "It's well documented in the Bible that people can live that long," Shebee had said, and though Christopher did not consider anything in the Bible to be well documented, he was still interested. Another of Shebee's clients had created a private language that she claimed was the only language God really understood, and she prayed for the world day after day. And another of Shebee's clients had hat boxes filled with models of tiny cities he had worked for years to build.

THEORY OF SOUND

And he wondered where sound really went, and why it dissipated all at once instead of slowly like water evaporating from a dish.

THEORY OF SOUND

He learned that sound dissipated right away because it travels fast. *So why don't you hear all that's been said whirring by you all the time like standing in steady wind...why isn't sound like a wall of water flooding you constantly...why isn't what you say lost in a sea of sound before it can even be heard?*

LOOKING FOR WESTY

Christopher was looking for his father, which was a mystery, since his father was sitting in the same room with him. He really didn't know how to look so that he could find him—how to look to be able to see what was right in front of him—to look through his father's distraction, like looking through churned water, to see what was underneath.

THEORY OF SOUND

Why doesn't sound accumulate until the buildings shake, and, anyway, what does it mean for sound to dissipate? When water evaporates, it goes into the clouds and condenses and falls—so why isn't there a torrent of sounds from the past? And if sound doesn't rise but sinks to the ground, then after centuries wouldn't it be miles deep? So why aren't you drowning in sound?

THE DAY WOULD ARRIVE

The day would arrive when Christopher would decide why his father had paid so little attention to him.

THE DREAM OF CARRYING GASOLINE

Christopher had a dream that he was carrying gasoline in paper bags and the paper bags were thinning and dripping trails of gasoline as he carried them. Thankfully, there was no fire *but for how long? In the dream he was hurrying. He was walking as fast as he could. And the outside of the thinning paper bags looked like wet wax, and the bags were dripping gasoline from their corners, and he was hurrying along with his hands clenched around the folded tops of the paper bags, his knees slightly bent so the bags would be close to the ground.* In the dream there was nothing unusual about what he was doing, except that he couldn't remember where the bags were supposed to go.

ALCOHOL AND DOMINOS

Jack O'Neal was a gentleman in that weak, deferential, self-damning way that some alcoholics are gentlemen—in that way that you never want to be noticed, because if you are not noticed, then nothing will interfere with your drinking. O'Neal was a gnarled, wiry man who had an index finger that he could not straighten, which fascinated Christopher. His voice was gravelly and syrupy at the same time, and he mumbled more than spoke. He was never rude, and he never swore and was never without a lit cigarette. He seemed to be Westy's best friend. Christopher never really heard his father and O'Neal have a conversation. It was mostly a series of grumbles, insults, snipes and barbs, interrupted with bursts of laughter. Often on Sunday afternoons Christopher would hear the clicking of the dominos from the living room.

RUGGER

That horrible Bob Boyeur and his wife, Elaine, invited Westy and Evelyn to their Russian Hill apartment for a small cocktail gathering. Evelyn went reluctantly. She and Elaine, who was childless and spent her life on the phone, chatted vapidly while Elaine doted on her corgi, named "Rugger." Rugger routinely welcomed visitors on arrival but attacked them as they left. No one said a word because Bob was important and Elaine was devoted, so her few friends suffered it as one suffers the children of one's friends, except that children rarely bite people on the leg as they are leaving.

SHEBEE'S CLIENTS

Shebee suggested that the things that her clients did were not any more absurd than what most people were doing.

BRIDGE

Evelyn insisted that Christopher learn to play contract bridge because she foresaw a future where a bachelor would be in demand as a fourth, and the type of young ladies he would meet would be the type of young ladies who played bridge. Christopher thought of the cards in bridge hands *as sets of indoor messengers like indoor animals that knew how to behave and not like the wild messengers he picked up on the streets and these tamed messengers made pristine little worlds when thrown together and together they made messages that turned out to be rules he had to figure out and follow and believe in for a little while until the cards were picked up and shuffled and dealt again.*

NATURAL HISTORY MUSEUM

The night sky in the diorama of the night-hunting caracal reminded him of his mother's cobalt tablecloth, scattered with spilt salt. The scene itself, frozen and quiet, reminded him of his house.

BRIDGE

Christopher was remarkably good at bridge. Actually, fairly quickly, he was more accomplished than his parents—something that they were constitutionally incapable of seeing.

THE UPSIDE DOWN DIAGONAL WORLD

Once as a child, while walking down Polk Street with Shebee and his mother, a man, bent forward, swinging his arms wildly and yelling "You don't know what you're talking about," over and over, rushed by them on the sidewalk. Christopher said of the man that he lived in the *upside down diagonal world.* Shebee said that he made a wonderful contribution by reminding everyone of this important truth.

THE UPSIDE DOWN DIAGONAL WORLD

The day would come when Christopher would see that the upside down diagonal world lay just beneath the carpentry of routines—that it could open under you at any time—and the carpentry starts to fall apart faster than you can hammer, and you reach a point where you throw the hammer down and you want to pull the boards away yourself; you want to tear your way into the upside down diagonal world and leave the world laid out in lines behind.

It's not a choice like the choice to go to the store, or the choice to become a lawyer. You are looking for something to use to tear the floorboards up, and the only tool left lying around is huge and hard and blunt and hard to use sparingly: the only tool left lying around is madness.

BHUTAN LECTURES

The professor introduced a key work by the Third Dodrupchen Rinpoche (1865-1926) explaining, in detail, the manner of concealment and rediscovery of the Dharma Treasures scattered by Guru Rinpoche. The title of this text was *Wonder Ocean*.

MEDITATION ON DROWNING

He started to notice his thoughts—flying particles—he noticed how much of his time he had spent carpentering an artificial past to produce a fantasized present, and for the first time he recognized this as flight, as a fierce swimming from what could not be fixed, and he faced the voracious emptiness that had inhabited the space just next to him all the time—he saw how he had run from it continuously—into fantasy, into dreaming, into planning. He witnessed the very moment of turning away, of fleeing.

SHEBEE'S CLIENTS

One afternoon while he was playing hangman with Morgan and thinking about Shebee and her clients, Christopher realized that all of Shebee's clients were strange, and while, until that moment, Shebee had always just been there in his life, it suddenly occurred to him that he and his family were, actually, Shebee's clients, and he wondered which of them was the strange person Shebee was there to serve.

TEST-DOCTOR'S OFFICE

The receptionist looked like the kind of person who should have a lazy eye or a therapeutic shoe. She signaled Christopher to sit. The test-doctor was so shiny that Christopher thought of the plastic fingers story, and the test-doctor's office did not smell like people; it smelled like the wax Westy used to polish his Austin Healy *and the people looked like wax people or people dipped in wax and men in white doctor's coats showed Christopher pictures of flies with five legs, a bird without a beak and a four-pointed starfish and what was wrong with this picture, and six plus six and nine times nine, and who wrote Romeo and Juliet and how many states can you name, and what color is this and what shape is that, and what do you get if you mix blue sand with red sand—read this aloud, put it down and tell me what it said— stand on one leg and touch your nose with your eyes closed, and an eye chart, and an ear test in a little booth with beeps and lights.* After what seemed like hours, Christopher went home with his mother.

PETS

Though she said that it had to do with the lease, even more than smells or furniture scratches, it was actually the inconvenience of death and goodbye that led to Evelyn's ban on pets of every kind.

HARPSICHORD

The sound of Wanda Landowska's harpsichord on the 78 was distant and muffled, echoing as if it were coming up from a great depth, as if time were a kind of *ocean and the farther back you went the deeper you were, so her notes arose from so long ago they took a while to reach the surface, and by the time they got there they were just a little bent from the change in pressure because time bends things as they rise through it; the surface is thin and light and the depths are dark and pressurized. He imagined her playing down there deep in the sea, her*

*harpsichord resting on a sea-shelf, her hair floating above her head. It
didn't matter that she was dead in the world where he was because she
was still sending music up, and when it broke the surface, it bent the
world a little where he sat in his room because there wasn't anything
left that conformed to it.* He sat in his chair and thought how if he
tried, he might follow the music back down into the depths and
touch her fingers as they flew across the keys.

THEORY OF SOUND

Maybe sound goes where the past goes. Maybe sound goes where
the dead go. Maybe the underworld is full of sound.

OUTSIDE THINGS

Christopher knew that he must learn to withstand the outside
things, the hard things; he must come to grips with desks, pencils
and chairs. He knew that he could never let these in, that he must
withstand them, but not in a way that would draw attention to
himself but in a supple, continuous, determined way. He knew that
he must keep them out while seeming to be involved with them.

WAR LETTER FROM WESTY TO HIS FATHER

Back at last after a trip that was anything but dull. Before I go any
further I might as well tell you I am well and very happy to be back
to the good old U.S.A., even though I haven't as yet set foot upon
beautiful earth, as we are now sailing up Chesapeake Bay bound
for Baltimore. I hope you have been well and that you received the
two letters I wrote you. Guess you would like to hear about the
trip, so here goes. We left New York just after midnight on the
morning of Jan. 13. What a night! Cold as hell and windy. I was
on the bridge until about seven; 19 hours of freezing. We formed
up the convoy, about 36 ships as I recall, and away we went. Our
escort was six destroyers of the latest type. The trip over was very

unexciting, but there was an awful lot of signaling as I was on duty from dawn 'till dark. During some bad weather several ships were separated from the convoy. We later learned that two of them were sunk, one by a torpedo, the other by shell fire from a sub; rotten break for those two.

THE ANONYMITY OF BIRDS

Christopher thought about the anonymity of birds and how he could not get back to it—how none of the birds flying through the branches beside his window had individual names, how flocks flew overhead, none named, no names among the birds, no striving to be known, no possibility of being remembered. He thought about how this was closed to him, how, even if he buried his name in a box in his mother's yard, it would still be his, and he would have to make a person beside it like a city built on a lake.

THE KEY

One morning, during his year home from school when he was nine, while playing bus, Christopher found a key on the sidewalk near his house. He had never received a messenger so *hard and sharp and sure of itself—it had the feeling of being lost because people almost never throw keys away, and it was stingy because keys are not supposed to tell.* He put it in his pocket and carried it around for many weeks.

THE CAROLERS

After the Christmas Eve tradition of drinking and decorating the tree into the small hours with Shebee and the ornaments shattering on the floor, came Christmas and the roast beef dinner that Evelyn prepared for *The Carolers,* a small band of English expatriates, who came to the flat, ate heartily, drank continuously, and sang traditional songs, ending with *The Parting Glass.*

CHRISTOPHER TRIED TO BE MORE LARGE

With Evelyn, Christopher tried to hammer himself thin like a sheet of gold, to confer a glistening sameness to every surface, because things that upset her could come from anywhere, and a gold-leafed surface is always a single surface safe from surprise.

GLASS

One Christmas a man came with *The Carolers* who had blown half of his face off while cleaning a shotgun. He looked like a melted plastic mask and had to eat his meals through a glass straw. Evelyn sat Christopher next to him at the Christmas dinner because she wanted him to understand how important it was to be able to be with someone who was disfigured and treat them exactly as if they were not, and to not, in any way, draw attention, even by the inference of a startled expression, to their condition or make them in any way less comfortable or welcome than had they been exactly normal.

HAIL

That the self was like hail—layer-on-layer of ice surrounding nothing.

BRIDGE

Evelyn would drill Christopher on how to count points and what a singleton was worth, what a void was worth, when to bid three, what the two bid meant and how you must not comment or gesture or exclaim because any indication beyond the bidding itself was cheating.

CHRISTOPHER DECIDED

Christopher decided that Shebee was there to look after his mother.

MIRROR-PERSON

A man was walking down Polk Street holding out a mirror; it looked like a car mirror he had found in the gutter, and he was disheveled and deranged and he was demanding that people look at themselves. But there was something else: when you looked at yourself in the mirror, he was holding you; you were in his hand and small, and though you were opposite him walking down the street, you were next to him where you stood in the mirror, and what were you carrying—all the sticky burdens of dailiness, those cosmic trifles that you parade around as your ceaseless unsolvable task—but now he was carrying you, and wasn't your initial discomfort at seeing him, that urge to cross the street, actually a sense of indebtedness—that it was he who was doing the heavy lifting of the world?

THE LAST MESSENGER

The City of Messengers was now almost complete, and he sat on the floor and placed the key by the empty space, near the center, where the last messenger would go if he ever found it.

WAR LETTER FROM WESTY TO HIS FATHER

We arrived in Casablanca, French Morocco, after 21 days at sea. After unloading, we were all set to sail back to New York when, bingo, our orders were changed and now the story gets hot and no fooling. We had taken on some iron ore for ballast and were laying at anchor, all ready to sail, when we were shifted back to a dock along with two other liberty ships to load a very hot cargo. It took us about a week to load and so we had plenty of time to think, and we did a lot of tall thinking—reason? Well, in our number one hold, which is forward, we had I don't know how many thousands of gallons of 100 octane gas; number two was OK, just tanks; number three, which goes under what were then my quarters, contained about one thousand tons of bombs ranging in size from nice little harmless 300 pounders up to big ugly 2000 pounders—ouch! Number four, which is aft, had squad cars, and number five another 1000 tons of bombs and iron pipe, very nice, what? About the bombs, they aren't as bad as they sound as they won't go off by concussion unless they have detonators in them, but they do give you the willies. On deck we had a couple more tanks and the detonators for the bombs, and they will go off and how! We knew that there was only one place we would be sent with that sort of cargo, the Mediterranean, which is still one of the hot spots for convoys.

TEST-DOCTOR RESULTS

The white-coated test-doctor shuffled Christopher's test results in his shiny hands and said in a voice like a *snapping three-ring-binder that his interest was in gifted children who did not reach their potential and that this was his interest in Christopher. He said that such children were called underachievers and wondered aloud if ungifted children could ever really be considered underachievers and what did Christopher think, though this of course did not apply to him, and Christopher didn't know, and the test-doctor continued that underachievers who did not have testable defects, and this did apply to him, were almost always quitters or dreamers or simply lazy and which was Christopher and what did he have to say for himself?* Christopher had nothing to say for himself. The test-doctor's words were like the shredded backs of cereal boxes read at random. The test-doctor pressed Christopher to respond but Christopher only asked in his softest voice and completely without malice, "Why are you so angry?"

WESTY AND THE CITY OF MESSENGERS

Evelyn asked Westy if he might take a bit more of an interest in Christopher, so one Sunday afternoon, Westy came to Christopher's door and saw Christopher on the floor arranging the scraps of paper and debris he'd found on the streets. Westy asked him what he was doing, and Christopher said, "I am building the City of Messengers."

EVELYN BECAME CONCERNED

Eventually, Evelyn became concerned about all the trash that Christopher was carrying around in his pockets and all the time he spent arranging it on his floor. "Don't you want to play with the other children? Aren't you lonely?" She asked Westy to intervene, so he bought Christopher a baseball glove and took him to a game at Candlestick. Christopher was very bored except that he got to visit the Stadium Club, which was always fascinating.

OTHER CHILDREN

Christopher said that the other children did not understand the messengers.

ALFRED AND THE MESSENGERS

And Evelyn began to be frantic and rebuke him, saying "this laundry list does not say anything but shirts and slacks and suits." Westy implied to Christopher that it might be best to throw the junk away. Christopher began to cry hysterically, and Evelyn called Uncle Alfred who said in no uncertain terms that neither she nor her husband were to meddle in Christopher's private dealings with his collection.

HIDING THE KEY

When Christopher thought that his father might destroy the messengers, he hid the key in the secret drawer of Evelyn's cherry desk.

WAR LETTER FROM WESTY TO HIS FATHER

In company with the other two liberties, who were similarly loaded, and 3 sub chasers, we slipped out of the harbor just at dark and headed up the coast for Gibraltar. The Rock is really quite a sight, but what impressed me most of all was the Spanish shore of the bay. It looks just like California around Monterey Bay; it's really beautiful. We lay at anchor over night and sailed at dawn the following day. As part of a convoy of about twenty ships, our escort was British, six corvettes. That day was as quiet and beautiful as any I have ever seen. About one o'clock in the morning I was awakened by gun fire and a heavy shock followed by the alarm bell which meant battle stations. My station was on a 20 millimeter machine gun, where I was on the phones to receive orders and relay them to the gunner and to help reload when necessary. The gun fire was from our ship and the shock I felt was the recoil from our 4 inch on the stern and 3 inch on the bow. The gunners had fired at what they thought was a sub; whether it was or not will never be known. We were at general quarters for about an hour and then back to bed. It seems strange now, in view of subsequent events, but this little show didn't bother me in the least. If anyone so much as fires a cap pistol now I'll jump at least a mile.

THE WONDER OCEAN

He saw the words on the page, all solid and lined up, and the moment he started to read them they become a blizzard. *He would pass through the page, barely brushing its sides as he fell through, and then he would come up a long way away in the teeming open water of thoughts and words and images and memories, and the little guided tour provided by the book was lost to him, but the Wonder Ocean was found.*

BRIDGE

When Westy was not playing dominoes with O'Neal, Sunday afternoons were often given to tutoring Christopher at bridge—

dealing out hand after hand, demanding that he bid and play them. They played on the card table with the folding legs in the living room overlooking the bay. Westy would have a cocktail, and Evelyn would have a glass of wine and they would play *as if* there were a fourth at the table. They wanted to be somewhat generous with Christopher's mistakes but, even seeming hard-pressed to comprehend the rules, he made few. They could not understand how he was able to play so *almost reasonably well* without *knowing* anything.

BARE MESSENGERS

Again and again he sensed *how some pieces of debris had almost no messages on them, again, like the parts of paintings that hold only sky or open space or a part of a field or expanses of tundra or a tablecloth or water or ice. Some messengers held only a sense of how light falls or that particular kind of waking in the dark after a sound but you're not sure that there was a sound or that second before a choir begins to sing or that sense of looking and looking for something lost. Some messengers were already in the past, like parts of photographs; some cast light across the city of messengers; some cast shadows; some fell across paths like trees; some were the falling itself; some rested like dust on everything; some were the resting itself; and he knew that even those with no message at all were still messengers.*

SECRETS

Have you ever considered how a secret opens dimensionality in a person—how duplicity is always the intentional pushing back of a flat wall so that it becomes the back wall of a room? Because a secret must have a place to reside, a place where it is kept, and that place cannot be on the surface; it must be a pushed-back place, spacious enough for a secret to disappear, spacious enough for intimacy to enter, even if only the intimacy of how one holds a secret.

SECRETS

Christopher wanted his father to have a secret so that there could be an inside to discover, an inside room where a shadow could be cast along the floor and up the opposite wall. And Christopher hoped that his father had a secret because he wanted to be held like a secret is held.

ALCOHOL

Maybe Westy used alcohol to try to open a room like that in himself.

TORN RECEIPT

Christopher carried half of a torn receipt in his pocket for many days trying to solve it—a narrowness, like being wedged or trying to fit where there wasn't any room. When he held it in his hand, he felt the crowdedness press in, someone trapped or hiding in a close place, and he couldn't solve it at first because the person wasn't there—only the tightness—and he couldn't solve it until he understood that the person was on the part of the receipt that had been torn away.

THE WONDER OCEAN

And Christopher saw that the Wonder Ocean was not just behind the words in books; the Wonder Ocean was behind everything.

WAR LETTER FROM WESTY TO HIS FATHER

The next morning at about quarter to nine the escort ran up a signal indicating that he was hunting a sub and started dropping depth charges, the first we had encountered. Boy, do they shake a ship! At about nine he ran his signal down and all was quiet. The third mate and I were discussing the sub situation and had just decided that it must be pretty well in hand in that locality when, boom! a tanker right in the center of the convoy was hit—I'll never forget that sight as long as I live. I was looking right at her when she got it. She was hit in the engine room, which is at the stern on tankers. There was a huge ball of fire, followed by stream and water, which came from her stack—those poor devils in the engine room never had a chance. We went to battle stations at once and the escort were dropping depth charges, "ash cans" we call them, all over the place. After about twenty minutes of this it was quiet and remained so for the balance of the day and night. We were all plenty jumpy by this time and every time a door slammed everyone would jump.

THE TRADITIONAL HOSPITAL

The day following their return from the Tiger's Nest, the group visited Thimphu's traditional hospital, with its pink and blue flag, the charts with all the cures, the benches surrounding the huge prayer wheel and the crowd waiting to be cured. Christopher pushed through the wall of disbelieving faces, sat on the bench by the prayer wheel and, reaching out, ran his hand along its spinning surface, lightly, so as not to burn himself or slow the wheel perceptibly. He sat and waited with his back to the charts and grids with all the animal parts, bird parts, scorpions and snakes pictured next to the organs of the body. He waited as people filed in around him. Numerous younger relatives accompanied elderly patients, some frail to the point of seeming near death. Babies, comforted by siblings as well as parents, fussed and cried. Patients who had traveled great distances sat impassively with members of their community. Christopher sat in the midst of all these people, neither claiming a place in line nor seeming concerned about going in. He looked at face after face, and noticed that no one had come to the clinic alone. The tour group moved on and it was actually quite a while before he was missed and the professor sent Dorji back to retrieve him. After this, the professor shuffled through his tourist-forms looking for more information about the strange young man. But, since Christopher had taken his assistant's place, and never filled out the forms, the professor found nothing.

READING TUTORS

Christopher was no stranger to reading tutors. There was Mr. Farb, who wore pince-nez and twitched, Mrs. Shane, who was large and coarse and whom Evelyn believed had never bathed, and little Miss Renfrew, who said OK OK, and shuffled papers and chewed the pencil eraser as well as her nails. The tutors were all confused about Christopher's problem: he could clearly and fairly quickly pronounce each word when reading aloud; he could even sound out words that he did not know, but he couldn't spell, and, after haltingly reading a paragraph aloud, he could hardly recall what he'd read. Yet he was articulate way beyond his years. The string of tutors came and went through the house and none could fix him.

THE LETTERS

The professor asked bluntly, "As you're not a pilgrim or a religious scholar or an anthropologist, why did you go to the trouble of coming to Bhutan?" Christopher paused, reached into the pocket of his coat, retrieved two letters and, holding them out said, "Because of these." The professor, not reaching for the letters, asked, "What are they?" "They're letters—they're why I'm here—I'm here to find out what they mean." "Where did they come from?" "From me…I sent them…to myself." "*You* sent them? So you've come to Bhutan to find the meaning of two letters *you sent to yourself?*" "Yes." The professor—incredulous and vexed—shook his head, turned, and walked away.

COAL

Most evenings were cold in San Francisco, so Westy routinely lit fires in the shallow coal-burning fireplace in the living room. The coal truck driver delivered the shiny chunks of coal in burlap bags to a bin on the back porch of the flat. Westy's fires were carefully constructed with kindling stacked on newspaper and chunks of coal, retrieved from a brass coal bucket, laid on top. There was a cylinder with a see-through plastic cap of long matches next to the fireplace with Westy's single fireplace tool—a black poker with a hook at the end—and there was a fire screen to stop sparks from popping out onto the wooden floor. Christopher was not allowed to touch the fire tool, move the screen, or play with the fire in any way. Sometimes Christopher would go down the back stairs and into the street just to smell the sweet sharp coal smoke in the clear night air.

WESTY

Maybe Westy was exactly what he seemed to be.

THIMPHU

After the incident at the traditional hospital and the encounter over the letters, the professor mentioned his concerns about Christopher to Dorji and asked his help in attending to the situation.

ANGLICAN ACADEMY

Evelyn did not want to send Christopher back to Grant. A new school, for boys, was opening at the Cathedral on Nob Hill, so she submitted an application for Christopher. After an interview, during which Christopher was flawlessly polite, he was accepted.

ANGLICAN ACADEMY

Anglican Academy was like a large and seamless replication of his mother's house, where all things had their place amid beauty, manners and propriety. Except for the boys themselves, nothing seemed to be alive—there was only a sense of years stretching back and back, held in by stone, glass and ritual. At Anglican, Christopher was referred to as *Mr. Westall*, and he had to stand by his desk when called upon to ask or answer a question.

WESTY'S BANKBOOK

One Saturday morning when Westy left Christopher in his office to go across the street to the club, Christopher decided to find the secret bankbook with Westy's account so that he could see how much his father made. It was in the lower right hand drawer of the desk in the private office, and Christopher carried it to the front windows so that he could watch the alley for his father. Leafing through he learned that, even though there was quite a bit of money in the account, his father seemed to make less and less each month and now was making not much more than the allowance checks to Evelyn. Aside from club dues and some checks written to cash, there was actually very little activity except, to his great surprise, checks written to Lydia, going back month after month, even though Westy never spoke of her and it had been years since she had been to the flat or Christopher had seen her.

SECRETS

Christopher wondered what secret Westy was paying Lydia to keep; what was it he didn't want Evelyn to know?

THE VERGER

Charles Newsom, the English verger and cathedral maintenance man, was considered odd by almost everyone. He lived in a small apartment on the grounds of the cathedral and collected clocks. He was pasty, prim, diminutive and taciturn, and he seemed to live in a world the width of a second hand. The verger, when not robed in purple and leading the procession to chapel, could be seen scurrying about the cathedral in his utilitarian gray slacks, black shoes and gray shirt. He could be heard from far away because of the jingling of what seemed like a hundred keys on a key ring attached to his belt, and the verger knew each key so well that he hardly had to glance at the ring when he wished to unlock a door, a locker, a corridor, a cabinet, a fuse-box or a closet.

WAR LETTER FROM WESTY TO HIS FATHER

The next day all was quiet until 5:20 P.M. I was just finishing my dinner when, wham, a loud explosion and one helluva jolt. I thought we had been hit, and so did most of the other boys. Man, you should have seen that mess room clear out! The ship ahead of us, another liberty loaded as we were, was the victim. She was hit in the fore-peak tanks, which are ballast tanks right in the bow, and did not sink. Had she been hit a little aft she would have taken it right where the gasoline was and would have blown higher than a kite. She dropped out of the convoy and we moved up to take her place. We were just about to leave our guns, as it had been a couple of hours without incident, when things started to happen again. The sun had gone down and there was just a little light in the sky to the west. The first sign of trouble were three very bright flashes of gun fire on the horizon to our left on the north. At first I thought it was a surface raider, when all of a sudden all hell broke loose. Every ship in the convoy opened fire with its anti-air-craft guns and machine guns. We were being attacked by torpedo planes. The first flashes we saw were from the escort. The air was full of tracers. The gun I was on was going hell bent for election and the one on the other side of the bridge behind me was shoot-ing just over my head. I could feel the bullets go by. The planes made several runs at the convoy but the gun fire was so heavy that they never had a chance to get set for a decent shot at us. After we were sure they had left and it was good and dark, we scurried down to the regular watch and went below. Our nerves were drawn tight as violin strings by now and sleep was darned near impossible.

CLOCKS

Each of the verger's clocks had keys and needed winding—some every day, some once a week, and many had chimes that struck on the quarter hour, the half hour, and the hour. Christopher spoke to Mr. Newsom every day, even if he was only hurrying past. Christopher would always smile at him and wish him good morning, good day or good afternoon. He called Mr. Newsom "Uncle Charlie" behind his back, which made the other boys laugh. Then one morning he slipped and called him "Uncle Charlie" to his face, and Mr. Newsom said, somewhat sharply, "Don't you think that's a bit disrespectful?" "Not if we're friends," Christopher replied, and Uncle Charlie invited Christopher to come over to his apartment for lunch that day and served white clam chowder, which Christopher did not like but ate anyway. He had never seen so many clocks. They seemed to be everywhere, in every nook and stacked on shelf after shelf. Christopher had lunch with Uncle Charlie about once every other week after that, and it was always exactly the same.

VERGER

One morning Uncle Charlie asked Christopher if he would like to lead the procession into chapel. Christopher, carrying the verger's silver wand with the crucifix at its tip, was so nervous and excited that he practically sprinted and left the whole procession running to catch up with him. Uncle Charlie was amused but felt responsible, so that afternoon he rehearsed the appropriate pace with Christopher. The next morning Christopher led the procession perfectly.

WINDING THE CLOCKS

When Uncle Charlie went back to England to visit his sister, he asked if Christopher would mind dropping by to wind his clocks. Christopher mapped the location of each and made a schedule.

He came by every day after school and, on the weekends, Evelyn, proud that her son was trusted with such a task, parked and waited. The furniture in Uncle Charley's apartment reminded Christopher of *Tea and Rarity*—so many ornate, precious, formal things all crammed together—and he grew comfortable there, sitting among the clocks.

THE PHILASCOPE

Christopher knew that his mother had never had a philascope because, if she'd had a philascope, why was she always frantic when he was late?

NORTH DAKOTA

Toward the end of the school year, everyone in Mr. Kent's fifth grade class at Anglican had to write a report about a state. Christopher wanted to write about North Dakota because he wasn't convinced that North Dakota actually existed. He'd never seen a North Dakota license plate or met anyone, ever, who had been there, or *ever, even once, seen a picture of North Dakota in the Chronicle. Plus, what kind of name was Bismarck for a capital? Wasn't Bismarck a German general...how was it possible for an actual state capital to be named after such a person? And in the encyclopedia, the pictures didn't look like pictures of a real place; they looked like someone went out into a field and took a picture and said it was North Dakota, and the picture of the state capitol was of a small skyscraper on a street somewhere, and everyone knows that state capitols have domes and are not skyscrapers, so someone had taken a picture of an office building and said it was the North Dakota capitol.* No one wanted him to write his report on North Dakota; everyone, Mr. Kent, Evelyn, and even the somewhat feared sixth grade teacher, Mr. Warner, wanted him to write his report on New York or Florida because they didn't want him to poke around and find out that North Dakota didn't really exist.

CONTINUOUS WITH THE FABRIC

Christopher saw that when Playland was built, it had fit into the fabric of the world, but then the world began to pull away and it remained until one day it was dated in that particular way that things once taken for granted become dated so that something once invisible suddenly shows itself, is suddenly visible, because the continuous fabric of which it was a part has gradually rewoven itself, and Playland had become a discontinuity, and could not help but stand out.

THE SURFACE OF THE SEA

And it struck him how whole worlds arise and go out, like the weavings of light on the surface of the sea.

FALLING

So when you actually see the world around you it is because you have fallen away from it—you see that there had seemed to be a constancy upon which everything rested, but now you know that there is no such constancy—now you can distinguish that you are falling—you can look back at the world as it recedes, and it can be suddenly vivid.

CITY OF MESSENGERS

And Christopher noticed that everyone was making *a city of messengers; out of bank slips, pay checks, phone numbers, date books, deadlines, due dates, and the defining events of their lives. No one lived without weight-bearing walls papered with found things, things found in the world, made private, made personal, set apart, made structural, made an inside place, made to stand inside against the cold.*

PRESSED AGAINST VANISHING

And all the things blowing down the street at their feet were deemed worthless, ignored, things pressed against vanishing, already almost invisible, so concealed in the familiar, so blocked by rules of evidence, a beautiful entirety that the days and weeks left out. These were not personal the way memories were; they did not justify your life the way your string of stories did; they did not define the inner walls or paper them or shield you from the cold; these things, when placed in the center, made another kind of life, a life pressed against vanishing, a sand-storm life; a fierce-guardian life; a life in the teeth of the cold—a life where you could not sleep.

WAR LETTER FROM WESTY TO HIS FATHER

We expected another attack at dawn and so just before it began to get light we went to our guns. Just as it was getting light a plane came in, whether he was out looking for us or just stumbled onto us I don't know, but I think he thought he could surprise us—a very bum guess on his part. He came in low from behind us and was met by a wall of machine gun fire. He passed right down between our column and the outside column, and I know damn good and well we hit him, as I could see the tracers from the gun I was on and another of our guns go into his belly. The last we saw of him he was flying low over the horizon and appeared to be on fire. About ten o'clock we turned into Phillipeville, which was our destination, and is about 60 miles from the front where Rommel is. Phillipeville is a beautiful little place. It rests on the side of a hill and is on a crescent-shaped bay. On our third night in port, just at sunset the air raid alarm sounded and those of us who were not ashore went to the guns. We thought it was just another false alarm, but no such luck. There were several bombers; some were the big heavy four-engined type and the rest the smaller two-engined type, and they came in from the sea. We opened fire and so did the shore batteries and other ships in the harbor. The planes split their formation and came in from all angles. I was on the central control phones on the bridge, but soon gave that up as they went out. Just as I left the phones to go to my gun, which was manned, I heard the scream of bombs and saw a plane directly overhead. It seemed ages while those bombs dropped, but at last they hit, big heavy babies, one hit on the other side of the dock, in the water, and sent up a regular tidal wave; others hit quite a good distance away on the docks. Boy, what a shaking up those babies give you. They really pack a wallop. I got back to my gun and found that we would soon need more ammunition. I also put on my helmet, which I hadn't had time to do before, so seeing there were no ammunition carriers, owing to the fact that we were short-handed, I grabbed a couple of empty magazines and started for the ship's magazine which is at the stern below decks. I must have made ten trips, I'm not sure of the exact number, but I hauled a hell of a lot of ammunition to our gun and all the others. I had to travel over about 150 feet of open deck to get to the stern, and during one of these trips I was hit in the wrist by a shell splinter, although I didn't know it at the time, as it didn't hurt a bit. When the raid was over I found out I had been hit, as I had a small cut in my wrist on the outside and another on the inside where the splinter had gone out, and my wrist was quite sore. I fixed it up for the night and after standing watch on the dock 'till midnight, went to bed. Next day I went to the British hospital and had my wrist X-rayed; no broken bones, very nice. It is all healed now.

DAYS AND WEEKS

And Christopher thought that life must be more than days and weeks—that days and weeks hid another world behind them—like a door hides something behind it when it's opened.

CHRISTOPHER'S RELIGIOUS SERVICES

Toward the end of his second year at Anglican, Christopher began to conduct religious services in the living room for Mrs. Blamey— the old, sweet, obese, devoutly Catholic former telephone operator who lived in a small apartment in the building on the corner and babysat for Westy and Evelyn. He would turn out the lights, light candles, wear an old sheet as a vestment, and, pretending to read from the Bible he was carrying, mutter *"Verily, verily and then sayeth; and unto the Lord came so and so and into such and such a land was sent and so forth," while leading a make-believe procession toward a makeshift altar that he had arranged on the mantel. Having forged through several lessons and hymns, Christopher would deliver an impassioned prayer for the fallen world—the infirm, the poor, the children of the poor, and the people with nowhere to go.* Mrs. Blamey, who thought this guileless display of devotion was the most beautiful thing that she had ever seen, would sit on the love seat, her huge bosom heaving as she wept, and quietly dab her eyes. When it was all over and Christopher had put everything away, she would reward him with one of her wretched Luden eucalyptus coughdrops, redish-amber and bitter, which, having spat the first several out, he came to actually crave.

CHRISTOPHER'S INTENTION
TO BECOME A MINISTER

It was during this time that Christopher proclaimed his intention to become a minister. Evelyn called Uncle Alfred in a panic, but he told her, "My dear, do not concern yourself, soon enough, Christopher will be an atheist."

THE CITY OF THROWN-AWAY THINGS

The messengers made a map because they were parts of people's lives— not the parts they thought of as themselves, but the parts they'd thrown away. So the City of Messengers was the City of Thrown-Away Things, and because of this, it stood opposite the world of days and weeks, the world of purposes—an opposite place, a parallel of no account and no expectancy, a city of vanishing, a city of standing on nothing—and, if you entered it, you stood outside *with it* and you could look across at the city of purposes and then *it* was the opposite place of no standing.

HIDING AND THE LITERAL

Christopher learned that he had to hide what the messengers said, that he had to act as if they were only things found on the street, as if they *were flat and actual, as if they didn't open onto oceans, as if, like other things, they only stood for themselves. He had to agree that the messengers didn't have worlds in them and weren't windows and weren't remnants, that they didn't whisper or gesture, that they weren't traces of lives, splinters, particles, maps of voices, but only rubbish pushed through literal streets by a literal wind.* So this is what he learned to say but for him it was never so.

INVISIBLE PLACES

And sometimes Christopher could not go to sleep, and he wanted to find invisible places in his atlas but the bedside light would disturb his mother, so maybe he could *go under the covers with a flashlight, but he wasn't sure that he could turn the pages silently enough, and it would be hot and steamy under there like the Hall of Flowers. Or he could try to shut the door, but it would be too squeaky, and his mother would wake and not be able to go back to sleep, so maybe he could go down to Patton's Hardware Store on Union Street and buy a tin of oil and oil the hinges, but then she would be concerned about the door being closed, so maybe he could open it when he finished looking at the maps, but then he'd have fallen asleep, and he'd wake in the middle of the night and go to open the door, but then he'd have to have gotten up for a reason, so he'd go down the hall and pretend to go to the bathroom but what if he actually had to go later? Then what would his mother think, being all concerned that he's going to the bathroom so much in the night and not let him have any water an hour before bed, so then he'd have to start sneaking water, so maybe he could keep a coffee can under his bed with the knife-people to pee in, but what if she found it—how would he ever explain a pee-can under his bed if his mother found it?*

WAR LETTER FROM WESTY TO HIS FATHER

The day after the raid we sailed for Oran and made it with only one alarm which came the first night out at dusk, when the escort dropped a lot of ash cans. Oran is a pretty good place. I went ashore once and wound up with the Captain of this ship and one of the cadets and we had a fine time. All got pretty tight, which I imagine even you will excuse after all the hell we went through, and didn't get back to the ship until one in the morning. I was due back at 10, but nothing was ever said as I was with the Captain. Left Oran on the 13th of March and started back for New York; were joined by a large number of ships at the Rock, and away we went. We had perfect weather until the evening of the 27th, when a terrific storm hit us. We were very light and as we were in the trough of the sea, rolled terribly. I stayed on watch to catch signals and try to see the other ships. About one o'clock the full force of the storm hit us. The wind was deafening and the rain was so heavy you couldn't see the mast, which is only about twelve feet in front of the bridge. With ships all around us it is just a miracle we didn't ram someone or that we weren't rammed. When the sun came up the wind was still a gale and the convoy was all over the Atlantic. We finally got in formation again and that afternoon I got a couple of hours sleep, the first in 36 hours.

THE SPEAKER

Once, in the middle of the night, Christopher woke to hear someone speaking to him through his closed bedroom door. Why was the door closed—who was on the other side—how could his mother not be awakened? He got up, tiptoed across the floor and pressed his ear to the door. The voice was *muffled like a radio far away, but it wasn't far away because he could hear the person's breathing—and it was rapid, as if they had been running, and he could not understand what the speaker was saying because they were so out-of-breath or their mouth was full of cloth or the words were in another language or an almost English language. Christopher could not tell at first if it was a man or a woman speaking, but he was trying, and after sitting on the floor and placing his ear lower on the door, he realized the voice was a child's, and the child must be kneeling. Christopher was terrified but strained to make out the message because there was an urgency in the voice, and he asked very softly if the speaker could speak more loudly, but the speaker's volume remained exactly the same. And then, all at once, like a broken vase flying back together in a film played backwards,* the words became whole and clear, and Christopher finally understood what the child was saying, and it was: *"Do not open the door."*

BENT-BACK-AND-FORTH PLASTIC THING

And to have something like this happen in his mother's house was like *being bent back and forth where a seam begins to form, like the seam in a bent-back-and-forth plastic thing,* and he knew that he must not break in his mother's house, and he knew that he must not appear to begin to break.

JAPANESE SCREEN

How relaxed and quiet he was sitting in front of the screen—sunlight from the north coming through the big window looking out onto the Marina District, the Palace of Fine Arts, and across the bay to Marin.

THE PALACE OF FINE ARTS

The Palace of Fine Arts was a favorite landmark in Christopher's early life. Its beautiful fluted columns and stately dome made it look like the center of a kingdom lodged in another time. Westy told him that it had never been meant to be permanent but it turned out that way, which reminded Christopher of what Evelyn had said about Doug Sutton's insurance career.

LIGHT

How do you know that nothing can travel faster than the speed of light?

JAPANESE SCREEN

Christopher looked at the Japanese screen to see if there were any scraps of paper blowing down the packed dirt streets. He looked with great care but he couldn't find a single one, so he imagined that someone in the picture had already collected them all. He tried to figure out which person it was, and after looking and looking, he settled on the inconspicuous middle-aged man with the little red satchel slung over his shoulder, walking, with his head slightly bowed, up the hill toward the halfway house.

LIGHT

You know that nothing can travel faster than the speed of light because, no matter from how far it comes, light always arrives brand new.

TRAIN OF THOUGHT

During his instruction on *The Elements of Style*, observing that

Christopher had drifted into daydreaming, Mr. Warner said sharply, "Mister Westall!" and, having been ignored, walked to the front of Christopher's desk, struck it and demanded, "Mister Westall, are you with us—are you following our train of thought?" At first, Christopher, said yes, in a muted voice, but under Mr. Warner's continuing glare, he asked confusedly, after a pause, if it was an actual train or a model train, for which he was sent to stand outside the classroom for half an hour.

THE IRONING BOARD DOOR

Christopher tried to crop himself so that he could be with his father, to be like the pollarded trees lining the band shell seating area in Golden Gate Park. He tried to cut himself back, to be straightforward and unswaying, and he tried to be interested in British cars and business stories and baseball. And Christopher thought that if he could just compress himself a bit more, maybe then he could be with his father.

THE IRONING BOARD DOOR

Have you ever had to crop yourself to be with someone else? Have you ever tried to fit yourself inside someone else's life, to fit yourself to someone so the edges were smooth and contiguous? You may have had to cut a lot of yourself away; you may have hardly known yourself when you were finished, but the other person will likely not have noticed this cost to you, because isn't the fit so perfect?

LIES

Westy told Christopher that all he had was his word—in relationships, in business, in everything, and if his word proved to be no good, then nothing would be possible other than lying for a living. Christopher did not know why his father was so upset. What did he think that Christopher had lied about?

LIGHT'S OPPOSITE

If light runs faster than time, so that time can't touch it at all, what is the thing that outruns space—can't be found anywhere—but constantly ages?

THE DREAM OF THE FOLDING YARDSTICK

And Christopher had a dream: he dreamed that he was not allowed to walk on the floors of the flat, so he carried a folding yardstick that he extended between tables, the arms of chairs and counters, and he walked across it like a balance-beam.

THE IRONING BOARD DOOR

Christopher tried to imagine what it would be like to be shaped as his father might wish; and he thought of the tall, very narrow door in the kitchen wall, of the built-in pull-down ironing board, that was always closed, and had scared him so when he was small, because what kind of person could fit through a door like that?

THE DREAM OF THE DUST SNOWSTORM

And Christopher dreamed that there was a dust snowstorm in the flat, glistening as it fell thicker and thicker—dust on the furniture, dust in the doorways, dust on the windowsills, dust in drifts in the corners of the hall.

BENT NAIL MESSENGER

You live in a world where people don't know their hands.

TOPOGRAPHICAL MAP OF NEBRASKA

Mr. Warner turned in utter frustration to Christopher saying "I have no idea what led you to believe that a topographical map of Nebraska was the weekend's assignment. I have no choice but to give you an F."

NULL SET

Though fascinated with the concept, Christopher could not understand why you'd ever need a set that was always empty.

TOPOGRAPHICAL MAP OF NEBRASKA

You might think that a topographical map of Nebraska did not amount to much, but this is not the case: there are hills, the depiction of which requires a subtlety more demanding, by far, than the Rockies.

WATER AND PAPER

You don't even know how there can be single things—why water instantly knits itself after being cut apart and paper can't.

CHRISTOPHER'S CONFIRMATION

Christopher was confirmed in the Episcopal Church on the Thursday before Palm Sunday 1964, by the Bishop of California, James Pike.

RITUAL

It was not hard to appear fully faithful, the memory of it still relatively fresh. And in the memory of it, the hint of it that still remained, the vestige knife-like blade of it. Christopher had a new appreciation of what ritual was for: it hid waning faith. Because the mannerisms of faith were well set, staged, automatically enacted, so you could hide all your doubt behind them—like some stilted, formal caricature of faith, like his mother's dinner parties were caricatures of parties, like he had become a formal, stilted caricature of a child.

WAR LETTER FROM WESTY TO HIS FATHER

I went back on watch about 5:30 and stayed on the bridge until midnight. The next day we were ordered to leave the convoy with seven other ships and started hell bent for Baltimore without any escort. We soon spread out and were fairly well scattered by sunset. We had no trouble, but were plenty relieved when we were met by a destroyer and a blimp about 10:30 this morning. From here on in there is nothing to it; we are in safe waters and will be in Baltimore in the morning. I don't know how long it will be before I go to sea again, but I'm ready to go as soon as I've had a little time ashore. You may wonder if I wasn't afraid during the attacks. Stop wondering—I was, and so was every man on this ship, but we got the stuff there and gave a good account of ourselves, and that is what counts. War is really hell, when you get right into it, and we will all be overjoyed when it is all over, but until then we are going to keep on taking the gas, bombs, tanks, men and food to the front, and if they get us there will be someone to fill the gap until we win this damned war. I will write again soon and let you know where I am and what I am going to do. Affectionately, Weston

THE SIXTH GRADE SPELLING FINAL

One morning at the end of the school year, after serving as acolyte at the early morning service and having a little wine with the bishop, Christopher sat in the hall with his back to the granite wall and devised a way to cheat on the spelling final.

THE SIXTH GRADE SPELLING FINAL

The spelling final was graded on the spot. Mr. Warner was very impressed with Christopher's improvement, so much so that, during the review, he triumphantly called on Christopher to give the correct spelling of words the other boy's had missed. "Mister Westall, tell them how it's spelled." But Christopher could not tell them how it was spelled. After this occurred several more times, Mr. Warner stopped dead still and stared quizzically at Christopher before proceeding; he didn't ask Christopher to spell any more of the words. At the end of the day, as the boys were shuffling out, Christopher stayed behind and approached Mr. Warner. After a nervous pause, he looked him straight in the eyes. "I cheated, Sir." Mr. Warner said he'd thought as much, and it didn't matter how but why. "My brain is broken, sir. I can study the words and repeat them again and again, but the letters move around, and I can't remember them." Mr. Warner softened and said that this was a mystery, and it must be difficult for Christopher. Then he asked how many test-words Christopher thought he could actually spell. Christopher responded that, on his luckiest day, he would get, perhaps, enough right to get a C. And Mr. Warner thanked him for coming forward and said that just this once he would give him a C on the final if he would keep it to himself and promise to never cheat again at Anglican. Christopher agreed.

BRIDGE

Evelyn routinely read the Chronicle bridge columns to Christopher with a crackling urgency in her voice because these things *mattered*. She used the sharpened tip of a No. 2 pencil to draw lines, make little check marks, and delineate the succession of play. Christopher found the entire exercise to be inscrutable.

BRIDGE

Her pop-quizzes could occur at any time, seemingly out of nowhere, like when he was coming out of the bathroom or coming in from outside or coming into the kitchen after school. "You have a very long weak suit and enough points to open, how do you bid?" Or, "you have a void in a hand that will not be bid no-trump, what is it worth?" He learned to focus and formulate an answer, and he started to understand a little about scoring, about what was meant by *doubling, redoubling, being vulnerable, above* and *below the line,* and *making game.*

THE DEATH OF THE GENUINE

After the death of the genuine, something must be made to stand in its place.

TOPOGRAPHICAL MAP OF NEBRASKA

Standing in Laurel Super speaking with little discretion to Evelyn, Mrs. Donnelly complained of how hard she had worked to raise Justin as a gentleman and how he was spoiled, rude, ruined and ungrateful. Evelyn was speechless, so Christopher told Mrs. Donnelly about working all weekend on his topographical map of Nebraska, and getting the assignment all wrong and getting an F.

WONDER OCEAN

Christopher knew that the Wonder Ocean was not just waiting like a sea at a shore; he felt it *pressing in like the water in the tank of the diving bell at Playland—pushing in through all the cracks and seams that people continuously labored to seal shut.*

WONDER OCEAN

And when you slept, the container split apart, and the Wonder Ocean rushed in—all the images, voices, strife and marveling.

NEVER ANSWERS ENOUGH FOR EVELYN

The world was like a plate fallen on a floor of tiles—the arduous piecework of putting it back together, the countless questions to which he thought she must surely know the answers: "Do all the students at your school speak like this? Does no one comb their hair anymore? Are all parents failing to raise their children properly?" But she did not know the answers, and though he was drawn into the bootless habit of trying to answer, there were never answers enough to make the world a single seamless thing, and there was a cost to answering and answering, and the cost was a wearing down, a wearing thin, a wearing through.

GLASS

A bus transfer, a piece of foil from a cigarette pack, a piece of fabric with a buttonhole, a bluish nugget of broken electrical glass from the top of a telephone pole.

PATERNITY

Christopher asked Evelyn why she and Westy had not had any more children.

THIMPHU DZONG

The travelers were driven just north of the city, to a prominent hilltop where the massive Thimphu Dzong, with its multi-storied, whitewashed walls glistening under tiered golden roofs, looked out over the valley. Monks in red robes were hurrying across the vast inner courtyard carrying scrolls between buildings. "The king's throne room is there." Dorji said, pointing to a towering building with red-latticed woodwork decorating its front. The professor, reading from a series of cards, recited the history of the fortress, from its construction in the early thirteenth century to its multiple fires and eventual establishment as the seat of religious doctrine and royal rule for the entire country.

ABANDONING THE MESSENGERS

And then one day while he was looking for the last messenger, leaves and foil and paper scraps were blowing by, and he didn't pick any of them up. It was sort of like the time he realized that not everyone drank like his father, which was something obvious he had never seen because it hid behind what he'd always thought was true. It wasn't that he'd come to see there were no meanings in the messengers, or that he'd made their meanings up, or put them on like stickers. It wasn't that he'd come to see there was no city, or that everything didn't belong to everything else or that the messengers were not parts of people's lives that they'd thrown away. It was not that he'd come to see them as merely childish; it was not as if he couldn't remember why they'd held his interest; it was not that they'd simply reverted to thrown-away things; it was not as if he'd woken from a spell; it was not that he wouldn't think of them now and then. It was very matter-of-fact, like clothes that don't fit anymore or walking home a different way from school, and he put the cigar box on a shelf at the back of his closet.

THE BOOK OF JOB

The Book of Job was a puzzle to Christopher; he wondered if God really smote his followers based on bets with the devil. In response to Christopher's question during sacred studies, Father Martins did a thundering rendition of the voice from the whirlwind: "Where were you when I laid the foundations of the earth?" Christopher found this to be as spellbinding as it was inadequate as an answer, but did not pursue it further, and Father Martins claimed that the part of the story where Job is restored to his wealth and position was a popularization added later to please the masses and that, in fact, Job perished in scabrous poverty but with perfectly tempered faith.

SIXTH GRADE SPELLING FINAL

The evening of his conversation with Christopher, Mr. Warner called the house and spoke to Evelyn. He did not mention Christopher's cheating on the test, saying instead that Christopher was bright and well-liked, but he simply *had* to settle down, and, while his career at Anglican was not in jeopardy, his prospects for admission to a select preparatory high school were growing dim, and that it wasn't too late for him to pull himself up. He must be pushed and not coddled; he must dedicate himself all summer long to bringing his work up to speed.

PROTECTION THREADS

The tour group was ushered into the antechamber of the senior lama at Thimphu. The professor proceeded into his presence and, after making appropriate offerings, indicated that each of the travelers had been invited to receive individual blessings. They entered the small room one by one where the lama sat on a cushion. Each prostrated themselves—knees, chest and foreheads flat on the polished floor—and he blessed them. When it was Christopher's turn, he entered reverently and knelt before the red-robed lama, who was old and boney and bright-eyed. The lama said a prayer and bid Christopher to come close, and then he loosely tied a red linen thread around Christopher's throat, then another, and Christopher prostrated himself in gratitude, knowing nothing of what the threads were for.

FINDING CARL

After her conversation with Mr. Warner, Evelyn called Vicky Landry, who lived across the street, to ask if she knew of any tutors who might help Christopher catch up. Mrs. Landry, who had graduated from Stanford when few women did and took pains that none forget it, said that she happened to know of a tutoring service, used by many of the best families, that employed lots of bright *Stanford* people looking for a little extra money to help with graduate school. Evelyn, who never refused advice from anyone she envied, called the service the moment she hung up.

CARL KIMMERY

Carl Kimmery was a graduate student at Stanford. He lived on campus, in adult student housing, and was working with an undergraduate theatre company on a production of *Guys and Dolls*.

He drove a maroon Buick coupe from the 1950's and he wore seersucker suits, gray and green. Sometimes he carried a silver-handled cane because of gout. There were supposed to be several boys in the summer reading class, but the other boys dropped out. Evelyn offered to pay a bit more if Carl would tutor Christopher privately.

SHEBEE'S MOVE TO KLAMATH FALLS

A few months before Christopher heard the speaker at his door, Shebee moved on short notice to Klamath Falls, Oregon. Evelyn told a tearful Christopher that government agents had warned her never to live in a port city again.

EVELYN AND CARL

Evelyn saw Carl Kimmery as a person without stain. She was willing to forgive his goatee because it was closely clipped and clean, and because she considered Carl an intellectual. She was willing to forgive that his clothes were rumpled because they were immaculate, and, after all, he was a single man with more important things than laundry to think about. She saw in Carl a person whom she could admire but needn't envy, and she was willing to forgive that Carl was hugely overweight because he was like a raja.

READING LESSONS

Carl drove up from Stanford three times a week to conduct the reading lessons in an empty classroom at the City School, which was over the hill from where Christopher lived, so he could walk. He looked forward to spending time with Carl. Nothing was going to be spilled, broken, lost or late, left behind or out of place. They started reading a history of *Lewis and Clark* and then *A Tale of Two Cities*. Carl took Christopher to see the guillotine at the wax museum at Fisherman's Wharf, and sometimes Carl brought books from his own collection. Sometimes he would let Christopher sit on his lap when he read to him.

READING LESSONS

Evelyn thanked Carl for his willingness to drive all the way from Palo Alto to tutor Christopher. Carl said that he had other business in the city and was in no way inconvenienced.

HEXT

Westy brought home a puzzle with nine curved and irregular pieces that needed to be fit into the irregular edges of its flat box, which served as the puzzle frame. The puzzle was called *Hext*. Christopher was fascinated that, even with so few pieces, it was seemingly impossible to assemble. The scattered pieces of *Hext* were kept next to its box on the game table in the living room. Everyone who came into the house was encouraged to try it, but the only person who could assemble *Hext* with little difficulty was Evelyn.

PLASTIC CAFETERIA PLATE

Evelyn was like one of those thick plastic cafeteria plates with the dividers where the things in the different compartments never touched.

CARL AT DINNER

Christopher was nervous that Carl's table manners would not be perfect or that he would say something inappropriate, and then his mother would not like Carl anymore. But Carl's table manners were perfect enough, and he said nothing all evening that failed to charm, as if he could see all the hidden rules of the house, the rules that lay like mines. He just skated around them, this huge man, with the most delicate mastery. Of course he did not smoke and showed great restraint, eating little for a man his size, enjoying a glass of wine and leaving just a bit of food on his plate, to Evelyn's delight. Christopher had never seen anyone quite as at ease as Carl. Westy saw Carl as little more than a passing barge.

THE TRIP TO STANFORD

The initial trip to Stanford was all arranged beforehand by Carl, who contacted Evelyn to gain her approval before saying anything to Christopher. Carl said he was working on a production of *Guys and Dolls* with the theatre department; he could see if there might be a thing or two for Christopher to do. Evelyn was excited that Christopher might work on a theatre production at Stanford, so, after an early dinner at the flat, Carl made the invitation to Christopher as if on the spur of the moment; might he be interested in spending the weekend at Stanford and working on the play? The subsequent trips to Stanford were frequent through the summer as *Guys and Dolls* progressed and Christopher helped.

WINDOWS

There was nothing that Carl needed Christopher to interpret, and Christopher did not need to keep Carl safe from things that broke. On the drive down to Stanford Christopher said that he liked the windows down, and, rolling his window down, Carl said "Roll them down! Roll them all down!" Christopher rolled his window down, climbed over the seat into the back, and rolled the back windows down, *and the wind of that warm summer night blew through the car, and he and Carl began to laugh as papers stacked on the floorboards rose and flew all around and some went out the windows.*

RETURN FROM STANFORD

The evening when Christopher returned from Stanford, his mother was in the living room holding a delicate Chinese bowl, so thin that you could see the shadowy outlines of your fingers through the painted surface of rearing horses and horse-handlers pulling them down with ropes. The house was quiet, almost cold. "Look," she whispered, "Come and see this. I know that you will be able to see the beauty in this." The bowl in her hands, the unspeakably fragile bowl, and her fragile grasp around its edges somehow let Christopher know that he was not, under any circumstances, to speak of what had happened to him at Stanford because he knew that if he did that bowl would fall to the floor and be shattered in such a way that it would never again be anything but dust.

IN CARL'S BED

At first, Christopher could not take Carl's large uncircumcised penis completely into his mouth without gagging, but Carl was patient. And at first, it hurt a lot when Carl slid his stubby oiled fingers into Christopher's anus. He wanted Carl to stop, but he did not push him away. There was *power in being craved, and he did not push it away, and Carl persisted and was almost tender, and after Carl gave him his bath, Christopher wanted to sleep in his pajamas, but Carl insisted that he sleep naked next to him. Carl's skin was rough and the wool blanket scratchy, and Christopher lay awake for hours while Carl slept soundly. He noticed how the pain was riding alongside like a noise; he thought of his mother weighing letters in her hand, and he tried to remember where all the keys were hidden in his house, and he listened for the knife-people, but they were not there, and he missed them.*

ROYALL LYME

Looking up from the horse-handler bowl cupped in her hands, Evelyn drew back just slightly from Christopher. "You smell like Carl." Then, after gauging Christopher's response, which was rather cool, she said, "I mean you smell like Carl's cologne." Christopher paused, fumbled only slightly and gathered himself enough to say this slowly "It's the Royall Lyme he wears. I like it, and he let me put some on." Evelyn fixed her gaze momentarily on his face and then let it pass.

ENTERING FREEZING WATER

When Christopher went to bed that night, he was very still, like someone *entering freezing water and having to stop and wait to grow numb before going further—numb first at the feet, then up to the knees, then from the knees to the waist, then up to the chest, then just the head above the water and now all numb and not wanting to get out because the air would seem unbearably cold.*

PROTECTION THREADS

Christopher asked Dorji what the red threads meant. Dorji responded that they were "protection threads" and that Christopher must wear them until they fell off of their own accord.

THE GAME OF THE WINTER STORM

Maybe because Carl seemed to live on a larger scale, his apartment at Stanford seemed small to Christopher. One night they played a game where Carl went out, stood in the hall, knocked on the door and pretended to be a person lost in a storm on a winter's night. Christopher played the abandoned little boy who had locked himself in a house deep in the woods. "And I sound like a person begging to come in, but I'm actually the wolf, and you know that you must not let me in, but you do because you are so alone and lonely and sorry for me." So Carl stood in the hallway, knocking softly while muttering plaintive requests for shelter, to share the fire and a little food, a crust of bread, a bit of straw on the floor to sleep out of the wind. Christopher stood on the other side of the door, which Carl had instructed him to bolt, and he listened to the droning through the door and at first he was playing along, but then he began to *freeze—the feeling was a freezing in his chest, like the time when he first heard the knife-people or when his mother froze him out for being late or breaking something or saying something wrong, and he was used to pushing this freezing feeling down, but, even so, he could*

not speak to the creature lost in the woods on the other side of the door
as he was supposed to, and for what seemed many minutes, he could not
move. Carl was growing impatient in the hall, the softness in his voice
was stiffening, growing more actually urgent and anxious—what if
someone heard him or happened to come along? Christopher moved in
that empty automatic way that he was used to when he pushed the
freezing down and slid the bolt and cracked the door. Carl burst in,
flicked the door closed with his foot and immediately seized Christopher,
picking him up as he pulled his pajama top off and then spilling him
out of his pajama pants so that he landed on the mattress rather hard.
Carl fell on him and began to eat him alive, starting at his throat, then
the nipples, then the naval and then moving quickly down between the
legs, licking the penis and scrotum, hoisting the hindquarters into the
air, pressing his tongue between the buttocks, licking the anus, licking
the tender place below the balls—all the time pinning Christopher's
shoulders against the sheets, growling softly, moving his head side-to-
side so his beard was scratching Christopher's skin, and Christopher was
squirming, actually trying to get away because that's what you do in a
game of being eaten alive.

PRETA

But not a wolf, but a starving outcast, a wilderness cannibal starving, a furtive, insatiable outcast—a man at the edges of being able to
speak who had to summon everything to be understood, to be convincing, to get the boy on the other side of the door to unlock and
open it, who had to pretend again and again to be an actual person
so he could be admitted into a house and eat its children, who had
to make himself understandable or starve, and his pleadings had to
be the perfect replicas of human pleadings or passable replicas or
plausible replicas or almost plausible replicas or where he was breaking apart had to be mistaken for the genuine breaking apart of the
human voice; he had to remember the human intonations, fetching
far back to find them, like trying to remember the taste of water.

PRETA

To remember the customs of asking, of entreating, of sincerity and the manners of reaching out and touching where the touch did not betray the hunger hiding in the fingers—of seeming to belong to that communion of capable people, of the self-restrained, of the civilized—the communion of bread and wine, heart and soul, of speech, touching and asking; the interlocking fibers of a blanket, of a world, a world inside instead of outside, with a fire, cooked food and conversation—as if you remembered houses, streets and customs, self-restraint and doors and locks and asking and accepting no.

IN CARL'S BED

Carl preferred that Christopher lie on his back with this knees drawn up so that he could look into Christopher's face while using him. Christopher learned to relax himself so it didn't hurt. It was neutral, like the beige walls of Carl's room, like the tap water Carl would drink when he was through.

PAPERWORK

Standing at the door of the bus, as the travelers boarded for the trip to Wangdiphodrang, the professor thrust the traveler information forms into Christopher's hands and told him to fill them out on the trip.

WANGDIPHODRANG

The group left Thimphu in the afternoon and took the narrow lateral road, through misty rain—first south, then northeast, ascending steeply and over Dochula Pass which, at 10,500 feet, separated Thimphu from Wangdi Province and was festooned with banners and lined with thin flapping vertical prayer flags. Then they traveled north, then south, then southeast, descending into driving rain, and there wasn't a straight hundred yards on the whole drive to Wangdiphodrang, a town so gritty, rundown and desolate that it led one to immediately long for Thimphu. They checked into a rabbit warren of a hotel with green chipping paint and the face of a saint painted next to an enormous winged rose-and-blue phallus on the west-facing outside wall.

PAPERWORK

Christopher, remembering that he'd put it in his backpack, handed the filled-out paperwork to the professor. Later, huddling with Dorji, the professor reviewed the forms, trying to decipher the script, jarred all over the page from the rough road. "He's a *banker*," the professor said with a slight edge of disapproval, "and he's from San Francisco." "A *banker?*" Dorji, acutely interested, responded. "He has no one, no relatives at all according to this, no one for us to contact in an emergency. Not that we *could* contact them, even if he did, but anyway, he's squarely on our shoulders." Dorji was far away, thinking of what it could mean to know a banker from San Francisco.

WITH CARL

And it's not like the ledge in the pool at the Day Club in Marin because it's not the kind of deep water that once you have gone in you can come back—*you have to stay there, even though your feet cannot touch bottom, even though you cannot swim well enough to be there and cannot really breathe deeply with the water in your mouth, and you know that you will be there from now on, and you can't let anyone know that you are there because then they will ask how you got there, and you will have to tell them, and then you will not only be drowning, you will be despised.*

PRETA

Like trying to remember the taste of water, how to fold a napkin, ask a question, close a window, wait for something, hold a fork or brush the hair back from another's face with your fingers—something as everyday as salt, soap, or cutting bread with a knife—something as everyday as speech, salt, stitching torn clothes, cutting hair or sweeping cut hair with a stiff-bristled broom—things slow, habitual, constant, invisible, impossible, pure and remote, when you don't enact them anymore, when your hands do not remember them, when you're not a person among people anymore.

WITH CARL

Carl did not threaten Christopher with death. He did not threaten to kill Christopher's parents or burn down their house if he told. He did not threaten to take Christopher away to another state or another country. He never told Christopher to roll his window up or not to sing. He took him to elegant restaurants. He took him to modern art galleries, gourmet stores, theatre performances, bookstores and the Stanford Library. Carl bought Christopher anything he wanted: bags of metal marbles, bubble gum, a set of pirate cards, a book of flags. He never put his hands around Christopher's throat. He never struck him, spoke harshly to him or failed to listen with his complete attention when Christopher spoke. Sometimes they played the stranger game or the game of the winter storm. They stayed very calm and controlled. The secrets brushed and sparked with no outward sign. By the end of the summer, they had special secret names for each other's private parts. They stayed up very late. Carl never treated Christopher like a child.

PRETA

Eater of children—enter a room as if you were capable of performing the thoughtlessly conducted human rituals of belonging, as if they were *natural to you, as if you were sated by them; enter a room as if you were capable of sufficiency and dailiness, eater of children; enter, starving so starved; enter a room as if you were not an always*

*outside person; a starving person so starved that the person is gone and
only the starving remains.*

PRETA

Eater of children walking concentric circles perfectly so no perturbation will be noticed, expert, exact, practiced in human ways, in
human habits, walking in circles perfectly, adorned in the habits of
normalcy, completely indistinguishable from every other everyday
ordinary thing; enter a room as if you had acquired the rituals of
belonging through natural progressions, like learning speech; enter a room as if you must not carpenter and cobble, feign, mimic,
emulate and devise.

SECRET SUN

The secret he shared with Carl was like a secret sun around which
he moved; it drew his thoughts into circles around and around,
and it had the effect of diminishing everything else, so everything
else in his life seemed small and without pull. Yet he had to build
a surface smoothed of its influence—a person whose orbit seemed
to center on school, chapel, homework and television. He was always in motion away from what was true and toward what must be
made to look like it was true. This pulling placed a sundering at his
center, a sundering that constantly swept toward the surface, that
had to be contained by that manufactured smoothness, where the
sun was not the sun, the center was not the center and the surface
was unremarkable and smooth like the fabric of noise and laughter
in the schoolyard during recess.

SECRET SUN

And he began to learn the costliness of semblance—how the fake
won't hold together by itself and must be revived with more and
more, how everywhere at the edges it was frayed and demanded

repair. And the hours became these restless sleepless things, and he was running from place to place inside to patch and paste, to make sure that what was there did not show through.

THE HIDDEN PERSON

For the first time, he began to see that the person he really was was the hidden person and that the outside person, the person on the surface, just gave the hidden person something to hide behind, and he saw that this was what was meant by *growing up*.

BLOOD

There would be some blood on the inside of Christopher's underpants every now and then, but he didn't want to say anything to Carl about how he was bleeding. He thought how he would have to throw his underpants away—then he'd have to figure out how to explain the pairs that were gone. He wouldn't be able to so, he'd have *to steal some money and buy new ones, but then he'd have to pay attention to get the right brand and the right size, and then he'd have to find a way to wash them without his mother noticing because why would he be buying new underwear? So maybe he could slip them into the laundry—but no, she would surely notice—or maybe he could find a laundromat, but then he'd have to use the same detergent that Evelyn used or she would notice the different smell, so maybe he could steal some in a little plastic bag and take it with him. Then he'd have to sneak the washed underpants into the house, fold them just like she did and put them in his drawer at the bottom of the stack.*

PRETA

To remember the taste of water—to know human rituals as if they resided reflexively in your body, like walking, as if they were like the automatic operations of hurricanes or roses opening, and not like making glass and making joists and hammering together the

many parts of the splintered world. The wind is not hiding itself behind itself; the rain is not hiding in rain. In an instant you
must borrow and emulate genuine things, to fashion a continuous
replica to live behind, to remember the taste of water, to be as inconspicuous, shaped to every edge—to be as the taste of water, in
every mouth, but unremembered.

PRETA

*Wrestling inside ropes, wishing this were that and now was then—
smoke, tears, and rain as hard as rice, miles of walls the tops of which to
walk upon, these human things that you no longer know but carry their
replicas in front of you through the world. And aren't you like other
people...aren't all persons replicas, cravings, light and memory...made
of these...complete private purposes...aren't these the calibrators? And
hurricanes don't operate like this, and roses opening don't, but persons do
and aren't you like these persons you tell yourself.*

THE STRANGER GAME

Late in the summer, more and more often, Carl wanted to play
the stranger game where he and Christopher pretended not to
know one another. Christopher would wait in a diner, in a bookstore or on a bench in a park, and Carl would approach as if they
had never met.

WANGDIPHODRANG

After dinner, the rains had stopped. Christopher, uninterested in
the lecture, sat on a bench outside of the hotel. It didn't matter that
it was soggy. He smoked a cigarette, and though he was shivering,
wasn't going to go back inside until everyone went to bed.

READING TEST RESULTS

Carl administered and graded Christopher's reading test at the end of the summer. It recorded great progress, and he submitted the results to Evelyn and to Anglican Academy.

CARL'S GOODBYE

Carl did not tell Christopher face-to-face that he was moving east to teach at a boys prep school in Massachusetts—he left that to Evelyn. So Christopher did not know that afternoon when Carl dropped him off that he would never see Carl again. There was a goodbye phone call, the contents of which Christopher could not remember even five seconds later, and there was a single postcard, showing some trees with fall colors, which said essentially nothing except that Carl would write again when he cleared his desk.

PRETA

But then again you don't really speak to yourself because you are never apart from what you want, you are never at a distance to speak across—you are never at a distance from yourself because you cannot push the want even an arm's length out; you are pressed against your hunger—you are not stepping back—you are not stepping back far enough to speak across a distance to yourself—you are not stepping back far enough to see yourself as anything other than what you want—you are pressed against a hunger—it is blind and blindingly close, because hunger cannot speak to itself except in seeking, because hunger is a single surface with only hunger underneath. But if you did speak to yourself, you would say that you were like other people wouldn't you?

PRETA

And you pray, but not as a prayer that passes from human lips to the ears of gods but more like a prayer of steps, a prayer of fixed roofs or mended walls or knots tied tight, that kind of prayer, and you pray *that the massive underneath, the massive hunger that powers you from underneath, will not show through, that the cobbled together mask will hold, be never seen as a mask, be taken for your face, and you rely on the vast inattention of everyone to everything but themselves, rely on the static layer of indifference that lies on everything—how everyone around you hurries toward something. But you do not. You do not hurry. You are slow and step by step as you approach, steady, step by step. You do not hurry. You cannot survive a misstep—the underneath will burst through any crack, any slip, any sigh, through any looking back or questioning, through any moment of regret, human thought, human touch, any ache, any stinging ache or ache of any kind that is not the hunger you know, the hunger you hide behind your step by step, the hunger that threatens to flood you, overtake you, flood and break you into edge after edge of rushing hungry knives.* This is your prayer of step by step, moment by slow-motion moment that you will hold together over the massive underneath that binds and guides you, the hunger that pushes outward from within you, that you will hold together until it is fed each time and each time again until it is sated for now and quieted.

THE DREAM OF FINDING CARL

And Christopher had a dream: he dreamed that he searched for Carl for years and years and finally found him in a foreign city, but Carl could not be made to recognize him—could not be made to stop playing the stranger game.

METAL

He woke with the taste of metal in his mouth.

THE SALE OF TAHOE

Of all of Evelyn's siblings, she was the only one who had ever had a job; and that but briefly just after the war, and before she married Westy. The rest had things that they "did," like buying a kit to make an electric car, yacht racing, brief marriages to boorish textile heirs, having horses, drinking, going from man to man and having trouble with the truth. Decades of these activities had rendered the siblings low on cash, and the once seemingly endless supply of assets to be sold was running out. This circumstance rendered a kind of hungry, eager look and a darting of the eyes that Christopher noted in several of them when they'd come to visit from San Diego. In the fall of 1964, talk arose among them of selling the last of land at Lake Tahoe, in which they each owned an undivided interest. There were three hundred acres remaining, more or less.

MISTER MUST

One night the knife-people slit the strings on a gunnysack and *something sticky and predatory uncoiled and came out. It closed all the windows and closed all the doors, pulled down the shades, pulled the curtains closed, filled all the spaces between cups in the cupboards and books on the bookshelves. It lay across the slits in the floor-furnace grates, filled the empty glasses, and found a way into him, gnawing tunnels through the words he was trying to say to himself, through the threads that stitched his feelings to memories. And it roomed in him, bunked in him, breathed in all the air, had him for its lamb and sweets, and hollowed him out where it lay curled, and it was icy and gripping, and he had that being eaten-alive-inside feeling, that feeling of trying to wrestle out of ropes.* He called it Mister Must and he made room for it and continued being himself on the sides and did not speak of it to anyone.

MISTER MUST

Do you know the meaning of plunge? Do you know the meaning of rasp, of rote? Do you know the tenacity of tar, how its fingers fill every crack?

MISTER MUST

Sometimes Christopher would lie awake waiting—you cannot believe the coldness—or wake with a start and be waiting, instantly cold—or at any moment during the day he would suddenly re-member Mister Must, that Mister Must was waiting and grown hungry. There was a wearing away, a thinning, and *it was like ev-erything was lifting off into a funnel cloud—all the memories and fa-miliar things uprooted and flying around, so nothing was where it was supposed to be, and he couldn't find his way back to what he knew.* But it wasn't like that exactly; it was more like being taken out and thrown into the sea so that everything you know is far away and small across a vast expanse of water, and you are *treading and trying to swim and the current is tugging you out and the waves are pushing you down and you are lying there in your bed,* and you are drowning.

THE SALE OF TAHOE

Evelyn was against the sale, believing that the day would come when the land would be immensely valuable. Her weak-willed younger brother, Chip, agreed with her but it was two against three, and Chip's vote really counted less than half because the other siblings thought that anything he supported had to be wrong. So the land was voted sold, and the highest bid was brought by the sharp, deal-making brother who was rapidly going broke. He said triumphantly that he had been in touch with the detested cousins who owned the adjoining land and had withheld an easement years before that would have allowed their family to develop the property. The brother proposed to sell the land to them, saying that the cousins were willing to put the falling-out behind them and pay top-dollar and that the siblings had no re-sources to develop the land anyway. At least it would stay in the family, he said, and they could avoid the embarrassment of put-ting it on the market publicly, get the proceeds right away, and on and on. The decision was made by the three who wished to sell that the land be sold to the cousins. Over the ensuing years, Chip sent articles to Evelyn from the Tahoe paper to which he contin-ued to subscribe, noting the rapid rise in property values and the fortunes being made, all with the intention of showing her again and again that they had been right. She repeatedly asked him to stop but knew he'd been right about so few things in his life that he would not be able to stop.

WITH MISTER MUST

And it was like his mouth was full of metal and his chest was being gripped like when you suck the air out of a plastic soda bottle and the sides collapse and there isn't anywhere else you are pressed so closely you are going to barely breathe one short shallow breath at a time and you cannot swing your legs out of your bed because where would you go because there isn't anywhere else there is only how like wet netting it is how cold and downward dragging.

WHITE GLOVES

Evelyn wore white gloves when she read the newspaper.

TAHOE PROCEEDS

Westy used the proceeds from the sale of the Tahoe property to open his investment banking business.

MR. KELTON'S DANCING SCHOOL

Edward Kelton ran a sniffy little invitation-only dance school on the other side of the hill from Pacific Heights, and all the seventh graders at Anglican and those at Banes School for Girls were invited to attend. The foxtrot and the waltz were de rigueur for those who hoped to one day attend the Christmas Cotillion at the Fairmont, so attendance at Mr. Kelton's was the first rung of a ladder. Mr. Kelton himself was a doughy, pompous man who stood in the center of the floor with a ballet master's cane while his assistant, a twittery little English lady named Miss Colt, cajoled the students and paired them in dance after dance. Christopher developed a crush on Deborah Burke and, finding her in the Social Register, called her one day just to talk. A few days later she returned the call, asking if he had the number of a classmate because she was having a party and wished to invite him. Christopher had cheerfully given her the number, and hung up, before realizing that she had not invited him. At the next dance class, Deborah drifted past Christopher and said in passing, "Of course, you're invited too," but Christopher had no intention of going to her party or ever saying another word to her.

THE WANGDIPHODRANG LECTURE

Thongdrols, huge wall hangings, embroidered, not painted, are unfurled once a year at religious festivals called *Tsechu*, the attendance to which earns merit. *Tsechu* means *day ten*, and the festivals are so named because it is said that Guru Rinpoche achieved all of his great deeds on the tenth of the month.

BROKEN PIECES

He knew that the world was not solid the way it seemed to be; he knew it was broken pieces put together.

THANK YOU NOTES

The Christmas after Westy left Pacific Bank to start his firm, there were very few thank you notes to write.

SUICIDE

Evelyn had said that she could not afford for death to arrive at some random time; she could not afford for just anyone to find her.

MEMORY

Now everything that had ever been between them was already memory.

THE PEARLS BY THE BED

By the dish with the note was the strand of pearls for which the entire flat had once been turned upside down when it was lost. It was cut, and a single pearl was set apart with the closed scissors resting next to it. Christopher gathered the single pearl with the strand, went to the kitchen, took a white towel from a drawer and, folding the pearl and strand into the towel, walked down the stairs to the basement where his mother's gardening jacket and red-handled tools hung on the wall. He took out his key, unlocked the deadbolt, then slid the upper bolt, the one that earlier the officer had checked so diligently, to the left, then turned the knob of the spring-lock and, pushing the backdoor open, stepped into the tiny garden that lay between the back of the house and the Presidio wall. Bending down, he dug a rectangular hole with his mother's trowel, dropped the towel into it, slid the dirt back in place with the side of his foot and pushed some gravel and leaves to cover the loose earth. It seemed as if the hole had never been there.

SUICIDE NOTE

The note was written in fountain pen in her strangely backward-slanting left-hand script: "The time had come to say goodbye. Everything hurts. Doors of wood and paper. I can't be vigilant anymore. I ask you to understand. I count on your understanding. Look carefully for all the hidden things. There's no hurry. I've paid the rent months in advance. Throw nothing away unexamined. Everything in the house is valuable. I love you all the while."

ALL THE HIDDEN THINGS

His mother had told him over and over again where everything was hidden in the house, so over the coming days Christopher would begin the task of going through the countless drawers of things, shelves of things, nooks, *and jewelry hidden in pots, silver dollars in pillowcases, cash in coat pockets at the backs of closets, trinkets collected over years and placed behind books and hidden in the bands of hats, an amber frog at the bottom of a drawer full of candles and her worn paper sandals by the bed.* Everything in the house is valuable she had said.

THE WANGDIPHODRANG LECTURE

The professor continued: *The dzong at Wangdi was constructed in 1638. The Wangdi Thongdrol, depicting Padmasambhava in his eight manifestations, carries the special significance of the seminal role of Guru Rinpoche in the seeding of the Terma and establishing The Treasure Cycles.* Only Dorji noticed Christopher's absence.

SEARCHING FOR MISTER MUST

Early one Saturday morning, awake in the dark, trying to talk to himself about Mister Must, Christopher decided that later, when his mother was working at the rummage sale and his father was playing dominoes at the club, he would search the flat for the *burlap bag where Mister Must slept during the day and he would take it to the middle of the Golden Gate Bridge and throw it off and then Mister Must would find out what it was like to be falling and frigid and out-to-sea and drowning.* He could hear the knife-people shushing themselves when he asked them where it was.

SEARCHING FOR MISTER MUST

The very day after Christopher searched for Mister Must, Evelyn confronted him about the papers in her desk having been disturbed. How dare he go through her private things. What was he thinking and how would she ever be able to trust him again? She was becoming increasingly agitated, and Christopher knew that soon she would be frantic, so he rushed into speech like leaping into rapids. "A man came into the house…a man came into me…

and I couldn't breathe…and I had to find him so I could throw him off the bridge…and I had to look…" Then Christopher stopped abruptly because his mother had frozen as if stabbed with an ice-knife. Her eyes were darting everywhere like someone pulled from the ocean after days. "What…man?" she said haltingly, and then more desperately, "*what man?*" and then she began to swat herself all over as if she were being attacked by bees.

WITH MISTER MUST

You are not with anyone: *if you look at corrugated cardboard from the side there is a honeycomb of cells. You are not with anyone: as if you are swallowed alive by something that can't be seen and you are in there swallowed up; so, what touches you doesn't touch you but touches that thing that has swallowed you; what brushes you brushes that thing; what speaks, speaks to it and asks it things, and you are trying to make yourself known from inside that thing. And do you forget that you are swallowed up? Do you forget that things can actually touch? Do you forget that you are a single thing inside of something else and not the inside of that other thing?*

THONGDROL

The professor told the group, sitting in a circle around him, that *Thongdrol* meant literally: *liberation on first sight.*

ON THE BENCH AT WANGDIPHODRANG

Dorji approached and settled in beside Christopher on the wet bench in the dim light. After a few rejected entreaties to rejoin the lectures, some groundless wispy pleasantries and a slightly uncomfortable silence, Dorji said, in a hushed voice, "Sir, I understand you are a *banker,*" Christopher said nothing, "from San Francisco," Dorji continued, "please, sir, tell me of that world, what is it like to be in such a world?" Christopher responded flatly "I'm not really a banker anymore." Dorji, taken aback, took a moment to regroup and then changed course. "Sir, the professor says you came to Bhutan because of two letters." His tone was warm but tentative. Christopher responded combatively, "They aren't *my* messages, they aren't *my hints*, I didn't *write* them...they're an *obligation*..." Dorji was clearly bewildered and abashed. Christopher calmed himself and, after offering a cigarette, which Dorji took and lit, started again: "I sent the letters long ago, on behalf of someone else. They turned out to be reminders, but not just of the past, but the way a remembered obligation reorients action, the way an archaeologist finds a shard that forces the reinterpretation of everything." Dorji was engaged but still completely lost. Christopher frustratedly withdrew the letters from his coat and, pressing them into Dorji's hands, turned away as if resting his case. Dorji put the cigarette in his mouth and, blinking back the smoke, tilted the letters toward the faint light from the hotel. He opened the raggedly torn envelope on top and withdrew its contents—a small square of white paper, blank on both sides. Dorji did not speak. He rose and returned both envelopes to Christopher, and he knew that Christopher *must* be attended to, and that he must be the one to do it.

SEARCHING FOR MISTER MUST

The morning after confronting Christopher about her desk, before he went to school, Evelyn sat him down in the living room. She was gelid and steely and composed. She told him that she and his father had searched the entire flat; there was no man; there had never been a man, and no one other than he had rifled her papers. She began to become upset all over again because he was such a liar, and what was going to become of him? And he was never to touch her things or speak of this man in the house ever again.

SEARCHING FOR MISTER MUST

Christopher had begun his search for Mister Must shortly after his mother left the house, but he'd waited a few minutes to make sure she wouldn't return having forgotten something. It was a zigzag search. Before he searched the cherry desk in his parent's bedroom, he started at the far end of the flat in the living room. He looked behind the love seat and the couch, and in the narrow space beneath his father's favorite chair, then stopped in front of the silver cabinet with the crisscross wood-and-glass front. It was locked, and though he knew the key was in the hollow under the fanstand, he simply looked through the glass at the monogrammed goblets, sugar bowls and creamers, and at Aunt Elly's birthday cup embossed from inside with the faces of animals. Mister Must was not there and he looked next in the oxblood vase on the mantel, finding a note explaining its age and value. He removed the Chinese lamp with the green dragonflies from the captain's chest, which was full of quilts and not locked. He knew that the black iron key in the keyhole was not its key, but fit the drawers in the tansu chest across the room, so he took it and walked across the large red and camel rug from Tabriz, which his mother had told him was not very fine but would have to do. He knelt in front of the tansu chest, turned the key in the lock of the middle drawer, which was the only one of the three which was locked, and, lifting it slightly, pulled it out. It contained paid bills grouped by month and secured with rubber bands, bank statements filled with cancelled checks, blue and red ledger books of Evelyn's household accounts going back to the year of her marriage, and old engagement calendars, leather bound, with the years stamped in gold on their covers. The calendars were grouped in threes, the newest on the top, and secured with rubber bands. He pulled a few out and thumbed through them. The boxes with the dates were filled with appointments, birthdays, notes of antiques purchased, luncheons, teas, rummage sale commitments and reminders—remember to tell Margot about the sale at Gump's; Christopher's first day at school; have Westy pick up cough syrup because Christopher may be developing a cold. He went to the bottom of the stack

and looked at the oldest book, 1947. There was nothing until July
7th where it said: "Marrying Weston 4:00, Grace Cathedral" and
"Honeymoon" with some subsequent days lined out. The bottom
drawer of the chest had old copies of magazines arranged by date,
and the top drawer was filled with bric-a-brac, small fine porcelain
dishes wrapped in white tissue paper, a small folded lacquer screen
depicting a tea ritual and a stack of Japanese iron sword handles
engraved with flowers.

SWINGING ON THE HOOK

Christopher called it *swinging on the hook*. At night sometimes,
before he went to sleep, he would take his pajama bottoms off, roll
onto his stomach, slide his pillow under him, slip his penis between
the pillow and the sheet and rock his pelvis back and forth, picturing *a medieval square with villagers milling around, restless children
tugging their mother's skirts and men facing a platform with their arms
folded over their chests. On the platform, a large metal hook hung at
the end of a tangle of chains and pulleys, and the executioner and his
assistant stood waiting for him. He was brought through the crowd in
a cart, naked except for a loose smock that nearly covered his buttocks
and genitals. He climbed the several stairs, his hands tied tightly behind
him. The hook would be inserted from the front with the executioner
facing him—reaching under and behind his scrotum, finding his anus
and guiding the hook into it while the assistant steadied Christopher
from behind. It didn't really hurt—it was more like what he'd heard
about worms having hooks put through them, that it didn't really hurt,
but he felt a pressure and a scissoring inside, a feeling of steadily deeper
puncturing. Now he was being tilted back, and he was mostly able to be
brave until he saw the tip of the hook push up under his naval and then
emerge. Now the executioner began to tug the chain and hoist him up
before the crowd, and he was arching and inverting, and the smock slid
down and bunched against his chin, and then, not meaning to at all, he
began to writhe, to try to work his insides around the hook so it would*

*not grip and stretch him so, and now, bent back he looked into the faces
of the crowd, and they were excited and eager to see his response to the
hook.* He was writhing now, faster and faster, moaning, moving his
penis in and out between the pillow and the sheet. Then, with a
muffled shriek, he died on the hook and lay dead still in his bed.

SEARCHING FOR MISTER MUST

There was nothing in the shallow drawer of the telephone table in
the hall except the Social Register. In the dining room there was
only the sideboard to search, filled with napkins, place mats, little
silver spoons, sterling salt dishes and candles the color of unsalted
butter. In a silver dish, beneath a flat jade carving of a bird, he
found the key to the cabinet underneath, which held silver soup
terrines, ladles, a wooden box containing monogrammed flatware,
and the hollow silver bottle, punched out all over with five-sided
stars, with which Evelyn had christened the submarine. He took
the bottle out and looked at it, running his fingers over the scuff
marks and slight dent where it had hit the hull. Exiting the room,
he paused in front of the six-paneled Japanese screen with its river,
streets, cherry blossoms, and people going about their lives. He
glanced at himself in the gilt oval mirror on the opposite wall and
pushed through the swinging door into the pantry. The built-in
cabinets housed everyday dishes, flower vases and salad tongs, and
he didn't search the liquor cabinet beneath because he knew what
was there, and it wasn't Mister Must.

SWINGING ON THE HOOK

Christopher was concerned that swinging on the hook would
wake his mother.

SEARCHING THE CHERRY DESK

The slightly red desk shone and smelled of wax. Christopher, having made a mental diagram, moved the many stationery items from the writing surface to the floor. He closed the drawbridge desk-front, reached down, opened the bottom drawer and, because of his theory of sound, muffled the knock of the brass drawer-handles against their plates and lifted the drawer very carefully as he pulled it out. It squeaked slightly anyway as he tilted it forward, nearly resting it on the floor. The inside of the drawer was elaborately partitioned with cardboard shirt-boards from the dry cleaners, and the contents of all the compartments were neatly stacked. Staring into the drawer, Christopher noticed that the stacks were arranged as if time moved left to right, like reading. He tried to discern which stack was Elly's because he wanted to see the map of her grand tour again, and the photo of her sitting on the camel. He found the photographs beneath a folded copy of her last Will and Testament; which he could not help but try to read and found the entry leaving Evelyn the sum of $20,000. Being careful to note the position of the photographs in the stack, he took them out and looked at her face, really for the first time. It was sturdier, more square and jowly than he had realized and he saw that she wasn't actually very tall. He put the photos back carefully on top of a series of monogrammed cards inviting Evelyn to her apartment on Russian Hill for tea, or inviting both Evelyn and Westy for cocktails.

TAHOE PHOTO ALBUM

Digging further down beneath the photos of Elly, the postcards of her grand tour, the folded map and a seemingly endless pile of letters written in Elly's Victorian cursive to Evelyn over the years, Christopher saw the cover of a black leather binder lying flat toward the bottom of the drawer. He unearthed it from beneath the pile, which he placed on the floor. "Photo Album" was embossed in gold on the cover of the binder and in the upper right, in white ink, was written Vol. 1., and, on the inside cover, over a topographical map of Lake Tahoe, was inscribed "Benjamin Brooks, Pictures from Summer, 1929." The pages of the album were black and all the writing was in white ink. The postcards and photographs were secured by little paste-on triangles at their corners, and included an aerial map in brown and green next to which Ben had written in white on the black paper, "Lake Tahoe California (in the Sierra Nevada Mts.) About 23 miles long, and 13 miles wide 6,225 ft. above the sea." His handwriting was clear and somewhat ornamental. There was a picture of the lake, "Taken from Mt. Tallac," and numerous other black and white photographs arranged roughly four to the page depending on their size. Ben had written notes or names next to many of them, and they included photographs taken from highways and hillsides, photographs of the family's boats and docks and boathouses—some clear, some grainy and out-of-focus—photographs of servants in uniforms, photographs of the main house, a photograph of a small pond just below the timber line, photos of the lake from Job's peak, of the trail to Pyramid Peak, of placid gentlemen fishing in tweedy suits and nubby ties, and women in dresses and big summer hats sipping tea on bright verandas overlooking the lake with servants in attendance standing around with their hands clasped in front of them awaiting orders.

TAHOE PHOTO ALBUM

Christopher leafed quietly through the photo album, sometimes lingering on an image, and it was as if the sense of leisure embodied in the photographs had spilled into the room. He studied the photographs of Virginia City Nevada, its dusty streets and boardwalks, of the old Episcopal Church, of the old Comstock Mine and the new Comstock Mine—the shafts and the ore-cars loaded with rock sitting on their rails—and an untitled photograph of a canyon wall banded with strata. There was a photograph of Uncle Henry sleeping in a chair on a veranda, and one of Elly, whose face was in shadow but still recognizable, standing beside her husband, and photographs of children standing indifferently at the water's edge, and one of a cluster of impassive people described as "Navajos," and one of Ben, whose face was a perfect replica of his mother's, sitting on a rock by the water, dangling a fish on a string—next to the photograph, the note in white, "three and a half pound rainbow." And, toward the center of the album, Christopher came upon a photograph so stunning and strange that, at first, he didn't know what he was looking at: a feral girl—hair knotted and littered with sticks and leaves—was holding the outstretched wings of a red-tailed hawk by her fingertips and staring directly and fiercely into the camera. The bottom of the photograph was bleached with glare, so she seemed to be standing on air. Just to the right of the image, written in Ben's careful script was "Evelyn." *How could it be? Who had she been?* He rushed through the remaining pages to see if there were other photos of Evelyn. There were not.

GLASS

He saw the hundreds of pieces *shattering out behind him, each with its part of the image—a plant, a door, a part of a dusty path, a horse, the scent of a garden, light through branches reflected on water, a point of land, two figures walking toward its tip and around its bend to a secret beach.*

TAHOE PHOTO ALBUM

Some pictures were loose in the back, behind numerous blank pages. Summer had ended, and these, Christopher knew, would never be put in their places, like the stamps at the back of his father's stamp collection. He closed the album and put it back, but after a pause took it out again, returning to the photograph of the fearsome girl, about his age, holding the hawk. How would the hawk let her hold it that way? Then, he realized, of course, it was dead, probably Ben's hunting prize of the day, and he realized that

Evelyn must have been looking at Ben when the picture was taken. He put the album away again and he sat on the floor with the sun slanting into the room. The house was very quiet and the shutter's diagonal shadows striped the wall. He thought of the light in the photograph, the blinding light at her feet, and he knew how Ben had died, and how Evelyn had come to live, so the pictures were like pictures of people being carried, small boat, toward a falls that they could not see, a falls, the entire enormous height of which, was before him. He thought of the light at her feet, and realized that he had never before thought of there being a glare in the past.

WEIGHT

What does fire weigh…what does falling water weigh…what does light weigh? Does a house of cards weigh more than a pack of cards… does an inch weigh more than a mile… does doubt weigh more than belief…does a promise weigh more before or after it's broken…does the horizon weigh more or less than the distance to it? What is the weight of the floodgate that keeps secrets safe from the rising river of speech?

SEARCHING THE CHERRY DESK

He continued, almost reflexively, for a while, closing the bottom drawer, then looking quickly through the middle one. He distract-edly shuffled through letters, photographs, newspaper clippings, cards from Shebee over the years, of which he scanned a few, a photo of Uncle Alfred and Doug shopping for plants at a nursery, with Alfred strolling in a casual suit and broad brimmed hat and Doug loaded down with pots, a note from Alfred to Evelyn's par-ents, a copy of which he'd sent to her "sub rosa," saying how strong, independent and capable she was, wedding pictures, Evelyn beam-ing in her beautiful white dress, the Marriage License, invitations, breathless letters of congratulation, and a clipping reporting the decommissioned Cachalot sold for scrap. He found no stack for

Lydia in his mother's cherry desk, but he did find an unmarked envelope containing a tracing of the assembled pieces of Hext. In the stacks of the top drawer, dedicated entirely to himself, he found his most recent report card and, digging down, notes from teachers, school papers, his admission letter from Anglican, and the green palm cross from his first communion, paper-clipped to a note saying that Evelyn had found it on the floor beneath his bed while cleaning his room. To the left were drawings in crayon and finger paintings, and far below he found a card with footprints in black ink from the day of his birth, his birth certificate, and letters congratulating the couple on their happy news. He knew that Mister Must was wound and waiting somewhere in the flat, but he could not pull his thoughts from the photo of Evelyn.

CLOSING THE DESK

Christopher wondered if a thousand things of momentary interest made a life. *How these had come to stand in for the breadth of her childhood: big houses full of cousins and servants, long unstructured summer days at Tahoe with Ben hunting, fishing, hiking and taking photographs while the adults stood around in dresses and country suits. The world then was black and white, like the photographs, everything standing out straightforwardly—strata of rocks, strata of people, hours stratified in layer on layer of leisure—money leaking away in every direction and no one noticing because it had always simply been there.* Christopher closed the top and middle drawers, lowered the drawbridge writing surface, and put everything back on the desk as perfectly as he could remember.

COAL

He walked from the flat toward the eucalyptus groves in the Presidio, stopping only briefly on the back porch to look through the coal sacks. The coal was *black and shiny and the coal dust was oily and sticky and smeary and it stuck to his fingers as he moved the coal*

around and the smell was intrusive and acrid but the coal was not
Mister Must.

THE SALE OF TAHOE

After the bitter sale of the Tahoe property, Evelyn never really
spoke to her brothers and sisters again.

KNIFE-PEOPLE

He found how pain flattens you, and thought how much pain the
knife-people must be in to be so flat, and he wondered if that was
why they had let Mister Must come out: because they needed him
to know what makes a person a knife-person—it was pain.

MEDITATION ON DROWNING

Forms of fleeing forged in forms of forgetting—everyone turning away,
from every kind of emptiness, from illness, despair, pain—turning
away into stories, engagements, agendas, activities, professions, pas-
times—drowning in that turning, drowning in that forgetting, in the
crush of immediate concerns—and he ran alongside, keeping contact
with the turned-from, the hardness of it, the costliness; the breaking-
heart hollowness.

SEARCHING FOR MISTER MUST

Some evenings later, Christopher sat in his room and tried to
think. Maybe he had overlooked the most obvious thing—that
his mother was right, that there was no man in the flat—*and it*
was as if he had been speaking a made-up language in his sleep, and
when he woke and spoke it again it made no sense—how had he ever
thought that he would find Mister Must in the flat? How had
he overlooked the most obvious thing: that *he* was where Mister
Must slept during the day.

KNIFE-PEOPLE

But I will never be a knife-person, he said to himself. I will never be a knife-person as long as I live. But Christopher *felt himself sharpening; every night before he'd go to sleep, he felt a coldness brushing him and part of his outer layering rubbing off, and he knew that he was sharpening and flattening. And as he sharpened he started not to trust his own edges. He started to be afraid that he would cut the things around him, which he knew was not a good thing to be happening in his mother's house, and he wanted to find a way to keep the cutting inside so that he would not shred the world.*

THE PRE-DAWN WALK TO WANGDIPHODRANG DZONG

A good while before dawn, the group was awakened and visited the dismal squat toilets in turn, and washed with hot water from bowls filled by attendants. They did not eat breakfast because they were fasting. Sonam signaled that it was time to depart. The rains had stopped in the middle of the night, and they walked in the dark down the long muddy street past hovels lit with butter lamps toward Wangdiphodrang Dzong. Christopher was slipping; he was very cold, and his shoes were already filled with water.

STRAIGHT LINES

Evelyn's writing paper was never lined but was thin enough to see through to a darkly lined page placed underneath and used for guidance.

THE DREAM OF THE SECRET GARDEN

Christopher dreamed that his mother had a secret garden behind a high ivy-covered wall. He was *running his fingers through the leaves, and he felt the little flat hinges, the outline of a door and the little circular latch that folded into the wall, but in the dream he couldn't put it together that this was a door, so he didn't even try to open it.* When he woke, he was struck with self-reproach: how could he not have known it was a door? How could he not have tried to open it? What would he have found on the other side?

THE OTHER BOY

After lunch one day, as Christopher washed his hands in the boy's room sink, a younger boy with reddish hair and his shirttails out, whom Christopher had seen around but did not know, approached him and began to speak in a level voice while looking Christopher directly in the face. "You're Carl's friend, aren't you?" "Yes." "I was Carl's friend too." "Well, we were really good friends…he used to take me to Stanford." "Carl used to take me to Stanford too." Christopher didn't respond. He stepped around the other boy, pulled the bathroom door open and pushed through the noisy crowd of classmates loitering in the hall. *His body was like a room with all the walls fallen down; every icy bit of blown debris was rushing into him, and he had no way to close himself off or keep anything out.* As he pushed past his classmates and rubbed his wet hands on his trousers, *a tumbling coldness entered him, and he had a sense of drowning, that there wasn't any air but only icy water all around him pouring in, and there weren't any boundaries between his body and the coldness everywhere.* He hurried along the granite corridors, past the cloakrooms and frescoed walls and he began to cry, but it wasn't the kind of crying where you think about something sad and it makes you cry. *It was the kind of crying where everything dissolves in you and rushes to get out, and you are the narrows and you are choking—your chest is clenched and heaving—you can't cry fast enough or hard enough—you can't get out of the way of everything trying to escape.*

AND HE WENT ABOUT HIS DAYS

And he went about his days of blue button-down shirts and tied ties, morning prayers and snapping three-ring-binders, gum erasers and stained glass windows, candles and pencil sharpeners and psalms and being on time and staying very quiet while others spoke and holding up his hand and waiting for his turn and wishing he were not so impatient to die.

BRIDGE

Christopher came softly up the back stairs, through the door into the kitchen. Evelyn, at the sink, wheeled and fired: "You have a balanced hand with twenty-one points and honors in every suit. How must you open?" Without pausing or breaking his stride, he said: "Two no trump," and he proceeded to his room and closed the door.

WITH MISTER MUST

You are not with anyone; the distance is cluttered with clotted moss; you are not with anyone; people are here right in front of you, and you are not with them; they are here; you are facing them, and you are not with anyone.

TEA PARTY

Evelyn gave a tea party for acquaintances she had met in the antiques business. Margaret from *Tea and Rarity* asked Christopher what he hoped to do when he grew up. He said that he was considering moving to North Dakota. "*What?* Leaving San Francisco to move to North Dakota? My dear—and what will you be doing there?" "I don't know, maybe I'll be a waiter." Standing on tiptoes, she exclaimed to her husband across the room, "Ceryl—Ceryl— Evelyn's son hopes to leave San Francisco to become a *waiter* in North Dakota!" The room went quiet; then there were titters and laughter, and Christopher saw that the people in the room had no use for places that did not exist because they were happy with the world in front of them.

LYDIA

In the photo Christopher had found in the box of pipes in his father's closet, he discovered that Lydia had once been beautiful.

ROYALL LYME

The Christmas after Carl moved east, Evelyn gave Christopher a bottle of Royall Lyme with the little pewter crown cap in his stocking, and he had to thank her for it but he could not look at her when he did, and he could not wear it. *But if he did not wear it, he would have to explain why he was not wearing it—he could not even look at it, but he could not throw it away because then he would have to explain why he had thrown it away*, so maybe he would put it on a shelf a little out of the way, and maybe he would wear it once in a while because his mother was always vigilant.

THEORY OF SOUND

Christopher told his teacher that all the sounds ever made were still here, humming lower and lower, and you could still hear them somehow in a part of yourself.

WESTY'S FATHER

In Byron Westall's wallet, Christopher had found an old five dollar bill, a lucky four-leaf clover taped to a card, and another card that gave the address of the sanitarium to which Byron was to be returned if found wandering or lost.

DEPTH

By definition, depth is where you can actually drown.

THEORY OF SOUND

And the teacher asked what was the oldest sound that you could hear? And Christopher said that you could hear the beginning of the world if you knew how to listen—if you knew how to sort through the noise—you could hear the beginning of everything.

SALT

The most important thing that Christopher would ever learn in school was the composition of salt.

YOU CAN'T WALK THE SUN WITH YOUR FINGERS

You can't take pictures of things that are smaller than light.

YOU CAN'T WALK THE SUN WITH YOUR FINGERS

A girl, Christopher's age, lost her father to a sudden illness. He was a minor liaison, in the French Consulate, who'd moved to San Francisco years before and married an American. Their daughter, Genevieve, refused to attend her father's funeral, or even to acknowledge that he was dead. After a while, she started telling strangers that she was an heiress, being kept from her inheritance by her wicked mother.

YOU CAN'T WALK THE SUN WITH YOUR FINGERS

Genevieve's mother, who would now have to raise a child by herself, was a schoolteacher, wore a cloth coat, drove a falling-apart VW Bug, and lived in a small rented house on Anza. She worried about her daughter incessantly.

DEPTH

In the depths you can't push the pressure away with your hands.

THE TSETSE FLY

Christopher wanted to do his seventh grade report on the tsetse fly, but Col. Easton made him do his report on the building of the Golden Gate Bridge.

WANGDIPHODRANG

The travelers stood among a throng of pilgrims at the gates of the dzong in the chill black pre-dawn air with puddles and frost on the ground and numerous fires lit to warm the hands of those waiting for admission to the Tsechu. Those waiting, even in their finest traditional dress, were settled in the ordinary—in natural proportion to what was asked. None had ever seen a dentist, driven a car or been in an elevator. They were people who belonged to each other in that way that belonging could not be noticed by them—not in the way that words can't notice how they fall together in sentences, not in the way that raindrops enter lakes, but more in the way that when you are walking, all the things that are balancing you and holding you up are invisible to you.

MINOR LIFE

And he thought that if there were really many lives, that this one must be a minor life, a toss-off, like a single tabletop of marginalia found in the second bedroom of an old person's house on a side-street in a nondescript town—*that kind of life, that kind of little clutter of private tumults kind of life, that clutch of private memories kind of life, that shamble of private meanings kind of life, that kind of life that someone later finds and clears in a single motion into a box that ends up on a table with folding legs at a rummage sale.*

FIRE

Christopher walked up to one of the fires, took the letters from his coat, and tossed them in.

THE FIRST THORN FIRE

In the early hours of the last Monday of May, 1965, when he was finishing the seventh grade, Christopher was lying awake in the dark, and heard fire engines approaching closer and closer until they were very loud. There were voices in the street of people hurrying past. He jumped out of bed, and his father was already standing in the hall. "Get your coat," he said. Soon they were heading down the stairs and into the street. The fire was around the corner, up the hill a little past the middle of the block on the west side of Broderick. Lots of people were already assembled across the street in their pajamas and overcoats. There was much excitement and chatter, neighbors greeting neighbors whom they hadn't seen in a while as they stood across from the burning house in the small hours of the morning. The fire ladder was already up, the middle front window broken out and a high volume hose was shooting water into the living room. Sparks were climbing the black air, billowing white smoke was hissing where the water hit, and a burning couch was hauled out of the house and placed on the curb. The owner was safely outside, speaking with the firefighters, and the fire was quickly extinguished so, after a little while, everyone went home.

RETRIEVING THE KEY

The day after the first Thorn fire, the acrid smell of smoke transfused the neighborhood. Before going to school, while his mother was making breakfast, Christopher snuck into his parent's bedroom, opened the secret drawer in the cherry desk and retrieved the key. He put it in his pocket, where it would stay for several days while he decided what to do.

ENTERING THE HOUSE

That Friday, after school, still in his uniform, with the fog already blowing through the streets, Christopher stood in front of the house that had had the fire with the key in his hand. Looking up to the second floor, he could see where the middle window was still broken out but now boarded up. The curtains that remained were stained gray with smoke, and the burned up couch still sat on the curb waiting to be picked up. An unmarked commercial van was parked in the driveway. Christopher stood for what seemed a long time, as if waiting for something to fall into place in himself, before approaching the door and ringing the bell, which did not seem to work. When there was no answer, he tried the key and found that it did not fit. But he also found that the door was not locked, so he opened it and entered, his motions slowed by the great cost of stepping into a stranger's house uninvited. Standing in a small foyer at the bottom of a flight of carpeted stairs, where the smell of smoke was bitter, soggy and stale, he couldn't hear a sound in the house. He thought of turning back, but when would he find the house unlocked again? So he walked up the stairs and, in a very tentative voice, inquired "Is anybody home?" Christopher arrived at the second floor landing, looked left into the dining room, then right into the living room. The immediate impression was not at all of wealth: books stacked on the floor, overflowing ashtrays, worn chairs and rugs, cluttered surfaces, and somewhat banged up furniture he knew was not valuable. There was a Persian rug his mother would have liked though it was far too worn for a collector. There was also, in all of this, a sense of comfort, so much so that any sense of apprehension vanished. The bookcase occupying the entire left-hand wall of the living room was so crowded with books that some were laid horizontally on the tops of the vertical ones. A halfheartedly erected scaffolding stood in the center of the room where the couch would have been, and a bucket of white paint, perched on a plank, sat under the few brush stokes applied to the ceiling, most of which was still black. The overwhelming sense was that little had been done to repair the room.

THE NOTEBOOK

Just off of the living room was a study with more books on the floor, another bookcase, a red leather chair by the window, a small couch with a side chair, and a table crowded with another over-flowing ashtray, a phone atop a phone book, a yellow legal pad, an open pack of Chesterfield regulars, and a black leather notebook with gilt-edged pages and a fountain pen resting on top. Christopher walked into the study, pulled a cigarette from the pack and put it in his mouth without lighting it. The raw tobacco was hot where he pressed his tongue. Flopping into the leather chair, he let his leg dangle over the arm and, placing the fountain pen on the table, picked the notebook up, opened it to a blank page in the middle and, leafing toward the front, found that it was entirely blank except for the first few pages, which had writing in dark green ink. There were smears and blops, like dark little suns, where drops of ink had fallen to the page when there had been hesitations. Christopher had turned to the first page and had read the first two jottings, both titled *Trace*, when a voice shook him into panic—"May I offer you a light?" Christopher looked up to see a tall, slender, older man in a gray herringbone jacket, unironed button-down white shirt, camel slacks and worn loafers standing before him, clicking a Zippo and lighting the cigarette dangling from his mouth, then holding the lighter out toward Christopher, who shook his head slowly and jumped to his feet. "Oh, I suppose you don't *actually* smoke." "No, sir." Christopher tugged the cigarette out of his mouth, and the paper had dried to his lower lip and tore it slightly. He tasted a little blood but the pain was nothing, and he put the cigarette on the table and fished in his pocket for the key. "Nasty habit—started this fire you know." "Yes, I know," and now Christopher, wanting to pursue his redemption, held the key outstretched toward the gentleman and blurted "I wanted to return this to you." The face of the slender man standing before him was handsome, though deeply lined, and there was not a hint of anger in his eyes. "Well, it's not mine, so keep it." Then, as if by habit, he reached for a volume on a bookshelf—*A History of Materialism*—"Not a thief are you?" he asked archly. Christopher stiffened, not knowing what to say. "Good," the man said, not waiting for an answer, "I keep my cash here," and, taking some bills from his pocket stuffed them inside the front cover and put the book back on the shelf. Christopher, now nervous beyond measure, was momentarily cast into some corner of his thinking associated with Anglican and said "I'm Mister Westall." The gentleman was somewhat taken aback. "Well, Mister Westall—I'm Dr. Thorn, but you can call me Andy if you like." Christopher continued, "I live around the corner on Green Street." A smile played at the corners of Dr. Thorn's mouth as he took a draw on his cigarette. "After the fire, I started keeping that journal you're holding." Christopher, who had forgotten that he was holding anything, put the journal quickly back on the table, and fumblingly placed the fountain pen on top. Dr. Thorn paused, then smiled broadly, "Now, are you interested in a little after school work to help me get this place back in shape?" "Well, yes sir, but I'll have to ask." "Fine, let me know." Christopher was relieved; now he would be able to explain why he smelled like smoke when he got home—because he had decided to ask the owner of the house that burned if he could be of help.

BLOOD

Evelyn asked Christopher why his lip was bleeding. He was caught off guard, and knew that the thing that he told her, which was anything but the truth, was not completely believed.

HELPING REPAIR THE HOUSE

Dr. Thorn took Christopher to Patton's, where they bought supplies and a sheet of glass to replace the front window. He told Christopher that they'd have to do it all themselves because the place was not insured, and he showed him how to remove the sharp shards, repair and prep the frame, and replace the glass with glazier's points and putty, and he showed him how to use trisodium phosphate to clean the ash from the ceiling so they could paint, and they went to a rental outlet for equipment, and Christopher steamed the rugs and the carpeted stairway. Dr. Thorn also had him call the city about removing the couch: "Tell them you're my representative," he'd said. Evelyn seemed OK with all of this, and Christopher even heard her tell Uncle Alfred over the phone, with a little pride, "He's helping Dr. Thorn repair his house." Over the coming weeks, things came together, even a little well, and Christopher had worked with his hands and, even over Evelyn's protestations to Dr. Thorn that Christopher needn't be paid, earned his first money ever.

TRACE

You must learn to distinguish the substantial from the unsubstantial—that which can bear weight from that which cannot.

ENCLOSURE

Dr. Thorn asked Christopher if he could think of an enclosure that was open on all sides.

DR. THORN

Christopher would never call Dr. Thorn "Andy," he would always call him Dr. Thorn.

TRACE

There is a bridge between the substantial and the unsubstantial. It is fire.

THE KEY

After Christopher had been coming to his house for a while, Dr. Thorn said, "Something's been puzzling me. Of all the houses in the neighborhood, why did you choose to come to *my* house with the key, and why did you *come in* even after the key didn't fit the door?" Christopher didn't pause. "Because the key was a messenger, and I came to your house because of what it said." "And what did it say?" "It said: *the door out of hell is hidden in a burning house.*"

THE CONTINUOUS CONSTRUCTION OF MEMORY

All these delicate structures built on the fault-lines, shaken down as they are made, built again and again and again.

WAGON OF SPELLS

You are trying to go home in your speaking, in the wagon of spells, in the cart heaped with straw, pulled by the great horses of language and longing.

DR. THORN'S

The doors were never locked; there were no particular schedules or procedures to attend to; the carpets were worn and warm; there was a globe and a huge book of maps on the table in the hall. There was an *Egyptian Book of The Dead* and a *Tibetan Book of the Dead*, books in German, books in Greek, art books with page after page of plates, books about the origins of words and the origins of the earth, the patterns of tides and the origins of the stars. *And his mother wasn't shaking like chandeliers in an earthquake, and his father wasn't roused from the dormancy of alcohol and history to run interference for her.* Christopher could go into the house at any time; and he could breathe there, and he could rest there, and no one was tightening and testing him like tuning a piano.

THE DISCOVERY OF PLUTO

Dr. Thorn told Christopher that, because of perturbations in the orbits of the outer planets, scientists knew of Pluto's existence before it was actually observed and that it wasn't unusual for unseen things to influence people's lives in a similar way.

WANGDIPHODRANG TSECHU

Christopher was pressed forward through the gates into a long corridor, then through another gate. The throng was like an invading force, and it was clear that the dzong had been architected as a fortress to be defended. The second gate opened onto a vast courtyard and Christopher was swept into a sea of masks—*but not the masks of the sales counter or the boardroom, not the masks of the job interview, not the masks designed to keep persons safe behind them or to present faces safe to look upon—not masks like that, but devil masks, fierce-guardians, skull-masks and hungry ghosts—everything pulled from underneath and worn as a face.*

JAPANESE

Evelyn began to study Japanese on her own. She kept a little notebook with words she was learning, written with the greatest of care. She would read them aloud to Christopher: "*Tokonoma*: an alcove reserved for one or two beautiful things—a painting, a poem written delicately on fine paper, an old piece of sculpture, a vase and a few flowers. *Kura*: strong box. *Fusuma*: doors of wood and paper. *Haori*: ceremonial clothes." She would say the words aloud again and again in Christopher's presence, and dutifully recite the definitions.

ORBITS

And Dr. Thorn told Christopher that if you looked carefully, you could discern, in the irregularities of people's lives, the presence of things that must be there outside of view; the influences pulling on them—hungers, expectations, memories, loss—and you could sense a cutting away of the attention toward something hidden, like a cutting of the eyes from what was present, and in that instant of absence a perturbation formed.

BONES

He felt his bones beneath his skin. He thought of the National Geographic pictures that he'd seen in the dentist's office of the scattered bones of diamond miners unearthed by the wind in an abandoned mining town in the Sub-Sahara—how the bones had nothing to say of whose they were, how like seashells they were, how unlike people. His bones too were like this—he could feel them, starting with his collarbone, then his sternum and following each of the ribs around to the back. He thought how unlike selves the bones were, how steady and everlasting. What part of a person remains in a femur tossed by itself on the sand? Nothing of names, nothing of desire: he felt his bones beneath his skin, inside his legs, inside his fingers. What did they have to do with him anyway?

GRAVITY

Christopher had always thought of gravity as a kind of long-distance magnetism, but Dr. Thorn said that, according to Einstein, gravity was actually caused by indentations in the fabric of space made by the presence of massive objects and that an orbit was a rolling around the edge of one of these indentations.

ORBITS

And Dr. Thorn said that, in consciousness, attention equaled mass, so people orbited what they paid attention to—that their lives were the trajectories created by their habits of attention.

THEORY OF BROKENNESS

Evelyn said the brokenness in everything was just waiting to be coaxed out.

ORBITS

Christopher knew that something unseen was pulling on his mother from a distance. He had it figured for an ice-orb.

SIEVE

Many afternoons he went to Dr. Thorn's house after school when Dr. Thorn wasn't there. He'd put coffee in the percolator and, though he *never* actually smoked there, would take a dead cigarette from an ashtray, put it in his mouth, flop on the couch and, having picked a book from the bookcase, leaf aimlessly through it. *He'd put some toast in the toaster, and the butter was out on the counter uncovered, and the jam was out on the counter and the lid was nowhere to be found—it was whole fruit and whole milk and orange juice loaded with pulp and no jelly and nothing in its place, and nothing special, and nothing strained through a sieve.*

THE WELL

The fog was rolling into Pacific Heights one afternoon, and Christopher, having taken a random book from Dr. Thorn's shelf, was sitting on the floor, trying not to spill the cup of coffee he'd set on the rug. The volume had a worn gray dust jacket with the title, *The I Ching*, and Christopher was wandering through its mysterious pages, divided by six line symbols with explanations, and, landing on *The Well*, he turned the pages slowly, trying to stay with the sentences...*Wood is below, water above...The wood goes down into the earth to bring up water...They come and go and draw from the well...They come and go...This is my heart's sorrow...In the well there* *is a clear, cold spring...*and he began to fall through the pages, as if into the well itself.

SHATTERING

And you will know shattering—not shattering where only something shatters, like a vase falling from a table onto a floor of tiles but shattering where everything shatters, inside and out, when, through the spraying shards of the shattered world, nothing of wholeness can be seen, no ground, no vantage, no person, no powers, nothing reflected or reflecting, nothing to grasp—everything flying from everything, everything singing with disintegration at the speed of absolute shattering. The flying blanket of shards wraps you, riddles you, seizes your every part as passenger and carries each aspect helter-skelter outward from the center. So are universes born—so are selves flown from themselves in the ceaseless mix, toward the stretched elastic limit of shattering, upon which there is a turning at the first muted tints of assemblage, of joining, of making, of return.

LANDRY'S

Dr. Thorn liked to walk, so he and Christopher took long walks together, sometimes all the way to Chinatown or Ocean Beach, or up to Arguello and over to Golden Gate Park, or down to the Marina. Sometimes they would just walk down to Union Street and stop at Landry's Pie Shop. And it was nothing out of the ordinary for a father and son, which is what they were taken for, to take a walk and have a piece of pie together.

PASSAGE FROM GRANT

Christopher turned to Dr. Thorn and, like a horse leaping over barricades, blurted out, "There's a secret passage from the play yard at Grant School to the piano in my den." Dr. Thorn stopped what he was doing and turned intently toward Christopher: "Tell me what you mean." "I mean one day during recess, I was playing by myself in a corner of the play yard and it suddenly seemed as if all the other kids had gone inside because I can't remember any yelling or laughing around me, and then I noticed a kind of outline in the cement, like a door—then I was just tumbling, and all at once, I was sitting on the floor of my den next to the piano. I called to my mom, but she wasn't in the flat, so I went back to school."

PASSAGE FROM GRANT

Christopher looked directly at Dr. Thorn. "Do you believe me?" After lighting a cigarette, Dr. Thorn said "Yes. There are all kinds of cracks in the world, wild cards in the deck, things that make people uncomfortable, so they set them aside as if they never happened. Did anything like it ever happen again?" "No." Christopher seemed suddenly impatient to change the topic and asked if he could make a pot of coffee.

CARTOGRAPHY

Holding his cup of black coffee, Christopher asked Dr. Thorn what *kind* of doctor he was. "My parents were older, had money and believed in education, and I never wanted to leave school. I drifted from subject to subject, year to year, but settled on Geographic Sciences—basically, I studied cartography." He glanced at Christopher to see if he understood. "Mapmaking," Christopher said. "Yes, but that was long ago and I never really used it." Christopher hardly heard this because he wanted to press Dr. Thorn about something important. "Do you think that *all* the places on maps *really* exist? Do you think North Dakota *really exists*? Do you think that *Bhutan* really exists?" "You're quite something, aren't you. Well, I don't know about North Dakota, but I actually happen to *have* a few stamps from Bhutan, somewhere around here, and if I can find them you can have them." Christopher was excited and, after digging in several drawers, Dr. Thorn produced two small wax paper envelopes, each containing two colorful stamps. Even though they did not prove that Bhutan existed, Christopher liked them so much that he didn't want his parents to see them or even know he had them, so he brought them home without mentioning them and hid them in his father's stamp collection at the back of his father's closet.

INVISIBLE PLACES

Dr. Thorn told Christopher that he was right; that the places on a map weren't really places, like the light in a photograph wasn't really light, and noticing some confusion on Christopher's face, he explained, "I mean, you can't read in the dark by the light of a photograph. Still, the light that was there when the picture was taken allows you to find your way through the images. The lines on a map are like that."

THE PRAYER RUG

It seemed that Dr. Thorn collected everything: old maps, rare books, religious artifacts, old letters, pottery shards and fossils, and everything was spread around, stacked in corners or pushed into bookcase nooks. There was a closet in the downstairs hall where coats were supposed to be hung, but it was stuffed with rolled Oriental rugs. One afternoon after school, Christopher pulled one out and unrolled it on the floor. It was a small red rectangle with cobalt bars, and at one end of the rug was a woven pair of hands, thumbs facing in, so it was their backs that you were seeing, so they must have been lying flat. Christopher got down on his knees and, in order to fit on the rug, he had to fold himself back and rest his weight on his ankles, which was hard and hurt, then he stretched to place his palms on the hands on the rug, which brought his forehead almost to the ground, and after holding that position for a while, he realized that he was praying.

CARTOGRAPHY

Christopher asked Dr. Thorn why he hadn't stayed a mapmaker. "I never cared for *employment*—I mean working for someone else—and there's not much call for a lone cartographer—couldn't have managed a *faculty* position—so, there you are, after the war, I struck out on my own, finding things to do, mostly with my hands, eventually going into business for myself." "Where did you fight in the war?" Christopher asked. "I didn't *fight* in the war, I had a desk job, probably arranged by my father, right over here at the Presidio." "*Desk* job," Christopher said faintly, "*arranged* by your *father*, you didn't *fight?*" "No, probably for the best, I never much believed in it anyway." Christopher, stunned, experienced a visceral, unwelcome ratcheting-down of his estimation of Dr. Thorn. "Didn't *believe, how could you not…?*" Dr. Thorn, eyes glistening, interrupted, "Didn't believe then, still don't." Christopher, struck into silence, was trying to recover himself. Dr. Thorn continued, "I'd studied history. I'd seen that *everything* burns itself away and war is just a means of trying to stop or accelerate that. But it never answers anything, it just makes the fire burn faster. And I'd studied religions, especially Buddhism." Christopher flashed on the map of the world's religions at the back of his atlas and interrupted, "So, you're a Buddhist?" "No, I couldn't stay with anything. I was always restlessness." Christopher wondered how Dr. Thorn's parents had felt about his pursuits, and asked if they were still living. When Dr. Thorn said that they were not, Christopher said nothing more.

THE BURIAL OF THE BROKEN

A few days later, looking up from a piece of apple pie at Landry's, Christopher said to Dr. Thorn "There's something I didn't tell you about the afternoon I came through the passage from Grant. I managed to get up from where I had landed by the piano—the light was so clear coming in through the window, and I called out to my mom, but I couldn't find her, so finally I went to the big window at the back of the flat and looked down into the garden. I saw her kneeling in her Japanese gardening jacket and the red-handled hand-rake was on the ground next to her, and she was digging with her trowel, and there was a kitchen towel next to her with something wrapped in it. She made a nearly perfect rectangle in the ground, like a little grave, and laid the towel in it, and covered it back over and smoothed it with the rake and sifted some soil through her gloved hands and tossed some dried leaves on it so you would never know that anything was there. I pulled away quickly from the window. I knew I had to hurry and it was good to have a secret, and even if I told the other kids about the passage, I would never tell anyone what I'd seen my mother doing. I went quickly back through the flat to the kitchen and down the back stairs and I trudged up the hill to school. The other kids were just going in from recess, so I slipped through the gate and fell into the line and went in."

PETRIFIED FOREST

The ad in the *Chronicle* lying on the floor in front of Dr. Thorn's couch boasted "majestic petrified redwood giants arrayed before you in a fascinating grove." Christopher was finishing a cup of coffee and slowly reading it when Dr. Thorn came in from a Saturday morning walk. Next to the ad for the Petrified Forest, was another, promoting the *Mystery Magnet House* with a fuzzy picture of kids seeming to walk up walls: "Just minutes from the Petrified Forest." Christopher exclaimed that he'd love to see the Petrified Forest and the Mystery House, and intimated that perhaps he and Dr. Thorn could go sometime. "Let's go *now!*" Dr. Thorn said. "We'll be back before anyone even knows we're gone." So they got in the van and went across the Golden Gate Bridge, driving from the chill of the fog to the blond, tree-dotted hills of sun-washed Marin, north for an hour and a half to Calistoga, then, taking a left into the woods, they arrived at the crooked little house, built on a slope, where nothing inside was right, where the compass did not point north, and you could sort of walk up the somewhat slanted walls.

STONE TREES PRONE

The trees of the Petrified Forest were over three million years old. They lay prone on the forest floor like fallen broken columns among pine needles and strewn stones. Christopher had imagined rows of stone trees standing in a grove, which was the actual source of his excitement in going. Now he was here and the stone trees were prone, and there were no stone leaves and no branches. How was he to be anything but disappointed? Yet, the whole of human history was contained in the shattered trunks on the ground before him. He pictured it; all rushing past, like the child rushing down the river in his dreams. The other children playing in the Petrified Forest were not stunned, awed or shaken by these sights. To them the trees of stone were merely rocks, a place to play, not even as good as a playground.

PETRIFIED FOREST

It was shortly after the trip to the Petrified Forest that Christopher told his mother that their lives were so short and small as to be next to nothing. Evelyn was in her apron, putting some plates away, and her entire response was to say that some people *saw* it and some people *didn't*, just as there were people who saw deeply into beauty and people who lived only with décor. And in that instant, Christopher saw that—even with all her idiosyncrasies, maddening quirks and arbitrary rules—they shared something beyond the flat cardboard enactments of routine—something that glistened at its edges—and he saw that they belonged to each other the way that diagonals do.

THE PAST

As if the past were the inside of something that the present was the outside of—as if the past had a shape which the present surrounds and, in the surrounding of that shape, takes on.

THE DREAM OF THE BROKEN PHOTOGRAPH

Christopher dreamed he had a photograph in a frame of himself and Dr. Thorn leaning against each other. The *frame broke to pieces in his hands and two photographs fell out, one of himself and one of Dr. Thorn. Christopher tried every way possible to put the two pictures back together again so that it would be one picture, but he could not put them back together—he could not arrange them back as they had been—one picture of two friends, leaning against one another.* In the dream he was sitting on the floor, like a child with two impossible puzzle pieces, trying to fit them together—this way, that way, turning them, this way, that way, with no way to fit them back together, with no way to make a single thing of them again.

THE PAST

The shore recedes and the surface walks toward you in waves. Where once, a name became where the wind had been. Where later, the wind regained what a name became. You will never know the cost of the hours you have taken, their true price, or the size of the cyclone that delivered them—poured them across the sieve of your outstretched hands.

THE TREASURE CYCLES

Terma can occur as objects, wisdom-scrolls, thoughts, and in other forms. The Terma must be retrieved at a particular time, in a particular place, and in a specific sequence. Terma discovered out-of-sequence must be re-concealed.

CIGARETTES

There was no shortage of half-smoked cigarettes—some stubbed out, some smoldering—in the ashtrays of Dr. Thorn's house.

CUTTING

Christopher came to Dr. Thorn's house often and just walked in the front door. Many afternoons Dr. Thorn would come home to find him tousle-haired, in his rumpled Anglican uniform, asleep on the couch. One afternoon Dr. Thorn came home to find Christopher sitting in the middle of a pile of shredded pillowcases, newspapers and books. When Christopher looked up, there was no remorse in his eyes.

FIRE

Dr. Thorn bent down and scooped up a double handful of shreds and threw them in the air. It was like the snow in a Christmas globe, and Dr. Thorn said, "It's cold in here and we have some shredded things to make use of, so help me build a fire and we'll throw them in."

FIRE

Sitting with the gathered pile of shreds, throwing them into the fire one by one, Christopher asked Dr. Thorn if he was being so nice to him because he wanted him in his bed.

MISTER MUST

And Dr. Thorn responded flatly, "No Christopher, I don't." Then there was a long, long silence with Dr. Thorn looking calmly and directly at Christopher; and then Christopher said somewhat hurriedly, "There's a man who comes into me every night, and I try to keep him out but I can't, and I can't sleep and it's like I'm drowning. He's not a man really, but I call him Mister Must, and he's like drinking ink, like being forced to drink ink, and you can't drink fast enough and he keeps pouring in and you start to drown." And he told Dr. Thorn about the knife-people, how he had looked and looked for where Mister Must slept during the day but couldn't find it, and the knife-people wouldn't tell him where it was, and after looking almost everywhere, he'd realized that *he* was where Mister Must slept, so it was *like trying to keep someone out on the other side of a door when they're breathing behind you,* so he *knew* he was already in there, but it didn't *matter* what he *knew* because he *still felt broken-into every night and he wanted to throw Mister Must off the Golden Gate Bridge and he was trying to push him out but he was sticky, eager and everywhere,* and Christopher's voice trailed off because he was starting to cry. He did not look directly at Dr. Thorn and Dr. Thorn sat very still through all of this and he made no attempt to dissuade Christopher, no suggestion that everything was not exactly as he had said, nor did he rush to comfort Christopher.

MISTER MUST

Fishing around in a near-empty pack of Chesterfields, Dr. Thorn told Christopher, almost casually, that he would never be able to escape Mister Must or keep him out. He finally retrieved a cigarette, tamped it, lit it, and continued, "There's a place in Death Valley, called the Amargosa Chaos, where great tensions broke the earth apart, splintered the strata and jumbled the geological layers so you can't figure anything out. The past is *actually* closer to the surface than the present. Mister Must comes from a place like that in yourself, a place so faulted and fractured that it can't be mapped. He brings that chaos to you night after night, he holds it out to you so you can look at it and name it, even if it feels like you're drowning. You named that chaos *Mister Must*, and you've been terrified by it, but you can't throw this messenger off the bridge without throwing yourself off with him, and my sense is he's come to keep you alive." Christopher was aghast, "*Keep me alive?* Do you *understand* how *hungry* and *empty* he is? How he puts all that emptiness *into me* and fills *himself* up? I get so empty and brittle that I think I'm going to break, but I have to stay in one piece because broken things don't last in my mother's house." A silence ensued. Christopher saw that Dr. Thorn was not to be reversed and said, a bit resignedly, "Well, anyway, what am I supposed to do?" "Let him in." "*What?*" "He's your cold, sticky guest, he pushes everything over and keeps you up, so you're going to give him a job to do, a chore around the house, you're going to give him the job of saving your life." "But *it's not safe!*" Christopher exclaimed, resuming his defense. Dr. Thorn looked at him intently and, after a pause, with the words pushing smoke from his mouth as he spoke, said in his quietest voice, "What's so good about being safe?" Christopher looked out the window and then at the floor, "*How* can he *save my life?*" "By making you fight for it, and you *can*, but not in the way you think, not by wrestling him off a bridge, but by learning to steady yourself, steady yourself and breathe in the chaos, in the crushed-foil center of things. He's come to make that possible for you, to give you a way to practice, so welcome him."

BLUE SMOKE

Christopher nodded and grew still, and he knew that Dr. Thorn cared about him, and he knew that he would *never* welcome Mister Must.

THE PAST

Distances narrow and widen, shattering flings all you've held, across the blinding fields and out of reach, and out of reach always, except where memory extracts the shattering from the shattered.

MR. THAYER

The man next door to Dr. Thorn was digging up his backyard, making a huge mud-mess of it. Dr. Thorn said that it had just gone on for years, and the man, whose name was Mr. Thayer, never finished it. No one ever really understood what it was that he was trying to finish, even though he talked incessantly of terracing, drainage and perfect slopes. It was all very physical—lots of wheelbarrows moving dirt around, shovels everywhere, levels, plumb lines and strings stretched out between stakes. When Christopher asked Dr. Thorn what he thought of Mr. Thayer, Dr. Thorn told Christopher that Mr. Thayer was a *complete presentation*, which was to say, *a lesson from which nothing was missing.*

MR. THAYER

Christopher tried to determine what Mr. Thayer was a complete presentation of.

THE DREAM OF HANDS

Christopher dreamed he woke in his bed, but the room was wrong. *He didn't know himself and decided if only he could find his hands in the crumpled sheets, he could find himself. But he couldn't recognize his hands, and he kept trying to throw the cardboard replica hands out of his bed and it never occurred to him to ask himself with whose hands was he picking up the cardboard hands and throwing them?*

AFTER THE SECOND FIRE

When Christopher went to search the rubble after the second fire, Mr. Thayer was in his back yard assessing the consequences of the fire on his project—all that water, fallen timber, ash and smoke. He was so engaged clearing away the debris, shoveling mounds of mud, working harder than ever, that he didn't seem to even notice Christopher.

INDUSTRIAL DISTRICT

In the industrial district south of Market Street, Dr. Thorn had a little warehouse with a rusted rail-siding, an office, a workshop, a couple of part-time employees who drifted in and out and customers calling every now and then. He oversaw a hodgepodge of enterprises like reconstructing conveyor belts and reconditioning hydraulic motors for fishing boats. When he was there, he spoke of these things as if they contained the entire world. Sometimes Christopher would ride along in his van and they'd eat lunch at a gritty café, order apple pie from the spinning glass case on the counter, and drink black coffee. Christopher remarked that he was amazed at how no one seemed to know who Dr. Thorn really was or the questions that he really cared about. Dr. Thorn responded that the spiritual was sheltered in the ordinary, housed in its difficulties, in the things people did every day with their hands. Christopher took a sip of coffee, and, though he did not believe that this was so, didn't argue.

WHERE THE WILD THINGS ARE

Dr. Thorn asked Christopher if he'd had a favorite children's book. Christopher said that it was *Where the Wild Things Are*, except that he didn't know why Max came back. Dr. Thorn said Max came back because he was bored and hungry, and because a person could never be a person by being a wild thing, even if they were king of the wild things. "So you have to come back and press forward into the world. This is what you have, what you must make something of—not hiding, not wrecking yourself on the rocks but walking into the world, and this is a sacred act because everything is at risk."

WHERE THE WILD THINGS ARE

And Christopher wondered if it wasn't so of all children that they want to be wild—at least in a part of them, the part of them that is being forced into shoes down at the shoe store on Chestnut Street with the spindly marionette of a salesman asking rhetorically: "How do they feel, pretty good?" But they don't feel pretty good. They hurt, and it's that *same hurt everywhere of the natural shape being forced into the made shape, and you can't even talk about this pain, it's so everywhere in your life, and you can't complain about this pain because the world has put the name "growing up" on it, and you want to grow up so that you can be as wild as you want, but by the time you do grow up you have forgotten how to be wild, forgotten why you wanted to be wild in the first place. You actually don't even like wild things anymore, and that's how you know that you've grown up.*

THE WONDER OCEAN

Christopher told Dr. Thorn about the Wonder Ocean that arose when he tried to read.

CASCADE FALLS

Several years later, lying outstretched on the rocks above Cascade Falls, Christopher would decide that Dr. Thorn had been wrong about *Where the Wild Things Are*, and he'd been wrong about it being a sacred act to enter the world because Cascade Falls was the sacrament, and *Where the Wild Things Are* was everything that had been buried in the false, the manufactured, the pretentious, the acquisitive and the gross.

BURIAL OF THE BROKEN

And he came to understand that the burial of the broken wasn't eccentric—this was what people did every day, stuffing their brokenness down, pushing it down, smoothing the surface over, making the surface look like nothing was broken underneath. Because, if people see that you are broken, they will not want to stand with you. They will migrate away from you the way groups of people walking down the street will move aside when a shambling ranting man approaches. They will look at the ground and look away so that such a person becomes invisible. So if you are such a person *or just an everyday person with some broken places, some places really bro-*

ken, you will pull them back from view so you can mingle with others without being seen as broken. Because if you have the look of a broken thing, if you are pushed aside and turned from, you will never find your footing again in the world.

UNCLE ALFRED'S NOTE TO EVELYN'S PARENTS

Christopher tried to imagine how the Evelyn *he knew* could have left her family, her friends, her whole past and ventured, by herself, to San Francisco.

THEORY OF BROKENNESS

As Christopher began to observe the world, he saw that Evelyn's theory of brokenness was true: that, as he began to break, her brokenness surfaced, showed itself, responded. And it was true *everywhere he looked, even in whole countries, when an earthquake broke the buildings, the brokenness in the people started to come out, and looters broke things more, and, when the money became broken and wasn't worth anything, people started to horde things and hurt each other, and when something happened to someone, something bad, like when little Phillip down the street got hit by the car with its trunk full of bricks so it couldn't stop, the parents started to break—the mother left the house and wouldn't come back and the father lost his job because he couldn't work and they got a divorce.* He saw why brokenness had to be stopped before it invited everything to be broken.

SOMETIMES BROKENNESS CANNOT BE STOPPED

But then he began to realize that sometimes brokenness cannot be stopped—*it has a separate life, like tides or seasons or something running its course, like when something cracks, breaks off and rolls downhill like jealousy where nothing will be enough, and then there is a hatred pushing through that cannot be contained or placated, and once it starts it can't be stopped by anything.*

FIRE

Dr. Thorn, while burning the scraps, said "when things are burned they don't turn into nothing."

THE MADMAN OF WANGDIPHODRANG

In the first brilliant light of dawn, the swirling costumed dancers, almost blindingly colorful and quick, were already enacting a narrative as the crowd filed up the narrow crooked stairs, burnished by centuries of footsteps, and into the slightly sloping wooden galleries. There was a kind of gritty boredom on the faces of some in the crowd; others were stoically marveling, and the children were restless, distracted or amazed. In a corner of the courtyard, by himself, a slender man with a scruffy beard and a scrawny dog was alternately muttering to himself and ranting at the lamas who were seated reverently on podiums. He was twirling around, singing out-of-key and seemingly mocking the dancers. Christopher asked Dorji, who was seated next to him, why this person was not attended to or removed. "No, he's revered. He's an incarnation of Drukpa Kunley, the Holy Madman, here to remind us of the folly and lost compassion of our piety." The motions of the dancers accelerated, and there ensued a frenzy for hours of things hidden, revealed and hidden again, dance after dance—dance of the four stags, dance of the twenty one black hats, dance of the three Kings of Ging, dance of the nobleman and the ladies, dance of the stag and the hounds—flutes, gongs and bells, clouds of incense, people pushing through people—and the professor offering sporadic commentary, in low tones, when the din died down.

CARL

One afternoon, on a walk to Union Street, Christopher told Dr. Thorn everything that had happened with Carl, except he did not mention the other boy.

CARL

Dr. Thorn had very little to say about Christopher's experience with Carl, so little that Christopher wondered if Dr. Thorn really understood what had happened. Dr. Thorn did not seem to be particularly interested in Carl. Dr. Thorn was interested in Mister Must.

DREAM OF THE RECKLESS DRIVER

And Christopher had a dream—he dreamed that he was *chasing a reckless driver up a steep winding mountain road with no guardrails. There were hay bales stacked on the right shoulder and a forest behind them. The reckless driver was driving a van with his meek and terrified wife and their five children. He would pause to light the bales of hay on fire with a branding iron, and Christopher would have to stop and put these fires out before continuing to chase him.* It ended in a courtroom with the reckless driver's lawyer saying what a good citizen his client was with five children, a church and a steady job.

THE PAST

As outcomes emerge, the past is continually re-weighted, reconstructed so that it *can* have caused the present, so that the present can retain its essential nature as inevitable given the past.

CHOICE

It never occurred to Christopher that what had happened with Carl had not been his choice.

CARL

And Christopher thought that he might murder Carl—*under cover of darkness, under cover of another identity, creating a story of a week away with a friend and hiding himself on a train—there would be no trace—and advance with the sheerest of stealth—who would ever know or connect him back—and open the door so quietly part way and slide through sideways—was Carl asleep—should he wake him—did he want him to know—brutal fierce sudden hammer blows relentless pitiless numerous countless.*

DESTINY

Christopher told Dr. Thorn that he did not believe in destiny.

FAR EAST CAFÉ

They would walk through Chinatown and sit in a curtained booth at the Far East Café on Grant Avenue, and Dr. Thorn would talk to Christopher about the underpinnings of everything.

DESTINY

"You may not believe in destiny. You may think that destiny is about things that are fated, but that's not what I mean by destiny at all. *To discharge the obligation of your gift*, that's what I mean by fulfilling your destiny—and it's not assured—it's not preordained. In fact, your destiny's what's most at risk in your life. And, Christopher, remember, that to discharge the obligation of your gift is not only to accomplish something, but also to express your gratitude—not gratitude for the gift itself, not really, but for the obligation that the gift bestowed, the obligation that provided a ground and a path, a way to inhabit being alive."

YOU MIGHT THINK

You might think that a boy of fourteen would not be interested in such things, but you would be wrong.

THE WORLD CEASES IN INCREMENTS
THE SIZES OF PERSONS

The world ceases in increments the sizes of persons. There is a handing off; the world the dead lose continues in remnants handed unevenly down to the living. How does something altogether stop and also continue? Have you ever touched the world as you would touch the face of someone you will lose?

DESTINY

"Your destiny is that which makes the carrying of dead weight impossible for you. Its essence, its necessity of being, is your attention to it—as the cut opens at the sharpened edge of the knife—as Mister Must comes in and displaces you—that kind of attention."

THE DREAM OF DISAPPEARING

Christopher dreamed that everything he knew had disappeared, his house, his block, the city, all were gone. In their place was another place that he did not know. He was walking the streets, trying to find his way, and the streets were becoming so narrow that his shoulders were brushing the buildings on either side.

SNOW

Dr. Thorn turned to Christopher as he entered the warm, smoky living room and began to speak while resting his opened notebook on the edge of the couch. "I've been thinking about the legend of Socrates standing, transfixed, in the snow for twenty-four hours... dawn to dawn...I think at Potidaea...the versions vary...anyway...he is traditionally characterized as having been *thinking* about something, some intractable problem...of logic, or some such, and, honestly, that's what I'd always imagined, but now I realize that that wasn't it at all...now I understand that he wasn't *thinking*...figuring something out...painstakingly fitting the pieces together hour after hour...he was *looking* at something...something was happening in the snow...he was *seeing* something...something was *showing it-self* to him...something *whole*...something *direct*...something *given in its entirety*."

SNOW

Later, walking down to Union Street, Christopher asked, "What do you think Socrates was *seeing* when he was standing there in the snow?" Dr. Thorn paused, took the cigarette out of his mouth, and said warmly, "I think he was seeing how the world...the cosmos... organizes itself...there in the falling snow...in the snowflakes... in their chaotic descent...up close...all day and against the black backdrop of night...snow pelting his face...ordering itself...even when it seemed without order...even with everything flying at him in flurries...I think he was standing outside...watching his mind engage the falling snow...seeing the self-ordering of everything... seeing how the workings of consciousness are the paradigm of that ordering."

SUN

When they got home they made some toast and coffee and sat in Dr. Thorn's study. Christopher asked, "What's the *real differ-ence* between *seeing* something and *thinking* about it?" "Well," Dr. Thorn said, glancing around the room, "look, come over here and sit in this chair," and he gestured toward the red leather chair by the window, "now, close your eyes and put your fingers slowly on the upholstery buttons at the end of the armrest, *slowly, one by one*, like a pianist playing a scale in slow motion, and leave them there as if you are holding the notes." Christopher did so and the brass buttons, warmed for hours in the sun, radiated heat through the tips of his fingers, warming them completely on contact, and Dr. Thorn said slowly, "*That's* the difference."

PHOTOGRAPHING HANDS

For his final eighth grade project at Anglican, Christopher conducted an experiment. He took photographs of the backs of the hands of the boys in his class, making a list of the order in which they were taken so that later he could match the hands with their owners. He had them developed, and then at the end of the week, he had the children put their hands behind their backs, and he laid the photos out on a big wooden table at the back of the classroom. Each photograph had a number next to it, and he asked that each boy pick the photograph, by number, of his hands. Some boys had arguments because they both thought one of the pairs of hands was theirs and some hands went unclaimed. There was jostling, joking and making-fun, but not a single child asked Christopher why he was doing this experiment. In the end he tallied how many boys had chosen their own hands, and it was none.

PHOTOGRAPHING HANDS

Later, the teacher asked Christopher to give a report to the class about what he had learned. The experiment caused quite a stir, so several teachers and even the headmaster came to hear Christopher explain how the experiment was conducted and how he had learned that it was *not only discarded things that were overlooked, invisible, unrecognized. It was not only thrown-away things that people couldn't see. It was also the things that were closest to them, the things that were even the closest parts of themselves, that they did not know these things, as if a stranger passed them on the street, as if a stranger brushed them and there was a sudden glance that produced not even a glint of recognition, that it was not only strangers being spoken of—it was things encountered every day; that this was not strangers being spoken of—this was their hands.* Some of the boys were restless, but the teachers were riveted. One of the teachers questioned Christopher, trying to discredit the experiment by saying the photos were too small and indistinct. Christopher responded, with even a little anger showing through, that he thought it wouldn't have mattered how large or clear the photos were because he had learned that we live in a world where people don't know their hands and that, when someone says they know something like the back of their hand, it means they don't know it at all. The entire room was speechless.

MEMORIZING HANDS

So Christopher vowed to memorize his hands because he knew that *you can't take your hands with you into sleep, so your hands in your dreams are always not your own, and if you are ever lost in a city with buildings closing in and unfamiliar streets and no people anywhere, you can look at your hands and know if you are dreaming, so if you know your hands, you will never be lost in believing a dream again.* And he practiced steadying his hands and looking at them. He learned the lines of his palms, the shape of his nails and the lengths of his fingers, and he studied the pattern of veins on the backs and the pattern of lines on his wrists, and promised himself to always remember them, because he knew that these markers of who he was were always there. He vowed to know them by heart.

SNOW

Just before leaving Dr. Thorn's to walk home for dinner, Christopher had asked, "What does the order of the world look like when you see it?" Dr. Thorn had looked up thoughtfully, hadn't answered right away, then had replied, "It looks like a snowstorm."

THE ARCHITECTURE OF MEMORY

Memory is a mirror in which you can see the vanished.

THE SECOND FIRE

Water from the fire engines and the hydrants cascaded down the steeply sloped street, overflowing the drain at the corner, rushing along the curb and curling against the tires of parked cars.

THE ARCHITECTURE OF MEMORY

What if the sense that memory takes hold of the past and pulls it forward is built into the act of remembering? What if memory opens the past inside like that? What if *seeming to open the past* is the action of memory?

THE DANCE OF THE LORD OF DEATH AND HIS CONSORT

Dance of the terrifying lord of death, guarder of the three worlds, portrayed in a buffalo mask—dance of the wrathful deities in sumptuous brocade dresses, boots and drawn daggers—dance of souls fleeing wrathful forms in the Bardo—through forests littered with traps and tangled vines—souls forgetful of teachings—who cannot recognize Buddha's fierce forms and run from paradise.

GALVANIZING

One Sunday afternoon, Dr. Thorn took Christopher to Richmond because an overhead conveyor system at a galvanizing plant had broken down. The plant manager was grateful to see Dr. Thorn, calling him Andy. Dr. Thorn introduced Christopher as "My assistant, Chris." Christopher carried some tools, trying to look like he knew what he was doing. The repair took about an hour, and Christopher got as much grease as possible on his hands and clothes. When they were finished, the conveyor transported sections of metal fencing to a vat filled with silver liquid; when the fencing was lowered into the vat, a sizzling, popping, explosive sound erupted, and Christopher jumped, but he didn't think anyone noticed. On the drive home, Dr. Thorn explained that an electrical current was actually being passed through the liquid metal in the vat, so the fencing and the liquid were bonded by being oppositely charged, and the resilient properties of the metal were conveyed to the surface of the fencing.

GALVANIZING

Christopher would never spend another afternoon with Dr. Thorn.

THE PAST

What is the past? The past is a house built again and again in such a way that it seems like the same single house.

THE SECOND FIRE

The fire emitted a kind of roar.

THE ARCHITECTURE OF MEMORY

It is the architecture of memory, its structural necessity, that what it holds appears to be at a distance; that what it holds appears to be the past. You think the past is built into the moment of re-membering, but what if what's built-in is not the past but the kind of opening out, the kind of seemingly almost infinite room, that two mirrors make when stood face-to-face? What if that sense of spaciousness is an architectural attribute of remembering, like the sense that every moment arrives new is an architectural attribute of the present?

THE SECOND FIRE

The fire was snapping like bones breaking.

THE ARCHITECTURE OF MEMORY

The past is formed of outcomes now at hand—in the angle of a glance from where you stand.

KNIFE-PEOPLE

After the second fire, the knife-people sharpened themselves completely away.

NULL SET

Now Christopher understood why you have to have a separate place in yourself that holds nothing.

MEDITATION ON DROWNING

The ground that you swim toward gives you that swimming for a life—your strokes are like hammer-blows fastening a floor, the underside of which is dark and empty and endless.

THE ARCHITECTURE OF MEMORY

What can you know of how you make the past? That it is made whole in an instant; that in this sense it replicates the present; that it is made to seem like the present brought back. But what if the past is not a brought-back thing? What if the past is the part of the present moment that you make? Wouldn't the present moment be small and flat if you didn't add this opening-out called memory? Isn't the present small and flat to those who cannot remember?

THE SECOND FIRE

The smell of the smoke lingered in the neighborhood for many days.

THE UNFURLING OF THE THONGDROL

The Thongdrol was unfurled from the uppermost gallery, just beneath the roofline, and covered the entire eastward facing inner wall of the dzong. As the red-robed monks congregated in front of it and the crowd gazed in awe, the red, yellow and blue clad dancers continued to swirl amid loudly banging gongs and intermittent gasps.

THE SECOND FIRE

In the days just after the second fire, Christopher could be found digging in the ashes, poking through the rubble, running his fingers along the ground. He would come home smeared with ash and smelling of smoke.

THE GALE FROM THE THONGDROL

The Thongdrol was dominated by the massive central figure of Guru Rinpoche, seated in lotus position, on a throne of flames, surrounded by his consorts whose gazes were turned to him. Along the edges of the tapestry were the peaceful and wrathful manifestations of the Guru. Everywhere there were clouds, flames, birds and brilliant blue skies. Beneath the throne was a wildly rolling sea. Christopher fixed on the incomparably gentle, questioning eyes of Guru Rinpoche and *sensed, after a while, something like a breeze coming from the Thongdrol, and he glanced around and noticed that no one else seemed affected, and the Thongdrol, initially flat, was becoming dimensional, as if the back wall was receding to form a large room into which you could step, and then the breeze, which was now a wind, at first silent, was carrying songs, and as it strengthened these became more clear, and still those around him seemed to notice nothing.*

THE VANISHED

People in the endless push of people—names in the sea of names— and Christopher saw that the enclosure, open on all sides, was consciousness.

THE ARCHITECTURE OF MEMORY

The room that two mirrors make when stood face to face; you *can* not-know that that room cannot be entered. As a child you do not know it—you do not know that that room is an attribute of mirrors. You can *not-know* that the opening out of the past in the act of remembering is an attribute of memory. You can be told that every memory is made fresh, but you cannot see a memory in this way. You do not see a house made over and over, but a single house that waits to be brought back.

THE SECOND FIRE

The smoke tucked itself up inside his nose so there was no room to smell anything else. He thought that he would never smell anything else ever again.

THE GALE FROM THE THONGDROL

There was a stripping away in the gaze of Guru Rinpoche, whose eyes were fixed on him, pulling him forward, *compelling every clinging ghost, every rotted baggage, every sewn-together story, to fall away—so rapidly that he felt like he was falling—and the figures in the Thongdrol floated free, and he was falling through the Thongdrol, so fast that the friction was like flames brushing his cheeks in the icy air.*

GLASS

One day Evelyn worked for hours making her special soup for guests and then struck the glass lid on the cast iron pot and noticed that it was chipped—and where was the missing chip—where was it—and was it in the soup—and if it was in the soup the entire batch would have to be destroyed because you cannot feed your guests a piece of glass. She searched for the chip—and was it chipped before and she hadn't noticed—she couldn't remember—and was the chip in the drawer with the other lids—and was the chip on the stove or on the floor—and what would she feed her guests if she threw the soup away to save their lives?

FALLING

Imagine you are falling. Imagine that when you are walking you are

falling, and falling when asleep and when you are standing still—
everything rushing toward you, through you, past you—that time
is uneven like the flow of water over a falls, that it slows, swirls,
billows and rushes forward bringing everything along. Imagine you
are falling through this rush of everything carried against the grain
of your going, that you are falling through your dreams, through
the faces of those you love, through your fears, through highways
and books and images, laughter and longings, through the smells of
kitchens, through your tears and the tears of others, through prayers,
wars, gardens and chandeliers, through the shadows of candles on
tables, falling through seasons and sunsets, cyclones, deliriums and
dailiness, falling through faltering steps on stairs, through sympho-
nies, sincerity and lies, falling ceaselessly in celebration or mourn-
ing, falling where everything scatters behind you—all pretense, all
possessions, all conclusions, all things said, all the hidden words, all
handholds—everything stripped away in the velocity of your going.

THE BOOK OF TRACE

A few days after the second fire, Christopher went down to Union
Street and into Schrader's stationery shop where he purchased a
Sheaffer cartridge fountain pen, a green ink cartridge, and a notebook with a black leather cover and pages with blue lines about a
quarter inch apart. He carried the notebook to the site of the fire
and, with his bare hands, rubbed ashes onto page after page until
the book was full of pages smeared with soot, and then he wrote
on the title page with his ash-dipped index finger, *Book of Trace*.
He thought of hiding the *Book of Trace* behind his secret box on
its shelf in his room, but he knew this book had no place in his
mother's house—this black book, this book of stench, this book
of fetid smoke, this book of teardown and trace, of shard, splinter, cinder, collapse and remnant—so he decided to bury it that
evening after sunset in the sand in the Presidio as the fog blew
through the eucalyptus trees.

THE BOOK OF TRACE

The ash was oily, sticky and thicker than he could ever have imagined, and it didn't want to come off of his hands. If it touched anything, even for a second, it stuck fast. He saw how like fire these ashes were, how tightly they held to anything that touched them.

OUTSIDE

He felt as if he could see the entire world, he was so outside.

THE GALE FROM THE THONGDROL

Now the wind from the Thongdrol was a gale: *Song of the lost mountain—Song of the man whose hands turned to money—Song of masks—Song of being hurled through a tunnel of fire—Song of needles—Song of not being able to stand—Song of pushing upward through floorboards toward a path—Song of thorns—Song of fears without anchors—Song of going through the house as it falls apart—Song of secrets—Song of unbreakable orbits—Song of land's end—Song of night one minute at a time—Song of tides—Song of moss—Song of relentless rowing—Song of knowing no one's name—Song of figures on a paper screen—Song of cupped hands brimming with cold water—Song of the last breath—Song of the last word—Song of people laughing before the flood—Song of embers—Song of halves—Song of history seeming to return—Song of nails—Song of tools—Song of the man whose hands have pulled you out—Song of mica—Song of frost—Song of talons—Song of tar—Song where someone thinks they know your past—Song of pretending to sleep while others speak—Song of mileage—Song of marvels—Song of leaf after leaf descending in the wind—Song of fevers—Song of magic performed on a stage of bones—Song of rafters—Song of rising—Song of the whirlwind—Song of the promise kept in a sea of stones—Song of whispers—Song of shallows—Song of no one seeming to know—Song of grasping—Song of grasping—Song of letting go.*

BURYING THE BOOK OF TRACE

He did not falter or waver. Tears did not well up. He did not try to remember or try not to remember. His hands steadily scooped the sand deeper and deeper. And he couldn't think of things being the way they were, and he couldn't think of things being any different, and he buried the Book of Trace and he closed the earth with his hands.

THE ACTION OF MEMORY

Hands extracting fire is the action of memory, so now whole solid things stand free of the fire that had consumed them. The action of memory—that memory is the holder of fire in bare hands.

THE MISSING LAST MESSENGER

After the second fire, Christopher saw that the missing last messenger was an empty messenger.

THE ACTION OF MEMORY

Extraction of fire is the action of memory. In memory the fire walks into being as vanishing and that which was burned walks into being as unfolding. Memory is making new, taking something out of the fire again—each time a new thing out of the fire, each time out of the ashes a newly made thing.

THE PAST

Christopher saw how easily others seemed to forget, *as if the past were only parts of speech or the barely brushing against the skin of a scarf. But for him, it was not a barely-brushing-against. For him, the past was always there, happening next to him, as if he could almost push through—familiar creased fabric, voices, palpable and warm—as if the past were the inside of something that the present was the outside of, and everything that you could run your fingers against was rushing into it, becoming slow, sheltered and broad.*

SINGLE FABRIC

The past and the present were like a single fabric, the underside of which you could not touch.

THE PAST

And he wondered if memory was made of the past or if the past was made of memory.

THE DANCE OF THE LORDS
OF THE CREMATION GROUNDS

Dance of the fierce thunderbolt, freeing demonic spirits from shackles of bone and leading them into bliss—dance of the heroes in brilliant yellow skirts and gold crowns swirling in a palace of radiant lotuses under a limitless sky, dancing in emanations without obstacle—dance of the lords of the cremation grounds, white skull-masks and black twirling skirts, the dipping dancing forms like flames, but black, like heatless lightless fires, furious, rising and falling, circular and fathomless.

DROPS OF WATER

Ten days after the second fire, Evelyn found Christopher sitting with his back to her on a tall stool in front of the kitchen sink. The faucet was dripping one drop at a time at somewhat lengthy and irregular intervals, and Christopher was just sitting there watching. She said nothing and backed quietly out of the room.

EVERYTHING FROM NOW ON

Everything from now on was just going to be made up: a manufactured floor, a pieced-together answer to anything asked, a fashioned self to walk around in the world, like a person for whom something could matter—a whole world cobbled together from bits and scraps, minor keys and mirror shards, the circular driveways of words and the drudgeries of stuff and common sense.

THE MOVE TO JACKSON STREET

In late July of 1966, one month after the second Thorn fire, Evelyn abruptly announced that the family would be moving. The timing seemed odd, since Westy's business was slow, but she was insistent and rented a small house in the last block of Jackson Street, along the Presidio wall.

EUCALYPTUS

The new neighborhood was drenched in the sharp scent of eucalyptus wafting from the groves in the Presidio.

FIRE

Sometime after the fire, Christopher realized that he had let the fire in. Different parts of himself were burning, and though it felt like he was freezing, *he saw that he was actually on fire, that the fire could not be put out, that the fire was alive in him, deadening him, part by part. And his thoughts were like birds in the treetops of a forest on fire, scattering outward, and the leaves and needles on fire were raining-down, and everything in him was in flight—everything in him was fleeing or in flames.*

THINGS END IN YOUR LIFE

Evelyn was concerned that something must be said to Christopher about his loss of Dr. Thorn and his unwillingness to accept it. She pressed Westy to speak to him, so the next Saturday morning he resumed the long-abandoned practice of inviting Christopher along on his rounds and, while driving to Rinken Annex, said— maybe thinking of his business, maybe thinking of something else, maybe thinking of a woman he'd known during the war—"Things end in your life, even things that you thought never would. Do you understand?" Christopher said "yes," so Westy continued, "I don't mean you thought they'd never end, as if you believed things last forever." Christopher shook his head slowly, acknowledging that he did not believe things lasted forever. Westy continued, "Only that it never occurred to you that they would end, it never occurred to you to picture your life without them." Then, after a pause, Westy said, "Your friend is gone, you have to accept it." Christopher looked out the window. He thought how stretched cellophane can look like the thinnest ice. He was not concerned with what his father thought he must accept, but nodded compliantly. The conversation was over.

FIRE

He knew that it must not be seen that he was burning because after the initial excitement of those watching, after he was all caved in, he would be abandoned, cordoned off, leveled and smoothed over—readied for his replacement to be built.

DANCE OF THE EIGHT MANIFESTATIONS OF GURU RINPOCHE

The professor, reading from notes, intoned: "Guru Rimpoche, who was born from a blue lotus, who renounced worldly treasures, who entered the whirlwind and perceived the deities in their multitude, who, condemned to burn, transformed the blazing pyre into a lake, who flew on the tiger's back, who shook the sky like a thunderbolt to waken all to the teachings, who gathered the radiant consorts of Knowledge and Wisdom that their emanations might benefit all beings."

FURNITURE

To the greatest degree possible, Evelyn arranged the furniture in the house on Jackson Street just as it had been in the Green Street flat.

WASHINGTON HIGH

Given his father's gradually eroding financial situation, and Evelyn's commitment to having money of her own that could not be touched, there was little to do after Anglican but to send Christopher to George Washington, a vast public high school on Geary Boulevard, while his classmates toddled off to private schools. Even Lowell, the public school for gifted kids, was out of the question given Christopher's mediocre grades and disastrous test scores.

WASHINGTON HIGH

Inundated—jostled—pushed—pressed—the smells of roast beef, gym-socks, industrial cleanser and gunpowder from the firecrackers set off earlier in the hall, fragments of shattered glass crunching under foot from an Asian gang having shot the overhead lights to bits with zip-guns, a relentless racket composed of screaming, hooting and slamming locker doors, the shrill reverberations of coded bells—it was a long way from Anglican Academy, from the cathedral, from uniforms, and from standing by one's desk when asked a question—a long way from the Social Register and Mr. Kelton's Dancing School.

WALKING

And Christopher woke every day with a question pressed against him, and he didn't even know what it was, the way time presses against you but you can't say what it is. But he sensed that, with the fog against his face as he walked, he could start to touch what was being asked.

STAND STILL

One afternoon, sitting in Dr. Thorn's office in the industrial district, eating a glazed doughnut from the mobile coffee stand that had just stopped by, Christopher had asked Dr. Thorn if he'd ever married. After a pause, he'd responded: "The woman I love is married to someone else, a powerful businessman, and she lives on a ranch in Marin." "Who is she?" "It doesn't matter, she has children and social obligations and we mustn't see one another." Christopher, suddenly ill at ease, had blurted: "Can't you love someone *else?*" Dr. Thorn had shaken his head and smiled as if marveling at something and, above the din of clanging machinery, with his feet on the desk, he'd said: "You can't always fix things, make things work, you can't always replace the past, sometimes you have to stand still in your own discomfort."

WEIGHT

If you lived in a country where the air was heavy as clear water—if you lived in the depths of that country and the air was pressing in with all its weight, and you were almost used to it except that when you woke you noticed it, like a question that is a kind of being leaned against, like the sea, when you walk beside it, is a question.

THE PAST

Christopher wondered how the past could *ever* be replaced.

IMPERMANENCE

One afternoon, walking along the Marina, thin clouds blowing overhead, barely looking at Christopher, Dr. Thorn had said that impermanence was the central issue, and most people responded by attempting to establish the permanent in their lives, by being in opposition to impermanence, and that this preference for the permanent over the impermanent was only a decision that people did not see as a decision.

SOME SEGMENTS OF TIME

What if some segments of time are laden with gain or loss, like some lengths of wind are laden with rain—but it's not wind—it's not rain—it's not figurative—what if time is actually this way?

THE MAN WHO VANISHED

Charles Everett Ruskin, who arrived in San Francisco in 1836, was, by the time of his death twenty years later, the largest landowner in the entire city. One morning, a dozen blocks from where Evelyn was making Christopher's high school lunch, having woken him a second time a few minutes earlier, Ruskin's direct descendant, Jonathan Augustus Ruskin, a man with everything—great wealth, a thriving business and a loving family—walked in his pajamas from his Pacific Heights mansion, as if to fetch the morning paper, and was never heard from again. The mystery of Ruskin's disappearance was splashed across the papers for several weeks and was never solved.

THE MAN WHO VANISHED

Christopher was drawn again and again to stories of people who had vanished, people who had abandoned their lives and started new ones—men with two families in two towns, people with multiple names, people who faked their own deaths.

MRS. RUSKIN AND HER DAUGHTERS

San Francisco society was divided as to how the disappeared Mr. Ruskin's wife, Elizabeth, should be treated. Were condolences to be offered as if she were a widow? Was she to be cloaked in protective silence and discretion as if she had been forsaken? Were righteous outrage and vigilance to be expressed as if her husband had been abducted? Or was she to be treated with circumspection, as if she was a party to a scandal that, though it had not yet come to light, surely would? For her part, Mrs. Ruskin, having no notion whatsoever as to what had become of her husband, and wholly preoccupied with caring for their two adolescent daughters, Jenean and Abigail, cared little how others regarded her.

IDENTITY

The thoughts came back like thirst: what would it be like to walk from your life, to find its outer boundary and cross over, to stand in that sudden emptiness? *If you chose new stars as constellations, if you walked down a street for the first time and invented a childhood there, if memory was a hardened-over lake you walked upon but could not see into anymore, so the past was white, so the past was whatever you said it was, so you could never drown in the past.*

DEAD AND ALIVE

And he saw that leaving your life and taking up another was a way of being dead and alive at the same time.

EQUINOX

After dinner one evening, Christopher, having made loose plans to spend time with Dr. Thorn, had left the flat, crossed the street, walked around the block, and entered the house. Calling out before climbing the stairs, he'd realized no one was home and found a note on the landing saying, "Had to go out...see you tomorrow?" He carried the note into the living room, flopped onto the couch, considered how out-of-the-ordinary this was, and wondered, intently, where Dr. Thorn had gone. Restless, he rose and went to the window—*yes, the van was in the driveway, so it wasn't work, and he'd walked*—then wandered into the study and quickly noticed the phonebook, open on the table by the phone. Scanning the listings, he fixed on a box with bold print, *Equinox*, which he knew to be a small, fashionable restaurant just over the hill and a few blocks west on Sacramento. He left the house, strode up the hill and down the other side, turned right, then slowed his pace as he approached the restaurant. Looking through the large front window from across the street, it took several moments for Christopher to locate Dr. Thorn, at a corner table toward the back, and he saw that Dr. Thorn was not alone. Christopher lingered behind a panel truck at the perfect angle to see but not be seen, though it hardly would have mattered, they were so absorbed. The woman's back was to Christopher. Her salt-and-pepper hair was long and loosely gathered in a knot and her beauty, though he could not see her face, was clearly reflected in Dr. Thorn's delight. She wore a dark silk blouse and he imagined a string of pearls though he could not see her throat. Their arms were stretched across the white tablecloth; their fingers were interlocked, and they were laughing as the waiter, in a white apron, poured red wine. Christopher was momentarily pulled to walk in and present himself, but knew that he must not. He stood there for a long time, just out of sight, as if waiting for something to happen, something that would admit him to that room, or was it something else? Maybe it had never really occurred to him how marginal he might be in Dr. Thorn's life, how he'd somehow assumed he was somewhere near the center when, actually, he was on the periphery. He stood stunned, then turned slowly, scurried across the street, and went straight home.

EQUINOX

The following day he wondered if he should ask. He wondered if Dr. Thorn would lie about where he'd been. He didn't want to know, so he wouldn't ask. And now there would be the measure, like the waterlines on the hulls of ships at the Embarcadero, now he would know the true depth of what they had.

THE TREASURE CYCLES

The Terma comes into being as the Terton retrieves it from its place of concealment. In essence, it is concealed in the inattention of the world and revealed in the particular attention of the Terton.

EQUINOX

That night, Dr. Thorn had been unmistakably glad to see Christopher, and he'd apologized for his absence the night before, saying that his lady friend from Marin had called unexpectedly and invited him out to dinner.

WALKING

Christopher walked to the Great Highway and along the seawall across from Playland, and the ocean was effortless, tireless, and indifferent to every outcome.

THE UPSIDE DOWN DIAGONAL WORLD

Hurled diagonally through the world, thrown through the world at an angle, the structures are visible, the architectures, strange and vivid. Thrown diagonally through the world, you will not be able to sleep—which is to say, live without question, which is to say, settle the world. Thrown diagonally, the world will not be granted. The world will have to be made into something, taken for something. So what are you to make of the world? What is the world to be taken for? These questions will hold you awake because they are like the sea that you walk beside—the sea that demands a response—but no response is ever an answer to the sea.

YOU CAN'T WALK THE SUN WITH YOUR FINGERS

One morning, Genevieve left her mother's house on Anza, boarded a bus on Geary, and headed downtown. Arriving on Market Street, she surveyed the various seedy establishments offering identification cards and settled on "True-To-Life ID" three floors above a consignment store that sold used motel furniture. The man behind the counter was pudgy and gruff. Genevieve explained, with great care, what she wanted—A flawless ID, issued by the state, with a picture and a birth date and an address in Pacific Heights. "What name do you want?" the man asked, "Abigail Remington Ruskin," she replied, "and it must be perfect, absolutely without flaw, completely believable." The man shrugged, demanded cash up front, stood her against a white wall, snapped her picture, and went to work. The result, produced in half an hour, was not as she had hoped—the grainy slightly blurred photograph, the print that seemed about to smear, and all its other deficiencies culminated in the flash realization, obvious to anyone, that it was fake. She threw it on the floor, shrieking and demanding her money back, "I told you it had to be *perfect!*" The man behind the counter kept her cash and told her to get out.

DISCREET INQUIRIES

Evelyn had made some discreet inquiries with the couple at *Tea and Rarity*. "Oh, with Christopher growing up, I'm at loose ends and might enjoy having something to do a few days a week." They had recommended her to Joyce and Jim Gossworth, who owned *The Golden Goose* on Union Street.

YOU CAN'T WALK THE SUN WITH YOUR FINGERS

Eventually, and at great expense, Genevieve obtained an identification card that met her specifications.

PHOTOGRAPHS

Christopher found a used bookstore on the edge of Chinatown. On a table in the back were boxes of old photographs of San Francisco, which Christopher thumbed through, one by one—*people in formal dress from the turn of the century, anonymous people standing on streets or bunched together in groups, people playing in the water at the Sutro Baths, people caught in everyday actions, carrying groceries, reading newspapers, smoking cigarettes, photos of the Ruskin building being built, two workers on a girder above the city, leaning into each other, laughing, the blur of old cars, the blur of people in mid-stride.*

THE PHOTOGRAPH OF THE GIRL

And there was one photograph in particular, to which Christopher returned again and again and eventually purchased for a dollar. It was of a girl about his age, perhaps from the 1880's. She was facing the camera with such consummate self-possession that it startled him. Her hair, which appeared to be ash-blond, was parted in the middle and pulled back tightly, perhaps in a bun at the back. She wore a frilled high-collared cotton blouse, and her features were fine but not overly delicate. Her eyes were warm, dark and clear, and her head was slightly tilted as though she were listening to a question. She wore the faintest smile across her lips. She was so simply beautiful—and it was only an accident of time that she was not standing next to him, in blue jeans and a simple cotton shirt, looking through a box of photographs. It was only an accident of time that he could not be in love with her.

THE PAST

As if the past were the inside of the self—a room, a house, a walled garden, a world to dwell in—built of everything brought inside from the outside edge called the present.

THE PAST

As if the past were the inside of the self—as if, if the past were gone, the self would be extinct.

EVELYN'S JOB ON UNION STREET

Evelyn secured a part-time job at *The Golden Goose*. Given that she was faultlessly polite, knowledgeable, and scrupulously honest, the eccentric Brits who owned it didn't seem to mind her birdlike manner, stilted formality or odd perspective. In fact, they found these to be charming.

PHOTOGRAPHS

Christopher wondered how people remembered the dead before there were photographs.

LEAVING WANGDIPHODRANG

As the bus pulled away from Wangdiphodrang toward Punakah, it lurched to a stop because Drukpa Kunley was standing in the road, waving his arms. After he stepped aside and the bus pulled slowly forward, Christopher's and the madman's eyes briefly locked. "Where will he go?" Christopher asked Dorji. "He is said to live under a river-bridge with his mermaid wife." "He looked at me as if he recognized me." "Oh, he looks at everyone that way."

WASHINGTON HIGH

In homeroom at the start of every day, they recited the pledge of allegiance and took roll and the voice of the principal crackled with indecipherable messages from a speaker in the wall above the homeroom teacher's desk.

BONES

The paper said a missing woman's skeleton had been found—that the bones had definitely been identified as hers. He wondered how your bones could be considered your own, as if you possessed them, and at what point during dying did they stop being your bones, like it stopped being your life?

BONES

Pressing from inside against the skin at the elbow—you don't own your bones the way you own cars or chairs or carpets—they aren't yours like that—*it's more like you harbor them the way you harbor speech, the way you inherit speech from a procession of speakers, as an inherited scaffolding, but not like speech but solid like property, but not property because how could you actually take ownership of them?* So they said that they had found her bones, but in what way were they hers and in what way was any part of the body ever owned?

TRIPS TO JAPAN

Evelyn began to compile travel brochures of the major cities and sites of Japan. She extolled the cultural virtues that these places espoused: the formal, the ritualized, the modest, the aesthetically stark. She lingered over photographs of temples, gardens of raked gravel, brilliant kimonos, and arched wooden bridges over streams.

GLASS

She still went to the Hall of Flowers from time to time. She would sit quietly, by herself, on the moist benches. Afterward, there was always time for a trip to the Japanese Garden for tea and rice crackers.

ORBITS

Christopher now saw what he could not, at the time, have distinguished—that his mother's response to his search for Mister Must was a perturbation created by a secret. Now he knew—and the larger the perturbation the larger the secret, and in the drawers of the cherry desk, in the stacks he'd thumbed through, there must have been the secret hidden latch of a door in the ivy wall, and his fingers had unwittingly stumbled across it and moved on.

WASHINGTON HIGH HISTORY CLASS

Niles Ardessy, a history teacher at Washington High, who insisted on being called by his first name, led his class into a pitch-dark room on the first day and everyone was stumbling over desks and trying to find a seat. "History is a blind walk," Niles said. This resulted in two preppies and three Chinese kids going to the office and requesting to be transferred to a *real* history class.

JAPANESE

Evelyn began taking Japanese lessons from a woman in Japantown and wearing some Japanese clothes around the house. She purchased a game of Go to put on the game table in the living room and sometimes, bowing slightly, she even greeted Christopher in Japanese when he got home from school.

RAINY SEASON IN THE TROPICS

Christopher's favorite painting at the Legion of Honor was Church's *Rainy Season in the Tropics*. Sometimes he'd walk from Washington High after school and sit on the hard narrow bench in front of it. He found the lush brilliant scene, fresh from recent rain, to be deeply calming. A vivid, translucent rainbow arched above a party of travelers who threaded a path on a jungle precipice among palm trees and impenetrable mists. Beneath them, shrouded in light and clouds, a vast valley, sheltered in sheer peaks, folded outward, far from everything.

ZIPPERS

You know how when something's overstuffed the zippers start coming down by themselves so what's inside starts coming unintentionally out—that was pretty much what socializing was like for Christopher.

ISOLA DE CALIFORNIA

There was an antique map of California, pictured as an island, on the wall of Niles's classroom. His first lecture concerned the type of knowledge that is taken for granted but is actually quite new, such as the shape and size of the continents. He pointed out that this map, specifically, was dated after the Spanish had discovered that California was *not* an island but was kept in circulation and even allowed to fall into the hands of foreign navies in the hope of one day bottling up an enemy fleet in the crotch of Baja.

ISOLA DE CALIFORNIA

Christopher wondered if high school was like this map—taken, on its face, as a way forward, but actually cornering those who pursued its course—trapping them in a life of work and debt and choices that narrowed and narrowed like the dead-end bottleneck of Baja.

MEDITATION ON DROWNING

You have already decided what it would be for you to drown—you are looking for things to grab—hungrily treading toward that which you think will save you—wary of anything that might grab you or weigh you down—everyone there in the river beside you—everyone drowning in the vicinity of each other.

YOU CAN'T WALK THE SUN WITH YOUR FINGERS

Have you ever seen someone so beautiful that you couldn't look at them, that you had to turn away as if from a glare? A person of such beauty was sitting on the bench in front of *Rainy Season in Tropics* one afternoon. It's not that she was classically beautiful or could have been a model; her face was too narrow and her nose too prominent for these, but that she was like a shell washed fresh from the sea—one single unguarded angle, glistening.

YOU CAN'T WALK THE SUN WITH YOUR FINGERS

Christopher approached her tentatively. She noticed him on the periphery and began to speak, in very proper English, not so much *to* him as simply in his presence. She said, disgruntledly, that her family had lent this very picture to the museum, over her strident protestations, and it was her favorite painting in the world and now she had to come to a *public place* just to see it, and it was almost as if her life wasn't *hers* anymore. She was in no way eliciting a response, but Christopher, in a state of bedazzled disequilibrium and seeking any foothold, blurted that *he* had been *looking* for a way to *become someone else*, even to the point of considering *faking his own death*. After a sharp brief glance, in his direction, she asked how he could *say such a thing* to her. "I thought we might be alike in some way," he said softly. "Well," she responded, seeming slightly shaken, "if we *do* have similarities, the similarities *end there*," and then she asked if he might please leave her to herself.

YOU CAN'T WALK THE SUN WITH YOUR FINGERS

If you think you have a second self and you want to burn the first away to find it, you can light a fire in your life, the way fear lights fires—the way lies start fires in lives—or fantasy, or alcohol, or delirium, or wishing your past was the past of someone else. Many selves are burned unintentionally away in fires like these. But this is not the case with you— you are an arsonist loose in yourself, you are looking for the ground, and until your surface-self curls in flames and recedes, you will not know if anything lies beneath it. Nothing now of beliefs—no gods or ghosts or afterlives—nothing of the questions that these evoke—but only the floor beneath your steps, and if you burn it away the question is—is there another under or behind it? But not "under" or "behind" the way a garage stands behind your house or a person is under a spell or your hands are held behind your back. But is there another self if you burn the first away with all its pasts and purposes and preferences? And of what is this other self made that it stands in the fire? Nothing of believing or disbelieving—you are willing to live with an empty self if nothing lies beneath—nothing of shelter or self-deception—nothing negligent—but burning to the ground.

YOU CAN'T WALK THE SUN WITH YOUR FINGERS

She sat in front of the Church painting, alone in the vast gallery, on the bench. In the painting it was raining in the distance and the arching rainbow glistened; in the painting the architectures of light were the only walls, and people were the smallest part of the world.

YOU CAN'T WALK THE SUN WITH YOUR FINGERS

After looking at the painting for a while, she rose, gathered her things, left the museum, walked south to Geary and boarded the bus to her mother's small, rented house.

WALKING

Christopher knew that he was walking *like fire burning hours* because he could not find home.

COUGH SYRUP

One Saturday morning, Westy privately and quietly insisted that Christopher come with him to his office, and there, made a phone call that resulted in him yelling. When he was finished, he was brusque, agitated and angry. He looked Christopher in the eyes, as if sizing him up, and then they went to a drugstore off of Market Street. Westy purchased several bottles of cough syrup, drove to the Hotel Royal Earl on Eddy in the Tenderloin and, waiting out front with the engine running, told Christopher to take the bottle-packed bag to room 503. The elevator was out of operation and the filthy hotel carpet smelled of urine and old cooking and there were TV's and radios on full-blast and someone drunk was screaming.

It was like going into a madhouse or hell, and Christopher was out of breath when he reached the fifth floor and knocked on 503. The door swung open to reveal the wild-eyed, frantic, blanched witch or beast in the person of his grandmother. He said, haltingly, "Grandma?" She growled "Not anymore, kiddo" and went for the bag, seizing it greedily, no, desperately. "Gimme that!" she shrieked and pulling one of the bottles out, let the others drop to the floor. Shaking, she unscrewed the bottle and chugged it down gulp after gulp. Christopher slowly withdrew, then ran down the stairs to the car. After a few blocks of driving in silence, Westy said, "Did you give the bag to your grandmother?" Christopher said "Yes." Then Westy asked, "Did she say anything?" "She said gimme that." "Did she say anything else?" Christopher said, "No."

FALLING

Evelyn was like someone tumbling down a ladder, grabbing for rungs, and she held to her mundane tasks at the Saint Luke's rummage sale as if there was nothing beneath her but thin air. And all of Westy's entreaties, for her to quit a task that she obviously loathed, only demonstrated how little he understood her.

HIDING BEHIND BROKENNESS

Christopher learned how people can hide their brokenness behind the brokenness of others and how common this was—*he noticed how people spoke of their husbands and wives, how one of them always seemed to be more broken than the other, how that meant that the less broken one could hide their brokenness behind the greater brokenness of the other because, next to the other person, it wasn't so obvious that they were broken.* And it was as if there was an agreement that one of them would be more broken and the other would hide their own brokenness in the storm of shards from the shattering of the one who was breaking apart in front of everyone.

HIDING BEHIND BROKENNESS

And Christopher saw that one could hide a lot in the storm of shards of one more broken than oneself.

MEDITATION ON DROWNING

You are saving yourself—attaching the drowning you fear to everything you touch.

YOU CAN'T WALK THE SUN WITH YOUR FINGERS

Every time Christopher returned to *Rainy Season in the Tropics*, which was often, he looked for the beautiful strange girl; he walked through gallery after gallery, into the gift shop, and back through the galleries again, but she was never there.

BONES

His bones were already those bones lying on the sands, already neither him nor his. His blood was on his side—his skin and his organs were on his side—but his bones were not. His blood was on his side—it had a stake in his being alive—but not his bones. His tissues and organs had a stake—they would dissolve when he dissolved—his eyes were his because they would dissolve like him when he dissolved but not his bones—his bones had no stake in his being alive—no more than any other outside thing—no more than girders, rocks or railroad tracks—no more than the moon—and his bones were like those outside things but embedded in him—his bones belonged to those lasting things and they had no stake in him. So right in the center of him were things that had no stake in his being alive—and this was the way he was built. There was no proper way to punish the bones, to punish the most disloyal things ever made, or come to grips or expel them. So the bones had him in just the very way that being alive had him—that trying to be a person had him—that having to be a person when there was no person to be had him—that everything aligned around him, solid, fixed and defined had him—and none of the outside things had a stake in his being alive—and his bones were with those things and not with him.

TEETH

And his teeth were with his bones but needed tending, and he hated them and refused to brush them, and when they began to decay he had no pity for them.

YOU CAN'T WALK THE SUN WITH YOUR FINGERS

The brass plaque on the wall next to *Rainy Season in the Tropics* said simply, "Anonymous Loan," and inquires in the office as to the lender, were rebuffed.

WALKING

He walked past houses at night filled with lights, rooms alive with voices, through the scent of coal smoke, past rows of businesses, brushing those settled into their lives, and walking became his version of the genuine.

WEIGHT

One afternoon, standing by the window in the living room, taking a cigarette from a pack of Chesterfields, Dr. Thorn had asked warmly, "what do you think you'd weigh on the moon?"

WEIGHT

And Dr. Thorn had said "In the world as you have made it, you know what everything weighs and your precious stories are the scales. Your experience weighs very little to someone else, but to you it is crushingly heavy, so heavy that you can't lift it, you can't move it from the center of your life."

WALKING

Every memory is a retouched photograph—every step. *He walked through the airbrush of hours, through the airbrush of fog, falling where that which approaches is hidden and that which scatters behind is vanishing.* Dr. Thorn had said that *impermanence was the central issue—change—vanishing—that vanishing was the issue—the thing to be faced—that when vanishing leaned into your life, the place where it put its weight was your destiny.* Christopher walked and walked, and he wondered how many times his heart could break over the same thing.

FIRES IN HIM EVERYWHERE

Fires in him everywhere—flames lightless and room temperature—smoke conforming to everything, like memory—he couldn't tell where the world was warped or what was on fire and what wasn't.

WESTY'S BUSINESS

There were rumors on Montgomery Street concerning the viability of Westy's firm.

STANDING ON NOTHING

Dr. Thorn had told Christopher that *everyone* was *standing on nothing.*

LYDIA

After the fight on the phone and the cough syrup incident at the Royal Earl, Christopher knew that Westy would not be sending any more money to Lydia.

HIDING BEHIND BROKENNESS

And Christopher started to wonder what brokenness his father was hiding behind Evelyn's brokenness, in the storm of shards from Evelyn's being frantic. He wanted to know what his father was hiding there, what his secret was, because a man like Westy could not be with a woman like Evelyn unless he was hiding something huge.

BONES

He lived in the space between the outside things and his bones that belonged to them. He lived in that narrow space, and his bones did not live with him but against him. His bones were like inside walls that he moved among, and his bones made a border inside that he could not cross, *and the bones had a place for the dead reserved in him, and the bones took all the hours and returned them as the past. The bones kept the hours like the walls of canyons keep hours, like granite outcroppings keep hours, like reefs keep hours, like all the things that throw time back like an echo when it touches them keep hours, like all the things that time can only brush on its way to consuming all the things that take the hours in. His bones made a border in him that he could not cross, between all the inside things that time pulls into the past and all the outside things that time must live beside. And only his bones were with the outside things, leading their double lives, leading their lives of lies, hiding inside as if they were part of him, hiding from harm in him like secrets held from speech, pretending not to return all his hours as ash, pretending not to know how they pushed time back into every other part of him, pretending to stand for him and pretending to sleep when he slept.*

LOST VIRGINITY

Christopher had already met the girl with whom he would first have sex—well, not exactly met her, but brushed her in the hall.

BONES

And one of his teachers told him that bones were alive and would knit if broken. But Christopher knew that they were not alive for him, that they only knit for themselves. He could be broken to bits, and they would not knit for him.

THONGDROL

And upon turning he saw that the Thongdrol was a galaxy of those who could not sleep.

FIRE

As if fire were the messenger enclosed in the fibers of everything, the smoldering inclination to be unmade, so closely sheltered that you cannot see it, but fire reminds you, and every falling-apart thing reminds you, instant after instant passing the whole world forward—not that things die, not that nothing lasts, but motion against motion and that friction kindling fire.

PRETA

He knew that the homelessness of his walking was the homelessness that the starving outcast had imparted—he knew it was only the semblance of refuge, the kind of shelter allotted to semblance-persons, walkers outside, persons who take shelter in not being seen, sheltered in motion, sheltered in blur.

M-OCEANVIEW

The M-Oceanview is the longest streetcar line in San Francisco.

RUSSIAN BONDS

Because of his purchase of a trunk-full of Czarist Russian Bonds and the subsequent overthrow of the monarchy, Alfred had to move from his apartment on Nob Hill to a far more humble dwelling. He remarked to Evelyn with a chuckle many years later, how untimely it had been for a five-hundred-year-old dynasty to have fallen on his bank account. "My brother, seeing my folly, tried to dissuade me and it caused a rift—*never* make the same mistake my dear, trying to spare loved ones from lessons they need to learn is thankless and bootless." Evelyn agreed. "You *know*, my dear," he said laughing out loud, "I *never* had *much sense—none* actually—*none at all.*"

LYDIA

Word arrived from the manager of the Hotel Royal Earl that Lydia was dead.

EVELYN

A bowl, a cup, a plate: these breakable things—when shattered on the floor—as much her body—her bones—her heart—into pieces.

CHRISTOPHER'S LOCKER

At the beginning of his junior year at Washington, Christopher received a locker number and a combination. He worked his way down the hall lugging his books and finally arrived at the locker, which did not work, even after repeated attempts. He went back to the office where a harried lady behind a crowded desk told him a maintenance man would look into it when he had time, which Christopher took to mean never, so he lugged all his books around with him from class to class to class.

THE PIT

Behind the cement bleachers of the football field, in an area that the students called "The Pit," there were a few benches and a graffiti of a purple wrinkled face with "Mr. Prunes" written in black beneath it. The hippie kids hung out there, and they would congregate between classes and during lunch to smoke cigarettes, listen to transistor radios and deal a little drugs. Christopher ended up there because he wasn't black, Chinese, a scholar, or a jock.

TERTON

Once the world was like a great bowl—a continuous edge. Then
it was smashed into a trillion separate things so its prior unity was
concealed in shattering. Human beings are the part of the world
designated to reassemble it, and the Terton embodies this designation, this capacity, as a way of being alive.

WEIGHT

*It was a room temperature heaviness, so you couldn't sense it and you
couldn't see it because it had become your way of seeing and you couldn't
tell how it was warping things, you couldn't see how seamlessly it applied itself, you couldn't see how it was lying under everything.*

THE DREAM OF THE UNDERWORLD

And Christopher had a dream: he dreamed that he spent the entire night with his father in the underworld. In the dream the
underworld was a grand hotel—in the final stages of decline—located in a spent industrial town of medium size and gray weather.
The money was extracted teeth with gold fillings. Christopher
had his father's and bought his whereabouts from a stranger with
them. His father was working for a furniture auctioneer and carried bleached-white business cards with lettering in raised red felt.
He did not remember Christopher but agreed to spend time with
him anyway. Communication was automatic and telepathic, so
there weren't any actual voices. His father still drank heavily but
looked younger by fifteen years or so. The hotel was packed in all
its widening cracks with paperback books of every type. Everywhere petty chiselers, pickpockets and low-end thieves plied their
trade. No one ever physically touched. Everyone was clothed all
the time. The hotel's larger rooms were subdivided with walls of
pressed books so the pages were opened and flattened—sometimes
varnished sometimes bare. His father did not remember him and

the word *son* seemed foreign to him, but he agreed to meet with Christopher awhile, jiggling a pocket full of teeth the entire time. He asked Christopher where the outskirts were and whether he had seen them. As in life, he drank heavily and seemed distracted. Now and then he directed words to Christopher in the automatic way—had he seen anyone seeming to be lost near the hotel entrance? Had he seen any rooms that seemed to be unoccupied? Could he tell him again the reason he wanted to see him?

WESTY'S FAILING BUSINESS

Westy had hired a spiffy young man from a wealthy family to work with him in his business. Then, toward the end, as the business was sputtering to a close, the young man simply disappeared— didn't show up for work days in a row and didn't call. Finally, when Westy tracked him down, he had taken a job in New York. Christopher overheard the phone conversation where Westy said this simply wasn't done, and there were emotions in Westy's voice that Christopher had never heard his father have before—indignation, hurt, humiliation and powerlessness.

DOOR

Christopher went to see if his father was all right. Westy's face was buried in his hands and he was crying. Watching his father cry was like standing at a door that was open and closed at the same time.

WALKING

You are not with anyone. You are walking outside. You are scrolling through face after face. You are not with anyone. If there is someone next to you it is chance like shuffling cards. Here is someone speaking. You are with no one. *If the sea is mountains moving, if fire is the footing onto nothing, if pine needles strew themselves in a crisscross thatch pointing everywhere—pointing eastward pointing northward pointing southward pointing westward—where is some-one?* There are lines of people everywhere. Have you ever stood opposite yourself, as if you could peel yourself from yourself and walk partly away? Have you ever done this and looked back and tried to be with someone?

TIME AND THE DEAD

If the past is assembled inside, is this why the dead have no past—because they have no place to bring things in—no place to arrange things—did being dead mean that now there was no inside?

NAME

What does your name really name? Your body actually does not have a name; it is your body—that is its name. Only its parts have names, and these are the same names as the parts of other people's bodies, so they don't belong to your body actually—they are applied. The name belongs to the person, but the person cannot be recognized except as the body, so that which is named is that which cannot be found except for that which does not have a name.

GLASS

Westy was in a bar, not the Trader's Exchange Club where he went less frequently now, turning his glass very slowly and eating pretzels, having closed his business and settled for a job at a brokerage house. The bristling bravery of being about to be blown to bits on the liberty ship was no good for this lusterless circumstance.

FIRE-DANCERS

During this time, in the evenings, Westy would pour a cognac, go into the basement and draw with charcoal and pastels on pads of newsprint—fire-dancers, trees on fire, sheer cliffs, blazing boats about to be swallowed by the sea, stained-glass-colored fish and broad blond empty beaches.

CHALK

And he would take the smallest shard of red pastel from the scattered nubs, chips and dust and strike it in a sweep across the bottom of a drawing, bringing it to life. He would draw drummers, cartoon persons walking in red shoes with tall whimsical hats, horses with braided fire for manes and women with brilliant robes. He put these along the walls with thumbtacks, sometimes calling Christopher to come down and refill his snifter with cognac. He didn't talk about his drawings and he didn't ask for comments or opinions.

NO PLACE FOR BROKEN THINGS

Evelyn said that the Japanese understood that there was no place for broken things, for lost face, for imperfect gestures, for cracked porcelain and chipped plates.

JUNIOR YEAR

Almost from the beginning of his junior year at Washington, Christopher began to become forgetful, lightheaded and disoriented.

NO PLACE FOR BROKEN THINGS

Evelyn told Christopher that young people in Japan would sometimes kill themselves if they failed at school or flunked an important test because it was clear they would never amount to anything, and they wanted to protect the honor of their families.

FURNITURE BODY

And he knew that it was OK to be already dead in his mother's house, but you couldn't be already dead and also broken. You can be furniture—almost invisible among the other furniture—but if you are broken, then you cannot be invisible. *If you are broken, you'll be singled out and sold or buried somewhere, so you'd better fix yourself quickly, like shattered mercury coming back together, and if you are broken and trying to hurry in putting yourself back together, you'd better not draw any attention to yourself or what you are doing, but this is really hard when you are just learning, when you are clumsy with yourself and unsure and some of the pieces are actually missing—you are trying to find them on the floor somewhere or fill in the blanks somehow before the blanks are noticed—and the blanks, the faults, the fallen-apart places, can always be noticed accidentally at any time but more commonly are found when the furniture is needed, so you'd better come back together before you're needed because furniture has duties and without notice must hold up something heavy or something delicate, that is itself breakable, and must be reliable in holding up whatever is placed upon it whether it is a plate or a platter or a porcelain horse or a heavy person settling in.* Christopher never knew when he was going to have to hold something up and be whole, sturdy and able. He had to appear always capable of bearing lots of weight reliably and not as if he was barely able to stand.

FURNITURE BODY

And cracks showed up whenever he was late, when he didn't eat his favorite foods or made a face when pressed about his homework or why his shirts were not in the hamper or on hangers in his closet or when, having forgotten his theory of sound, he talked too loudly to himself in his room with the door closed or when he couldn't remember something someone told him just a few minutes ago or said something not entirely on topic or interrupted or didn't put his knife and fork across his plate when he was finished or didn't ask to be excused.

FURNITURE BODY

And he tried to find things in himself to put over the cracks so they wouldn't be visible from the outside, something to seal himself with from inside so that what was in there wasn't going to leak out like light or smoke through a crack. He reached for things in himself—like smiles, nods, words and gestures—anything lying around on the floor of himself, like a story from school, a compliment, a memory that put him in a good light, a humorous phrase but not a complaint or anything that could be construed as disagreeing or disagreeable or out-of-sorts or out-of-line. And he was pushing these things up against the cracks so fast he thought that at any minute he would run out of things to paste on his inside walls and then all the brokenness of which he was really made would come to light in a single moment. Then there would be no way to regain his footing ever again, and it would be noticed how incapable he was of bearing weight and holding things up, and he would be of no use in his mother's house.

SALT

Christopher's science class with Mr. Tolliver was his last before lunch. Mr. Tolliver was a soft rumpled man with a round balding head, a gray beard and a baby blue cardigan sweater. He spoke so softly that the class grew quiet the moment he began, and the clamber in the halls, that spilled into every other class that Christopher had, was absent in Mr. Tolliver's science class. There wasn't much of a lab, just a metal sink set in a linoleum counter at the front, some beakers, a Periodic Table on the wall, a yellowed plastic skeleton in the corner and a few anatomical charts of frogs and human beings. At the beginning of the year, Mr. Tolliver told the students they would be studying rocks, minerals, elements, compounds and mixtures.

VANISHING

Everything in Christopher's life was vanishing: he couldn't remember where his wallet was or where he had put that piece of paper with the phone number written on it. He began to lose things everywhere—his bag lunch, his homework—and he couldn't remember where he'd hidden the candy bar the day before, and he was tired all the time and his stomach was queasy and there was a gauzy feeling as if packing material was pressing in and slowly smothering him. Evelyn kept trying to get him to eat because she said she was worried about him.

LOST VIRGINITY

A slight, inconspicuous girl of sixteen sat next to Christopher in science class. She had slightly curly, mousy-brown hair and wore large black-rimmed glasses, loose sweaters, bellbottomed jeans, a macramé belt with a large silver buckle and several silver rings with stones that looked so big it seemed she would have trouble lifting her small hands. She was not un-pretty if you took the time to notice her, but she was quiet and in the background and Christopher was not aware of her.

LOST VIRGINITY

One morning, watching him stack his books on his desk and under it, the quiet girl in science class asked him why he carried all of them around with him. He told her his locker didn't work, and they wouldn't fix it. She smiled and went back to what she was doing. At the end of class, which covered rocks and minerals, she asked if he'd like to share her locker, and they walked down the crowded halls together and she opened it and gave Christopher the combination, which he wrote on a promptly lost piece of paper, and they piled his books on top of hers and went to the pit for lunch. She commented on how beautifully wrapped his sandwiches were.

LOST VIRGINITY

Christopher by now was no longer short. He wore his ash-blond hair, which he rarely combed, to his shoulders. He was still very thin and always appeared to be restless and distracted like someone searching for something lost. Often, he would walk to the Legion of Honor after school—*where was she*—and he'd walk to the Great Highway and huddle in the steady misty rain against the seawall.

LOST VIRGINITY

There in the Pit with Mr. Prunes while sharing a cigarette, the girl from science class asked him if he would like to come home with her after school and listen to some records. They took the bus down Geary to Second Avenue. The apartment building was white, nondescript, and on the wrong side of Geary. Her father was not in her life and her mother worked all day, so no one was there. She sat him down on a cheap white couch, and there was thick carpeting everywhere, and nothing beautiful or valuable anywhere, and she went to the kitchen and came back with some carrots and celery, asking if he ate vegetables, and he said only coffee. She put a record on, sat beside him, kicked off her shoes, leaned against him, ran her hand up his thigh and put her face in front of his, keeping it there until he kissed her again and again. Then she got up, loosened her belt, unbuttoned her jeans, and let them fall to the floor. Now she was standing in front of him in her panties and he impulsively yanked them down. She said she was glad he did and stepped from the pants at her feet. Then she did that thing where you run the toes of the opposite foot down your heels to remove your socks and, nearly toppling, tugged his hand and led him back to her bedroom. *It was all white and lacy except for some rock star posters on the walls and the bed was covered with binders, papers and books which she pushed onto the floor—clearly none of this was new to her—and she flopped onto her back with a laugh, pulled her sweater*

*and undershirt off in a single motion and she wasn't wearing a bra
and her nipples were small and stiff and her breasts were barely more
rounded than a boy's.* She told him to take off his pants and while
he did she rolled onto her stomach and asked him to rub her back.
*She spread her legs wide so he could kneel between them and he gently
pressed his thumbs against the edges of her shoulder blades, following
them down and around to her ribs, and then he ran his fingers down
her spine and rested his hands in the hollow of her back, and the bones
were just there beneath the skin and it was wondrous how their shapes
were so clear to the touch.* As he pulled off his shirt and threw it on
the floor, she reached under herself and her breathing changed. He
placed his palms flat on her buttocks and pulled them apart. She
drew a sharp breath, rolled onto her back, and looked into his face.
Her eyes were glittery and black and he was kissing her and prob-
ing clumsily between her legs with his erection because he couldn't
find the opening. Suddenly everything stopped. She looked at him
quizzically and asked with tender urgency, "Are you a *virgin?*"
Christopher didn't reply. "Oh—you're a *virgin*," she said, and seeing the concern on his face said very softly, "I won't *say anything.*"
Then, reaching under him, she said "here," and gently guided his
penis into her. She closed her eyes, smiled, and shifted her fingers
upward to play with herself, *and it felt so achingly warm inside of her,
and he was rocking back and forth and she was moaning softly and for
a while he was buoyed and everything was actual and close, but then
something intervened and the pleasure began to be far away and he
started to sink into something gummy like tar and his penis began to
soften because it wasn't part of him anymore, so he had to hurry, and he
was pumping automatically like treading water, and he had to reach for
something to pull him out, and the boy is brought through the crowd in
the cart and the hook is guided in and worked upward and the pulling
upward and the tilting back and the tip of the hook coming out and the
crowd watching and the not meaning to writhe and the writhing faster
and faster and the muffled scream and the dying and the being dead.*

WALKING

He walked in the Presidio for over an hour after this. The air was cold and the fog was blowing through the eucalyptus trees. Their scent was sharp and strong, clinging inside his nose and in his throat when he tried to swallow. He walked past the swings at Julius Kahn, past the clubhouse, over the softball field and into the woods. And it was as if he was outside of himself and could watch himself walking among the trees—as if he had borrowed his mother's philascope. He walked and walked and "it's all pretzel pieces," he said to himself.

LOST VIRGINITY

The following morning, Christopher was consumed with rage. He didn't know why, but he knew that he did not want to look at her, be seen by her or hear her voice. *It was like the teeth of a trap had torn into him, or like he was a toy she had brought home and wound up and let loose in her room for her amusement, and everything was pushing into him, using him, coring him, extracting him from himself and putting wood paste where he had been.* When he got to school he *couldn't* look at her.

WESTY FIRED

Westy had been fired from his brokerage job and sat in a coffee shop a few blocks off of Montgomery Street with nowhere to go, day after day after day. Later, he walked along the Embarcadero and sat on benches. He got up every morning at the usual time, put on his suit, drove downtown and spent the afternoons in bars or at Candlestick Park. He said nothing to Evelyn, Jack O'Neal, or anyone else about his circumstances.

SYPHILIS

Christopher woke in the middle of the night, cold and shivering.

He knew that he was dying of syphilis—he could almost feel the little screwworms boring through his brain, tangling and erasing everything.

POSTAGE DUE

One day Evelyn received a letter, postage due, from Mrs. Donnelly. It became the topic, the fountain of questions: she could understand if she simply forgot to put postage on but to put too little? It clearly weighed more than a single stamp would carry; was this intentional? The very rich were always tight; they always treated the less wealthy with that casual indifference, as if Evelyn ought to pay something for the privilege of receiving a letter. Why should she be slapped in the face like that? What had she done to deserve this kind of treatment? Maybe she should have sent the letter back. The rich are always tight; should she be tight as well?

THE FREE CLINIC

There were numerous free clinics, scattered around the city, run by various agencies and nonprofits. Christopher found them, listed in the phone book of a pay phone near his school. Imagining anonymity, he chose the one run by the county. It was located south of Market, in an area Christopher only knew as a drive-through to Candlestick. He sat in the crowded, shabby, indifferent institutional waiting area with its welded-together chairs, cheap worn upholstery, stained rug and all the being-eaten-alive people crammed together and taking numbers—prostitutes, pimps, street people, junkies, disoriented souls come in from the cold—everyone smoking and coughing with broken yellow teeth, tics and tremors. He was so repulsed that he had to leave, but his gnawing fear so galvanized him that halfway down the block he stopped and returned, shouldering again through the cat-calling men loitering near the front—"I've been waiting for you!" "Hey girl, I'm talkin' to you!" When Christopher's number was finally called, a weary but sympathetic doctor in a cramped office papered with public health announcements asked why he had come. "I have syphilis, or at least I've been with someone who later told me they have syphilis, so I need to know." "Do you have any symptoms?" "I don't feel well." "Have you had any kind of sore on your penis?" "No, I don't think so." "Any discharge?" "No." "How long ago were you exposed?" "I don't know exactly. It seems like a long time ago, maybe it's already quite advanced." The doctor looked puzzled. "How old are you?" "Sixteen." "Where do you go to school?" "Washington High." "Are you taking any drugs?" "No." The doctor eyed the information Christopher had filled out, examined him and found nothing. "I'll order a workup. If anything's wrong, we'll call and say it's the school library so you'll know to come back." Christopher was shuffled off to a little bathroom for a urine sample and then was left sitting in a hall waiting for a large black nurse to take a blood sample. He sat in the row of gray steel chairs by himself, swinging his legs back and forth, *his shoes scuffing the stained rug, and he felt completely stripped away and hollowed out, like an empty building with all the doors taken off and all the windows broken out and the weather just blowing through, and he didn't have any way to hide behind anything—he was rungless and falling and every filthy way that he was stained and used was simply there to be had like a thing in the broken window of a looted shop.* After the blood test the nurse said "We'll call and say it's the library so you come back," but the call never came. At first he was relieved, but then the nagging fear returned, and then it was as if he had never gone to the clinic because he knew that in that chaotic place, they had lost his sample, mislabeled it, mixed it up with someone else's, lost his phone number or simply botched the test. He wanted to go to a real doctor, but then he would have to explain how he contracted syphilis, from Carl, at the age of twelve, and he could never do that.

SYPHILIS

Chills and sweats—being eaten alive inside by little screwworms day after day, test after test, clinic after clinic, like putting a fiend to sleep for a little while but knowing it will wake, and you are trying to skirt it in a tiny room; in a hot wet tiny room with no doors and no windows.

SYPHILIS

He got tested only on days when Evelyn was working on Union Street so he'd get home before she did and no one would know. It was not that it was probable that all these labs were losing his samples or losing his number or mixing his samples up with someone else's. It was only that it was not impossible.

SYPHILIS

Now it was night after night, one minute at a time—held in place—as if clutched in the hot-cold current of an electric fence.

WALKING

And he walked and walked and walked, as if he were trying to walk out of himself, *and there was a kind of violence in the way he walked, in the way that his feet punched the pavement, his face against the fog—and not the fog as metaphor but the literal chill curtain blown from the sea; and he could not distinguish the substantial from the unsubstantial. He walked as if he were trying to walk out of himself, but you cannot walk out of yourself, even in the fog where you are lost. You cannot leave yourself in the fog, even if you cannot distinguish yourself from the unsubstantial.*

TRIP TO THE COUNTRY

Evelyn announced that the family would be taking a trip to the country, perhaps to Mt. Shasta, to get everyone out of the city and into the beauty of nature and some fresh air.

TRIP TO THE COUNTRY

Christopher was well aware that his family was not the kind of family that took trips to the country.

THE FOLDED-OVER FILM

Sitting by himself in the hallway of a clinic, waiting for a blood test, Christopher's attention was drawn to the push-lid of the trashcan in front and to the right of him. It was suddenly swinging on its hinge, not as if someone had just thrown something in, but as if someone had thrown something in some seconds before so the lid was in the latter stages of swinging *and was already slowing down. But there was no one there; no one had been there, and there had been no sound of anything hitting the lid. So the event was like an insert, as if time was a film that could fold over on itself so things from different times could be superimposed on one another or lie side-by-side. It was happening here in this clinic, so maybe the tests he had taken folded over to a time before he was infected, so the results were negative, or there was a folded-over future after he was cured, so the tests were negative. But now he was being devoured, which could not be noticed because everything they tested was from a folded-over other time—and the future of his being dead was folded-over next to him, factual and stark.* He started to sweat profusely. Nothing in the clinic was going to be the truth. He stood up, walked down the hall, through the crowded waiting room and out the door.

THONGDROL

The Thongdrol can begin everything again, and, in that new beginning, realign everything that has led to it.

THE FOLDED-OVER FUTURE

Hurrying down the street, he had the sense that nothing was happening now; that everything, like the swinging trash can lid, was happening in a folded-over moment of the future. And he wondered, since now he was in the future, what could he remember that had not yet happened, and he thought that he could remember murder.

GOLD DISC

Evelyn wore a braided gold bracelet with a dangling gold disk charm stamped with various dates. Westy had given it to her and she called it her *happy day* bracelet. Her birthday was there and Westy's; their anniversary was there, and Christopher's birthday, and another date that wasn't familiar to Christopher at all. Evelyn said it was just an especially happy day.

SOME THINGS ARE NOT SINGLE THINGS

Some things are not single things, like mileage, like confluences, like inch by inch, like erosion and like rust—things inhabited by other things, things merged, things in increments, things taken from themselves, not all at once but the way the moon's orbit subtracts the light of the moon from the wall of the room where you cannot sleep.

THE HARDNESS OF SHELTERING QUESTIONS

If you shelter questions, you will be worn away and the questions will stand, and it is hard to hold questions and be steadily worn away. It's easier to leave the questions outside, to give them over to the wearing away that the world brings to every exposed thing, to let the questions be worn away so that you can stand unworn in the world, or, if not unworn, at least not torn to bits.

WALKING

Christopher walked as if the answers were in motion just ahead of him.

M-OCEANVIEW

Sometimes he would walk to Market Street and board the M-Oceanview and roll past decrepit gaudy shops and drug dealers standing in doorways and ride west down Market Street to the longest streetcar tunnel in the world—under Twin Peaks to West Portal. The inside of the streetcar always seemed too small, as if it had been built on another scale. The upholstery had been worn glossy, and the tracks ran through alleys behind the houses of Saint Francis Wood. People who had real reasons to ride got on and off with shopping bags and children—people looking at watches, impatient with traffic lights and traffic jams. The tracks ended next to the ocean.

NITRO

Westy had angina—took nitroglycerin—told no one.

SOME THINGS ARE NOT SINGLE THINGS

Some things are not single things—like rain, like doubt, like depth.

SHATTERING

Christopher saw that there was shelter on the other side of shattering, on the other side of the habits of days and weeks and the lock-step lives of persons tied to tasks.

TRIP TO THE COUNTRY

Evelyn brought up the trip to the country again.

SYPHILIS

Should he tell the first girl that she'd been exposed? He imagined how, in a year or two, she would lose her mind. But she hadn't been a virgin when they'd had sex, so she wouldn't know it was him and, in fact, would suspect him last, since she thought he was a virgin. But he couldn't let this happen to her, so he made up his mind to tell her. Standing in the hall trying to be heard above the bells and slamming lockers—"I have something that I need to tell you." "What is it?" "You may have syphilis. I mean, I *may* have given you syphilis." "*What?*" "I'm sorry, I just had to tell you so you wouldn't get sick and go mad someday." She was all outward-flying arrows. "Some *virgin!* You are such a *dick*—you are *such* a liar. You just *go to hell!*" And she stormed off down the hall, knocking into people—books flying and everyone cursing—Christopher turned and walked the other way.

SALT

When Christopher came into science class the next morning, he found all his books dumped on his desk. The girl had swapped seats with a pimple-faced boy and moved to the back of the room. Christopher had chills and was shaky and disoriented. He was about to put the books on the floor and his head on the desk when Mr. Tolliver began to rapidly jot a formula on the board.

THONGDROL

The Thongdrol can begin everything again—a turning, wonder simply untying your preference for settling the past in such a way that it settles the present.

SALT

The formula that Mr. Tolliver wrote rapidly on the board was this:

23 parts Na + 35.5 parts Cl = NaCl (Sodium chloride / table salt)

The click, click, squeak of the chalk was mostly what managed to enter Christopher's mind while Mr. Tolliver continued softly by saying that the formula contained everything the students needed to know about compounds. Christopher's head was halfway to his folded arms on the desk when he was jolted into alertness as Mr. Tolliver murmured that the two components of table salt were both poisonous. These were Na (Sodium)—a shiny silvery white metal so reactive that it had to be stored out of contact with the air—and Cl (Chlorine), a yellowish green poisonous gas. When these deadly partners were combined they created a substance absolutely essential to life. Mr. Tolliver continued by explaining that it was a central property of compounds that their constitutive elements did not retain their individual properties, and asked if there were any questions. Christopher raised his hand and asked tentatively, "was it possible to break the parts of salt back into poisons again?" Mr. Tolliver stated that it would take a great deal of energy because of the strength of the ionic bonds holding the sodium and chlorine atoms together. "You would have to pass an electrical current through molten salt to separate its elements." "But it would be possible?" Christopher continued. "Yes."

POISONING

At the end of the class on salt, Christopher walked up to the girl and, looking her in the eyes, told her that he had not given her syphilis, and he was sorry about how he had treated her. Then he abandoned the pile of books that crowded his desk and with steady strides walked through the halls. Clutching his lunch, he went down the staircase and outside, past the bleachers, down the stone stairs, past the pit and, lighting a cigarette, left Washington High and walked the eight blocks down Geary to Doug Sutton's office.

POISONING

Christopher entered the shabby little office with the bell above the door, the Statue of Liberty clock on the wall and the raspy receptionist who by now had grown rather small, like the Sibyl, and whose hair was dyed blond and pulled back and the dye seemed to have bled down into her scalp because the skin just below the hairline looked slightly green. He asked to see Mr. Sutton and she called out that Mrs. Westall's boy was here. Doug came out of his office with a big smile and invited Christopher back. They sat at his desk with the pencil sharpener bolted to it and Doug offered him the last of the powdered sugar doughnuts from the little cylindrical package with the cardboard and the torn thin cellophane. Christopher declined and said that he had brought Doug a decent lunch, spilling the contents of the bag on Doug's desk. Doug was taken aback but muttered "Thanks." Christopher gave him a hug and left the office.

CASCADE FALLS

After dropping off his lunch at Loudon and Sutton, Christopher walked the several blocks to Park Presidio, crossed the street and put out his thumb. A VW bus picked him up and the hippies packed inside asked where he was going. "I don't know," he said, and they said that they were going to Cascade Reservoir to go swimming and asked if he wanted to come. "I don't have a swimming suit," he said, and laughing they said he didn't need one. So he said OK, and they drove north over the bridge through the fog and the Rainbow Tunnel into sunny Marin and down the Waldo Grade past Sausalito, through Mill Valley to Old Mill Park and up a steep winding road to its end. The journey had taken less than half an hour. Everyone piled out, climbed a narrow well-worn path up an embankment and pushed through the chain link fence cut and bent back long ago. There was a throng of naked long-haired kids lying flat on the rocks, their clothes strewn everywhere. Many were well-tanned and some were smoking pot, and there was a rope-swing over a roughly round not very large reservoir and some of the kids were laughing and some were swimming and some played guitars. Christopher's companions abandoned him at once, stripping down and diving into the water. He stumbled forward; starting to take off his shirt reflexively, then seeing that he couldn't do any of this, backed toward the entrance, slipped through the fence and started walking back down the steep road.

CASCADE FALLS

About half a mile down the road from the reservoir, Christopher came upon a small parking area demarcated by a couple of logs and some gravel. Behind it was a path somewhat hidden by overhanging branches. He pushed his way in, following the path into the forest. If you have ever walked into a redwood stand, you will know how much cooler the air becomes, almost cold at first, and it seemed even more so because of a rushing stream that zig-zagged beside the path, and over which Christopher walked on some rotting moss-covered boards. Just on the other side of the trees, steep walls rose, so he was walking in a ravine. The fragrance of the forest floor was sweet, and jumbles of ferns grew everywhere and intermittent light was pouring through, and as he proceeded, slowly, he heard the steady thunderous clap of a waterfall.

CASCADE FALLS

The path was relatively straight and led to the foot of the waterfall which stood about twenty feet high. At the bottom was a shallow pool and a cluster of boulders. The walls were moss-covered and bright, and a cold mist rose where the falling water struck the rocks. Christopher stood for a long time watching the falling water, trying to trace the particles as they fell, and there was nothing pushing in on him and there was no one there but himself.

CASCADE FALLS

After standing in front of the falls for a long time, he doubled-back and climbed a narrow slippery path to the top where a small pool gave itself continuously over the lip. He sat down on the rocks, took off his shoes and socks, rolled up his jeans, swung his legs around and put his feet in the cold cold pool at the top of Cascade Falls. There was a moment of suddenness, like brilliant light it was so cold, but he left his feet in the water until they were used to it.

CASCADE FALLS

And he lay back on the rocks at the top, beside the pool, with his arms behind his head, his knees bent, and his bare feet flat, and he knew that his mother was poisoning him by breaking salt apart somehow, or in some other way, and it didn't matter exactly what the mechanism was or exactly how she was doing it because he knew that she was taking something ordinary, some household thing, and cracking it into its lethal parts and putting the poisons steadily, patiently and remorselessly into his lunch. All that mattered was that now he knew.

THE NATURE OF COMPOUNDS

And he saw that sometimes things brought together lost themselves and became something else; and a person going to a job day after day had a life that was compounded with that job, and in a marriage two people were not themselves anymore. He could see it all around him—people entering into combinations where they lost themselves and the kind of force it would take to break them out.

THE NATURE OF COMPOUNDS

The way he could lie on the rocks like a fallen tree, like a tree in the petrified forest, looking into the past as if it were the face of someone just here; or looking down at himself as if this was already memory.

POISONING

And he wasn't sure that he didn't want to die, but he didn't want to be buried like a broken glass and he didn't want to be pulled in the pony cart.

IDENTITY AS AN EDGE

He knew that identity occurred as an edge, how salt too was an edge; just taste it. And identity was an edge that pressed itself to the present like any other thing; you find it *by tracing the edge with your eye or in your thoughts or with your tongue or by tracing the edge with your fingers, like tracing the shoulder blade of a girl or in memory you find its edge as an image, and when identity is there, something takes hold; you are held in touching it—even in memory you are held, taken hold of, even if only what holds you is memory, something combines and is solid, even when you know that memory has no edges.*

TRIP TO THE COUNTRY

And Christopher wondered what kind of father would dig the hole and bury his son in the country to appease his wife.

PATERNITY

Christopher decided that the kind of father who would dig a hole like that was the kind of father who was not his father at all.

SALT

You cannot break consciousness apart because the only thing that you have to break it apart with is consciousness itself. It isn't like having a handful of salt to hold and run through your fingers or like putting a pinch of salt into your mouth.

GOLD

And gold does not wear away—silver does not, copper does not but mica, iron and tin all wear away, rust away, fall apart in heat or weather or under pressure, and consciousness was like these and not like gold, so he knew that consciousness was a put-together thing, a thing made of other things that bonded and became unrecognizable as themselves.

MICA

Consciousness was a thing made of other things, a put-together thing, *fragile and layered, like mica, separating into thin almost elastic leaves, like stacks of windowpanes made slightly pliant by heat.*

THE NATURE OF COMPOUNDS

And he knew that the bonds that held consciousness together could be worn away—that the parts would dissolve when they hit the air, and that pulled apart, they would kill you.

GOLD

But gold will flatten almost forever, one atom thick, until it curls and is so light that a breath can carry it, like consciousness is transported on single breaths.

FIRE

Or was consciousness like fire—in constant motion, dependent on things to appropriate; transforming things into the past? You do not think of fire as fragile because it can't be held or dropped or broken to bits, but nothing is more fragile, dependent, or homeless than fire.

CASCADE FALLS

He lay flat on the cold flat rocks, placed his right hand in the icy pool and left it there. The water falling over the edge *struck the rocks below in a single extended hammer blow—he felt struck far away like that, his bones more like rocks than part of him, more like rocks at some distance down below, his whole body boulder-like, immobile, taking the downward thrust on its shoulders, on its back, in its crotch, taking the thrust like a blunt unbroken fall. He knew no numbness comparable to this, no coldness of water on skin; no struck skin, even skin struck bluntly and repeatedly, was numb like this; no coldness of water was numb like this, no silence, no flatness was flat like this, no knife blade, no razor blade, no file, no planed plank was flat like this. There, by the fluid motion of the water, by the tumbling over the edge of the fresh first water, the never before, the never again water, the once water, rushing and rushing over his numb flat hand, the water once rushing over the numb flat hand resting stone-like under it.*

POISONING

After the science class where he learned about salt, Christopher didn't go to classes anymore, except for homeroom first thing in the morning so he wouldn't be counted absent. He left his lunch every day at Doug's office. But, after the first few times, the receptionist said that Doug was on the phone or with a client and could not be disturbed, so he left it for her to give to him. Christopher essentially lived on candy and cigarettes, except for dinner, when everyone ate the same thing.

LISTENING

He would lie in his bed awake early in the morning, listening to his mother in the kitchen, with the radio on very softly, making his lunch.

BLIND MOTHER

And it was like a boy with a blind mother in a world of cliffs—how could he protect her from herself and himself from her at the same time?

THONGDROL

Transmission is the substantiation of the non-private nature of consciousness. It is neither exceptional nor miraculous but serves as the most immediate and subversive engagement with the fallacy of the self as private property.

POISONING

At first he thought of throwing the sandwiches away, but he knew that then the poisoning would never stop.

THE WASP DREAM

Christopher dreamed that he was shoeless in a large empty room where a red wasp was tumbling over and over to the bare wooden floor in front of him. At the far end of the room was a fireplace with no back wall. It was full of ashes and large enough to walk through. In the dream, Christopher had to cross the room barefooted and step through the ashes to a little room on the other side and climb a hidden staircase. The wasp, its wings covered with ash, could fly no higher than Christopher's knees and fell, again and again, where he was about to step. In the fireplace, a little boy stood ankle-deep in ashes—holding out his hand—offering to guide him.

THONGDROL

If you are looking back, there are only fires sweeping toward you. If you are looking forward, there is only the precipice—you cannot carry anything over its edge, not latitudes, not longitudes, not gold, not silver, not lacquer, not precious stories.

THE MOVE

Christopher knew that his mother would not move lightly.

RETURNING TO THE CHERRY DESK

One morning, in the new house on Jackson Street, when the house was empty, Christopher returned to the cherry desk. He touched nothing on the writing surface, moved nothing, altered nothing because, this time, his intrusion can't be noticed because he can't have to explain it. So he got down on his knees, pulled the heavy middle drawer out very quietly, and rested it on the floor. He was looking for only one thing, something he had seen before but not imagined the importance of. Going to the Shebee stack, he thumbed his way down toward the bottom, and found an envelope, sent from a Pine Street address to Evelyn at 2100 Sacramento Street Apt. A. It was a get-well card, in Shebee's loopy script, that said: "Hope you are better after your fall. We'll have a cup of tea in a day or two. Remember you can always count on me. C.B." He realized that it was signed "C.B." because he hadn't been born so no one had called her "Shebee" yet. He focused on the date of the postmark—April 3, 1951—nine months and five days before his birth. After reading the card again, he put it back, put the drawer back and hurriedly left the room.

ENGAGEMENT CALENDAR

Christopher went quickly down the hall to the living room, took the iron key from the captain's chest, and opened the middle drawer of the tansu. He grabbed a bundle of engagement calendars near the bottom, trying to pull them apart carefully, just enough to see the years embossed in gold, but the rotted rubber band broke, and how was he going to replace it? He pulled out the calendar for 1951, opened it to March and early April and nowhere was there a mention of the fall. He continued leafing through the pages to May 15th where the entry said, "Move to Green Street."

GOLD DISC

The happy day bracelet was coiled in the cloisonné bowl beside their bed. Christopher stole in, picked it up and wrote down the mystery date, June 13, 1951, on a piece of paper that he folded and put in his pocket.

WALKING

He walked the streets for hours through the fog, and there arose a sense of falling, as if the objects of the world were flying past him—*lights, phone poles, people, houses, voices, buses, intersections. Spun through the floorless world, the smooth chill brushing him as he fell, the things of the world rising up, miles and miles of unconnected things, things marooned, abandoned, forsaken, things chucked overboard of the flying universe—his feet, once bound to pavement, now unhinged—nothing to consider but the fact of rushing forward, nothing of thought or remembrance, no goal or destination, only the fact of falling through the fog.*

PUNAKAH

The tour group entered Punakah, a mountain city which was once the capital of Bhutan. The huge dzong sat at the confluence of the Mo Chhu and the Pho Chhu rivers and was accessible only by a covered pedestrian bridge. Then there were steep steps to climb, and multiple gateways through the thick fortress walls, to the inner courtyard.

THE APARTMENT

The apartment building on Sacramento Street, between Laguna and Gough, was an undistinguished orange brick affair. Christopher caught sight of it as he rounded the hill in Lafayette Park across the Street. He dodged his way through dogs chasing balls, palm trees, and shrieking children pushing around the swing set. A mother was scolding her child especially harshly to please the other mother whose child had had sand thrown in her eyes at the sandbox. He went down the stone stairs, and had to wait a while to cross the heavily trafficked street in the middle of the block. After he rang the bell of apartment "A," the voice of an elderly man came through the speaker. Christopher said that his parents had lived in the apartment before he was born, and he was very interested in seeing it. Could he possibly impose? It would only take a minute. "What was your name again? Well, I don't know." After some additional pleading and a long pause, the man buzzed the buzzer and let Christopher in. The carpet in the hall was beige and worn; and the building smelled of toast and steam heat. Why did all these buildings smell the same? The man waiting at the opened apartment door was gaunt and gentle, wearing a beige cardigan and, except for a bit of apprehension, seemed pleased for any company.

THE MOVE TO GREEN STREET

The afternoon of his visit to the apartment on Sacramento Street, over tea and with as much nonchalance as he could muster, Christopher asked Evelyn why they had moved from Sacramento to Green. He watched closely to see if she bristled a bit, but she was calm and steady. "We moved because you were on your way and the apartment was too small."

THE APARTMENT

Christopher knew that the apartment on Sacramento was not too small.

TIME AND THE DEAD

What can the dead put at risk—is to live without risk to live as if you are dead—is that what being dead is?

RETURNING FROM CASCADE FALLS

Late one afternoon, hitching back from Cascade Falls across the bridge, the fog blowing hard between the towers, *the sea no sea at all, the city no city.*

SECRETS

Christopher knew that Westy hadn't paid Lydia to keep a secret from Evelyn that Evelyn was already keeping, and Westy had not paid Lydia to keep something from himself that he already knew. This was a secret that Lydia had been paid to keep from Christopher.

HAVING IT OUT WITH WESTY

One day, when it was raining lightly, Christopher decided to have it out with Westy. He would tell him the truth about the poisoning and maybe even ask for the truth about his paternity. Instead of hitching a ride to Cascade Falls, he took a bus downtown and went into the Alexander Building at the corner of Montgomery and Bush. He went up the elevator to the brokerage reception desk and asked to see his father. The receptionist was bewildered, then brusque, saying that Mr. Westall hadn't worked there for many weeks.

PUNAKAH

Christopher stood in the bright inner courtyard of Punakah Dzong. A girl of maybe ten approached with her younger brother, their clothes ratty but clean, their faces thin but washed. She wore her hair in braids and approached with no little urgency saying "one pen, one pen." Christopher patted and searched his pockets but found no pen to offer. Finally, he shrugged and shook his head. After the girl and her brother turned and left, Christopher stood looking at a painting on a chipped white plaster wall of a blue, haloed mermaid floating above a turbulent sea, holding a flaming lamp in her outstretched left hand. After a while, the girl returned with her brother. She held a pencil-nub with a shiny rounded eraser out to Christopher and, moving closer, pressed it into his hand. He was speechless. The girl and her brother then hurried around the corner of the building. At first he was too stunned to move, but then went after them. They were gone, but maybe they had entered the doorway that stood fractionally opened before him. He entered and it seemed black as obsidian. He felt his way over to a wall and sat on the floor.

WESTY FALLING FROM THE WORLD

Christopher saw that no one actually stood in the world, that you were never really situated anywhere, that you had to be continuously ped-dling, that if you fell from the context of common pursuits, you no longer existed to those who remained within it.

TRUANCY

He continued to cut classes, drop his lunches off at Doug's office and go to Cascade Falls or sometimes to Golden Gate Park, or sometimes he'd ride the M-Oceanview to the end of the line or walk up Telegraph Hill to Coit Tower or go to the Legion of Honor, which was almost deserted, and look at the art then have a cup of coffee in the café, or he'd walk out past the Cliff House to the sea or walk down the Great Highway to Fleishhacker Zoo or go to Marina Green with the stone kiosk selling pink popcorn or sit by the Palace of Fine Arts, which was now an Exploratorium, and look up the hill and find the back window of the old flat on Green, the window from which he'd looked into the garden after coming through the passage from Grant School, and he knew that memory was not the same for everyone, and he walked and walked until it was time to go home.

THE DREAM OF THE WILD BOY

And Christopher had a dream—he dreamed that he was standing in his room and there was a black wasp perched on the corner of his desk. It lifted off and started to fly toward him but *in midair transformed into a crow, which pivoted and swerved in front of his*

*face, so close that the tip of its wing nearly brushed his cheek, then glided
and dove behind his bed. Almost at once the head of a boy popped up
behind the bed—it was a wild boy, nearly naked, fierce and unable to
speak, and it had to be decided where this wild boy would sleep because
there was no question that he had to be kept.* It was left to the boy
to decide. In the dream there were broad stone steps behind the
house, and the boy decided to sleep on one of these, under a thin
wool blanket.

THE LAST TIME CHRISTOPHER
SAW UNCLE ALFRED

The last time Christopher saw Uncle Alfred alive was on a Sunday. Evelyn had taken him out to the house on Taraval because
Alfred was not feeling well, not even well enough to go out into
the garden with Evelyn. He asked Doug to show her the garden
and he and Christopher sat in the living room. There was so much
swelling in Alfred's feet that he couldn't wear shoes and had to
wear socks under those rubber covers that people put on their
shoes to go out in the rain. After a little chat about nothing in
particular, Christopher asked if he could ask a question in strictest
confidence. Alfred responded jovially "anything, my dear, just between ourselves." Christopher asked if Alfred had any idea why his
parents had moved so suddenly from the apartment on Sacramento to the flat on Green. Alfred paused, considering the question
carefully. "Though your mother, I think, would be loathe to admit
it, I suspect that the source of your precipitous change of address
was the Social Register, or rather, your mother's quest for inclusion therein, not for vanity, mind you, but in service to your father's
business standing. How was she, with all due respect, to offer tea
to Mrs. Brink and Mrs. Beckwith and the rest, in that dumpy little
abode on Sacramento Street? Well, it was out of the question if
she hoped to be admitted to polite society." Christopher feigned
satisfaction with this answer. Then Alfred asked Christopher to

help him up and walk beside him to the window, so they might see what their loved ones were up to in the garden.

THE AFTERLIFE OF THOUGHTS

The professor stated that just as prayers blown from a prayer flag have a continuing life in the community, so too do thoughts have an afterlife, even thoughts kept to oneself—not only in that sense that they reverberate, as do all things set in motion, but that they reside in the Sea of Mind.

RUSHING WATER

His days were like rushing water, like reading, like reading where the pages were the eyes of needles, being pulled through like that, like stepping into water that was rushing, and how do you find your place in rushing water?

POISONING

And he lay flat on the rocks as he would lie dead at their feet, and after he was buried in the woods on the trip to the country, they'd just come home and tell the school that he'd transferred, and tell their friends that he'd had to be sent away.

THE BLINDNESS OF THE ORGANS

His kidneys were making urine; and his heart was pushing blood, his stomach was grinding food. He marveled at the blindness of the organs, at their dull continuous motions, their automatic indifference to loss, their dull, smooth, continuous functioning in the face of everything ending, and he noticed that none of his body was part of him—it moved with mechanical separateness, like a windup box in the corner of a room where someone is pinned to a wall—and the windup box purrs on— and the heart and lungs and liver continue to work like traffic signals facing empty streets in the dead of night.

THE SOUND OF WATER

Lying by the falls, he wondered how the sound of water rushing over rocks, after countless centuries, remained so new.

BUYING A COMPASS

Christopher went into Schrader's on Union Street because the woman at the Legion of Honor gift shop had told him that he could find a compass at a stationery store. Miss Schrader sprung to her feet—"Good afternoon young man." "Good afternoon Miss Schrader." "And what may I do for *you* this afternoon?" "I wondered, do you have a compass?" "I have the best compass in town," she said decisively. Leading him to a showcase and sliding the little glass door at the back, she brought forth a large black felt pouch from which she removed the glistening silver instrument and began to present its many features and advantages, including its numerous interchangeable points, its breadth and the fact that the little adjusting gear with the turning stem at the top was calibrated in tiny increments so Christopher would be able to be precise when he drew his circles. At no point could Christopher have interrupted, and at no point could he have begun to say that this was not the kind of compass he had meant. He couldn't begin to say it, so she continued to discuss her best compass in town, and he was frozen there in front of the display case, and the compass was very expensive and the store was empty and he knew that if he bought it he would not be able to afford the compass that he needed to save his life, but he bought it anyway because he realized that he would actually rather die than walk out of that store and leave Miss Schrader standing behind the counter with the compass spread out in front of her and he'd just have to figure out another way to get out of the woods alive.

THE TRUANCY LETTER

When Christopher arrived home, with his compass from Schrader's in its blue paper bag, Evelyn met him at the top of the stairs, and she had a letter in her hand. Almost right away she was waving it up and down, saying "This says you haven't been going to school—for weeks!" Her voice grew shrill. "Where have you *been?* What have you been *doing* all this time?" She backed him into the living room, and he did not answer. "Well, what do you have to say?" He did not have anything to say, and he continued to back toward the bookcase at the far end of the room. "And Alfred called today and apologized for not remembering to thank me for the sandwiches that Doug has been bringing home. He says that they are delicious. *What is this all about?* You're *not* going to school and you're *not* eating lunch..." She was starting to ice over. Christopher's eyes were darting everywhere and settled on the Chinese horse-handler bowl resting on its shelf. He put the compass down on the small teak table with the cloisonné lamp, reached for the bowl, took it in his hands and cupped it there as she advanced and continued her strident questioning. Then he looked straight into her eyes and, after the briefest pause, let the bowl drop to the floor.

VIEWING ALFRED'S BODY

The morning after Christopher broke the bowl the phone rang before he was to leave for school. It was Doug, distraught, because Alfred had died in the night. Would Evelyn and Christopher be willing to come out and be with him for a little while? They drove together to the house on Taraval and Doug met them at the door and he'd been crying. "He's in there," he said, pointing to Alfred's room. Alfred was tucked in his bed—his face placid and strangely youthful. Evelyn was shaken and unsure, unsuspecting that she would be presented with Alfred's body and clearly swept into some far corner of herself on seeing it. "He looks...he looks so...," and Doug, collapsing in tears, stumbled toward her, and she embraced him. Not then, nor ever, did Christopher observe a hint of disappointment that Alfred had died first—that the house would now pass to Doug's nephew—nor of Evelyn's certain knowledge of how Alfred had been killed.

PUNAKAH

After a while, the door to the dark temple swung open, flooding the vast room with light. Dorji entered. Christopher was squinting and Dorji sat beside him on the floor. Neither spoke. The faint light of the butter lamps on the distant altar played on the walls and Christopher said to Dorji under his breath, "there's something huge painted on the ceiling." Looking up, Dorji pulled his flashlight from his pack and shined it across the outlines of a figure stretched out across mountain ranges. "It's the Buddha, reclining over the Land of Snows," he whispered. Christopher could see that there were lines with markings along the limbs and inside the figure. He quietly asked what they were. Dorji said that the lines were meridians and the markings were dzongs, temples, chorten, and holy places marked with prayer flags. They had been placed along paths cleared to correspond with the meridians. Christopher was astonished, and asked if Dorji meant that the lines were *actual* paths across the landscape and that the markings were actual places with *actual* structures. Dorji said "Yes," so Christopher asked "where are we now? Where is Punakah on this map?" Dorji ran the beam of light up along a line to a spot where another line converged. "We are here. This dot on this small peninsula, right here." "Show me where we've been. Show me where we're going." Dorji moved the light back and forth, whispering, "here is Thimphu and here is Paro. Up here, along this line, is the Tiger's Nest, and here is the road to Wangdiphodrang. We will be going here, to Tongsa, and then along this line to Bhumthang, then here, along this path, to Tarpoling, then back this way, to Thimphu."

THE END OF THE POISONING

On the drive home from seeing Alfred's body, looking out the window through the rain at Lake Merced, he knew that there would be no more talk of a trip to the country, and he knew that the poisoning would stop because now she knew that he was capable of *anything*, and he knew that to be capable of *anything* meant that you would *not* amount to *nothing* in the world.

PRETA

You have taken the starving outcast's semblance into you. This is how he has truly devoured you. And, if semblance is the necessity of your being, then you can shatter and still seem a single thing, seem whole, comport yourself as an entirety, and shattered you can speak whole words, take whole steps and press the broken pieces so tightly together that the lines the breaks have made will disappear.

THE DREAM OF THE BROKEN PHOTOGRAPH

The photograph that fell apart in the dream did not have to be real.

LETTER TO GOD

Trying to walk out of the numbness, trying to burn the wooden sheaths from his hands and heart in the velocity of going, trying to burn the plywood sheets away, trying to splinter through with his hammering steps, with his pounding feet on the pavement, trying to wake whatever lay beneath the ice-sheet, the tundra, whatever seeds lay strewn, ice-sheathed, silent, encased, forgotten, dormant, trying to hammer down, to waken, to feel something in his fingertips, to have some sensation return to the surface of his skin, to make a web of cracks in the sheet of ice, to make a web of cracks as a letter to God in the hard self-leveling ice, in the ordered ice, in the blank, in the hard self-leveling blank of day after day spread out like a sheet of ice, the blank self-leveling days, serene and blank, smooth, cold and dead, the finely wrought wooden sheaths on his hands and heart that he knew were there because he couldn't feel anything, because glass is wood is ice is rain is smoke is fog. You cannot just sit still, being numb, cold and self-leveling like the ice. You must walk out, you must, and walk and walk.

MEDITATION ON DROWNING

The fierce turning of running alongside your own drowning life. To have lived seeking personal safety, *drowning in that seeking, drowning in the rush of everything pulling apart, trying to paste it back together in the torrent, like trying to make a papier-mâché doll under rushing water—the frantically busy hands—drowning in that busyness, drowning in trying to establish yourself on solid footing, arrangement after arrangement, plan after plan, imagining a future where all your present problems will be solved, drowning in that imagining, marshaling everything and everyone at hand toward your desired outcome, pushing away that the present is never solved.* That this is the life you have—the life in the unsolved present—the life that you keep drowning in the future.

ICE CRACKED WITH A HAMMER

The hammer against the ice again and again to write to God in the calligraphy of cracks, and chips and rupture, the web of cracks—a letter to God in God's own handwriting that God cannot help but read and understand—that the web of cracks is a letter to God—even if there is no God, it is still a letter to God in God's own hand, in God's own script, in the hand of God, in the letters God uses, like strewn pine needles, ragged clouds and the ragged edges of coasts—even if there is no God, even if these are not really writing, it is still a letter to God in God's own hand, like the curl and collapse of waves.

ICE CRACKED WITH A HAMMER

Not prayers in your words, not prayers in the manners of entreaties, but a hammer striking the ice of a frozen lake; and the ice, so struck, cracking. These lines of fracture are prayers—but not requests—not asking that anything be fixed—they are themselves the entire prayer, the entire address, the hammer striking the ice, the spreading web of cracks, the thuds and flying chips and finally breaking through where nothing solid waits, where depth waits open and endless, or it will be endless if you enter it because you will never reach the end of it, the bottom of it, before you become its empty creature of ice, its flooded closet, its boat, its swamped boat. Not prayers in your words, not human ambitions uttered under the breath, not plans requiring hopes of intervention, but breaking, breakage, broken—shattering as the only prayer of this praying. Give nothing, forgive nothing, redeem not, receive these sounds, these flying shards, these dents and cracks and fractures in the self-solid surface—receive these blows as prayers, as portents, as speech.

MR. MARQUAND'S STUDIO

After returning home from viewing Alfred's body, Evelyn made a phone call and said that there was something that they must do. She packed Christopher into the car with the shards and dust of the bowl wrapped in their towel from the day before and took him to McAllester Street, and up the shabby narrow stairs to Mr. Marquand's porcelain studio—all crowded with cups, dishes, bowls, tubes of glue, paint and glazing powders—a total chaotic mess. In a corner there was a kind of working desk where Mr. Marquand sat bathed in artificial light from a gooseneck lamp. He wore a loose gray smock and a jeweler's loop and looked as if he had never seen the sun. He was slight and slightly feral, as if he were uncomfortable in the presence of people, but his eyes were clear and keen. His voice seemed as far away as if he were speaking to you from another room. "Can you do anything with this, Mr. Marquand?

Mrs. Buck so highly recommends you. Is there anything you can do?" "Oh, Mrs. Westall," he said from far away "there is always something to be done." Evelyn approached the desk as if it were an altar, and gently placed the towel in front of him. He opened it a little rudely and eyed the rubble therein. "We can improve on this considerably, though it cannot be as it was, I hope you know." "Oh, I only want it fixed for the memory of it, to have something that reminds me of what it was." Looking over the pieces as an archaeologist looks over an ancient shattered city, he said, "old, and very fine. What has become of you old friend, what trouble have you found yourself in this time?" "Oh...I was heartbroken," Evelyn said before stopping herself. "Well, there's beauty in a broken thing as well, a stubborn beauty. We'll see what we can do with our old friend." A scrap of paper served as a claim check, and he asked that she call him in a week. On the way to the car, among blowing papers, garbage, and people smoking in doorways, she reached for his hand. He took hers, squeezing it tightly, and they drew close and leaned into one another as they walked down the street.

THE ROAD TO TONGSA

The small bus rattled its way out of Punakah, backtracking through Wandiphodrang, then east on the lateral road toward the mountain town of Tongsa with its majestic dzong visible across the Tongsa River Valley from half an hour away.

TOUCHING THE PAST

One afternoon, sitting in his room, Christopher was holding a book—*The Dialogues of Plato*—that Dr. Thorn had inscribed to him. He was reading what Dr. Thorn had written when startlingly, his fingers sensed the minute traces of Dr. Thorn's inscription on the underside of the page. He shut his eyes to concentrate and slowly traced the ridges on the other side of the writing, and it was like touching the past.

TOUCHING THE PAST

He shut his eyes more tightly. This was the remnant, where the muscles of Dr. Thorn's hand had written his name but now not a name to the fingers, *only shapes pressed from the other side of the page, when he and Dr. Thorn stood maybe a foot apart.*

TOUCHING THE PAST

The other side of writing is the past—the other side of speaking, seeing, saying, dreaming—the pressed-through gestures of hands, voices, motions, are the past—the past stored in those shapes, just there under your fingers, there, closed in the covers of a book and discovered unexpectedly, maybe a year later, maybe a decade, maybe almost a lifetime later— found by your fingers where your eyes had noticed nothing, there, with vanishing pressing against you, there, at the vertical incursion of loss, where the words were nowhere, found on the verso of time—a trace, a remnant, on the underside-page called the past, that only the fingers running absently over it could read, and not a reading like reading words, but like reading the temperature of water on your face, or your bare feet reading the rungs of a ladder in the dark, that kind of reading, that kind of touching—intimate like that.

TOUCHING THE PAST

Nothing stood in the way of the actual other side of that moment, of that moment as it entered the past, like a moment of light across film, but not an image, and not what he wrote, not the words or what they meant, but the pressing down of his hand, not even noticed as it was done, but here, under the passing over of your fingers—shapes that are another kind of word—word of the vanished body, word of ash, word made thoughtlessly and preserved in a secondary station—to touch the past like this—here, your fingertips can linger and rest—no pictures, no thoughts, no story, not memory, but here—the past at hand—the way the present moment rests in the indentation left by the moment before—the way cupped hands hold water.

MONTGOMERY STREET

After his father's death, Christopher would go to work on Montgomery Street.

THE BOWL REPAIRED AND PUT BACK
ON ITS SHELF

Mr. Marquand repaired the bowl remarkably well. Evelyn put it back on its shelf in the living room.

AFTER ALFRED'S DEATH

Months after Alfred's death, Evelyn and Christopher went to visit Doug at the house on Taraval. It had become so much a part of Doug's routine to set Alfred's place at the table that he forgot to conceal this habit. Welling up with tears he said, "He's *actually here* and he talks to me and I answer." Evelyn reached for his hand and Christopher, starring bitterly at the empty place at the table, wondered if Alfred would tell how he'd been inadvertently poisoned by Evelyn's sandwiches. But then, Christopher knew that Alfred would never be so indiscreet.

TOUCHING THE PAST

The writing on the page, the indentations underneath—how the past and the present occur in a single motion.

ICE CRACKED WITH A HAMMER

Even if there is no God, even if there is only how ice organizes itself while being struck, it is still a letter to God, even if there is only the pattern of pine needles fallen on the forest floor, ordered like yourself, falling in crisscross heaps. Even if the thinned and torn-to-tatters edges of clouds are the only God, even if only volumes of water crashing on curved rocks—it is still a letter to God in God's own writing—things moving, torn, thrown, these flying fragments—these the ground you cannot see as ground, the ground where you stand, here where the hammer strikes.

AFTER THE BROKEN BOWL

Over time, the brittleness returned—the special egg carton, the "lucky mailbox" for important letters, the frozen garbage, the forks in their appropriate slots stacked perfectly.

PAPER-THIN TIN ORNAMENT

He felt like one of the paper-thin tin ornaments that Evelyn hung from the Christmas tree. He felt that thin and stamped-out. He spun in any breeze, even a breath, even a child's breath spun him around.

THE ROAD TO TONGSA

People laboring on bright green terraced plots, water trickling through moss on roadside cliffs—oxen, dogs, stone steps, paths, prayer flags, chorten, high peaks, lush forests, shop stalls, and shacks with chillies hung to dry from window boxes with flowers overflowing. No one threadbare, hungry, left out, scuttled, torn apart, and the pace of life was the pace of walking—there was time to give to each step, to touching things exactly, to the making of a robe, the painting of a mask, the lighting of a lamp, to the unhurried journey over a rocky path to a dzong. These marked time—these single stitches, these single brush-strokes, these single fires, these single steps, these turns of the prayer-wheel initiated by hand.

GOD OF SCATTERING

God of scattering, god of tearing, god of no purpose, god out of vanishing, semblance and shattering, uninvited god, empty handed god, god of no comfort, god of no reward—the thing that you think death is, this

god is. Who would take the god of this as their god? Who would swim
toward this empty god? You cannot know that this pitiless thorn-cradle
god is generous, that this god holds you up, that this pitiless god of thorns
is the god of the no-ground you stand on.

PATERNITY

Christopher walked to the Main Library on Larkin near the Civic
Center to the newspaper archive room, which was musty and un-
derused. The archivist looked like Mr. Marquand. Christopher
needed some help threading the microfiche through the big awk-
ward reader but then he was stunned at how fast the pages flew by
as he turned the little crank and the days and weeks made a whirring sound as they passed and after several attempts he landed on
the front page of the Chronicle for June 13, 1951. He found only
articles about cigarette tax boosts, an abortionist being convicted
of tax evasion, Hedy Lamar's fourth marriage and her retirement
to please her new husband, a Chesterfield ad boasting "No un-
pleasant aftertaste" and an article about how the winds from the
west were expected to be soft that day. He scrolled aimlessly backwards, page after page. A trio of confessed kidnappers was there,
and the bloodstained Lincoln sedan of a missing gambler with a
.38 cartridge found on the floorboard and an actor dropped from a
TV show because his name had appeared on a list of communists.

MOVING OUT

Early in the summer after his senior year at Washington, Christopher got a job waiting tables at a café in the Haight, and he rented
a room with a small bath and a hotplate in a shabby Victorian on
Carl Street, next to the N Judah tracks, just west of the Sunset
Tunnel. He shared the top floor with a man who had recently
returned from Viet Nam, had a scorpion tattoo, ground lenses for
a living and liked to speed off the tops of hills on his Harley. A
woman lived on the top floor as well. She wore only blue, worked

as a veterinarian's assistant, and seemed the type of person you could trust to make pie from scratch. Each of them kept to themselves.

THE TREASURE CYCLES

"By *appointed* time," the professor said, "we don't mean that the Terma pop into being as the clock strikes nine. Here we are speaking of spiritual time—a time for which the Terton makes ready, a time when the Terma is compelled into being by the imbalances of the world."

BLANK WALL

Christopher had the sense of being pressed against a blank wall, a wall he woke facing every morning. He was literally pressed up against this wall that said nothing, revealed nothing and was so close that he could not see its size or shape. It demanded something of him that he did not grasp, a demand as persistent as it was unintelligible. And there was no turning from it. And he wondered if anyone else woke facing this wall.

YOU CAN'T WALK THE SUN WITH YOUR FINGERS

A strikingly lovely young woman was sitting alone at a table in Christopher's section. He approached and ventured, "Do you still visit your family's painting at the Legion of Honor?" Glancing whimsically out the window she inquired, "Are you still thinking of faking your own death?" Christopher hesitated, looking down as she continued, "Maybe you could do what *most* people do— fake your own death by *getting a career*." He looked at her directly. "That stuff about faking my death was just something I told you to get your attention." Without responding, she reached into a large, loosely constructed purse, pulled out a tidal chart, and handed it to him. "How do you think they figure these things out?" she asked, "Does someone stand by the shore and draw lines in the sand and make entries in a notebook, or do you think it's all math?" Then, as if coming to her senses, and before Christopher had any opportunity to answer, "Oh, I'll have a cappuccino, three lumps of sugar on the side…what do you have that's chocolate…oh, never mind, I'll have a panna cotta." When Christopher returned, after placing the cappuccino on the table, having completely forgotten the panna cotta, and not looking at her at all, he said, handing back the opened tidal chart, "High tide's at 7:10 would you like to go with me and watch the ocean turn?" "That's an *Atlantic* chart," she sniffed, "it's from my trip to the Cape." Wrong-footed and embarrassed, Christopher tried to recover but she was already on to something else, fishing in her purse she asked distractedly "Can you explain exactly *how* the exception proves the rule?" and, before he could respond "where's my panna cotta?" Christopher, flustered, turned on his heels and headed for the kitchen, meanwhile, several of his other tables were beginning to feel ignored and a woman practically grabbed him by the sleeve as he rushed by "May we *please* order?" He heard this request as if through a delay-mechanism and paid no attention to it. By the time he returned with the panna cotta, the young woman had a sketchpad out and was drawing a portrait, in pencil, of the angry customer. "I think you've landed on her wrong side," she said mischievously as she dashed several violent strokes on the pad and, not looking up, "Well, no matter, the world is *full* of people like her." Christopher stood unhurriedly, looking at her "The world is *not* full of people like you," he said slowly, "beauty like yours is the exception, and it proves the mundane rule of everything else." She looked up, shaking her blond hair slightly, and for a moment became very calm. His eyes rested uninterruptedly on her face, on her eyes, blue-gray like the centers of waves, and, after a long while, she said, "You can't look at me that way without my having to kiss you."

SECRET ROOM

With barely an explanation to the manager, Christopher abandoned his post. Walking from the restaurant, she slipped her arm through his, "I'm Abigail," she said, then pointedly, "*never, ever, even once, call me Abby.*" "I'm Christopher Westall," he said, "where would you like to go?" "I want to take you to a secret place," she whispered. They walked to the lower Haight, up Fillmore Street, through an alley, and into a shabby apartment house. "My family owns this awful building," she said, "and the manger lets me use this little room." At the end of a glaringly lit hallway, next to a shared toilet and sink behind a half-opened frosted-glass door, was another, crudely padlocked door. Pulling a key from her purse, Abigail popped the lock, pushed open the door, which scraped the slightly bowed floor, flicked on the light and led him in. From nowhere, she said, "My *father* faked his own death." "He *did?*" "Yes, vanished without a trace—walked off in his pajamas one morning and was never heard from again." "You mean Jonathan Ruskin? You're *Jonathan Ruskin's* daughter?" "Yes, I suppose you've heard the story, everyone has." She scraped the door closed behind her and threw the inside bolt. The room was more like a very large closet than a bedroom. A narrow window overlooked a light well, and a blue silk lantern covered the single low-wattage bulb in the ceiling. A large, ratty daybed, taking up most of the room, was pushed against the wall under the window. It looked like it had come from the Salvation Army. Along the walls were several low shelves that could have been discarded from closed kindergartens. Even before his eyes adjusted fully to the dimness, Christopher was clearly taken aback by the location, size and condition of Abigail's *secret place*. Observing this, she blurted, "I don't *live* here." She sat on the edge of the daybed and explained that she could barely stand to be in the family house in Pacific Heights. "My mother drove my father away, had him declared dead, and expunged him piece by piece from the house. Even our favorite picture, *Rainy*

Season, was sent away. Never, *ever* ask to meet her, and never call or come by, because she'll get wind of it, and I simply couldn't *bear* it. She's strangling my trusts in her clenched little fists—I'm a beggar in my *own house*—she won't even buy me a *car* or *decent clothes,* she made me go to that disgusting public *Lowell!*" Christopher imagined she might have been pleased with Lowell if she'd seen Washington, but she was clearly indignant, so he didn't say so. He looked at her sympathetically and, as there was hardly room to stand, sat on the daybed beside her. "I smuggled my father's favorite things," she continued, "in my purse, one by one, to this room, and none was really valuable, so none was ever missed." "Where do you think your father *went?*" Christopher asked softly. Abigail pulled a scrapbook from under the bed, laid it on her lap, and leafed quickly through it—article after article about the disappearance. "I borrowed money, from a cousin, to hire private detectives, one after another, to no avail. Tell me, Christopher Westall, do you think a question that will never have an answer is still *actually* a question?" Christopher looked at her piercingly. "Yes, I do," he said. She put the scrapbook down and he looked anew at the contents of the cluttered shelves. Many of the things were unremarkable, but mixed among them, many fine things shone, many very fine things, things very valuable and rare. "I smuggled them out" she repeated, "just the things I could carry, his favorite things, gradually, one at a time." Christopher blinked, never had he seen such a strange profusion of objects—trashy bric-a-brac, folded teak plate stands, a sterling colonial inkwell, antique fountain pens, fine porcelain jars, gold boxes, an inexpensive watch, small, perfect bronzes, jewel-encrusted frames holding miniature portraits, and, lying on their sides, a few Moroccan bound books with gilt pages and titles in French.

SECRET ROOM

Christopher tentatively waded a little deeper, "Can't you just *talk* to your mother?" Abigail responded sharply, "I *suppose* you haven't *noticed* that *narcissism* is a *safe* that can only be *cracked* from *inside*." Christopher tried to suppress a smile, "Oh, and I suppose *you* could talk to *your* mother." "Not exactly," he said. Then, leaning forward, he playfully placed an ear near her heart while mimicking, in the air, the turning of a safe's combination dial. "You just *stop it*," she said, starting to laugh and kicking off her shoes. There was little heat in the room, and he drew her close. She guided his hand to her breast and kissed him on the mouth. She pulled him onto her, unbuttoning his shirt then pulling off her blouse. Soon, they had stripped completely.

SECRET ROOM

Of her naked body this: that he had never seen anything so beautiful.

ROOF OF ASH

He was almost desperate with desire for her. But then that *feeling came as she touched him—like numbness from holding ice. He could feel all the airways closing in the crowded room. He felt the numbness climbing up inside of him, and though he continued to touch her breasts and stroke the warm inner curves of her thighs, it was all becoming wooden and made up, and he couldn't feel any of it anymore, only the trying to make it seem like real touching and real feeling and real responses. Now she was only a distant, formal enactment of something he could not reach, and the more she reached for him and wanted him, the deeper the buffering became, and now he was falling through countless shatterings, through myriad glistening shards fanning him, and his penis was not a part of him—his hands were not parts of him—his thoughts were not his thoughts. He was all cut off.* Now she was growing cold, closing down, asking what was wrong with tears in her eyes. He rose to his feet that felt like they were wrapped in woolen layers, reached for his clothes, said some things that didn't make sentences and fled. It was cold and windy and he was naked and trying to put his clothes on as he hurried down the alley and his life was falling in like a roof of ash.

LIGHT'S OPPOSITE

Just under the present how everything was gone—something gone like that—on the underside of the fabric called light, how light rested in the hollow of its clearing, in the hollow it made, in the clearing, against an unfindable edge that could never rest, upheld in motion, as the past upholds the present as it flees.

LIGHT'S OPPOSITE

A perfect hiding: hiding where the hidden assumes the shape of the hiding place, like mercury folded in the curves of a silver pitcher, like the meaning of a word, hiding in the letters of an unknown language, like one side of a piece of fabric hidden just underneath, that can never touch its own other side, except if bent—if he could only find a corner, lift it and fold it over into light.

LIGHT'S OPPOSITE

And he knew that the opposite thing was a hand-in-hand thing with light, the way the indentations in the page were a hand-in-hand thing with words. He knew that light hid its opposite just underneath, on the opposite side, the way the pen, pressed downward in a moment of automatic movement, transmitted a double world.

LIGHT'S OPPOSITE

And he knew that he would never see the opposite thing for all the light, that even pitch-black hid it perfectly.

YOU CAN'T WALK THE SUN WITH YOUR FINGERS

The next afternoon, Abigail came to the restaurant and said that she wished he'd stayed with her—that they didn't have to hurry anything—that she already missed him.

LOCATING ABIGAIL

Christopher could never seem to *locate* Abigail. She always seemed to be somewhat somewhere else. Like trying to find the source of a voice in a large unfamiliar house—now closer—now closer—now suddenly farther away. And, there was something in her bearing, an immateriality, a breathless, assumptive, restlessness that put her, at least for Christopher, beyond reproach or question.

BRIDGE

"I *don't suppose* you play *bridge*," she inquired haughtily. "In fact, I do." "Well, my *bridge* friends and I play *practically* at the *tournament* level, of course we can't be *bothered* to compete, but we'll have to get together and try you out." Christopher agreed, but this, like so many other promised gatherings, never materialized. In fact, Christopher never met *any* of Abigail's seemingly countless friends.

SECRET ROOM

They met, irregularly, at the secret room and at his apartment in the Haight. She had the feet of a ballerina and the temperament of a harpsichord, and she possessed a certain willingness to be cold.

NIGHT-DRAWINGS

She left a pad and pencil by the bed. Sometimes, in the middle of the night, she'd sit up, turn on the bedside light, and start to draw. One time she said that when she couldn't be awakened by the muse, the muse donned a little scuba suit and dove into her dreams. Often, she slept fitfully.

LOCATING ABIGAIL

She said that she had to go sailing with friends. She said that her mother never left the house and managed to be indifferent and interfering both at once. She said that she would be at her grand-parent's house in Tiburon all weekend. She apologized that she couldn't bring a waiter to their home. She said she was going to a private opening, a party at the Clay Jones, the opera as an obliga-tion to her aunt. He felt like he was barely able to cling to the edge of her life, as if her life was a spinning disk and the centrifugal force was pushing him constantly out of her attention.

THE DOOR YOU HAVE OPENED

The door you have opened is not actually part of the room you will enter.

SEX

She said, "Whatever you have sexually, it will be enough." But it was not enough.

LIGHT'S OPPOSITE

He knew that there were no corners that you could see because seeing requires light, and he wondered—if he could walk his fingers along a seam to an edge and in an instant roll them underneath, could his fingers touch it?

STINSON BEACH

One morning, Christopher heard furious honking outside of his apartment window—Abigail, seated in a gorgeous eggshell con-vertible Mercedes with red leather seats, was gesturing wildly for him to come down. "My aunt's in Europe and her driver slipped me the keys. I don't really have a license, but you don't mind, do you?" Crossing the Golden Gate Bridge, at high speed, her eyes fixed on the road, Abigail asked, a little loudly above the hum, "Do you think that neurosis is when you lie to yourself so much that other people start to notice?" Christopher, who'd been looking through the blurred bridge railing down to the boats on the bay, turned and responded, "I think it's when your past is like a floor set on water and it won't right itself, so you're shifting your weight and contorting yourself in ways that only make sense to you because no one else can see how you're trying to balance yourself, how you're trying just to stand." On the other side of the Rainbow Tunnel, having slowed a bit, she continued "Like when your father walks out of the house one morning and never comes back, a past like that?" "Yes, like that, and you're trying to balance your life against that loss, or like when your father is in your house somewhere but you can't ever seem to find him." Abigail did not turn her eyes from the road. Neither said anything more.

STINSON BEACH

They swerved down the steep winding road to Stinson Beach. In the trunk she had a blanket and a basket of fruit, dark chocolate, soft cheese and French bread, along with a bottle of fine white Burgundy, two glasses and a corkscrew. They spread the blanket on the beach, took off their shoes, ate, drank, and fell asleep, side-by-side, in the sun.

TONGSA

Looking down the hill at all the houses lit in the dim light of late evening, each with its customs, altars, histories, tended outer gardens, patched roofs, and cluster of neighbors—looking down the hill at the houses settled on slopes against the night, against the weather, within the cycles of crops, of abundance, want, birth, death and uncertainty—looking down the hill at the containers of human struggle, the brightly ordered enclosures snug against the slope, boards, nails, windows, doors, and within them, the little laddered hierarchies of immediate concerns.

SEX

"Where do you go when we have sex?" Abigail asked. He would not answer.

TIME AND THE DEAD

Do you think that the past is all that the dead may have—that the past is theirs but they have no means to hold it? The dead have no means because aren't all means for holding found at edges, and all meanings, aren't all meanings housed in edges? Where are the edges of being dead? If you have no edges, you can't take hold. Is being dead like that?

THE MAN GROWING SMALLER
AS HE WALKS DOWN THE BEACH

One afternoon in October, when it was warm and clear, Christopher's father took him out to the Great Highway. They parked and walked along the beach, the Farallons visible on the horizon. Christopher paused to look at something in the sand and his father continued to walk and then Christopher just sat down and watched him grow smaller and smaller and never look back.

HELL OF SAND

And Christopher had a dream—*he dreamed that he was in the hell of sand and sand was clotting in his eyes and stuck to his hands and sand was blowing around him everywhere and coating his hair and people on their knees were stuffing sand into their starving mouths and not knowing why they were still starving.*

TIME AND THE DEAD

If you have an edge like identity, the past is always on the inside of that edge and the present is on the outside.

SLEEPING ALONE

Abigail shrieked, "I'm tired of sleeping *as if I'm alone!*" He had no response but only a sudden desperate futile urge to reach and grasp, like watching a gold coin fall through an open grate.

TONGSA

The night was rushing, carrying all of these in its current. They were falling, and in that falling everything holding them together was gradually peeling off. Looking down the hill, how the edges evaded capture in the night, how the falling was a falling away from boundaries, each household pressing itself against the flow, the wear and tear on the faces, on the fences and rain-clogged gutters, how all that pressing against falling, against drowning, all that pressing toward shore against the current, was itself a life or a life could be made of it, a life of not being swept away at any cost.

IN A CORNER CALLED FIERCE NIGHT

These found in the Wonder Ocean, in a corner called fierce night, fierce depth, fierce heat—these scattered on a field of ice, a field of salt, a field of fire. Know no person; possess no measure; stand on no structure, stride nothing, forged in brevity, brushed, grasped partially— brought out of smoke and ash, a procession like grasp over grasp as if you climbed a rope.

WONDER OCEAN

Next to second hands, next to sleet, next to gone in a gale—don't think for a second that these are not your own—next to all things tossed aside, next to things gone instantly, gone in a gasp, like the brevity of bees—if you could see the trajectories of birds, if you could go outside and upon turning see the shape of your life—awake at once—a brevity like that—just upon turning once.

SECRET ROOM

Christopher had the ability to notice space that was not accounted for, like the space that a secret makes inside a person, like a secret room in a house. He started to notice that there was an unaccounted-for-space in Abigail's life, which she was trying to hide, as if behind a bookcase or a mirror. But actually she hid it behind all kinds of explanations about absences, for hours and whole days, that could not really be explained. He didn't say anything. He just watched this other secret room grow larger. Finally, it occupied most of their relationship, and he knew that in this other secret room, she was sleeping with someone else.

COSMOS

In the darkness, as the bus inched along the rutted road toward the hotel in Jakar in the Bhumthang valley, a patch of cosmos bobbed in the steady breeze, not now pink-petaled, not now yellow-centered, only a motion like a single slate gray wave pressed against a field of amaranth.

JAKAR

The travelers settled into a hotel that should have been named the *Palace of Scorpions*.

COSMOS

Setting out for the path to Tarpoling in the morning chill, no one seeming yet to be fully awake, and the flowers now glistening with dew—riotous, brilliant, joyous, bent, blown, bountiful.

THE GOLDEN GOOSE

Christopher and Abigail were walking down Union Street when it occurred to him that his mother might be on duty at *The Golden*

Goose and that popping in would afford the two a chance to meet casually without exposing Abigail to the rigors of a more formal meeting at the house. Looking through the window, he saw Evelyn dusting a vase. "Come meet my mom," he said to Abigail. They entered, and Evelyn, initially delighted at seeing her son with his friend, became instantly cool with the introduction. She lightly took Abigail's hand and said with a squint of slight confusion, "*Libby* Ruskin's daughter?" Abigail nodded. Evelyn, in a voice like slicing ice, said, "My *dear*, how you've grown up, the transformation is...*remarkable*." Abigail merely smiled faintly at this and, freeing her hand, strode quickly past Evelyn, who continued, "We were all *so* delighted at your mother's return to her duties at the rummage sale, we were simply *lost* without her." Abigail stopped at a table and picked up a small platter. "I'd not have expected to find such an obvious reproduction in a store of this caliber," she quipped. Christopher could see that things were not going well. Evelyn pounced, "An obvious reproduction is acceptable, precisely because it's obvious, the little platter's a *fun* piece, priced accordingly, something for your mother's pool house in Atherton perhaps." Abigail turned the piece over and looked at the price. Evelyn continued, "It's the *clever* copies, the ones intended to deceive, that must not be tolerated, wouldn't you agree?" Abigail did not respond to this but put the platter down very gently. Evelyn turned and directed her attention to her son and, while they spoke, Abigail opened a glass-front display cabinet and deftly slipped a finely carved jade perfume bottle with a solid-gold-clasped stopper into her cavernous purse, leaving the cabinet door slightly ajar. "I must have something to eat, Christopher," she said suddenly, interrupting their conversation. As she breezed toward the door, she said to Evelyn, "I'm sorry you're not able to join us, Mrs. Westall." "Another time," Evelyn said calmly. Moments later, Christopher found himself hauled across the street and onto a bus heading toward Chinatown.

SILENCE

Evelyn, following Alfred's dictum to not attempt to spare a loved one from lessons they needed to learn, never said a word to Christopher about Abigail not being who she claimed to be.

ON THE BUS

Blocks went by in silence. Abigail, looking out the window, was visibly distracted and chilly. Christopher explained that his mother was not always sympathetic to wealthy people because of her enviousness. Abigail offered no olive branch, saying only that she had encountered such treatment before. In fact, she had contended with it all her life. She said ruefully, "My life is a month with five Mondays," and then she mumbled a string of phrases in French that sounded like curses. They rode in silence the rest of the way.

ABIGAIL BORED

It turned out that Abigail had little appetite by the time they reached the Far East Café. She said that she was bored and left Christopher sitting at the table before the food even arrived. Christopher knew that she had someone else to go to. Soon, somewhere in the city, on a street, in a doorway, on a stairway, in a room, they would be embracing.

CHASING ABIGAIL

He could not let her go like that and bolted from the restaurant catching up with her half a block away. Her face was cold and wooden, "I feel like I don't love you anymore," she said flatly. And it wasn't only that the first he'd learned of her loving him was her declaration that she didn't, but that he'd never had the experience of loving someone and then not loving them anymore, so he'd always thought of love as a weight-bearing wall and not just a place to hang pictures or put a door. *There was a spectacular and sponta-*

neous dislocation. He began to recoil, trying to pull all of himself away from her, all those parts of himself that he had rested in her arms, and now he was trying to take all of it back at once, and it was all raining down and smashing at his feet.

GENEVIEVE

Genevieve left Christopher standing speechless on the street, in the crush and clatter of tourists and Chinese shoppers. She walked briskly away like someone who was late for an appointment. But there was no appointment, it was more like when something needs to be done and there is nothing to do, like when something prized has been borrowed and broken and then returned and it can't be fixed and you want to break it more, and she channeled this wanting-to-break-something-more into haste because she couldn't decide even what had been handed-back-broken, and what were the edges that couldn't be connected anymore and she couldn't say, even to herself, what they were. Just as something transparent is never transparent to itself—can't see through its own transparency—in just this way she couldn't stand outside to see into herself, to see what part was broken, and this could not be fixed, like the handed-back broken thing could not be fixed, and she walked past her bus stop and down to Market Street and took a streetcar to the ocean and the ocean was white-maned and furious. She walked along the beach, picked up a broken shell and a small piece of driftwood and put them in her purse. Eventually, late in the evening, her hair soaked with salt, she circled back and arrived at the house on Anza. She entered and her mother asked how she was. She said in a slightly cheery singsong voice, "pas mal," and went into her room and closed the door.

GENEVIEVE'S ROOM

The shelves in her room were cluttered with sticks and rocks, shards of pottery, cheap secondhand books, fossils, feathers, bird bones and pieces of fruit so withered and dried as to be nearly mummified. She lay on her bed, folded her arms behind her head, looked at the planets she'd penciled, then carefully painted on her ceiling, and closed her eyes. Inside was like the motions of stars—solar flares—red giants—sapphires.

THE DREAM OF THE CYCLONE PAGES

She dreamed of papers flying in cyclones all around her—the slanting edges of pages glinting, cross-thatched, dancing, but not glinting like quarter moons or scythes or flying knives because there is neither wind in dreams nor is gravity the same, so things don't have to fall, and, like the crackling sounds of fire, the words lifted off and disjoined like persons in open water, and proper things she saw become partial things, and actual things she saw become sheaths of ice wrapping leaves and falling away and every message inscribed by chance, not more or less than sleet or shale or rain, so all the pages were written and thrown off like hurtling carriages, but no horses, no engines, no standing angles lines or lights, but like the painted ceiling of the world, peeling and falling.

REIMBURSING THE GOSSWORTHS

Evelyn insisted on reimbursing the Gossworths for the valuable perfume bottle that had disappeared on her watch. She did so by declining a week's pay.

EMPTY WALK

The following night, Abigail showed up at Christopher's door. She was cool and distracted, no, disoriented, not seeming to want to be with him, but neither would she leave. Her voice was not her voice, and her presence made him restless, so they took an empty walk past shops, cafés and darkened bars. He felt the past folding over into the present, so even as they walked it was all already over, already yesterday, already a year ago, already many years ago.

FINALLY

Finally, lying in bed, having barely touched one another, Christopher said that he knew she was seeing someone else and did she want to talk about it? She said "No." And still she wouldn't leave. Christopher rolled over, turning his back to her, and pretended to go to sleep.

GENEVIEVE

In the middle of the night, Genevieve sat up in bed while Christopher slept, and, reaching into her purse on the floor beside the bed, retrieved a brilliant, perfect lemon she had stolen, and began to eat it, tearing it into pieces there in bed, and she was sitting up and crying haltingly, a kind of cold crying, a kind of frozen fury kind of crying, sitting up, and she ate the entire lemon and left the peel on the covers, and then she left and she was never there again.

THE GENUINE

What is the genuine? Isn't the genuine always what's at risk, where you stepped into the open, unshielded? The genuine can never be put in the past because in the past, there is nothing to put at risk.

WESTY DIED

Westy died of a heart attack at the Stadium Club.

FATHER'S ASHES

Christopher promised Evelyn that he would go out on the boat and spread his father's ashes because she said that she simply couldn't.

DAYS OF THE WEEK

Christopher knew that it would never be possible to know what year it actually was, that the numbering of years and the naming of the days of the week, were only ways of making the passage of time seem familiar and navigable. Christopher knew that days did not come back, that it wasn't "Saturday again," *that the days were like breath, never the same one again. Naming the days was like naming a thing that you wanted to own and use, and the things you own and use become familiar, and anything made familiar stopped being visible, so the passage of days had become invisible, and it was their naming that transported them into vanishing.*

NYINGMA DIETIES

Nyingma deities can arise in many forms. They can even be persons. They aren't "gods" in the western sense of the word.

THE DEAD PIGEON

When he was eight years old, Christopher found a dead pigeon lying on the sidewalk in front of his house. It was surprisingly supple and delicate. At first, he handled it with care and a bit of awe. It didn't weigh as much as he thought it would, and he was holding it in his hands, *fingering through the feathers, when something began to erupt from far underneath, a savagery fresh and foreign as the first struck match. He dug his fingers in and tore at the bird, at its chest. He tore it open—the organs were blue, sticky and slick, and the downy feathers were sticking to his hands, and he pulled a length of string from his pocket, tied it around the bird's neck and began to swing the dead bird overhead in a rampaging heartlessness faster and faster and the insides were flying out and some children hurried over from across the street to watch and they were giggling and yelping and one of the younger boys threw up when entrails hit his cheek and this only increased the frenzy and it was like a bonfire raging in front of his mother's flat.* Then, in a sudden jolting panic, Christopher stopped short. What had he done? Now he had to hide this terrible thing. He took the bird in his hands, told the children to go away, cleaned up all the innards and stuffed it all deep in the big garbage can at the foot of the back stairs. He snuck upstairs and stripped and stuffed his clothes deep in the hamper and ran a bath and stayed in the water until the water was cold—until his mother knocked and asked through the bathroom door if there was something wrong.

SOMETHING BETTER

Westy died the September after Christopher barely graduated from Washington High. When Jack O'Neal called to check on Evelyn, he learned that Christopher was waiting tables and said, "We have to do better for him than that." Better for him than that turned out to be a government-bond-clerking job in the back-office of Pacific Bank.

FATHER'S ASHES

Christopher did not keep his promise to go out on the boat and spread Westy's ashes in the Pacific.

THE PATH TO TARPOLING

The footpath to Tarpoling was arduous, rising nearly vertically out of the Bumthang Valley into forests of spruce and fir, bristling with cones, clamorous birds and gray langur monkeys. Streams and waterfalls were tumbling from the summits with some of the rushing waters used to turn prayer-wheels placed in the torrents.

FATHER'S ASHES

Christopher rehearsed his fabricated responses many times, but Evelyn never asked him anything about the scattering of Westy's ashes.

MEDITATION ON DROWNING

Attending to your own drowning life that cannot be saved—attending to it in the very moment of its being swept, not turning toward wish, plan, hope, but staying alongside, running alongside, armless.

TEETH

The Poseidon Society returned Westy's gold and enamel dental bridges, wrapped in cotton, in a small stiff cardboard box with a sliding top and an accompanying letter. Evelyn refused to open the box and gave it to Christopher.

SECRET ROOM

He thought of leaving a note on the door of her secret room, but something blocked him.

THE DREAM OF THE SNOW-STACKED ROAD

And Christopher had a dream—*he dreamed he was driving on a narrow road up a steep mountain and walls of plowed snow stood on either side, and as he drove, the walls grew higher and higher, so high he could see nothing but the winding asphalt corridor between them. As he progressed, the walls drew closer and closer until they were nearly scraping the sides of the car, so there was no turning back and he mustn't stop because the snow could start again at any time and bury him.* How did he get on this road? He could not remember. Where had he wanted to go? He could not remember. And he couldn't remember ever having seen another car.

THE BASEMENT

After Westy's death, Evelyn couldn't bear to go into the basement.

TIME AND THE DEAD

If time does not exist for the dead then in what way does time exist?

SHEBEE

Christopher called Shebee every other week just to check on her.

BOX OF BUTTONS

A box of buttons thrown on the floor: no one can know what it means, what is sheltered in its shapes. Even if a button finds a coat and holds it closed, this does not conclude anything. Use is bent in the blur of constant motion, like chips of glass tumbled in a kaleidoscope. But it isn't chips of glass that are tumbling here—it is whole lives tossed across time, some rolling on their edges great distances from the others, some bunched together, some touching, some overlapping, some lost. None is an explanation. Even if one finds buttonholes enough to use them all, even if they are carried all over the city performing their tasks, this only answers how they spent their time.

TOUCHING THE PAST

The inscription on *The Dialogues of Plato* read:
> To Mr. W,
> E Unus Pluribum (from the one, many) Dr. T. 6/12/66

DISCOMFORT

And Christopher had asked Dr. Thorn why anyone would want to stand still in their own discomfort? Dr. Thorn had replied that if you can stand still in your own discomfort, then you will not make a life of trying to transfer it onto others, and he'd said that it wouldn't matter, if people didn't always find a way to make themselves uncomfortable.

THE CONTINUITY OF IDENTITY

If the past does not exist, in what way can identity be continuous?

THE ARCHITECTURE OF MEMORY

If every memory is made new, of what is it made that it always seems the same? You have no sense that memories are torn down as you turn from them, so aren't they always there to be summoned forward from where they rest? Aren't they really there? You *can* not-know that they do not wait somewhere.

WALKING

Walking past Equinox, after hours and empty, he thought of how, that early summer evening, he could have stepped into that room, but he didn't, he could have not lingered looking in, but he did, her back to him so he could not see her face, that very table, there, right there, now stripped, bare wood, chairs upended, like a moment full to bursting, folded over into vanishing, the palpable imposition of everything now absent, if only the moment could be unfastened and back-folded and made full, and now he would walk into that room and push past the people waiting to be seated, and stand in front of that table and gaze into her face and now he would know who she was and now he would be able to find her.

THE ARCHITECTURE OF MEMORY

You know that the past cannot be opened out. The past is that part of the present that seems to open out behind itself—not an opening out in the way that space opens out a street and holds the houses on either side but an opening out so the present arrives as continuous.

EQUINOX

If he ever found himself on that threshold again, pressed against that window, looking in, pressed against any surface holding him out, he vowed that he would plunge.

THE WOMAN WHO WALKED
INTO BEING AS BEAUTIFUL

One afternoon when they were having pie at Landry's, a woman walked in, strode really, and Dr. Thorn, astounded with delight remarked "Look how she is walking into being." "What do you mean?" "Well, just look. You don't see that very often. She is walking into being *as* beautiful, and see how plainly human that is, how effortless. We've all forgotten how effortless beauty is—then she walks in front of us, all of us, and reminds us."

THE WELL

In the well there is a clear, cold spring.

GRIEF

Grief keeps coming back with the same things in its hands—Grief comes back again, its hands full of the same things arranged differently—Again and again, grief only has a few things in its hands to show to you—With its few things arranged differently, grief seems always fresh—Grief comes back with its hands held out again—Again and again, grief holds the same few things—These few things grief comes back with over and over.

MEDITATION ON DROWNING

Swept in the assembled elements of drowning—reaching, grasping, trying to manufacture solid ground—he saw that he was not, had never been, these strivings—*that he was only drowning when he turned from the emptiness—when he turned his frantic hands toward somehow trying to fix it—how this had been his life—what a full-time job it had been to paper the emptiness over: every surface placed upon it eaten away almost at once—everything pasted upon it eaten away—and the frantic grabbing of the next element of papering to paste on the well-mouth of emptiness, and eaten away, and reaching for another over and over, second after second, minute after minute—and that this activity itself was the drowning of his life.*

MEDITATION ON DROWNING

To see that your swimming from emptiness is what is exhausting you, is why you are always tired, that this is what's spending you. In his meditation on drowning, he saw that he could enter the emptiness, could swim toward drowning, and that this was a kind of swimming with no arms, and that this kind of swimming did not fix drowning but opened it, so there was a kind of joy in this kind of swimming, a kind of gratitude, a kind of breathing, a kind of breathing under water, a way of being armless in the river, a way of attending to drowning instead of pushing it away, a way of being carried by groundlessness, of being cradled there.

THE TERMA IN THE LAKE

On the path to Tarpoling, Dorji and Sonam carried backpacks with water, bread, cheese, chilies and hardboiled eggs. The professor was lecturing on the great Nyingma saint and treasure-finder, Pema Lingpa, who was born in Bumthang in the mid-fifteenth century, founded many of the regions monasteries and who, in front of a multitude, entered Lake Mebar holding a lit butter lamp, went to the black lake-bottom and, after a long time emerged, with the lamp still lit, holding a treasure trove under his arm. During his long life he brought forth innumerable treasures from air, water, earth and mind, including images of Guru Rinpoche, manuscripts, chorten, and sacred objects. Still, he found only half of the treasures placed in his care to recover. The travelers stopped by a waterfall to eat. There was a hollow in the rocks behind the falls, and Christopher put his head through the rushing water, and he could breathe behind the torrent, and the water was pounding the back of his neck like a cold continuous hammer-blow, and he closed his eyes as tightly as he could and there wasn't anything else.

THE ARCHITECTURE OF MEMORY

What if memory is a replica of spaciousness, the way you open a house of cards from a small flat deck, the way you slant drawn lines toward a vanishing point to open out the surface of the paper, the way you speak in such a way that a world grows wide and deepens as if words could make a world—each thinnest surface balanced on the instant underneath, a house of cards like that, but not a house of cards made with your hands but an inside house, like the self is an inside house, like the self is mirrors standing face to face.

GRIEF

Grief has no hands—you know this. Grief keeps coming back with the same things in its hands—you know this. You know that the hands of grief are memory. Again and again, grief holds the same few things. Things so ordinary that you didn't used to notice them.

WESTY'S ESTATE

Westy left Evelyn a meager portfolio of bonds and stocks, a decent life insurance policy and the bank account he'd used for buying presents, paying personal bills, and buying cars. In his safe-deposit box at Crocker Bank, Christopher found only old cancelled car titles, loose papers and the documents incorporating his firm.

THE DREAM OF EVELYN
FOLDING ABIGAIL'S SHEETS

Christopher dreamed that he and Abigail and Evelyn were crowded together in Abigail's secret room. It was all very matter-of-fact. Evelyn was stripping Abigail's daybed, though the sheets had not been used. She and Abigail were chatting casually, as if he was not there, and Evelyn was folding the spotless sheets and putting them away.

THE TRIP TO KLAMATH FALLS

The next morning, a Saturday, Christopher slung a small pack over his shoulders, took the N Judah to Market Street, then walked south to the Greyhound station. After an hour's wait in a grimy row of bolted-together plastic seats, with his pack on his lap because he didn't want to put it on the floor, he boarded a bus that traveled to Oakland, then to Sacramento, then, turning North, to Red Bluff and Redding, past Mount Shasta, to Weed and finally, nine hours after departure, to the ratty little depot at Klamath Falls. Initially he'd been pleased to secure the last available window seat, but then, in Oakland, a huge and hugely intoxicated wind-burned vagrant boarded, sat beside him and began to talk in a slurry of words like slush sliding from a roof, and his breath was beefy and syrupy like liver and Romilar, and he wouldn't stop talking until, somewhere north of Redding, he fell asleep more or less on top of Christopher.

THE PATH TO TARPOLING

An elderly man, slender, nearly toothless, and delighted to meet the travelers along the way, carried a vertical basket on his back, half-filled with brilliant marigolds. Dorji said that he was returning from Tarpoling, walking from monastery to monastery, delivering flowers to the altars.

THE TRIP TO KLAMATH FALLS

Christopher found Shebee living in a small, rundown wood frame house behind a bungalow whose owner's face was puttylike and pocked from decades of alcoholism. Shebee did some chores for him in lieu of rent. There wasn't much food in the cupboard, the wood stove looked like something from the Gold Rush, and some wood had been cut by a neighbor and stacked in a shed. There was an old soft couch in the living room, and the bedroom was just large enough for her bed and a bedside table. The kitchen had a tiny electric stove. Shebee was cheerful as ever and uttered not a syllable of complaint.

TARPOLING

The travelers straggled along as the terrain leveled off and the trees on the knobby knolls became sparse. The rocky soil and uneven surface made travel slow and even the professor fell into silence. Late in the afternoon, Dorji called out, pointing to a vague cluster of buildings across a ravine and down a steep slope in the trees. About half an hour later, the group arrived at the gates of Tarpoling.

THE GHOST IN THE HALL

The evening of Christopher's arrival, when he was sitting on the couch drinking a cup of tea, Shebee exclaimed, seemingly out of nowhere, that she'd never forget the time he'd seen Elly's ghost in the hall when he was five, how his mother had seen it too and been so terrified that she was frozen in the doorway calling for him to come and how Elly had known that Evelyn was deeply afraid of dying and had always promised to come back and give her a sign if there was anything after death. Christopher tried to remember the face of the woman in the hall, the face of Elly on the camel and her face in his dream of the animal cup. He couldn't be sure that they were all the same. He tried to envision her with all the life subtracted out, motionless and lost, and he still could not be sure. But Shebee could not have been *more sure*. She dug around in a trunk and pulled out a packet of photographs, handing him one she had taken at his christening. He was in Elly's arms, her white hair was pulled back in a bun and she was wearing the dark dress with tiny white polka-dots. Shebee said that Elly was dead within a month.

FIERCE GUARDIAN

The fierce guardian is there, not only to keep you from the Terma, but also to summon you to it—to make a vehicle of your fear.

THE FALL

Late that night, sitting by the stove-fire in the backhouse in Klamath Falls, Christopher noticed how little Shebee seemed to have aged year after year. It wasn't only the steady warmth of her smile or the sameness of her voice, it was as if she had not been in the world in the same way as everyone else. She had been in the world in a way where she took little notice of herself, and time, in the same way, seemed to have overlooked her. Leaning forward, and looking directly at Shebee, he gathered himself with all the force of the history that they shared. "I have something to ask you and I *have* to know." "All right, what is it?" "What happened to my mother?" The smile dissipated at once and Shebee looked at him confusedly. "In the apartment on Sacramento Street, before my parents moved to the flat on Green, what happened to my mother?" Shebee's face turned sharply, almost involuntarily, as if she had been struck, and she looked at him askance then faced him fully, her eyes slightly squinted and burning, as if she was now having to reassess him entirely, having to look at him all over again. Then she drew a deep breath and said, "I was living on Pine Street. Late one morning the phone rang, and it was your mother. She was crying, crying a lot, saying she had fallen off the ladder in the kitchen and she mustn't bother Mister Westall at work, and could I help her? I asked if she was OK and she said she was bruised and banged up and I told her to sit down and hold on and it was going to be OK and I ran out the door and stopped at the Chinese Herbalist on my way to the bus and I was there in about half an hour. "What did she say when you arrived?" "Well, she was very upset and pale. She was shaking and she said 'Make me beautiful again.' I put the kettle on for nerve tea and drew her a bath and she bathed and drank the tea and I made a salve for her bruises and she calmed down and rested and I sat with her all afternoon. I got her to eat a little something and then I helped her get dressed. She put some powder and perfume and makeup on and the salve had helped with the bruises a bit and when it was almost time for your father to come home, she looked well enough and I slipped out. "Where was she bruised?" "On her forearms, and on her left cheek." Christopher looked unflinchingly into her eyes—"Is that everything?" Shebee looked at him as a person looks when handing something priceless away that they will never be able to take back. "While your mother was in the bath, I went to the kitchen and climbed the ladder and took a small platter from the top shelf of the cupboard and dropped it so it would hit the edge of the counter and it smashed and the pieces went everywhere." Christopher shook his head slowly, saying softly, "You didn't buy it." Shebee continued, "When I arrived at the apartment, I tried to come in through the back door like I always did, but this time it was locked." Then, reaching across and clasping his hands in hers, she said, "I *don't know for sure* what happened, and no one else does, at least no one *you can ask*." After squeezing his hands hard, she pulled back and placed a raised index finger firmly over her closed lips, and he knew that nothing more was going to be said and that nothing of this conversation was ever to be repeated.

THE PAST

What if the past is unevenly distributed across consciousness so that some people hold more of the past than others, like some indentations in stones are deeper and hold more rain? Maybe consciousness curves more deeply into some people than into others. Maybe consciousness is almost flat in some people and everything just runs off. Have you ever noticed how, for some people, everything just runs off? Maybe some other people are like places where all the waters converge in ever deepening pools. Have you ever noticed how some people seem to be nearly drowning in the past?

THE FALL

Lying awake on the shabby couch after Shebee had gone to bed, Christopher pictured Evelyn standing in a corner of the living room on Jackson Street, in her light yellow house smock, with her hair brushed back, and her back to him, thumbing through an antiques book. On hearing him enter, he pictured how she turned and smiled at seeing him. Now he knew the cost. Now, for the first time ever in his life, he saw how brave she was.

THE FALL

Awake into the night, Christopher knew that Lydia, keen as gleaners, had pieced it together somehow.

TARPOLING

The walled monastery was not large, but there was an imposing white stone turret facing the valley. The forests thickened quickly as the terrain fell off. About a dozen novices crowded the arriving travelers. They were little more than boys and hard to herd. Their beautiful scrubbed faces and cropped black hair shone against the brilliant red of their robes, and they were whispering and giggling and embarrassed and leaning on one another. An ancient, docile monk looked on, resigned and contented, like an elderly gardener who has given a part of the garden over to weeds. Dorji and Sonam spoke to him, while the professor, speaking haltingly, offered gifts. The travelers, all very tired, were admitted to the central courtyard and, dropping their backpacks by the pilgrim's guesthouse, were led to the temple for prayers of gratitude for a safe arrival and to receive a blessing from the presiding lama.

RETURN FROM KLAMATH FALLS

The horizon had gone pink and orange and red and then to slate before the returning bus pulled into Weed. He pictured Westy and

Evelyn over dinner, those many years ago—candles, white table-cloths and wine—the truth now told—how a secret was preferable to a scandal—how everything was pressing them to wall-off the unspeakable—his career, her social standing, their entire future. In the eyes of the world there would never be a question. All that would be required was to keep it from the child.

CARE

Care is empty and armless, running along the bank. Care is always empty, which is to say that it must be sheltered spaciously, which is to say that care is a fierce guardian, difficult to shelter, because you must drop so much to shelter it—the business of your busy hands must go, and your clingy eager need to make things right. Care is always armless, which is to say it holds the fiercest pain without condition, without the condition that anything can be fixed.

CARE

Nature herself cares in this empty way, in this way that does not show itself as care, in a care that is hard to hold, hard to shelter, because you want care to be otherwise, a kind of comfort, but care is sheltered in the fiercest evenness—hard to welcome.

CARE

And if you could care for yourself in this fierce empty way, what would it mean?

CHALK

The day after returning from Klamath Falls, Christopher went down to the drawing table in the basement and saw the chips of charcoal and the ends of pastels—their edges flat on one side where Westy had rubbed them hard against the paper and put them down in the chaotic geometry of things set aside thoughtlessly and you don't consider, ever, that the moment when you will never pick them up again has already come.

TARPOLING

The travelers were filing into the temple and doing their prostrations as they moved toward the opulent altar. Christopher lingered at the back of the line, glancing down an outside corridor between two buildings. On the back wall was a brilliantly colored, circular image. He moved away from the group and walked between the buildings, closer and closer. The image was a wondrously detailed topographical map with clouds above peaks, rivers, a lake, knolls and tiny clusters of prayer flags. Within the larger circle there were two smaller ones which appeared to be stone walls. Within one of them he thought he recognized the Tarpoling turret, and beneath it was a path leading down the mountain to the other circle which contained a few small buildings. As the travelers knelt before the altar in prayer, Christopher studied the painted map intently, memorizing its details, trying to imagine the scale and the distances—where the path was relative to the turret—where the second circle was relative to the path. The other travelers, amid tiers of flickering butter lamps, bright flowers, and the hushed tones of the professor, were now reverently examining blazing red statues of fierce guardians with boots on the throats of defeated demons, elaborate tankas with hundreds of saints and deities floating in seas of cloud or surrounded by fire, wall-paintings depicting the miracles of Pema Lingpa, and a huge gold-leafed Buddha sitting with stern tranquility on a podium above it all. Dorji noticed that Christopher was missing and discreetly left the temple to look for him. Several novices were standing at a distance from Christopher as he studied the map on the wall. Dorji came up behind him and Christopher, sensing his arrival said, pointing to the map, "Is *this* where we are right now?" Dorji confirmed with the oldest of the novices that this was a map of Tarpoling and the surrounding area.

Christopher asked, "What is this other circle, this other monastery?" Dorji translated that it was called Santamling but it wasn't there anymore because it had burned. "It *burned?*" Christopher asked urgently. Dorji, as if trying to placate him, said softly, "Such fires are not uncommon." Christopher turned with stony deliberation, marched back into the courtyard, located Dorji's backpack and rifled it for some hard-boiled eggs, bread, a bottle of water and a flashlight. He stuffed these quickly into his own pack and, flinging it over his shoulder, hurried past the novices, out the front gate and around the outer wall. His socks were filling with burs, but he found the path beneath the turret. He half ran, half slid down the steep slope. At one point, his feet came out from under him, and he landed hard, tearing the blister on his tailbone from the horseback ride to the Tiger's Nest that had only stopped bothering him a few days before. He hastily picked himself up, brushed his wet backside off, and continued down the mountain into the thick forest.

CHALK

Christopher stood for a long time in front of the large flat drawing table because he wanted to remember the bits and pieces of chalk where Westy had left them among the accumulations of brightly colored dust blown or shaken from drawings over years. He walked up the back stairs, through the kitchen and across the hall to his father's dressing room. Opening the sock drawer, he found a handkerchief that was ironed and folded. He took it down to the basement, scraped the dust and chips into it with a flat-edged knife and brought the sides up, making a sack, which he tied tight and put in the pocket of his coat.

CHALK

Most days the wind came sharply from the sea, but today the wind was calm. Most days the gray swift fog blew hard against your face and through your hair, but today was clear all the way to the Farallons. Most days the Great Highway looked desolate and bleak, but today the decrepit remnants of Playland didn't bother Christopher as he held the handkerchief tightly in his hand because he knew that the hammered-together world would fold away, and also the sky with all its transiting forms, and the earth beneath it also, and the stars.

CHALK

Taking off his shoes and socks and rolling up his jeans, he walked a little way into the cold sea and bending down unfurled the handkerchief with a single snap. The brightly colored dust and chips of chalk settled for an instant like a scarf on the water and then were gone.

CHALK

And he wondered if you got to start over, if all the clotted secrets, grief and longing liquefied and fell, even if starting over meant never finding a world again, even if starting over meant universes ceaselessly folding back on themselves, even if you were not aware of any of it, even if wheeling galaxies were nothing more than pinwheels on a porch, even if that was what starting over meant—streets, faces, flatteries, forgeries, vanities, hands holding hands, feet against the hardness of the earth—even if starting over meant none of these again—and he walked from the water and he turned from the sea.

WONDER OCEAN

And he had known that the Wonder Ocean was behind the messengers, behind other people's dreams, behind everything—but now he saw how it was wasn't exactly *behind* everything, but sheltered there, *in* everything, *the way beauty is sheltered in a face, the way beauty carries a person in that clinging-nettle life that the beau-*

tiful lead, the way the wind is sheltered in the air, the way the tide is sheltered in the sea—that these are not behind the things that shelter them—they are held whole, concealed in surfaces, borne forward, embodied. Here is your hand—it shelters grasping. Here is the world—it shelters the Wonder Ocean.

AFTER THE TRIP TO KLAMATH FALLS

After his return from Klamath Falls, Christopher began to send Shebee a little money every month.

TARPOLING

Dorji, nearly dumbstruck at Christopher's having fled, had to collect himself before returning to the temple, going through the prostrations and interrupting the professor to notify him of Christopher's abrupt departure. The professor was simmering. Dorji would have to follow Christopher and bring him back. Dorji came out of the temple into the courtyard, seized his backpack in mid-stride, and the novices, who had watched from atop the walls, pointed to where Christopher had gone. Dorji set out in pursuit.

CLABERT WYCROFT

Clayton Burton Wycroft, whom everyone called *Clabert*, was what the community of decent people would commonly call a feckless, vacillating, worthless drunk whose sloshy nature and intermittent acerbic wit created the overall impression of a swamp with a single snake.

CLABERT WYCROFT

Clabert was born to a wealthy banking family, one that prided itself on having numerous motivated children. Apparently, by his own report, he disappointed from the start when, essentially, he refused to leave his playpen for days at a time. His absolute lack of eagerness infused the rest of his life with a serious pointlessness that failed to amuse his siblings and his parents, though it did give them something with which to bolster themselves. His brothers, Warren and Marshall, managed family properties and investment portfolios. Several of his sisters, whose names he seldom uttered, married high profile lawyers, architects and social statuary. The family owned a string of community banks in California and his father, Warren Sr., secured a job at Pacific Bank for Clabert, where he sold securities to the banks his family owned and to banks owned by a few of his father's friends. He had little interest in any of this, but his family had so tightened the financial screws that he was left with little choice. His own marriage was routinely unhappy, as his wife joined the line of those whom Clabert disappointed with his unreconstructed intoxication and indifference. She'd thrown him out three weeks before Christopher arrived to work at his bond clerk job, so he was living in his Lincoln Continental among empty pizza boxes, paper napkins and crumpled magazines. A pole stretched across the back seat from which he hung clothes worn again and again, and he had a small TV he'd somehow rigged to work through the cigarette lighter.

CLABERT WYCROFT

Clabert's skin was not really a skin color. Sometimes it would seem almost opalescent when, blinking in the light, he'd arrive at the sales floor, having risen from the cot he'd hidden in the utility closet down the hall.

LITTLE WESTY

Christopher sat at a desk in the dingy clearing room among a group of older women, all of whom had known his father. He quickly learned to sort, match and clear the government bond trading tickets. The Pacific Bank bond traders, led by A. Craig Caples, and bitter teasers all, were expert at sniffing out and exploiting any weakness. They started calling Christopher "Little Westy," which they soon shortened to "LW," and that's what they insisted on calling him when he came to collect their tickets, and they wouldn't call him anything else, and he hated it unspeakably and he had to learn to live with it.

CLABERT WYCROFT

Confiding a secret in Clabert was like putting a cup of coffee on the roof of your car and driving off.

CLABERT AND CAPLES

The Director of Trading, whom everyone simply called *Caples*, felt toward Clabert the way lions feel toward hyenas, which is to say, murderous. Clabert would shamble up to the trading desk clutching orders, some days old, and be met with withering taunts and tossed paper wads which increased in exact proportion to his indifference to them.

LW

The bond salesmen also called Christopher LW, except for Clabert, who took a liking to the young, disoriented clerk, and spoke respectfully and never made fun of him. Christopher had the season tickets Westy had bought in advance at a discount, so sometimes after work Clabert would make room in the passenger seat of his car, and he and Christopher would go to the game at Candlestick because Clabert loved to drink beer and watch the Giants.

PROSTITUTES

It was shortly after he went to work at Pacific Bank that Christopher started visiting prostitutes in the Tenderloin. At first, he was terrified of what he would find and how it would be. Would he be attacked or arrested, contract a disease or get beaten up by some pimp, or ripped off in some scam? He didn't even know how to get started, so he just started walking down Ellis Street on the west side of Union Square. Before very long, a woman standing in a doorway spoke to him.

SHEBEE

One Saturday, several months after his trip to Klamath Falls, when Christopher spoke with Shebee, she thanked him profusely for the money. She told him that the first two months she'd given the money to a man who was going blind and sold papers and gum at a stand on a corner downtown, and the next two she'd given to a woman who'd moved from Walla Walla with two kids because her husband beat her, and the money from last month she'd used to buy toys for the child who lived across the street.

THE FIRST PROSTITUTE

The first prostitute was hard and impatient and Christopher could not perform at all. He had watched her backside as she climbed the hotel stairs, and had thought that he could make this work, that this was something he wanted, but she had more or less barked his choices—handjob, blowjob, lay, and what did he intend to spend, and it was extra for her to take off her top and it was extra if he wanted to touch her tits. Christopher had never known such loneliness. He gave her twenty dollars and pulled off his pants. She pulled a condom out of a drawer, and, after some mechanical repetitive jerking of his penis, saw that nothing was happening. "I can't do anything with *that*," she said. He didn't argue, put his pants back on, and left.

AFTER RENO

After the company trip to Reno, no one would call Christopher LW anymore.

SCHEPPLING

Frederick Scheppling, the market technician who occupied a cluttered corner of the trading room, expounded his theory of critical mass and parabolic motion to Christopher. He explained how markets reflect geophysical laws, like waves through water or like the seismicity of mines, how human intervention generates its own series of events that could be traced and charted and predicted. He claimed that a knowledge of initial conditions and the shape and duration of prevailing forces was all that was needed to predict the future prices of securities.

SCHEPPLING

Scheppling stood slightly hunched and alert, like a feeding mantis, amid his array of dusty books, seismic charts and tidal calendars. If you caught his eye, he began to speak to you and would not stop, so people in the trading room looked away as they approached, as if he were someone gathering signatures on the street.

SCHEPPLING

Scheppling, whom Clabert referred to as "Shempling," after one of The Three Stooges, spoke at an angle to everything, so if you asked him a question, initially his answer made no sense because he began with a series of qualifiers that framed the question without addressing it. Every morning he gave a speech to the trading floor encompassing his outlook. Most of the traders spoke on the phone, did crossword puzzles or chuckled as he held up posterboards with jagged lines and dotted lines projecting market patterns forward in time. Christopher stood at the back of the room, trying to figure out if Scheppling was ever right.

ARRIVING EMPTY

You must pass through an abyss to reach the Terma, and the abyss is fiercely guarded. You must toss aside as much as you can as you walk to face the guardian. You must arrive as empty as possible—without armor, with no weapon or shield, and on foot.

STANDING ON NOTHING

In practice, standing on nothing means showing yourself to others as one who is falling.

THE SEISMICITY OF MINES

Scheppling showed Christopher a book about earth tremors created by mining—a book with lots of fold-out charts showing the manmade waves of force as they moved through existing rock. Scheppling placed one of the charts next to a recent price chart of the ten year treasury note; they were virtually the same. He said that *correlations were plentiful because manmade forces move through natural structures in patterns and that prices of bonds were just the building and releasing of pressures moving to breaking points through buyers and sellers, so to predict the markets you simply had to understand the manner in which things shatter.*

SHEBEE

At the end of one of their Saturday phone conversations, Shebee said that the spirits had come to her window the night before from across the field and told her that her time to join them would soon be at hand. She'd told them that she was ready. Christopher was stunned and agitated and resistant, but she told him not to be upset—she'd had a wonderful life, filled with people to love and help, and she told him to never ever be sad for her. Then she said that she'd felt a bit chilled so she'd put her map in the woodstove so now the future was bright, warm and empty. Now she was going to bed because she was a little tired and she told him that she loved him.

SHEBEE

The Tuesday after the conversation about the spirits coming to her window, Shebee was dead.

THE DREAM OF COLD DAWN

Christopher had a dream—he dreamed that dawn was cold, that sunlight was ice—that everything was freezing as the sun came up.

PROSTITUTES

Gradually he learned to be comfortable and the prostitutes weren't asking anything of him but his money and they didn't care if he went away someplace while having sex with them because they were far away as well and what they were doing wasn't part of them either. He felt a consistent tenderness toward them even when they were indifferent or stoned, even when he felt their hatred of him. A few were actually sweet and careful with him, and he never hated any of them the following day and they made it all right for him to keep to himself the rest of the time. Nobody had to know, and he didn't have to pretend to himself about anything.

SCHEPPLING

Scheppling's decline was rapid after his termination. He ended up in the upside down diagonal world, the *you-don't-know-what-you're-talking-about* world, the world of people swinging in compass-arcs around you. He walked Montgomery Street, saying *wave*, saying *points along an oscillator's output*, saying *arc*, saying *rising water*, saying *plunge*—offering to make rich any passerby who paused.

THE DREAM OF COLD DAWN

Christopher dreamed again that the dawn was cold, that sunlight was ice, that everything was freezing as the sun came up.

SUICIDE

Evelyn's suicide plans recurred like the trips to Japan. But only once did she tell him the time and the method. She asked if he could have the courage to find her so she would know that she would not have to suffer the humiliation of being found by a stranger.

ROCK FACE

On a rock face every handhold matters. In the vertical world there isn't any bending down to pick things up when they fall; there isn't a horizon like you're used to because here, the horizon is above you, and the surface is pushing you off instead of holding you.

SINGLE THINGS

Some things are not single things; some things are like stacking where weight accumulates.

TIME AND THE DEAD

So if you try to put nothing at risk in your life, are you trying to be dead?

THE PATH TO SANTAMLING

Eventually, Dorji caught up with Christopher but could not persuade him to turn back and rejoin the group. Christopher *did* promise to return after they were finished at Santamling. Dorji had little choice but to agree.

TIME AND THE DEAD

Christopher had seen that Evelyn had been trying to be dead for a very long time.

GLASS

Now, striding down the mountain through splintered light, he saw that brokenness was the only place where glass was safe—how his broken-to-ashes mother was safe in the sea.

TIME AND THE DEAD

And he promised himself that he would never try to be dead again.

EVELYN SLEPT

After Westy's death, Evelyn slept in Christopher's old room toward the front of the house.

DAYS AND NIGHTS

There was a small, clean, all-night coffee shop off of Eddy where the Tenderloin prostitutes congregated during their off-hours. Christopher would go there for coffee. For many months, even those women he'd been with failed to recognize him, looked through him, past him, but after the first year or so, some would nod, some would say a word or two, and a few would even sit with him now and then and make small talk the way any two people, slightly familiar with each other, would converse about sports or the weather or how nothing would ever get better at City Hall— all things out of reach—all things beyond blame—all things peripheral and passing.

DAYS AND WEEKS

Several years *did* pass. In a time of forgetting, in a time of empty saying, in a time of cosmetic face and rotating adornments, Christopher shouldered through weeks, through months, through streets, in and out of rooms, routines, transactions and lucid dreams.

MEDITATION ON DROWNING

And he saw that what had pressed in to drown him was that which was most his own, that that which he had pushed away was that which had most insistently called to him—fierce guardian, fierce weapons clutched in clawed hands, guardian at the doorway of drowning—a drowning in opening everything to risk, a fierce sheltering, a sheltering he had swum from all his life.

PROTECTION THREADS

Without explanation, Christopher borrowed Dorji's pocket knife and cut the red threads from his throat.

THE PATH TO SANTAMLING

They continued down the mountain toward Santamling, neither with any firm idea of how far it was. They hiked steadily for a long time, and a three-quarter moon was rising over the valley which still lay far below. The light had softened markedly. They stopped to drink some water and Christopher ate an egg. Dorji ate nothing. Neither had noticed any significant tributary running off the main path and they wondered if they had missed Santamling altogether but continued down the mountain in silence. Christopher's lower back began to spasm from where he'd wrenched it falling down but he did not complain and after another long while, with the pair steadily descending and the light rapidly fading, Christopher tripped over a root and involuntarily cried out and quite a distance in front and to the left of them, through the trees, a dog began to bark.

THE COMPANY TRIP TO RENO

After an extended period of low volume and unmet sales quotas, Christopher noticed that the volume of tickets and subsequent trade confirmations was increasing dramatically, exponentially it seemed. His desk was flooded with trades to match and process and he had to look at them more rapidly and they were becoming nearly continuous, like the slow-motion frames of a movie, and he was falling behind.

WONDER OCEAN

One morning at the bank, while washing his hands in the men's room sink, *he sensed a separating-out from himself, and the ordinary water turned into light where his hands had been, glowed as if laden with phosphorous, as if the fabric of the world had torn and behind it was a field of light holding everything up and seeping into everything from behind—but now it was opened directly—nothing mediating—and all the trade and commerce and margins and profits and balance sheets and cashflows and debits and credits and timelines and settlement dates were embodiments of its underlying order, and people who thought that they were merely going to work to do some job to feed themselves and have a little place in the social order were really refractions of the choreographic web-work of the sacred—he stood there stunned, holding the glistening water in his hands.*

SANTAMLING

Christopher and Dorji moved forward with renewed vigor, finding a small trail to the left, which they followed in the direction of the barking dog. When the trail soon petered out, they struggled through thickets, vines, clumps of trees and low branches and, after wedging between trunks and boulders, they came to a shallow ravine across which the dog, large and black, stood issuing a guttural growl accompanied by bristling hackles and bared teeth. The

animal began to move steadily toward them with increasing feroc-
ity. At first Dorji froze, but then continued as Christopher moved
forward into the ravine. Then, a voice from behind the dog, nearly
as wild as the animal itself, called out in choppy reproachful barks
and a disheveled man of sturdy build appeared in faded monk's
robes. Dorji leaned close "Another incarnation of Drukpa Kun..."
"I *know* who he is," Christopher whispered brusquely. The dog
barked several more times and the monk waved his hand as if to
hit him. The dog yelped and sat.

THE COMPANY TRIP TO RENO

The avalanche of tickets was testimony to both the volatility of
the market and the success of the sales incentive, and the CEO
announced to the entire floor that the goals had been exceeded
and that all employees and their spouses would go, by chartered
bus, for an all-expenses-paid weekend at the Nugget Casino in
Nevada.

THE COMPANY TRIP TO RENO

The bus was filled with fumes, people playing cards, and a constant
din of laughter and loud talk. Christopher looked out the window
as the valley floor gave way to the Sierra Nevada Mountains and
Donner Pass. On the other side of the Nevada border, almost at
once, the trees stopped and were replaced by blond sandy ground
with stubby rabbit bush and sage. The buildings became immediately more tacky; signs advertising shows sprouted up and neon
arrows pointed to cigarette stores, slot machine parlors and buffet
specials. On the other side of Reno, in Sparks, the Nugget's single
sand-colored tower stood above its thickly carpeted, gold-braided
slot-clanging lobby with its VIP Welcome Desk and framed photographs of local students who'd been provided scholarships from
the casino's winnings.

THE COMPANY TRIP TO RENO

Several top executives, traders and salesmen, saying they had business to attend to, did not take the bus to Reno but arrived with their wives in their Cadillacs and Mercedes in the late afternoon. Christopher was wandering through the lobby when Caples, rouge-faced and loud, arrived with his wife, Blythe, a worn beauty wrapped in white furs. Caples didn't acknowledge Christopher at all, treated the bellhops badly and was condescending to the check-in staff, insisting that his room be upgraded at no charge because he was a player, and demanding to see the manager. Blythe sat quietly on a lobby couch, like someone in a car waiting for a long freight train to pass.

DEAD AND ALIVE

Standing in the casino, looking at the faces of the people at the tables, the automatic, neutral joylessness, the mechanical responses to the cards, he saw that gambling was a way of being dead and alive at the same time—the first self burned away, the empty self exposed, the dealer sending cards like striking matches—the whole place built on this.

COMPANY TRIP TO RENO

To no one's surprise, Clabert missed the bus and showed up in his car six hours late, having stopped in a bar in Truckee and fallen asleep there.

SANTAMLING

In near darkness, Christopher and Dorji stood in the overgrown courtyard of Santamling with the lone monk eyeing them skeptically and the dog now lying in the shadow of a wall so that only his opened eyes were plainly visible. Dorji was digging in his pack to find some sort of offering, while the monk, whose weathered face and tangled hair made his age hard to guess, seemed a little impatient to see what Dorji would bring forth. Christopher suddenly stepped in front of Dorji, pulled the flashlight from his pack, turned it on and off and on again, then presented it to the monk, who looked at it with wonderment as he shined it around the courtyard, across charred timbers lying in heaps, crumbled blackened walls, and fallen-in roofs. It looked like the temple of wreckage, the temple of ash, the temple of the destroyed. There was a single two-story building left standing and it sagged as if structurally compromised. With little ceremony, a few minutes later, Christopher and Dorji were seated in a room on the second floor being offered tea.

BLYTHE

Later, while Caples whooped it up with some traders at the craps tables, Christopher saw Blythe sitting silently with another wife in the window of the Gold Dust Lounge, and she looked like a cardboard display-cake in the window of a bakery in North Beach— sun-bleached, brittle at the edges, iced—yet the beauty she had been was not so entirely lost as to be spared the bitter counterpoint of what she had become.

SANTAMLING

The moon shone through the glassless window frames. Butter lamps burned in the corners. The flashlight was on in the monk's lap as he sat cross-legged behind a low, simple, wooden table and poured tea from a metal pot heated over some embers in a shallow fireplace at the back of the room, opposite a small altar with a modest wooden Buddha, a little smoldering incense, and a few dried flowers. Dorji and the monk spoke in measured tones between sips of tea, and the monk asked what they were doing here. Dorji said they were on a pilgrimage to seek blessings and merit. Christopher interrupted, asked what they were saying, and then said, "tell him I am here as a matter of destiny." The monk shined the flashlight in Christopher's face, then fumblingly turned it off and said that they would pray. He led them to the altar where they lay flat on the floor in front of the chipped-paint Buddha. Then they sat on their heels and the monk chanted prayers. Christopher was stiff, his legs were full of pain, and his tailbone ached. *The monk rocked gently back and forth, chanting for what seemed at least an hour. Moonlight washed the room, moving steadily across the floor—was there a floor—were they actually here? Stars were now glistening above the trees. Was this the pivot-point of the entire wheeling world? The sounds of the prayers were cracking open like lit wood, and Christopher was thankful and tired and calm.* The monk rose and spoke softly to Dorji who said to Christopher, "he is going to show us the Terma that were saved from the fire."

COMPANY TRIP TO RENO

Standing in the lobby as Christopher happened through, several shiny red-faced boisterous traders, led by Caples and elbowing one another drunkenly, pushily offered to take Christopher to a whorehouse. "Come on LW, what you need is to get laid," one chuckled and another whispered audibly, "you can't drive a spike with a tack hammer," and they all burst into laugher. This was exactly what they did in every situation. This was the way that he was naked to them, and he emphatically refused to go, because he knew what it was to *be naked like the furniture-women were naked, the made-of-wood women, the upholstery women, numb, consigned, available, in the cold—how he was naked at everyone's whim like that, at the whim of these asshole traders, and strangers on the street, and just a glance or a word and he was naked, naked in the way the ignored are naked, that the mocked are naked, that the spoken of in whispers are naked, that the shunted aside are naked, that those standing outside are naked, available for handling and private use, for use by anyone, being pulled up and sat on like a roller-chair, like the always-available-to-anyone are always naked—naked like that.* These men, these cocky, drunken, aware-of-nothing men were never naked like that, were never in the cold like that, were pressing their purposes, were stationed to press their purposes at will—mule-masters, handlers, talkers, spinners-of-worlds, deal-makers, switch-masters, dead-makers, kings. He would never be party to their Roman Empire coldness. He would never give them a hint of who he really was, never an inkling, never an inch, and he said that he could never do anything like that and he walked away.

PYRAMID LAKE

After the encounter with Caples and the traders about the brothel, Christopher went looking for Clabert. The door to Clabert's room—key still in the lock—stood slightly ajar, and Christopher found him inside, fully clothed and asleep in a chair, bent down as if about to untie his shoes. His car keys were on the lamp table next to him with the valet parking ticket. Christopher took them, went to the lobby and claimed the car. It smelled like pet shop and pizza and he had to shove a nest of crushed wrappers and wadded shirts aside just to sit in the driver's seat. With no destination in mind he drove north on Pyramid Way to an empty two-lane state road, and into the deep desert night. He was amazed at how quickly there was nothing on either side of him, at how cold and clear things were, and he rolled his window down and put the heat on and he had never known the piercing scent of sage or a night-horizon devoid of lights, except when he'd looked out to sea, and the stars seemed sharp as pinholes punched in backlit carbon paper. After a while, he arrived at Pyramid Lake on the Paiute Reservation. He parked on a rise above the lake's west bank, and fell asleep. He woke as dawn broke across the silver-turquoise sheet of water, lighting the blond bare hills behind him.

MEDITATION ON DROWNING

When he entered this emptiness, having spent so much of his life push-ing it away, what did he find? He found that this emptiness was warm, that he was sustained without effort. He found, to his astonishment, that the emptiness at the center of everything was generous—that this emptiness, this which he had feared, was that which was most his own.

SANTAMLING

The monk opened a small wooden casket beneath the altar and lifted a linen bundle. The three returned to their positions at the low table, which Dorji cleared of the kettle and teacups. The monk unfolded the cloth, which contained a number of objects, each wrapped in silk. In succession he displayed a muted gold statue, about the size of a thumb, a piece of a yellow scroll with writing in black ink, and a sacred dagger with a fierce face on the handle. In each case, the monk recited which Terton had retrieved the treasure, when, and from where. Christopher expressed his grati-tude and then asked, through Dorji, how long ago the fire had been. The monk seemed almost unable to grasp the question, then muttered a response, "some years ago, how many, he can't be sure," Dorji said.

BLACKJACK

On his return from Pyramid Lake, Christopher wandered through the casino. Caples and the traders had stumbled in after their big night at the brothel and their all-night poker game. They hadn't slept and were now settled in drinking coffee and playing blackjack.

SANTAMLING

The monk unwrapped a slightly warped, graying piece of reflec-tive glass, about an inch wide at the base and tapering for sev-eral inches to a knifepoint. He placed the black cloth, on which it rested, in front of Christopher and spoke to Dorji ,who said very softly, "a shard of the future-seeing mirror of Pema Lingpa, a sublime treasure." Christopher tried to find his reflection in the shard, moving his face back and forth, closer and closer—was it even *actually* a mirror—*shadow-nest, blank-lake, face of fracturing, cleaving and tear-down, shred-dark, shatter-ice, lichen-light, climb-steps—and was he falling asleep—deliriums of grasping and make-sense—foreground buckled, background sheer, blinded, burst, un-coupled, all adhesiveness checked, doused, undone*—Christopher was jarred by Dorji's voice. "And this—this is the last treasure saved from the fire, at least the last that they still have." Christopher saw that the mirror-shard had been removed and replaced by a small, intricate, black metal scepter. "He says it is thunderbolt metal and confers great merit to look upon." Christopher studied the scepter for a long time, not wanting to seem impatient to ask what he urgently wanted to know. "What does he mean—*the last that they still have?*" Dorji responded after listening to the monk. "He says an out-of-sequence Terma was brought from the fire but had to be re-concealed." "Who brought it out?" "He says it was a fierce guardian, in flames, who emerged from the building and carried the treasure away." "Where did he take it? Where was it re-con-cealed?" Dorji reluctantly asked the monk in a halting, tentative voice. "He says, of course, he does not know." "Ask him: *if a pyre can be turned into a lake, can a lake be turned into a burning house?*" Dorji, exhausted and incredulous shook his head, not wanting to continue. He thought of Namita—how she had warned him—now he sat in a ruin, translating gibberish. "*Ask* him," Christopher demanded, and Dorji did. Drukpa Kunley said nothing, but rose and, looking directly at Christopher, *began to move fluidly around the room, his arms stroking the air as if he were swimming, and then he was running in circles, making gestures as if scattering seed, but clearly these were flames flying from him, and he was escaping something, a flood, a fire, and he was looking with feigned terror over his shoulder and now he was clawing the air, like a man trying to climb a steep bank to escape rising water when, as if changed in an instant, he paused, and turned, his face grown tranquil, and dove into the torrent, the flames, swimming deeper and deeper until he settled on the floor, like a river-bottom.* The monk folded his legs, held the palms of his hands toward Dorji and Christopher, and the three sat in absolute silence.

SANTAMLING

The Terma were gathered, wrapped tightly, and returned to their casket. A few more prayers were uttered in low tones, then Dorji excused himself to go outside. On his return, Christopher borrowed the flashlight and did the same. The dog, lying in the courtyard by the door, barely stirred on seeing them. The three shared some thin soup, bread, and the remaining eggs. Then, the monk pulled blankets from a shelf, unrolled some mats in front of the fire and offered a place for the night. They would sleep in their clothes.

FORMS OF FLEEING

Christopher lay awake on the hard floor at Santamling. Low clouds now blocked the stars. *Had anything ever really happened in his life? Had anything, other than fleeing, ever happened? Fleeing from pain and into pain—from shelter and into shelter—from solitude and into solitude—from the past and into the past—forms of fleeing, everywhere he looked.*

FLIGHT'S ENGINE

What had he fled—what stood at the roiling center of his flight—not the forms of fleeing but the engine—the source of flight—what was it—what did the present hold that was unbearable?

BLACKJACK

Christopher stood at a distance and watched the drowsy, hungover traders play blackjack, hand after hand. After quite a while, he approached and stood behind Caples, who was dejectedly reviewing the prospects of his hand. "I don't know what to do with this shit," he said. "Hit," Christopher said softly. Caples, startled, turned around defiantly. "Oh, it's *you*. Hey guys, it's LW telling me to hit. OK—hit." The dealer tossed the card face up and Caples had 21. Then, hand after hand, Christopher told him what to do, and he continued to win and win and win.

BLACKJACK

It wasn't that Christopher knew what card was coming up next; it was more as if there was a current running hot and cold through the air that connected to him—hit or stand was simply automatic, effortless. He stood in this humming-surround where there was nothing to decide—it was clear, in a warm and cold way, what would happen next. It was the absolute opposite of calculation or thought—there was nothing to it at all.

READING THE CONFIRMATIONS

Christopher returned on the company bus from Reno because Clabert could not be found and he went to work very early the following morning. The guard in the lobby let him into the building. He took the stairs and he sat on the floor of the clearing room with the hundreds of trade confirmations needing to be paired-off spread out like a vast patchwork quilt in front of him. He moved them here and there, side-by-side, this one next to that. Something began to *coalesce like a cumulative message—the patterns of buying and selling, profit and loss, right and wrong decisions—and he saw the markets moving in and out, like tides over days, waves breaking over rocks, filling and emptying pools. It was all there in front of him—ambient, apparent, obvious, clear—how each brief, culminating energy, would roll, break, reach and then withdraw—how each motion followed within the whole, and he could tell which positions the trading desk still held and he could see the market withdrawing its strength from them.* Shortly before the market was to open, he brushed himself off, went upstairs to the trading floor and standing in front of Caples said "you should not own all those bonds right now." Caples seemed incredulous in front of the other traders, but because of the blackjack incident, he sold a little after Christopher left. Within an hour the market began to plunge.

DRINKS WITH CAPLES

That afternoon the phone rang on Christopher's desk. It was Caples asking him if he'd like to go out for a drink after work. They went to an out-of-the way bar on Front Street and spoke amid the background noise of dice-cups hitting the bar and a radio broadcasting an afternoon Giants game, just the two of them. It was all in the shadow of the brothel teasing, the subsequent blackjack run, and now the market prediction, so Caples had some repositioning to do and, somewhat surprisingly, even to himself, Christopher was happy to make this easy and act like nothing had ever happened.

THE DREAM OF THE ANGRY DOLL

And Christopher had a dream—he dreamed that he had been carrying a little doll on his hip and it was an angry doll and at some point he wanted to put it down but when he tried to pull it away from his side he found that it was fastened there and he opened his shirt and saw that the doll had knitted itself through his shirt to his skin and when he tugged the doll his skin pulled with it and it didn't hurt but he saw that he couldn't remove the doll without cutting away the patch of skin to which it had knitted itself.

MEDITATION ON DROWNING

That which was most his own was that part of his life that made everything else impossible—that you cannot go on living your cobbled-together pastime of a life in the face of it.

SANTAMLING

Christopher woke in the dark. He could not be sure how long he'd been asleep. He rose quietly, not wanting to wake either Dorji or the monk, and grabbed his backpack, his coat, and the flashlight, which the monk had placed by the door. In stocking feet he went down the narrow stairs, found his shoes, put them on, entered the courtyard, and turned the flashlight on. The dog, instantly awake by the doorway, stood, scratched, shook himself, then followed Christopher through the trees. Christopher slid down the ravine and, even finding footholds hard to come by, climbed up the other side. *And he saw that fire was a single thing, the canceler of multiplicity, the maker of one from many, the maker of ash from multitudes. And he saw that single things were always hard and unforgiving because how can a single thing be otherwise in a world of multiples?* He looked back briefly, futilely tried to shoo the dog away, then moved forward quickly, *and he knew that the fire at Santamling, and second Thorn fire, were the same fire—and where would you hide a Terma if you were on fire—of course, in water—the maker of multitudes—the maker of many from one.* Striding urgently, he tripped over a vine and slammed into a tree trunk. He didn't pause, finding the fallen flashlight in the leaves and pushing through branches and underbrush. He found the main trail and proceeded down the mountain. The dog was close behind.

CONFIRMATIONS

After the markets closed, for many afternoons, Christopher could be found in the back office conference room with the day's trade confirmations spread out on the long rectangular table, on the chairs and on the floor. He was examining the time-stamps, the amounts bought and sold, and the coupons and maturities of the bonds involved in the trades. After numerous additional accurate market predictions and a trip, *this time* to Caple's *favorite* bar,

Christopher's days of clerking were over and he was promoted to Assistant Trader, provided an immediate bonus, and given the seat next to Caples on the trading desk. Now he was able to see the flow of tickets as they were written and to talk to traders at other firms about order flow. His predictions became even more precise and accurate.

RECKONING

Clabert leaned against the glossy bar and, twirling the ice in his bourbon said, "I'd rather have my eyelids removed than be sidled up to that creature all day long." Christopher said not a word in Caples' defense, nor in his own. "It's just not *like you*," Clabert continued. "*I'm not like me*," Christopher replied curtly, then, as if to compensate, leaned deliberately forward and, whispering, disclosed a plan.

THE DREAM OF THE DEAD AT THEIR DESKS

Christopher dreamed he was back at the office after many years of being away and being shown around by the man who had taken his place. Everyone at their desks was dead. The silence struck him first. In the dream he was unable to say that they were dead, so he walked through without comment, without question, the way things in dreams present themselves as beyond question. Everyone was dead in their suits, heads bowed as if reading papers, or looking across the room at offerings on the board—everything as if nothing remarkable was happening, the way things in dreams present themselves as unremarkable.

MEDITATION ON DROWNING

Not the flailing drowning of the thrown overboard, not the drowning of those who stretch their frantic hands toward land, not the drowning of the damned in the flood from heaven, not the drowning by accident of a child in a rapid river, but the drowning that one moves toward steadily, without negligence, without self-indulgence—steadily outward, away from certainty, toward open water.

LADY OR THE TIGER

Clabert had been drinking all afternoon and had finally settled in at Caples' favorite watering hole a block east of Montgomery Street. Half slumped in a booth with a bourbon on the rocks and a bull-dice cup, he was fingering the dice when Caples blustered in with another trader and ordered a martini at the bar. "Care for some dice *mister* head trader?" Clabert blurted banging the dice cup on the table, "You're a gambling man aren't you, or at least you *used* to be." Caples left his associate at the bar and swaggered over. "Well, still able to form sentences and it's almost the cocktail hour." Banging the dice cup again, Clabert flashed a marshy smile and continued, "but now there's not much risk is there, now that you've got a guide." Still standing, Caples said "your friend has talent." His smile deepening, Clabert said, at a volume that led Caples to bend closer, "yea, talent. Ambition too, though you wouldn't know it, and he knows what's behind the doors—buy or sell, lady or the tiger, and all you have to do is open the door he points to" and trailing off in a maundering slur, "she loves me she loves me not—lady or the tiger." "What the hell are you talking about?" Caples said like scissors. Clabert wheeled upward and looked Caples sharply in the face. "Why should he make *you* a fortune when he can make one *without* you?" and then, trailing off, "lady or the tiger, follow him or fade him, bet *with* him or *against* him, he loves me, he loves me not," then, suddenly sharp again, "I mean, *mister* head trader, if *you knew* what *he knows*, and *you* were working for *him*, what would *you* do?"

WONDER OCEAN

Wind tunnels like flutes and the drumheads of the sea—all the debris of language marking the edges of transactions, like coins rolling on their edges, like the rolling edges of galaxies falling through space.

OUTLAND

The outland at the edge of the carpentered world, beyond the shovels and picks of letters and numbers, the outland like a sheet of open water, beyond hammers and things to be done—if you could find the edge of your life and kneel there—you could almost touch your lips to that lake.

RECKONING

Christopher knew that he would never have to mislead Caples about the market to demolish him: Caples' assumption of deception, and consequent positioning, was all that it would take.

THE PATH TO THE LAKE

Christopher reached the path to the lake at first light. The dog sat at the juncture and followed him no further. He put the flashlight in his pack and followed a narrow path that was littered with loose rocks and fallen limbs. Christopher was fumbling through his thoughts, trying to assess the distance based on the earlier journey and the map at Tarpoling. But it wasn't that it mattered how far it was. He found his way along a rock face—with small clay replicas of chorten stacked in crevices—and across a rickety wooden bridge, festooned with prayer-flags, over a rushing stream.

RECKONING

After Evelyn's suicide, Christopher would never think of Caples again.

THE TURNING

The spray from the stream hit his face. He thought of the monk's dance. *In flames where the self was a handful of unlike things thrown*

*skyward—in depths where the self was held breath—at the turning—
could he take up the math of no preference—the hard math of nothing
solved or solvable—the math of seas?*

LIGHT'S OPPOSITE

*And he thought that if he could bend himself into the light that he could
see what light's opposite was—that he could see it where a corner was
laid flat against the light—if he could find an edge, a start or stop, a
corner to fold over where the opposite thing would touch the light—that
he could see it, even if it flashed away like lit gunpowder. If he could
bend himself into the light, if he could become his own opposite thing—
the opposite of who he was, what he preferred, where he stood, what he
insisted on—if he could find a corner and bend the fierce guardian of all
that he'd decided into the light, pressing this opposite self into himself,
even if it flashed away at once, he would catch a glimpse, and rest in
that glimpse as light rests—in constant motion.*

THE LAKE

To reach the lake, Christopher had to climb a steep embankment.
Gravel was pressing into his palms and he looked at his hands in
the soft light, and studied them, and he remembered standing at
the back of the classroom with the photos arranged on the table—
how not a single boy had recognized his hands, how several hands
had several children claim them, and some had none.

MEDITATION ON DROWNING

And he saw that that which was most his own did *not* clothe or
shelter him; did *not* tell him what things were for or what they
meant or what to do with them—*from the depths of the world's
drowning, breathing in, finding home with vanishing things, ancient
as the speech of fingers touching frost, ancient as tides—as torrents—as
salt—as nothing known—ancient as everything at risk.*

PHOTOGRAPHING HANDS

He pictured the faces of the boys—now as much made up as remembered—and wondered how many had continued to take up
the hands of others—and had pursued the work of those hands—
because they had never known their own hands, or what they were
really for.

THE LAKE

He touched the surface of the water, like you would touch the
black wall at the back of your life with your flattened palm. He
took off his shoes and socks—he took off his clothes, all of them,
and folded and stacked them on his pack, which lay flat on the
ground. He knew that the Terma was deep in the lake, and he
picked up two heavy stones, one in each hand, and entered the water and waded until the ground began to drop. He inhaled deeply
several times, then dove. It was like falling.

GLASS

The last time Christopher saw Evelyn alive, she was quiet, almost
transparent—no hardness, nothing fortified. She looked at him
with unflinching tenderness while she sat at the kitchen table in
her blue and white Japanese robe, her hands folded in front of
her. When he rose to leave, she rose also, and when he turned the
corner into the hall and looked back over his shoulder, he was sure
that she was about to cry, and the *seconds turned where they stood;*
the seconds turned like persons taken by their shoulders and turned to
face you, just upon turning once, these taken at the horizon, these cloud
formations in motion, these taken from vanishing, and the pull to re-
turn was not like the pull of the moon on the ocean's face; it was not like
riptides pulling you out to sea; it was like thick cumbrous weights pull-
ing you over as you try to walk.

ROTE BOATMAN

He sat in the living room, and watched as she was wheeled into the hall under a sheet on a lusterless aluminum gurney with black wheels and scuffed bumpers—*boat of the dead* he thought. The coroner said that they would take good care of her—*rote boatman, rote oarsman, man of wire and wood.* They carried her down the stairs and out the door. He did not watch them load her into the van but heard it drive away.

SWIMMING TOWARD DROWNING

Though the surface had been cold, the water just underneath seemed surprisingly warm. He pushed through the pressure building in his ears. He saw that he'd been practicing for this, that he could do this kind of swimming, this kind of straight-down swimming, this swimming toward drowning.

THE TERMA IN THE LAKE

And he sensed, in the grip of the depths, the tenderest access—*intimations of an opening vast and inviting just at the other side of a certain confining impasse, just beyond the burning tightness in his chest, beyond a searing like staring at the keyhole of a door closed on the sun—just there at the falling edge in the blackness—a mirror, a scepter, a scroll, a memory, a clearing—he knew that if he could pass through—pass through the wall of tightening, pass through the way that his thoughts pressed toward the surface—how far away it was, how foreign, that maybe it was raining, maybe rain was making rings on the surface above him—and he knew that on the underside of the water there was an impression where something had pushed through, like indentations on the underside of a page, and he only had to reach it for his fingers to read it, to read the underside of falling steps, of rivers over rocks, of splintered hearts, of unchained fires, to touch the underside*

of faithlessness and faith in their double orbit around the inexplicable,
and the burning became a fuse, a thread of fire, pulling him rapidly back
into his body, its heat, its hold, its keep, and his hands released the stones,
and he was carried upward, and now he was stroking hard to reach the
surface and he broke it gasping and gulping the air.

WALKING

In the days after Evelyn's death, Christopher was walking the
streets again, sometimes the same streets as long ago, sometimes
all day, sometimes into the night, sometimes the same ground,
against that wall again, that face of fog, that question again, pushing in, that wall of water that you can't see over.

RETURNING TO THE CHERRY DESK

In a cold, clear moment he walked to his mother's old bedroom,
to the starkly beautiful colonial cherry desk, thinking of what he
would do with everything, curious to consider the contents again
and began, at first carefully, very carefully, to move his mother's
pens, paper, stamp dish and sterling letter opener—the old habit
of diligence asserting itself. But now for whom—and he pushed all
these things aside with disregard, lifted the drawbridge writing-
surface and bent down to open the bottom drawer. How could it
be so light? He pulled it out quickly, and it was empty—empty.
It was like a slap. How could it be empty? How could she have
thrown those things away—Ben's Tahoe album, the photograph
of Elly, everything? He reached for the middle drawer and tugged
it open. It was empty too, except for a very few letters and articles, stacked to the right of the drawer. He hurriedly pulled the
top drawer halfway open. It was heavy—full of papers, photos and
articles. He closed it most of the way and returned to the slender
stack in the middle drawer.

LAST THINGS

At the bottom of these few things, Christopher found Westy's obituary from 1970 and, at the top, a recent, unopened letter from her addled brother, Chip. In the four years between the two, there had been very little to her life: a lavish article from Laura, in La Jolla, about the wedding of her daughter to a laundry detergent heir, with a little note saying that Evelyn had been missed; a going-out-of business ad for *The Golden Goose*; a series of articles from the *Tahoe Times*, sent by Chip and stuffed back into their envelopes—about the accelerating pace of development at the lake, and the rapidly rising prices. Christopher opened the recent letter. It was an article with pictures of the grand opening of Tahoe Shores, with flags, smiling faces, and large new houses, "with every amenity." Scrawled in red across the top and underlined was "The bastards got it all!" He put the article back in the drawer and closed it.

RUBICON

At first it had seemed a slicing selfishness: to keep him, finally, from her cherished things. But, through the emptiness of the drawer, in the empty quiet of the house, having held the last of them, he saw that she'd had to put herself on a footing of no return, and the destruction of everything treasured is a way of no-going-back, and he saw that she had left the things behind that she could not face, the things that would force her forward, the things that she could not bear to return to ever again.

FIRE

Christopher paused a long time before opening the top drawer of the desk. When he did, he saw, to the right, a newspaper clipping titled *Professionals on the Move*, with a few lines, circled in pencil, concerning his having been named to the trading desk at Pacific Bank after several years of serving as a clerk. Christopher shuffled rapidly downward, past his high school diploma, Mr. Marquand's bill for fixing the bowl, and the truancy letter from the time of the poisoning. Beneath more years of report cards, photographs and papers, he found the *Chronicle* article about the Thorn fire case being closed. It was dated July 21, 1966. The article said that the coroner had ruled Dr. Thorn's death an accident; that it was not uncommon for people to stay in burning houses collecting things or even to return to the flames in search of valuables, so the case was closed. But the article implied that the mystery of Dr. Thorn's actions that night would likely never be solved. It described how, according to witnesses, he had freed himself from the flames, brushed himself off, and looked to be in good spirits. Then, he had turned and looked back at the fire and, saying nothing, had bolted back into the house short minutes before its collapse.

FIRE

Christopher knew that Dr. Thorn had not returned to the flames to retrieve some *trivial thing*, some *valuable*. Christopher knew that Dr. Thorn had returned to the burning house because something was *showing itself* to him, because he was *seeing* something, because something was being *held out* to him.

THE LETTERS

Under more articles with theories about the fire, Christopher found a letter *addressed to himself* at the old address on Green Street— never opened, stamped *postage due*, and obviously kept from him and hidden by his mother. *Never opened*, because she would never open another's mail and *not destroyed*, because she did not throw things away that were not her own—never given him, *withheld*. The writing on the envelope was in green ink and the two stamps at the upper right were brightly colored and exotic. He held the sealed letter in his hand, and he was trying to turn things around in his mind, to find an angle from which he could *actually* see what he was holding, because he could not comprehend what he was looking at—tightly sealed, never opened, pristine, hidden away, from the time just after the fire. He grew suddenly voraciously impatient and didn't bother with the silver letter opener but tore the envelope open hastily and pulled a small square piece of notepad paper from it that looked like it had been torn from one of those blocks of notepaper held together at the back with that gummy rubbery glue. The facing side of the note was clean and the underside was smudged with dirt and, almost as once, he saw that the surface was indented with an image. Tracing the shape with his fingers and holding the note to the light, he determined that *two dots, inside a circle,* had been pressed into the otherwise blank paper, and it was clear from the dirt on the bottom, which now was clearly a scuff-mark, that the note was a messenger, and *it was like something rising through deep water, something sunken, something returning, something the memory of which had been sunken with it, something rising through sleep, returning when you wake, something from far away arriving new.*

STAMPS

He held the note in his left hand, rubbing it between his fingertips, and focused on the opened envelope held in his right. The stamps were both from Bhutan and cancelled. He remembered the afternoon when Dr. Thorn had given them to him. Christopher rubbed the messenger between his fingers again and again, and became aware, gradually at first, then blindingly, that it had been *sent forward—across years*—through the unintended agency of Evelyn's concerns—to reach him *now—to remind him*—and it was like touching the past again—but this was not the past—in that moment of recognition—of obligation—he was touching the future.

THE LETTERS

Christopher wanted to pull the stack apart, looking for other withheld items, but he resolved to be glacial, stolid and deliberate, because he knew that the sequencing would matter and could never be reestablished with certainty if disturbed. Beneath the letter with the stamps from Bhutan was a brief article saying that Dr. Thorn's remains had been found in the ruins, and it was now believed that the fire had started in the study, probably a lit cigarette dropped behind seat cushions and smoldering for days before igniting a conflagration. Beneath this article was the folded page of a newspaper dated July 12, 1966 with a circled ad for the rental house on Jackson Street—"Rare Opportunity to Rent in Presidio Heights"—the house to which they had moved in August of that year—the house in which he now stood.

THE LETTERS

Under the rental ad he found a second envelope, posted with the other pair of Dr. Thorn's Bhutanese stamps. He opened it more carefully this time. The note he pulled out was the same size and shape as the first, but this one was marked, deeply in blue ballpoint pen, with the circle and two dots, and the surface was slightly curled as if it had been lying in the sun—stained and smudged as if taken from a gutter, and the underside was clean and blank. He pressed the two notes together and saw that they were a single messenger, pulled apart and mailed separately, and he saw that the move to Jackson Street had been the result of the letters having arrived at the flat.

THE CITY OF MESSENGERS

Underneath the second letter he found a large manila envelope addressed to Dr. Thorn at his address on Broderick Street, and posted with a multitude of now cancelled U.S. stamps, some very old—3 cent, 5 cent, 7 cent, 10 cent—airplanes, buildings, bridges, birds and presidents all cancelled now, postmarked July 1, 1966. Below and to the right of the address was written in red and underlined twice "Please Forward" and Christopher's return address was meticulously penned in the upper left, and below and to the right of it was stamped a red hand with its index finger pointing to his address—"return to sender / unable to forward." He lifted the envelope out of the drawer and its contents bunched at the bottom. Beneath it was the front-page article about the fire, with a photograph showing billowing smoke, unfurled hoses and firefighters soaking the roofs of adjoining houses. The article reported how fiercely the fire had burned, how many alarms had been sounded, about the crowd spilling into the street and the owner, emerging and then returning to the flames and presumed dead. Christopher sat on the polished floor holding the manila envelope. He tore it open and dumped its contents in front of him—a jumble of laundry lists, bus transfers, chunks of colored glass, business cards, notes smeared with dirt, cigarette foil, an empty book of matches with a phone number written inside, part of an envelope, the bent nail, the key, the torn corner of a photograph showing only a person's shoulder, and all the other bits of debris picked up from the streets over years, and a folded piece of spiral notebook paper which he opened and found to be a crudely fashioned diagram with drawings and brief descriptions next to those drawings that were hard to recognize. The diagram showed the proper placement of each thing. Some of the writing was barely legible and some not legible at all. At the top of the page was written with painstaking clarity, "I am sending the City of Messengers so you can find your way home through its open gate."

THE LAST MESSENGER

He sat and placed the diagram flat on the hardwood floor and, making a simple initial geometry, began to assemble the City of

Messengers. The key was next to the empty center, and he saw that the two letters were to be received *as instructions—not from the world of stuff and common sense, but from the Wonder Ocean—to be taken, against all logic, at face value, as Dr. Thorn's response to the City of Messengers, and to be acted on as such.* The note with the markings had been mailed first and the one with the indentations had followed, so the one seeming to be blank was the empty last messenger—*between the substantial and the unsubstantial, between single things, fused multitudes and discarded fragments—the hint, the map, the origin and the arc*—and he held it in his hand.

SHORE

Christopher walked to shore unsteadily. Drukpa Kunley was waiting on the bank, twirling and chanting, astonished at the sight of him, naked, emerging from the water. The black dog was bounding and barking, and the monk was holding a blanket between outstretched arms. Christopher was chattering and shivering, stumbling across sharp rocks in that feet-hurting quick way of walking. The monk received him, wrapping the blanket tightly around him. Christopher sat on a flat rock while the monk gathered dry brush and sticks to build a fire. The dog approached and sat close beside him.

WEIGHT

The dawn was cold. The blanket smelled of soot and soured milk. The sky was a shattering sheet of blue slate. The sun's rays were needles. A place in the world would never be straightforward. He saw that this was so for everyone—everyone pressed forward—groundless—swept in swift water. His eyes filled with tears for those he had loved. He buried his face in the dog's black fur. If waking is winter—if waking is weights falling like limbs shaking acres of snow from their backs—he saw that the present moment arises without a cause, that the origin of the past is always new, like light.

FIRE

Embers crackled and danced. He sat straight up. He could feel the cold air on his face. He could feel the cold flat rock on which he sat. The weight of his body was with him. He held his hands over the fire. Drukpa Kunley was standing behind him. Christopher felt a soft tugging on the back of his head and heard a slight swift metallic sound like a series of sharp breaths. Drukpa Kunley was cutting his hair.

FIRE

The dawn was cold. The monk was sprinkling clippings into the fire and the acrid smell filled the chill air. Christopher drew a deep breath, exhaled, leaned back, and let his full weight fall on the monk's front.

OF JOINING, OF MAKING, OF RETURN

He belonged to those who could not sleep—who could not live without question—who could not settle the world. These were his he knew. These he would reach through broken glass to reach. He would make the long climb back to Tarpoling, against hard ground, through broken light, against the collapsing sides of his falling life, and he would see his past, not replaced, but refracted through the future of his hands, as treasure-finders, in the discarded world. He would enter the hardness of days and weeks— the tangle of unsolvable instants—on broken streets charged with discarded beauty—through houses on fire—in the upside down diagonal orbits of ash, abrasion and care.

Author's Notes and Acknowledgments

The poem serving as epigraph was originally published in 2008, under the title "Sea of Hooks," as a limited-edition letterpress chapbook from Arundel Press, Seattle.

The sections titled WAR LETTER FROM WESTY TO HIS FATHER are excerpted from an actual letter written by my father, Houston Hill Jr. to his father, Houston Hill Sr., and dated April 1, 1943.

The image of the mother running, armless, along the bank, watching her drowning child (which appears on pages 13-14 and thereafter), is derived from *Words of my Perfect Teacher*, by Patrul Rinpoche (1808-1887): translated by Padmakara Translation Group, and published by AltaMira Press, a division of Sage Publications, Inc. in association with Harper Collins, 1994, page 212.

"Hansel and Gretel," the Brothers Grimm's fairy tale, is summarized on page 44.

The title WONDER OCEAN, (used on page 97 and thereafter, and credited on page 102), is the title of a text by the Third Dondrupchen Rinpoche (1865-1926). A complete translation of this text can be found in *The Hidden Treasures of Tibet*, Tulku Thondrop Rinpoche, Wisdom Publications, 1986.

The sections titled WHERE THE WILD THINGS ARE (page 194) refer to Maurice Sendak's book of the same title.

Portions of the sections titled THE WELL (pages 182-183, and page 301) are quoted directly from the *I-Ching* or *Book of Changes*, translated by Richard Wilhelm and Cary F. Baynes, copyright © 1950 by Bollingen Foundation, Inc., New York, N.Y. New material copyright © 1967 by Bollingen Foundation. Copyright © renewed 1977 by Princeton University Press. Published by Princeton University Press, Princeton, New Jersey.

"The Lady or the Tiger," a short story by Frank R. Stockton (first published 1882), is referenced in the section of the same title on page 336.

I would like to acknowledge the loving and continuous support of my wife, Nita Hill, during the entire composition of this work.

I thank my brother, Houston Hill III, for a lifetime of friendship.

Thanks also to Gregory Kramer, Gale Czerski, H.C. ten Berge, Billy Panda, and Eric Matchett for their friendship and insights.

Special thanks are extended to Paul Naylor for his extensive editorial support, and to Caryl and Clayton Eshleman, for their work on, and support of, the manuscript.